BISON FRONTIERS OF IMAGINATION

CLARK ASHTON SMITH

Out Of Space And Time

Introduction to the Bison Books Edition by
JEFF VANDERMEER

UNIVERSITY OF NEBRASKA PRESS
LINCOLN AND LONDON

© 1971 by Neville Spearman Ltd.
Reprinted by arrangements with Arkham House Publishers, Inc., and
CASina Literary Enterprises, Inc.
Introduction © 2006 by the Board of Regents of the University of Nebraska
All rights reserved
Manufactured in the United States of America

First Nebraska paperback printing: 2006

The End of the Story, © 1930, by The Popular Fiction Publishing Company.
A Rendezvous in Averoigne, © 1931, by The Popular Fiction Publishing Company.
A Night in Malnéant, © 1931, by The Popular Fiction Publishing Company.
The City of the Singing Flame, © 1931, by Continental Publications, Inc.
The Uncharted Isle, © 1930, by The Popular Fiction Publishing Company.
The Monster of the Prophecy, © 1931, by The Popular Fiction Publishing Company.
The Vaults of Yoh-Vombis, © 1932, by The Popular Fiction Publishing Company.
The Second Interment, © 1932, The Clayton Magazines, Inc.
The Double Shadow, © 1939, by The Popular Fiction Publishing Company.
The Chain of Aforgomon, © 1935, by The Popular Fiction Publishing Company.
The Dark Eidolon, © 1934, by The Popular Fiction Publishing Company.
The Last Hieroglyph, © 1935, by The Popular Fiction Publishing Company.
Sadastor, © 1930, by The Popular Fiction Publishing Company.
The Death of Ilalotha, © 1937, by The Popular Fiction Publishing Company.
The Return of the Sorcerer, © 1931, by The Clayton Magazines, Inc.
The Testament of Athammaus, © 1932, by The Popular Fiction Publishing Company.
The Weird of Avoosl Wuthoqquan, © 1932, by The Popular Fiction Publishing Company.
From the Crypts of Memory, © 1922, by Clark Ashton Smith.
The Shadows, © 1922, by Clark Ashton Smith.

Library of Congress Cataloging-in-Publication Data
Smith, Clark Ashton, 1893–1961.
Out of space and time / Clark Ashton Smith; introduction to the Bison Books
edition by Jeff VanderMeer.
p. cm.—(Bison frontiers of imagination)
ISBN-13: 978-0-8032-9352-6 (pbk.: alk. paper)
ISBN-10: 0-8032-9352-6 (pbk.: alk. paper)
I. Title. II. Series.
PS3537.M335O88 2006
813'.52—dc22   2006012467

INTRODUCTION
JEFF VANDERMEER

When Clark Ashton Smith was twenty, Marcel Proust published *Swann's Way* and D. H. Lawrence published *Sons and Lovers*. By the time Smith was twenty-five, James Joyce had written *Dubliners*, Virginia Woolf had written *The Voyage Out*, and Oswald Spengler had completed *The Decline of the West*. Throughout his thirties and forties, Smith could have encountered new works by Pirandello, Eliot, Mansfield, Hemingway, Kafka, Breton, Faulkner, and even Nabokov. He would have had the opportunity to read all of the twentieth century's modernists and the godfathers of postmodernism.

However, it doesn't appear that *any* of these writers, with the possible exception of Kafka, had any influence on Smith's own work. He focused instead on French Symbolists, already well in decline by the time Smith became an adult—although it is probably more honest to say that he focused on the French Decadents as well. (Many of the "Symbolists" were identified as "Decadents" before academia legitimized them.)

This identification with a literary group that influenced other important writers but that largely did not reflect the mainstream of American literature is one reason why Smith remained obscure during his lifetime. Another, of course, was his love of pulp fiction, in the form of H. P. Lovecraft's work, among others. Is it any surprise that aligning himself with two "outsider" groups led to his own obscurity? Smith's reputation may also have improved had he written novels rather than poetry and short stories, since it seems to be an unspoken rule of writing careers that novels usually lead to greater recognition.

We can find evidence of Smith's dual highbrow-lowbrow sensibility in his personal life as well. As August Derleth and Donald Wandrei pointed out in the original introduction to *Out of Space and Time*, Smith was the descendent of Norman-French counts and barons, of Lancashire baronets and Crusaders. One of his Ashton forebears was beheaded for his part in the famed Gunpowder Plot. His mother's family, the Gaylords, came to New England in 1630—Huguenot Gaillards who fled persecution in France after the revocation of the Edict of Nantes. Smith's father, Timeus Smith, was a world-traveler in his early years, but settled at last in Auburn, where he died less than a decade ago.

But Smith's experiences as a "journalist, a fruit picker and packer, a woodchopper, a typist, a cement-mixer, a gardener, a hard-rock miner, mucker, and windlasser" can hardly be called aristocratic. Just because he used a diverse, archaic, and formidable vocabulary does not mean readers should assume that Smith was an erudite man of letters. It is precisely his overreaching for literary authenticity in some of his stories that shows us he was not.

And it is in a proletarian, pulp mode that Smith has been rescued from complete obscurity—through genre publications and publishers. This detail of his resurrection initially resulted in his work being discussed in terms of other pulp writers or with vague generalizations and nods to the Symbolists (who perhaps more specifically influenced his poetry). The pulp-genre comparison seems valid in terms of the purported "purple" quality of Smith's prose. At first glance, and sometimes second, Smith's writing does seem overwrought. It's easy to dismiss it as amateurish, in much the same way as others have dismissed Lovecraft's writing. I don't believe that this conclusion is false so much as incomplete.

Smith's prose is not always lush—it tends to *become* lush as he adds more and more descriptive passages to a particular story. In scenes dominated by dialog, however, the lushness recedes into the background, and the action tends to be better paced as a result. This is not always a good thing, given that we read Smith's prose precisely *for* a certain amount of escapism, for those flights of fancy that some critics condemn. (Is it odd to suggest that the French seem to like Smith because in translation a translator can flense those flights that are just a bit too fanciful?)

INTRODUCTION

In the more banal tales, this sense of prose poetry seems rather restrained, as in "A Rendezvous in Averoigne," which, with its chateaus and chivalry, exists all too clearly in a recognizably real world. While lovely, the descriptions of a "purling brook," a "tarn of waters that were dark and dull as clotting blood," and "skeletons of rotting osiers" seem oddly muted in the context of the story. There is no real resonance to the images—they do not seem illuminated from within but curiously immutable, mere description. Conversely, in "The City of the Singing Flame," transdimensional travel interferes with Smith's effectiveness because of his need to explain, or attempt to explain, through his narrator, with passages like:

> I had read a number of transdimensional stories—in fact, I had written one or two myself; and I had often pondered the possibility of other worlds or material planes which may co-exist in the same space with ours, invisible and impalpable to human senses. Of course, I realised at once that I had fallen into some such dimension.

Or, "My brain reeled before the infinite vistas of surmise that were opened by such questions". Or, "Inevitably, I began to speculate as to the relationship between the columns in this new dimension and the boulders in my own world".

All of this "business," as one would say in the world of theater, dilutes the poetic quality of the prose and the reader's sense of wonder. Regardless of whether this criticism is merely symptomatic of the difference in focus between the weird fiction of the 1920s and modern weird fiction—few writers today would bother with much of an explanation or extrapolation about the transdimensional factor—this is one reason why Smith can seem dated. However, his ability at other times to ignore the need for pedantic explanation preserves the transcendent quality of some of his stories.

Once Smith feels confident that the reader will not reject his initial premise, he relaxes into the story, and the imagery begins to exert an inexorable power:

> I returned to the town; and once again I sought to make my presence known to the inhabitants, but all in vain. And after awhile, as I trudged from street to street, the sun went down behind the island, and the stars came swiftly out in a heaven of purpureal velvet. The stars were large and lustrous and were innumerably thick: with the eye of a practised mariner, I studied them eagerly; but I could not trace the wonted constellations, though here and there I thought that I perceived a distortion or elongation of some familiar grouping.

The difference between Smith trying to defend his creations and Smith living comfortably inside of them is often the difference between success and failure. At times it seems that Smith would like nothing better than to discard the pulp trappings of his plots, abandon the cardboard cut outs of his first person narrators, and dive headfirst into the worlds themselves, to immerse himself in them without conforming to the needs of narrative. Luckily, the core of *Out of Space and Time* consists of stories such as "A Night in Malnéant," "The Chain of Aforgomon," "The Last Hieroglyph" (with its many delights, including a talking salamander guide), "The Vaults of Yoh-Vombis," and others in which the need to explain is generally subsumed by the visualization of a world or wondrously alien place.

In rereading these stories I did begin to feel that Smith's strengths and his weaknesses might be so intertwined that surgery would be required to separate them. It's a theory—some would say an excuse—that writers like the new weird's China Mieville have put forth about several pulp-era writers, including Lovecraft. Smith's pieces of self-taught sculpture and drawing have an amateur sheen to them—a sincerity and originality that goes hand-in-hand with an unfinished or rough draft quality. Why should we assume his prose is any different?

Smith's acknowledged influences—writers of pulp fiction and the Symbolists/Decadents—have all, at one time or another, been considered illegitimate or disreputable, outsiders on the margins. (Sometimes the writers associated with these groups wanted it that way, sometimes not.) Smith, however, truly was an outsider artist, not in the narrow European definition of art or writing by the mentally disturbed, but in the broader definition that includes folk art and creative endeavors by those with no formal training.

There are few writers who seem to write so wholly for themselves, who seem so enraptured by a vision only they can see that they sacrifice accessibility for that vision. Smith, it seems to me, is an outsider precisely because, in pursuit of his own gratification, he makes the *reader* an outsider. This voyeuristic sense of peering in on a world and worldview never meant for us is what attracts us to Smith's writing—and at the same time can repel us from it. I do not believe Smith cared one way or the other about the reader, so long as he could write what he wanted to write, in the way he wanted to write it. His visions may thus be incomplete, sometimes cloudy, but they are also, ironically enough given his pulp origins, undiluted by any appreciable commercial taint.

To Genevieve K. Sully

CONTENTS

CLARK ASHTON SMITH: MASTER OF FANTASY	XV
OUT OF SPACE AND TIME	
The End of the Story	3
A Rendezvous in Averoigne	25
A Night in Malnéant	43
The City of the Singing Flame	51
The Uncharted Isle	100
JUDGMENTS AND DOOMS	
The Second Interment	115
The Double Shadow	129
The Chain of Aforgomon	144
The Dark Eidolon	165
The Last Hieroglyph	198
Sadastor	218
The Death of Ilalotha	222
The Return of the Sorcerer	236
HYPERBOREAN GROTESQUES	
The Testament of Athammaus	257
The Weird of Avoosl Wuthoqquan	280
Ubbo-Sathla	291
INTERPLANETARIES	
The Monster of the Prophecy	303
The Vaults of Yoh-Vombis	347
From the Crypts of Memory	367
The Shadows	369

CLARK ASHTON SMITH: MASTER OF FANTASY

CLARK ASHTON SMITH was born on January 13, 1893, in Long Valley, California. He began to write at the comparatively early age of eleven. Apart from five years in the grammar grades, Smith is wholly self-educated; that he did not neglect his education is amply attested by the superb quality of his work in verse, prose, painting and sculpture.

At seventeen, Smith was selling stories to *The Black Cat, The Overland Monthly,* and other magazines. His first collection of verse was published only two years later, and was hailed as the work of a prodigy and classed with work of Chatterton, Rossetti, and Bryant. He resumed the writing of short stories as a profession when he was past thirty-five, and it was then, with publication in *Weird Tales* of *The End of the Story,* that he came into his own in prose. The success of that story inspired others, all weird, macabre, fantastic or pseudo-scientific, all equally popular with readers. Since that time he has contributed poetry and fiction to over fifty magazines, including *The Yale Review, The London Mercury, Munsey's, Asia, Wings, Poetry: A Magazine of Verse, The Philippine Magazine,* and the *Mencken Smart Set.* His poetry has been included in more than a dozen anthologies, and some of his translations from Baudelaire have been used in an anthology of *The Flowers of Evil* published by the Limited Editions Club.

His book-length publications were all printed in limited editions, with the result that all are collectors' items today. Four of his five volumes are of verse—*The Star-Treader, Odes and Sonnets, Ebony and Crystal, Sandal-Wood;* the fifth is a pamphlet of tales: *The Double Shadow and Other Fantasies,* most of which are included in the present volume.

Out of Space and Time is the first volume of prose to present to his readers here and abroad the cream of Clark Ashton Smith, who himself selected the stories to appear between these covers. He has three new volumes of verse in preparation, and the publishers hope that the success of *Out of Space and Time* will assure publication of a second collection of the tales of Clark Ashton Smith.

Apart from his prose and poetry, Smith is a painter and sculptor, and has exhibited many of his outré and exotic pictures and carvings in Western cities. His sculptures, which are especially powerful and fascinating, are cut largely from strange and unusual minerals, and have been compared to pre-Columbian art. While not widely circulated—they are never cast, but each one is original and has no copy—Smith's sculptures have found numerous purchasers, not limited to the coterie of fellow writers with whom Smith is in constant touch. Nor have his paintings been without acclaim; most common is the ranking with or above those of Odilon Redon, the famed French symbolist.

In his forty-eight years Smith has been a variety of things —a journalist, a fruit picker and packer, a woodchopper, a typist, a cement-mixer, a gardener, a hard-rock miner, mucker, and windlasser. Though his verse may occasionally sound as if Smith lived in an ivory tower, this is far indeed from the facts.

Moreover, Smith's lineage is almost as long in this country as was the late great H. P. Lovecraft's. He is the descendant of Norman-French counts and barons, of Lancashire baronets and Crusaders. One of his Ashton forebears was beheaded for his part in the famed Gunpowder Plot. His mother's family, the Gaylords, came to New England in 1630—Huguenot Gaillards who fled persecution in France after the revocation of the Edict of Nantes. Smith's father, Timeus Smith, was a world-traveler in his early years, but settled at last in Auburn, where he died less than a decade ago.

Of the stories in this collection, there is much to be said, and yet perhaps they speak best for themselves. Just as in poetry Smith was undoubtedly influenced not only by the French symbolists but also by his great and good friend, the late George Sterling, so in prose he was constantly encouraged and influenced in large part by another friend, the late great H. P. Lovecraft. Readers of weird lore in our time are familiar with the famed Cthulhu mythology of H. P. Lovecraft, the mythology to which other writers added bits and portions; of those writers, none added so much as Clark Ashton Smith—and this despite the fact that Smith had created a fantastic setting all his own: the fabled land of Averoigne, which had taken hold of many readers and fired their imagination. His hyperborean settings have achieved a popularity equalled only by the lore of legend-haunted Arkham that was Lovecraft's. Indeed, so completely did Smith identify many of his settings with those of Lovecraft's, with the aid and at the behest of Lovecraft himself, that today many of his remarkable sculptures bear such recognizable names as *Cthulhu, The Outsider, Tsathoggua, Yuggoth, Hastur,* etc. With consummate skill, Smith has added characters, enlarged on settings, spun his stories to embrace a far wider area in time for the Ancient Ones and the Elder Gods; he has himself invented the *Book of Eibon, Tsathoggua,* and many other place-names and characters in the mythos, used by Lovecraft as well as himself.

The stories in *Out of Space and Time* represent a variety and reveal most of the facets of Smith's unique abilities in prose, abilities which make it possible to say of him that he is the greatest living American writer of macabre and fantastic tales, and certainly the greatest living stylist in the genre. There are tales here of Averoigne, tales belonging to the Cthulhu Mythos, stories of sheer horror and one or two of sardonic comedy, such as *The Weird of Avoosl Wuthoqquan*. Such a popular science-fiction novelette as *The City of the Singing Flame,* together with its sequel under a single title, is here; and so are such classics of the weird as *The End of the Story, A Night in Malnéant, The Double Shadow, The Return of the Sorcerer,* and *The Dark Eidolon.*

Smith lives today in Auburn, California, in the heart of an old and rich placer-mining region, only six miles from the place of his birth. Still young at forty-eight, he feels that his best work is yet to be done.

—AUGUST DERLETH
DONALD WANDREI

OUT OF SPACE AND TIME

THE END OF THE STORY

THE following narrative was found among the papers of Christophe Morand, a young law-student of Tours, after his unaccountable disappearance during a visit at his father's home near Moulins, in November, 1789:

A sinister brownish-purple autumn twilight, made premature by the imminence of a sudden thunderstorm, had filled the forest of Averoigne. The trees along my road were already blurred to ebon masses, and the road itself, pale and spectral before me in the thickening gloom, seemed to waver and quiver slightly, as with the tremor of some mysterious earthquake. I spurred my horse, who was woefully tired with a journey begun at dawn, and had fallen hours ago to a protesting and reluctant trot, and we galloped adown the darkening road between enormous oaks that seemed to lean toward us with boughs like clutching fingers as we passed.

With dreadful rapidity, the night was upon us, the blackness became a tangible clinging veil; a nightmare confusion and desperation drove me to spur my mount again with a more cruel rigor; and now, as we went, the first far-off mutter of the storm mingled with the clatter of my horse's hoofs, and the first lightning flashes illumed our way, which, to my amazement (since I believed myself on the main highway through Averoigne), had inexplicably narrowed to a well-trodden footpath. Feeling sure that I had gone astray, but not caring to retrace my steps in the teeth of darkness and the towering clouds of the tempest, I hurried on, hoping, as seemed reasonable, that a path so plainly worn would lead eventually to some house or chateau where I could find refuge for the night. My hope was well-founded, for within a few minutes I descried a glimmering light through the forest-boughs, and came suddenly to an open glade, where, on a gentle eminence, a large building loomed, with several litten windows in the lower story, and a top that was well-nigh indistinguishable against the bulks of driven cloud.

"Doubtless a monastery," I thought, as I drew rein, and descending from my exhausted mount, lifted the heavy brazen knocker in the form of a dog's head and let it fall on the oaken door. The sound was unexpectedly loud and sonorous, with a reverberation almost sepulchral, and I shivered involuntarily, with a sense of startlement, of unwonted dismay. This, a moment later, was wholly dissipated when the door was thrown open and a tall, ruddy-featured monk stood before me in the cheerful glow of the cressets that illumed a capacious hallway.

"I bid you welcome to the abbey of Perigon," he said, in a suave rumble, and even as he spoke, another robed and hooded figure appeared and took my horse in charge. As I murmured my thanks and acknowledgments, the storm broke and tremendous gusts of rain, accompanied by ever-nearing peals of thunder, drove with demoniac fury on the door that had closed behind me.

"It is fortunate that you found us when you did," observed my host. "'Twere ill for man and beast to be abroad in such a hell-brew."

Divining without question that I was hungry as well as tired, he led me to the refectory and set before me a bountiful meal of mutton, brown bread, lentils, and a strong excellent red wine.

He sat opposite me at the refectory table while I ate, and, with my hunger a little mollified, I took occasion to scan him more attentively. He was both tall and stoutly built, and his features, where the brow was no less broad than the powerful jaw, betokened intellect as well as a love for good living. A certain delicacy and refinement, an air of scholarship, of good taste and good breeding, emanated from him, and I thought to myself: "This monk is probably a connoisseur of books as well as of wines." Doubtless my expression betrayed the quickening of my curiosity, for he said, as if in answer:

"I am Hilaire, the abbot of Perigon. We are a Benedictine order, who live in amity with God and with all men, and we do not hold that the spirit is to be enriched by the mortification or impoverishment of the body. We have in our butteries an abundance of wholesome fare, in our cellars the best and oldest vintages of the district of Averoigne. And, if such things interest you, as mayhap they do, we have a library that is stocked with rare tomes, with precious manuscripts, with the finest works of heathendom and Christendom, even to certain unique writings that survived the holocaust of Alexandria."

"I appreciate your hospitality," I said, bowing. "I am Christophe Morand, a law-student, on my way home from Tours to my father's estate near Moulins. I, too, am a lover of books, and nothing would delight me more than the privilege of inspecting a library so rich and curious as the one whereof you speak."

Forthwith, while I finished my meal, we fell to discussing the classics, and to quoting and capping passages from Latin, Greek, or Christian authors. My host, I soon discovered, was a scholar of uncommon attainments, with an erudition, a ready familiarity with both ancient and modern literature that made my own seem as that of the merest beginner by comparison. He, on his part, was so good as to commend my far from perfect Latin, and by the time I had emptied my bottle of red wine we were chatting familiarly like old friends.

All my fatigue had now flown, to be succeeded by a rare sense of well-being, of physical comfort combined with mental alertness and keenness. So, when the abbot suggested that we pay a visit to the library, I assented with alacrity.

He led me down a long corridor, on each side of which were cells belonging to the brothers of the order, and unlocked, with a large brazen key that depended from his girdle, the door of a great room with lofty ceiling and several deep-set windows. Truly, he had not exaggerated the resources of the library; for the long shelves were overcrowded with books, and many volumes were piled high on the tables or stacked in corners. There were rolls of papyrus, of parchment, of vellum; there were strange Byzantine or Coptic bibles; there were old Arabic and Persian manuscripts with floriated or jewel-studded covers; there were scores of incunabula from the first printing-presses; there were innumerable monkish copies of antique authors, bound in wood or ivory, with rich illuminations and lettering that was often in itself a work of art.

With a care that was both loving and meticulous, the abbot Hilaire brought out volume after volume for my inspection. Many of them I had never seen before; some were unknown to me even by fame or rumor. My excited interest, my unfeigned enthusiasm, evidently pleased him, for at length he pressed a hidden spring in one of the library tables and drew out a long drawer, in which, he told me, were certain treasures that he did not care to bring forth for the edification or delectation of many, and whose very existence was undreamed of by the monks.

"Here," he continued, "are three odes by Catullus which you will not find in any published edition of his works. Here, also, is an original manuscript of Sappho—a complete copy of a poem otherwise extant only in brief fragments; here are two of the lost tales of Miletus, a letter of Pericles to Aspasia, an unknown dialogue of Plato, and an old Arabian work on astronomy, by some anonymous author, in which the theories of Copernicus are anticipated. And, lastly, here is the somewhat infamous *Histoire d'Amour*, by Bernard de Vaillantcoeur, which was destroyed immediately upon publication, and of which only one other copy is known to exist."

As I gazed with mingled awe and curiosity on the unique, unheard-of treasures he displayed, I saw in one corner of the drawer what appeared to be a thin volume with plain untitled binding of dark leather. I ventured to pick it up, and found that it contained a few sheets of closely written manuscript in old French.

"And this?" I queried, turning to look at Hilaire, whose face, to my amazement, had suddenly assumed a melancholy and troubled expression.

"It were better not to ask, my son." He crossed himself as he spoke, and his voice was no longer mellow, but harsh, agitated, full of a sorrowful perturbation. "There is a curse on the pages that you hold in your hand: an evil spell, a malign power is attached to them, and he who would venture to peruse them is henceforward in dire peril both of body and soul." He took the little volume from me as he spoke, and returned it to the drawer, again crossing himself carefully as he did so.

"But, father," I dared to expostulate, "how can such things be? How can there be danger in a few written sheets of parchment?"

"Christophe, there are things beyond your understanding, things that it were not well for you to know. The might of Satan is manifestable in devious modes, in diverse manners; there are other temptations than those of the world and the flesh, there are evils no less subtle than irresistable, there are hidden heresies, and necromancies other than those which sorcerers practise."

"With what, then, are these pages concerned, that such occult peril, such unholy power lurks within them?"

"I forbid you to ask." His tone was one of great rigor, with a finality that dissuaded me from further questioning.

"For you, my son," he went on, "the danger would be doubly great, because you are young, ardent, full of desires and curiosities. Believe me, it is better to forget that you have even seen this manuscript." He closed the hidden drawer, and as he did so, the melancholy troubled look was replaced by his former benignity.

"Now," he said, as he turned to one of the book-shelves, "I will show you the copy of Ovid that was owned by the poet Petrarch." He was again the mellow scholar, the kindly, jovial host, and it was evident that the mysterious manuscript was not to be referred to again. But his odd perturbation, the dark and awful hints he had let fall, the vague terrific terms of his proscription, had all served to awaken my wildest curiosity, and, though I felt the obsession to be unreasonable, I was quite unable to think of anything else for the rest of the evening. All manner of speculations, fantastic, absurd, outrageous, ludicrous, terrible, defiled through my brain as I duly admired the incunabula which Hilaire took down so tenderly from the shelves for my delectation.

At last, toward midnight, he led me to my room—a room especially reserved for visitors, and with more of comfort, of actual luxury in its hangings, carpets and deeply quilted bed than was allowable in the cells of the monks or of the abbot himself. Even when Hilaire had withdrawn, and I had proved for my satisfaction the softness of the bed allotted me, my brain still whirled with questions concerning the forbidden manuscript. Though the storm had now ceased, it was long before I fell asleep; but slumber, when it finally came, was dreamless and profound.

When I awoke, a river of sunshine clear as molten gold was pouring through my window. The storm had wholly vanished, and no lightest tatter of cloud was visible anywhere in the pale-blue October heavens. I ran to the window and peered out on a world of autumnal forest and fields all a-sparkle with the diamonds of rain. All was beautiful, all was idyllic to a degree that could be fully appreciated only by one who had lived for a long time, as I had, within the walls of a city, with towered buildings in lieu of trees and cobbled pavements where grass should be. But, charming as it was, the foreground held my gaze only for a few moments; then, beyond the tops of the trees, I saw a hill, not more than a mile distant, on whose summit there stood the ruins of some old chateau, the crumbling, broken-down condition of whose walls and towers was plainly visible. It drew my gaze irresistibly, with an overpowering sense of romantic attraction, which somehow seemed so natural, so inevitable, that I did not pause to analyze or wonder; and once having seen it, I could not take my eyes away, but lingered at the window for how long I knew not, scrutinizing as closely as I could the details of each time-shaken turret and bastion. Some undefinable fascination was inherent in the very form, the extent, the disposition of the pile—some fascination not dissimilar to that exerted by a strain of music, by a magical combination of words in poetry, by the features of a beloved face. Gazing, I lost myself in reveries that I could not recall afterward, but which left behind them the same tantalizing sense of innominable delight which forgotten nocturnal dreams may sometimes leave.

I was recalled to the actualities of life by a gentle knock at my door, and realized that I had forgotten to dress myself. It was the abbot, who came to inquire how I had passed the night, and to tell me that breakfast was ready whenever

I should care to arise. For some reason, I felt a little embarrassed, even shamefaced, to have been caught daydreaming; and, though this was doubtless unnecessary, I apologized for my dilatoriness. Hilaire, I thought, gave me a keen, inquiring look, which was quickly withdrawn, as, with the suave courtesy of a good host, he assured me that there was nothing whatever for which I need apologize.

When I had breakfasted, I told Hilaire, with many expressions of gratitude for his hospitality, that it was time for me to resume my journey. But his regret at the announcement of my departure was so unfeigned, his invitation to tarry for at least another night was so genuinely hearty, so sincerely urgent, that I consented to remain. In truth, I required no great amount of solicitation, for, apart from the real liking I had taken to Hilaire, the mystery of the forbidden manuscript had entirely enslaved my imagination, and I was loth to leave without having learned more concerning it. Also, for a youth with scholastic leanings, the freedom of the abbot's library was a rare privilege, a precious opportunity not to be passed over.

"I should like," I said, "to pursue certain studies while I am here, with the aid of your incomparable collection."

"My son, you are more than welcome to remain for any length of time, and you can have access to my books whenever it suits your need or inclination." So saying, Hilaire detached the key of the library from his girdle and gave it to me. "There are duties," he went on, "which will call me away from the monastery for a few hours today, and doubtless you will desire to study in my absence."

A little later, he excused himself and departed. With inward felicitations on the longed-for opportunity that had fallen so readily into my hands, I hastened to the library, with no thought save to the read the proscribed manuscript. Giving scarcely a glance at the laden shelves, I sought the table with the secret drawer, and fumbled for the spring. After a little anxious delay, I pressed the proper spot and drew forth the drawer. An impulsion that had become a veritable obsession, a fever of curiosity that bordered upon actual madness, drove me, and if the safety of my soul had really depended upon it, I could not have denied the desire which forced me to take from the drawer the thin volume with plain unlettered binding.

Seating myself in a chair near one of the windows, I began to peruse the pages, which were only six in number. The writing was peculiar, with letter-forms of a fantasticality I had never met before, and the French was not only old but well-nigh barbarous in its quaint singularity. Notwithstanding the difficulty I found in deciphering them, a mad, unaccountable thrill ran through me at the first words, and I read on with all the sensations of a man who had been bewitched or who had drunken a philtre of bewildering potency.

There was no title, no date, and the writing was a narrative which began almost as abruptly as it ended. It concerned one Gerard, Comte de Venteillon, who, on the eve of his marriage to the renowned and beautiful demoiselle, Eleanor des Lys, had met in the forest near his chateau a strange, half-human creature with hoofs and horns. Now Gerard, as the narrative explained, was a knightly youth of indisputably proven valor, as well as a true Christian; so, in the name of our Savior, Jesus Christ, he bade the creature stand and give an account of itself.

Laughing wildly in the twilight, the bizarre being capered before him, and cried:

"I am a satyr, and your Christ is less to me than the weeds that grow on your kitchen-middens."

Appalled by such blasphemy, Gerard would have drawn his sword to slay the creature, but again it cried, saying:

"Stay, Gerard de Venteillon, and I will tell you a secret, knowing which, you will forget the worship of Christ, and forget your beautiful bride of tomorrow, and turn your back on the world and on the very sun itself with no reluctance and no regret."

Now, albeit half unwillingly, Gerard lent the satyr an ear and it came closer and whispered to him. And that which it whispered is not known; but before it vanished amid the blackening shadows of the forest, the satyr spoke aloud once more, and said:

"The power of Christ has prevailed like a black frost on all the woods, the fields, the rivers, the mountains, where abode in their felicity the glad, immortal goddesses and nymphs of yore. But still, in the cryptic caverns of earth, in places far underground, like the hell your priests have fabled, there dwells the pagan loveliness, there cry the pagan ecstasies." And with the last words, the creature laughed again its wild unhuman laugh, and disappeared among the darkening boles of the twilight trees.

From that moment, a change was upon Gerard de Venteillon. He returned to his chateau with downcast mien, speaking no cheery or kindly word to his retainers, as was his wont, but sitting or pacing always in silence, and scarcely heeding the food that was set before him. Nor did he go that evening to visit his betrothed, as he had promised; but, toward midnight, when a waning moon had arisen red as from a bath of blood, he went forth clandestinely by the postern door of the chateau, and following an old, half-obliterated trail through the woods, found his way to the ruins of the Chateau des Faussesflammes, which stands on a hill opposite the Benedictine abbey of Perigon.

Now these ruins (said the manuscript) are very old, and have long been avoided by the people of the district; for a legendry of immemorial evil clings about them, and it is said that they are the dwelling-place of foul spirits, the rendezvous of sorcerers and succubi. But Gerard, as if oblivious or fearless of their ill renown, plunged like one who is devil-driven into the shadow of the crumbling walls, and went, with the careful groping of a man who follows some given direction, to the northern end of the courtyard. There, directly between and below the two centermost windows, which, it may be, looked forth from the chamber of forgotten chatelaines, he pressed with his right foot on a flagstone differing from those about it in being of a triangular form. And the flagstone moved and tilted beneath his foot, revealing a flight of granite steps that went down into the earth. Then, lighting a taper he had brought with him, Gerard descended the steps, and the flagstone swung into place behind him.

On the morrow, his betrothed, Eleanor des Lys, and all her bridal train, waited vainly for him at the cathedral of Vyones, the principal town of Averoigne, where the wedding had been set. And from that time his face was beheld by no man, and no vaguest rumor of Gerard de Venteillon or of the fate that befell him has ever passed among the living. . . .

Such was the substance of the forbidden manuscript, and thus it ended. As I have said before, there was no date, nor was there anything to indicate by whom it had been written or how the knowledge of the happenings related had come into the writer's possession. But, oddly enough, it did not occur to me to doubt their veridity for a moment; and the curiosity I had felt concerning the contents of the manuscript was now replaced by a burning desire, a thousandfold more powerful, more obsessive, to know the ending of the story and to learn what Gerard de Venteillon had found when he descended the hidden steps.

In reading the tale, it had of course occurred to me that

the ruins of the Chateau des Faussesflammes, described therein, were the very same ruins I had seen that morning from my chamber window; and pondering this, I became more and more possessed by an insane fever, by a frenetic, unholy excitement. Returning the manuscript to the secret drawer, I left the library and wandered for awhile in an aimless fashion about the corridors of the monastery. Chancing to meet there the same monk who had taken my horse in charge the previous evening, I ventured to question him, as discreetly and casually as I could, regarding the ruins which were visible from the abbey windows.

He crossed himself, and a frightened look came over his broad, placid face at my query.

"The ruins are those of the Chateau des Faussesflammes," he replied. "For untold years, men say, they have been the haunt of unholy spirits, of witches and demons; and festivals not to be described or even named are held within their walls. No weapon known to man, no exorcism or holy water, has ever prevailed against these demons; many brave cavaliers and monks have disappeared amid the shadows of Faussesflammes, never to return; and once, it is told, an abbot of Perigon went thither to make war on the powers of evil; but what befell him at the hands of the succubi is not known or conjectured. Some say that the demons are abominable hags whose bodies terminate in serpentine coils; others, that they are women of more than mortal beauty, whose kisses are a diabolic delight that consumes the flesh of men with the fierceness of hell-fire. . . . As for me, I know not whether such tales are true; but I should not care to venture within the walls of Faussesflammes."

Before he had finished speaking, a resolve had sprung to life full-born in my mind: I felt that I must go to the Chateau des Faussesflammes and learn for myself, if possible, all that could be learned. The impulse was immediate, overwhelming, ineluctable; and even if I had so desired, I could no more have fought against it than if I had been the victim of some sorcerer's invultuation. The proscription of the abbot Hilaire, the strange unfinished tale in the old manuscript, the evil legendry at which the monk had now hinted—all these, it would seem, should have served to frighten and deter me from such a resolve; but, on the contrary, by some bizarre inversion of thought, they seemed to conceal some delectable mystery, to denote a hidden world of ineffable things, of vague undreamable pleasures that set my brain on fire and made my pulses throb deliriously. I did not know, I could not conceive, of what these pleasures would consist; but in some mystical manner I was as sure of their ultimate reality as the abbot Hilaire was sure of heaven.

I determined to go that very afternoon, in the absence of Hilaire, who, I felt instinctively, might be suspicious of any such intention on my part and would surely be inimical toward its fulfilment.

My preparations were very simple: I put in my pockets a small taper from my room and the heel of a loaf of bread from the refectory; and making sure that a little dagger which I always carried was in its sheath, I left the monastery forthwith. Meeting two of the brothers in the courtyard, I told them I was going for a short walk in the neighboring woods. They gave me a jovial *"pax vobiscum"* and went upon their way in the spirit of the words.

Heading as directly as I could for Faussesflammes, whose turrets were often lost behind the high and interlacing boughs, I entered the forest. There were no paths, and often I was compelled to brief detours and divagations by the thickness of the underbrush. In my feverous hurry to reach the ruins, it seemed hours before I came to the top of the hill which Faussesflammes surmounted, but probably it was little more than thirty minutes. Climbing the last declivity of the boulder-strewn slope, I came suddenly within view of the chateau, standing close at hand in the center of the level table which formed the summit. Trees had taken root in its broken-down walls, and the ruinous gateway that gave on the courtyard was half-choked by bushes, brambles and nettle-plants. Forcing my way through, not without difficulty, and with clothing that had suffered from the bramble-thorns, I went, like Gerard de Venteillon in the old manuscript, to the northern end of the court. Enormous evil-looking weeds were rooted between the flagstones, rearing their thick and fleshy leaves that had turned to dull sinister maroons and purples with the onset of autumn. But I soon found the triangular flagstone indicated in the tale, and without the slightest delay or hesitation I pressed upon it with my right foot.

A mad shiver, a thrill of adventurous triumph that was mingled with something of trepidation, leaped through me when the great flagstone tilted easily beneath my foot, disclosing dark steps of granite, even as in the story. Now, for a moment, the vaguely hinted horrors of the monkish legends became imminently real in my imagination, and I paused before the black opening that was to engulf me, wondering if some satanic spell had not drawn me thither to perils of unknown terror and inconceivable gravity.

Only for a few instants, however, did I hesitate. Then the sense of peril faded, the monkish horrors became a fantastic dream, and the charm of things unformulable, but ever closer at hand, always more readily attainable, tightened about me like the embrace of amorous arms. I lit my taper, I descended the stair; and even as behind Gerard de Venteillon, the triangular block of stone silently resumed its place in the paving of the court above me. Doubtless it was moved by some mechanism operable by a man's weight on one of the steps; but I did not pause to consider its modus operandi, or to wonder if there were any way by which it could be worked from beneath to permit my return.

There were perhaps a dozen steps, terminating in a low, narrow, musty vault that was void of anything more substantial than ancient, dust-encumbered cobwebs. At the end, a small doorway admitted me to a second vault that differed from the first only in being larger and dustier. I passed through several such vaults, and then found myself in a long passage or tunnel, half blocked in places by boulders or heaps of rubble that had fallen from the crumbling sides. It was very damp, and full of the noisome odor of stagnant waters and subterranean mold. My feet splashed more than once in little pools, and drops fell upon me from above, fetid and foul as if they had oozed from a charnel. Beyond the wavering circle of light that my taper maintained, it seemed to me that the coils of dim and shadowy serpents slithered away in the darkness at my approach; but I could not be sure whether they really were serpents, or only the troubled and retreating shadows, seen by an eye that was still unaccustomed to the gloom of the vaults.

Rounding a sudden turn in the passage, I saw the last thing I had dreamt of seeing—the gleam of sunlight at what was apparently the tunnel's end. I scarcely know what I had expected to find, but such an eventuation was somehow altogether unanticipated. I hurried on, in some confusion of thought, and stumbled through the opening, to find myself blinking in the full rays of the sun.

Even before I had sufficiently recovered my wits and my eyesight to take note of the landscape before me, I was struck by a strange circumstance: Though it had been early afternoon when I entered the vaults, and though my passage through them could have been a matter of no more than a few minutes, the sun was now nearing the horizon. There was also a difference in its light, which was both brighter and mellower than the sun I had seen above Averoigne; and the sky itself was intensely blue, with no hint of autumnal pallor.

Now, with ever-increasing stupefaction, I stared about me, and could find nothing familiar or even credible in the scene upon which I had emerged. Contrary to all reasonable expectation, there was no semblance of the hill upon which Faussesflammes stood, or of the adjoining country; but around me was a placid land of rolling meadows, through which a golden-gleaming river meandered toward a sea of deepest azure that was visible beyond the tops of laurel-trees. . . . But there are no laurel-trees in Averoigne, and the sea is hundreds of miles away: judge, then, my complete confusion and dumfoundment.

It was a scene of such loveliness as I have never before beheld. The meadow-grass at my feet was softer and more lustrous than emerald velvet, and was full of violets and many-colored asphodels. The dark green of ilex-trees was mirrored in the golden river, and far away I saw the pale gleam of a marble acropolis on a low summit above the plain. All things bore the aspect of a mild and clement spring that was verging upon an opulent summer. I felt as if I had stepped into a land of classic myth, of Grecian legend; and moment by moment, all surprise, all wonder as to how I could have come there, was drowned in a sense of ever-growing ecstasy before the utter, ineffable beauty of the landscape.

Near by, in a laurel-grove, a white roof shone in the late rays of the sun. I was drawn toward it by the same allurement, only far more potent and urgent, which I had felt on seeing the forbidden manuscript and the ruins of Faussesflammes. Here, I knew with an esoteric certainty, was the culmination of my quest, the reward of all my mad and perhaps impious curiosity.

As I entered the grove, I heard laughter among the trees, blending harmoniously with the low murmur of their leaves in a soft, balmy wind. I thought I saw vague forms that melted among the boles at my approach; and once a shaggy, goat-like creature with human head and body ran across my path, as if in pursuit of a flying nymph.

In the heart of the grove, I found a marble place with a portico of Doric columns. As I neared it, I was greeted by two women in the costume of ancient slaves; and though my Greek is of the meagerest, I found no difficulty whatever in comprehending their speech, which was of Attic purity.

"Our mistress, Nycea, awaits you," they told me. I could no longer marvel at anything, but accepted my situation without question or surmise, like one who resigns himself to the progress of some delightful dream. Probably, I thought, it was a dream, and I was still lying in my bed at the monastery; but never before had I been favored by nocturnal visions of such clarity and surpassing loveliness.

The interior of the palace was full of a luxury that verged upon the barbaric, and which evidently belonged to the period of Greek decadence, with its intermingling of Oriental influences. I was led through a hallway gleaming with onyx and polished porphyry, into an opulently furnished room, where, on a couch of gorgeous fabrics, there reclined a woman of goddess-like beauty.

At sight of her, I trembled from head to foot with the violence of a strange emotion. I had heard of the sudden mad loves by which men are seized on beholding for the first time a certain face and form; but never before had I experienced a passion of such intensity, such all-consuming ardor, as the one I conceived immediately for this woman. Indeed, it seemed as if I had loved her for a long time, without knowing that it was she whom I loved, and without being able to identify the nature of my emotion or to orient the feeling in any manner.

She was not tall, but was formed with exquisite voluptuous purity of line and contour. Her eyes were of a dark sapphire blue, with molten depths into which the soul was fain to plunge as into the soft abysses of a summer ocean. The curve of her lips was enigmatic, a little mournful, and gravely tender as the lips of an antique Venus. Her hair, brownish rather than blond, fell over her neck and ears and forehead in delicious ripples confined by a plain fillet of silver. In her expression, there was a mixture of pride and voluptuousness, of regal imperiousness and feminine yielding. Her movements were all as effortless and graceful as those of a serpent.

"I knew you would come," she murmured in the same soft-voweled Greek I had heard from the lips of her servants. "I have waited for you long; but when you sought refuge from the storm in the abbey of Perigon, and saw the manuscript in the secret drawer, I knew that the hour of your arrival was at hand. Ah! you did not dream that the spell which drew you so irresistibly, with such unaccountable potency, was the spell of my beauty, the magical allurement of my love!"

"Who are you?" I queried. I spoke readily in Greek, which would have surprised me greatly an hour before. But now, I was prepared to accept anything whatever, no matter how fantastic or preposterous, as part of the miraculous fortune, the unbelievable adventure which had befallen me.

"I am Nycea," she replied to my question. "I love you, and the hospitality of my palace and of my arms is at your disposal. Need you know anything more?"

The slaves had disappeared. I flung myself beside the couch and kissed the hand she offered me, pouring out protestations that were no doubt incoherent, but were nevertheless full of an ardor that made her smile tenderly.

Her hand was cool to my lips, but the touch of it fired my passion. I ventured to seat myself beside her on the couch, and she did not deny my familiarity. While a soft purple twilight began to fill the corners of the chamber, we conversed happily, saying over and over again all the sweet absurd litanies, all the felicitous nothings that come instinctively to the lips of lovers. She was incredibly soft in my arms, and it seemed almost as if the completeness of her yielding was unhindered by the presence of bones in her lovely body.

The servants entered noiselessly, lighting rich lamps of intricately carven gold, and setting before us a meal of spicy meats, of unknown savorous fruits and potent wines. But I could eat little, and while I drank, I thirsted for the sweeter wine of Nycea's mouth.

I do not know when we fell asleep; but the evening had flown like an enchanted moment. Heavy with felicity, I drifted off on a silken tide of drowsiness, and the golden lamps and the face of Nycea blurred in a blissful mist and were seen no more.

Suddenly, from the depths of a slumber beyond all dreams, I found myself compelled into full wakefulness. For an instant, I did not even realize where I was, still less what had aroused me. Then I heard a footfall in the open doorway of the room, and peering across the sleeping head of Nycea, saw in the lamplight the abbot Hilaire, who had paused on the threshold. A look of absolute horror was imprinted upon his face, and as he caught sight of me, he began to gibber in Latin, in tones where something of fear was blended with fanatical abhorrence and hatred. I saw that he carried in his hands a large bottle and an aspergillus. I felt sure that the bottle was full of holy water, and of course divined the use for which it was intended.

Looking at Nycea, I saw that she too was awake, and

knew that she was aware of the abbot's presence. She gave me a strange smile, in which I read an affectionate pity, mingled with the reassurance that a woman offers a frightened child.

"Do not fear for me," she whispered.

"Foul vampire! accursed lamia! she-serpent of hell!" thundered the abbot suddenly, as he crossed the threshold of the room, raising the aspergillus aloft. At the same moment, Nycia glided from the couch, with an unbelievable swiftness of motion, and vanished through an outer door that gave upon the forest of laurels. Her voice hovered in my ear, seeming to come from an immense distance:

"Farewell for awhile, Christophe. But have no fear. You shall find me again if you are brave and patient."

As the words ended, the holy water from the aspergillus fell on the floor of the chamber and on the couch where Nycea had lain beside me. There was a crash as of many thunders, and the golden lamps went out in a darkness that seemed full of falling dust, of raining fragments. I lost all consciousness, and when I recovered, I found myself lying on a heap of rubble in one of the vaults I had traversed earlier in the day. With a taper in his hand, and an expression of great solicitude, of infinite pity upon his face, Hilaire was stooping over me. Beside him lay the bottle and the dripping aspergillus.

"I thank God, my son, that I found you in good time," he said. "When I returned to the abbey this evening and learned that you were gone, I surmised all that had happened. I knew you had read the accursed manuscript in my absence, and had fallen under its baleful spell, as have so many others, even to a certain reverend abbot, one of my predecessors. All of them, alas! beginning hundreds of years ago with Gerard de Venteillon, have fallen victims to the lamia who dwells in these vaults."

"The lamia?" I questioned, hardly comprehending his words.

"Yes, my son, the beautiful Nycea who lay in your arms this night is a lamia, an ancient vampire, who maintains in these noisome vaults her palace of beatific illusions. How she came to take up her abode at Faussesflammes is not known, for her coming antedates the memory of men. She is old as paganism; the Greeks knew her; she was exorcised by Apollonius of Tyana; and if you could behold her as she really is, you would see, in lieu of her voluptuous body, the folds of a foul and monstrous serpent. All those whom she loves and admits to her hospitality, she devours in the end, after she has drained them of life and vigor with the diabolic delight of her kisses. The laurel-wooded plain you saw, the ilex-bordered river, the marble palace and all the luxury therein, were no more than a satanic delusion, a lovely bubble that arose from the dust and mold of immemorial death, of ancient corruption. They crumbled at the kiss of the holy water I brought with me when I followed you. But Nycea, alas! has escaped, and I fear she will still survive, to build again her palace of demoniacal enchantments, to commit again and again the unspeakable abomination of her sins."

Still in a sort of stupor at the ruin of my new-found happiness, at the singular revelations made by the abbot, I followed him obediently as he led the way through the vaults of Faussesflammes. He mounted the stairway by which I had descended, and as he neared the top and was forced to stoop a little, the great flagstone swung upward, letting in a stream of chill moonlight. We emerged, and I permitted him to take me back to the monastery.

As my brain began to clear, and the confusion into which I had been thrown resolved itself, a feeling of resentment grew apace—a keen anger at the interference of Hilaire.

Unheedful whether or not he had rescued me from dire physical and spiritual perils, I lamented the beautiful dream of which he had deprived me. The kisses of Nycea burned softly in my memory, and I knew that whatever she was, woman or demon or serpent, there was no one in all the world who could ever arouse in me the same love and the same delight. I took care, however, to conceal my feelings from Hilaire, realizing that a betrayal of such emotions would merely lead him to look upon me as a soul that was lost beyond redemption.

On the morrow, pleading the urgency of my return home, I departed from Perigon. Now, in the library of my father's house near Moulins, I write this account of my adventures. The memory of Nycea is magically clear, ineffably dear as if she were still beside me, and still I see the rich draperies of a midnight chamber illumined by lamps of curiously carven gold, and still I hear the words of her farewell:

"Have no fear. You shall find me again if you are brave and patient."

Soon I shall return, to visit again the ruins of the Chateau des Faussesflammes, and redescend into the vaults below the triangular flagstone. But, in spite of the nearness of Perigon to Faussesflammes, in spite of my esteem for the abbot, my gratitude for his hospitality, and my admiration for his incomparable library, I shall not care to revisit my friend Hilaire.

A RENDEZVOUS IN AVEROIGNE

GERARD DE L'AUTOMNE was meditating the rimes of a new ballade in honor of Fleurette, as he followed the leaf-arrassed pathway toward Vyones through the woodland of Averoigne. Since he was on his way to meet Fleurette, who had promised to keep a rendezvous among the oaks and beeches like any peasant girl, Gerard himself made better progress than the ballade. His love was at that stage which, even for a professional troubadour, is more productive of distraction than inspiration; and he was recurrently absorbed in a meditation upon other than merely verbal felicities.

The grass and trees had assumed the fresh enamel of a mediaeval May; the turf was figured with little blossoms of azure and white and yellow, like an ornate broidery; and there was a pebbly stream that murmured beside the way, as if the voices of undines were parleying deliciously beneath its waters. The sun-lulled air was laden with a wafture of youth and romance; and the longing that welled from the heart of Gerard seemed to mingle mystically with the balsams of the wood.

Gerard was a trouvère whose scant years and many wanderings had brought him a certain renown. After the fashion of his kind he had roamed from court to court, from chateau to chateau; and he was now the guest of the Comte de la Frênaie, whose high castle held dominion over half the surrounding forest. Visiting one day that quaint cathedral town, Vyones, which lies so near to the ancient wood of Averoigne, Gerard had seen Fleurette, the daughter of a well-to-do mercer named Guillaume Cochin; and had become more sincerely enamored of her blond piquancy than was to be expected from one who had been so frequently susceptible in such matters. He had managed to make his feelings known to her; and, after a month of billets-doux, ballads and stolen interviews contrived by the help of a complaisant waiting-woman, she had made this woodland tryst with him in the absence of her father from Vyones. Accompanied by her maid and a man-servant, she was to leave the town early that afternoon and meet Gerard under a certain beech-tree of enormous age and size. The servants would then withdraw discreetly; and the lovers, to all intents and purposes, would be alone. It was not likely that they would be seen or interrupted; for the gnarled and immemorial wood possessed an ill-repute among the peasantry. Somewhere in this wood there was the ruinous and haunted Chateau des Faussesflammes; and, also, there was a double tomb, within which the Sieur Hugh du Malinbois and his chatelaine, who were notorious for sorcery in their time, had lain unconsecrated for more than two hundred years. Of these, and their phantoms, there were grisly tales; and there were stories of loup-garous and goblins, of fays and devils and vampires that infested Averoigne. But to these tales Gerard had given little heed, considering it improbable that such creatures would fare abroad in open daylight. The madcap Fleurette had professed herself unafraid also; but it had been necessary to promise the servants a substantial *pourboire,* since they shared fully the local superstitions.

Gerard had wholly forgotten the lengendry of Averoigne, as he hastened along the sun-flecked path. He was nearing the appointed beech-tree, which a turn of the path would soon reveal; and his pulses quickened and became tremulous, as he wondered if Fleurette had already reached the trysting-place. He abandoned all effort to continue his ballade, which, in the three miles we had walked from La Frênaie, had not progressed beyond the middle of a tentative first stanza.

His thoughts were such as would befit an ardent and impatient lover. They were now interrupted by a shrill scream that rose to an unendurable pitch of fear and horror, issuing from the green stillness of the pines beside the way. Startled, he peered at the thick branches; and as the scream fell back to silence, he heard the sound of dull and hurrying footfalls, and a scuffling as of several bodies. Again the scream arose. It was plainly the voice of a woman in some distressful peril. Loosening his dagger in its sheath, and clutching more firmly a long hornbeam staff which he had brought with him as a protection against the vipers which were said to lurk in Averoigne, he plunged without hesitation or premeditation among the low-hanging boughs from which the voice had seemed to emerge.

In a small open space beyond the trees, he saw a woman who was struggling with three ruffians of exceptionally brutal and evil aspect. Even in the haste and vehemence of the moment, Gerard realized that he had never before seen such men or such a woman. The woman was clad in a gown of emerald green that matched her eyes; in her face was the pallor of dead things, together with a faery beauty; and her lips were dyed as with the scarlet of newly flowing blood. The men were dark as Moors, and their eyes were red slits of flame beneath oblique brows with animal-like bristles. There was something very peculiar in the shape of their feet; but Gerard did not realize the exact nature of the peculiarity till long afterward. Then he remembered that all of them were seemingly club-footed, though they were able to move with surpassing agility. Somehow, he could never recall what sort of clothing they had worn.

The woman turned a beseeching gaze upon Gerard as he sprang forth from amid the boughs. The men, however, did not seem to heed his coming; though one of them caught in a hairy clutch the hands which the woman sought to reach toward her rescuer.

Lifting his staff, Gerard rushed upon the ruffians. He struck a tremendous blow at the head of the nearest one—a blow that should have leveled the fellow to earth. But the staff came down on unresisting air, and Gerard staggered and almost fell headlong in trying to recover his equilibrium. Dazed and uncomprehending, he saw that the knot of struggling figures had vanished utterly. At least, the three men had vanished; but from the middle branches of a tall pine beyond the open space, the death-white features of the woman smiled upon him for a moment with faint, inscrutable guile ere they melted among the needles.

Gerard understood now; and he shivered as he crossed himself. He had been deluded by phantoms or demons, doubtless for no good purpose; he had been the gull of a questionable enchantment. Plainly there was something after all in the legends he had heard, in the ill-renown of the forest of Averoigne.

He retraced his way toward the path he had been following. But when he thought to reach again the spot from which he had heard that shrill unearthly scream, he saw that there was no longer a path; nor, indeed, any feature of the forest which he could remember or recognize. The foliage about him no longer displayed a brilliant verdure; it was sad and funereal, and the trees themselves were either cypress-like, or were already sere with autumn or decay. In lieu of the purling brook there lay before him a tarn of waters that were dark and dull as clotting blood, and which gave back no reflection of the brown autumnal sedges that trailed therein like the hair of suicides, and the skeletons of rotting osiers that writhed above them.

Now, beyond all question, Gerard knew that he was the victim of an evil enchantment. In answering that beguileful cry for succor, he had exposed himself to the spell, had been lured within the circle of its power. He could not know what forces of wizardry or demonry had willed to draw him thus; but he knew that his situation was fraught with supernatural menace. He gripped the hornbeam staff more tightly in his hand, and prayed to all the saints he could remember, as he peered about for some tangible bodily presence of ill.

The scene was utterly desolate and lifeless, like a place where cadavers might keep their tryst with demons. Nothing stirred, not even a dead leaf; and there was no whisper of dry grass or foliage, no song of birds nor murmuring of bees, no sigh nor chuckle of water. The corpse-gray heavens above seemed never to have held a sun; and the chill, unchanging light was without source or destination, without beams or shadows.

Gerard surveyed his environment with a cautious eye; and the more he looked the less he liked it: for some new and disagreeable detail was manifest at every glance. There were moving lights in the wood that vanished if he eyed them intently; there were drowned faces in the tarn that came and went like livid bubbles before he could discern their features. And, peering across the lake, he wondered why he had not seen the many-turreted castle of hoary stone whose nearer walls were based in the dead waters. It was so gray and still and vasty, that it seemed to have stood for incomputable ages between the stagnant tarn and the equally stagnant heavens. It was ancienter than the world, it was older than the light: it was coeval with fear and darkness; and a horror dwelt upon it and crept unseen but palpable along its bastions.

There was no sign of life about the castle; and no banners flew above its turrets or its donjon. But Gerard knew, as surely as if a voice had spoken aloud to warn him, that here was the fountainhead of the sorcery by which he had been beguiled. A growing panic whispered in his brain, he seemed to hear the rustle of malignant plumes, the mutter of demonian threats and plottings. He turned, and fled among the funereal trees.

Amid his dismay and wilderment, even as he fled, he thought of Fleurette and wondered if she were awaiting him at their place of rendezvous, or if she and her companions had also been enticed and led astray in a realm of damnable unrealities. He renewed his prayers, and implored the saints for her safety as well as his own.

The forest through which he ran was a maze of bafflement and eeriness. There were no landmarks, there were no tracks of animals or men; and the swart cypresses and sere autumnal trees grew thicker and thicker as if some malevolent will were marshalling them against his progress. The boughs were like implacable arms that strove to retard him; he could have sworn that he felt them twine about him with the strength and suppleness of living things. He fought them, insanely, desperately, and seemed to hear a crackling of infernal laughter in their twigs as he fought. At last, with a sob of relief, he broke through into a sort of trail. Along this trail, in the mad hope of eventual escape, he ran like one whom a fiend pursues; and after a short interval he came again to the shores of the tarn, above whose motionless waters the high and hoary turrets of that time-forgotten castle were still dominant. Again he turned and fled; and once more, after similar wanderings and like struggles, he came back to the inevitable tarn.

With a leaden sinking of his heart, as into some ultimate slough of despair and terror, he resigned himself and made no further effort to escape. His very will was benumbed, was crushed down as by the incumbence of a superior volition that would no longer permit his puny recalcitrance. He was unable to resist when a strong and hateful compulsion drew his footsteps along the margent of the tarn toward the looming castle.

When he came nearer, he saw that the edifice was surrounded by a moat whose waters were stagnant as those of the lake, and were mantled with the iridescent scum of corruption. The drawbridge was down and the gates were open, as if to receive an expected guest. But still there was no sign of human occupancy; and the walls of the great gray building were silent as those of a sepulcher. And more tomb-like even than the rest was the square and overtowering bulk of the mighty donjon.

Impelled by the same power that had drawn him along the lake-shore, Gerard crossed the drawbridge and passed beneath the frowning barbican into a vacant courtyard. Barred windows looked blankly down; and at the opposite end of the court a door stood mysteriously open, revealing a dark hall. As he approached the doorway, he saw that a man was standing on the threshold; though a moment previous he could have sworn that it was untenanted by any visible form.

Gerard had retained his hornbeam staff; and though his reason told him that such a weapon was futile against any supernatural foe, some obscure instinct prompted him to clasp it valiantly as he neared the waiting figure on the sill.

The man was inordinately tall and cadaverous, and was dressed in black garments of a superannuate mode. His lips were strangely red, amid his bluish beard and the mortuary whiteness of his face. They were like the lips of the woman who, with her assailants, had disappeared in a manner so dubious when Gerard had approached them. His eyes were pale and luminous as marsh-lights; and Gerard shuddered at his gaze and at the cold, ironic smile of his scarlet lips, that seemed to reserve a world of secrets all too dreadful and hideous to be disclosed.

"I am the Sieur du Malinbois," the man announced. His tones were both unctuous and hollow, and served to increase the repugnance felt by the young troubadour. And when his lips parted, Gerard had a glimpse of teeth that were unnaturally small and were pointed like the fangs of some fierce animal.

"Fortune has willed that you should become my guest," the man went on. "The hospitality which I can proffer you is rough and inadequate, and it may be that you will find my abode a trifle dismal. But at least I can assure you of a welcome no less ready than sincere."

"I thank you for your kind offer," said Gerard. "But I have an appointment with a friend; and I seem in some unaccountable manner to have lost my way. I should be profoundly grateful if you would direct me toward Vyones. There should be a path not far from here; and I have been so stupid as to stray from it."

The words rang empty and hopeless in his own ears even as he uttered them; and the name that his strange host had given—the Sieur du Malinbois—was haunting his mind like the funereal accents of a knell; though he could not recall at that moment the macabre and spectral ideas which the name tended to evoke.

"Unfortunately, there are no paths from my chateau to Vyones," the stranger replied. "As for your rendezvous, it will be kept in another manner, at another place, than the one appointed. I must therefore insist that you accept my hospitality. Enter, I pray; but leave your hornbeam staff at the door. You will have no need of it any longer."

Gerard thought that he made a moue of distaste and aversion with his over-red lips as he spoke the last sentences; and that his eyes lingered on the staff with an obscure apprehensiveness. And the strange emphasis of his words and demeanor served to awaken other fantasmal and macabre thoughts in Gerard's brain; though he could not formulate them fully till afterward. And somehow he was prompted to retain the weapon, no matter how useless it might be against an enemy of spectral or diabolic nature. So he said:

"I must crave your indulgence if I retain the staff. I have made a vow to carry it with me, in my right hand or never beyond arm's reach, till I have slain two vipers."

"That is a queer vow," rejoined his host. "However, bring it with you if you like. It is of no matter to me if you choose to encumber yourself with a wooden stick."

He turned abruptly, motioning Gerard to follow him. The troubadour obeyed unwillingly, with one rearward glance at the vacant heavens and the empty courtyard. He saw with no great surprise that a sudden and furtive darkness had closed in upon the chateau without moon or star, as if it had been merely waiting for him to enter before it descended. It was thick as the folds of a serecloth, it was airless and stifling like the gloom of a sepulcher that has been sealed for ages; and Gerard was aware of a veritable oppression, a corporeal and psychic difficulty in breathing, as he crossed the threshold.

He saw that cressets were now burning in the dim hall to which his host had admitted him; though he had not perceived the time and agency of their lighting. The illumination they afforded was singularly vague and indistinct, and the thronging shadows of the hall were unexplainably numerous, and moved with a mysterious disquiet; though the flames themselves were still as tapers that burn for the dead in a windless vault.

At the end of the passage, the Sieur du Malinbois flung open a heavy door of dark and somber wood. Beyond, in what was plainly the eating-room of the chateau, several people were seated about a long table by the light of cressets no less dreary and dismal than those in the hall. In the strange, uncertain glow, their faces were touched with a gloomy dubiety, with a lurid distortion; and it seemed to

Gerard that shadows hardly distinguishable from the figures were gathered around the board. But nevertheless he recognized the woman in emerald green who had vanished in so doubtful a fashion amid the pines when Gerard answered her call for succor. At one side, looking very pale and forlorn and frightened, was Fleurette Cochin. At the lower end reserved for retainers and inferiors, there sat the maid and the man-servant who had accompanied Fleurette to her rendezvous with Gerard.

The Sieur du Malinbois turned to the troubadour with a smile of sardonic amusement.

"I believe you have already met every one assembled," he observed. "But you have not yet been formally presented to my wife, Agathe, who is presiding over the board. Agathe, I bring to you Gerard de l'Automne, a young troubadour of much note and merit."

The woman nodded slightly, without speaking, and pointed to a chair opposite Fleurette. Gerard seated himself, and the Sieur du Malinbois assumed according to feudal custom a place at the head of the table beside his wife.

Now, for the first time, Gerard noticed that there were servitors who came and went in the room, setting upon the table various wines and viands. The servitors were preternaturally swift and noiseless, and somehow it was very difficult to be sure of their precise features or their costumes. They seemed to walk in an adumbration of sinister insoluble twilight. But the troubadour was disturbed by a feeling that they resembled the swart demoniac ruffians who had disappeared together with the woman in green when he approached them.

The meal that ensued was a weird and funereal affair. A sense of insuperable constraint, of smothering horror and hideous oppression, was upon Gerard; and though he wanted to ask Fleurette a hundred questions, and also demand an explanation of sundry matters from his host and hostess, he was totally unable to frame the words or to utter them. He could only look at Fleurette, and read in her eyes a duplication of his own helpless bewilderment and nightmare thralldom. Nothing was said by the Sieur du Malinbois and his lady, who were exchanging glances of a secret and baleful intelligence all through the meal; and Fleurette's maid and manservant were obviously paralyzed by terror, like birds beneath the hypnotic gaze of deadly serpents.

The foods were rich and of strange savor; and the wines were fabulously old, and seemed to retain in their topaz or violet depths the unextinguished fire of buried centuries. But Gerard and Fleurette could barely touch them; and they saw that the Sieur du Malinbois and his lady did not eat or drink at all. The gloom of the chamber deepened; the servitors became more furtive and spectral in their movements; the stifling air was laden with unformulable menace, was constrained by the spell of a black and lethal necromancy. Above the aromas of the rare foods, the bouquets of the antique wines, there crept forth the choking mustiness of hidden vaults and embalmed centurial corruption, together with the ghostly spice of a strange perfume that seemed to emanate from the person of the chatelaine. And now Gerard was remembering many tales from the legendry of Averoigne, which he had heard and disregarded; was recalling the story of a Sieur du Malinbois and his lady, the last of the name and the most evil, who had been buried somewhere in this forest hundreds of years ago; and whose tomb was shunned by the peasantry since they were said to continue their sorceries even in death. He wondered what influence had bedrugged his memory, that he had not recalled it wholly when he had first heard the name. And he was remembering other things and other stories, all of which confirmed his instinctive belief regarding the nature of the people into whose hands he had fallen. Also, he recalled a folklore superstition concerning the use to which a wooden stake can be put; and realized why the Sieur du Malinbois had shown a peculiar interest in the hornbeam staff. Gerard had laid the staff beside his chair when he sat down; and he was reassured to find that it had not vanished. Very quietly and unobtrusively, he placed his foot upon it.

The uncanny meal came to an end; and the host and his chatelaine arose.

"I shall now conduct you to your rooms," said the Sieur du Malinbois, including all of his guests in a dark, inscrutable glance. "Each of you can have a separate chamber, if you so desire; or Fleurette Cochin and her maid Angelique can remain together; and the man-servant Raoul can sleep in the same room with Messire Gerard."

A preference for the latter procedure was voiced by Fleurette and the troubadour. The thought of uncompanioned solitude in that castle of timeless midnight and nameless mystery was abhorrent to an insupportable degree.

The four were now led to their respective chambers, on opposite sides of a hall whose length was but indeterminately revealed by the dismal lights. Fleurette and Gerard bade each other a dismayed and reluctant good-night beneath the constraining eye of their host. Their rendezvous was hardly the one which they had thought to keep; and both were overwhelmed by the supernatural situation amid whose dubious horrors and ineluctable sorceries they had somehow become involved. And no sooner had Gerard left Fleurette than he began to curse himself for a poltroon because he had not refused to part from her side; and he marvelled at the spell of drug-like involition that had bedrowsed all his faculties. It seemed that his will was not his own, but had been thrust down and throttled by an alien power.

The room assigned to Gerard and Raoul was furnished with a couch, and a great bed whose curtains were of antique fashion and fabric. It was lighted with tapers that had a funereal suggestion in their form, and which burned dully in an air that was stagnant with the mustiness of dead years.

"May you sleep soundly," said the Sieur du Malinbois. The smile that accompanied and followed the words was no less unpleasant than the oily and sepulchral tone in which they were uttered. The troubadour and the servant were conscious of profound relief when he went out and closed the leaden-clanging door. And their relief was hardly diminished even when they heard the click of a key in the lock.

Gerard was now inspecting the room; and he went to the one window, through whose small and deep-set panes he could see only the pressing darkness of a night that was veritably solid, as if the whole place were buried beneath the earth and were closed in by clinging mold. Then, with an access of unsmothered rage at his separation from Fleurette, he ran to the door and hurled himself against it, he beat upon it with his clenched fists, but in vain. Realizing his folly, and desisting at last, he turned to Raoul.

"Well, Raoul," he said, "what do you think of all this?"

Raoul crossed himself before he answered; and his face had assumed the vizard of a mortal fear.

"I think, Messire," he finally replied, "that we have all been decoyed by a malefic sorcery; and that you, myself, the demoiselle Fleurette, and the maid Angelique, are all in deadly peril of both soul and body."

"That, also, is my thought," said Gerard. "And I believe it would be well that you and I should sleep only by turns;

and that he who keeps vigil should retain in his hands my hornbeam staff, whose end I shall now sharpen with my dagger. I am sure that you know the manner in which it should be employed if there are any intruders; for if such should come, there would be no doubt as to their character and their intentions. We are in a castle which has no legitimate existence, as the guests of people who have been dead, or supposedly dead, for more than two hundred years. And such people, when they stir abroad, are prone to habits which I need not specify."

"Yes, Messire." Raoul shuddered; but he watched the sharpening of the staff with considerable interest. Gerard whittled the hard wood to a lance-like point, and hid the shavings carefully. He even carved the outline of a little cross near the middle of the staff, thinking that this might increase its efficacy or save it from molestation. Then, with the staff in his hand, he sat down upon the bed, where he could survey the litten room from between the curtains.

"You can sleep first, Raoul." He indicated the couch, which was near the door.

The two conversed in a fitful manner for some minutes. After hearing Raoul's tale of how Fleurette, Angelique and himself had been led astray by the sobbing of a woman amid the pines, and had been unable to retrace their way, the troubadour changed the theme. And henceforth he spoke idly and of matters remote from his real preoccupations, to fight down his torturing concern for the safety of Fleurette. Suddenly he became aware that Raoul had ceased to reply; and saw that the servant had fallen asleep on the couch. At the same time an irresistable drowsiness surged upon Gerard himself in spite of all his volition, in spite of the eldritch terrors and forebodings that still murmured in his brain. He heard through his growing hebetude a whisper as of shadowy wings in the castle halls; he caught the sibilation of ominous voices, like those of familiars that respond to the summoning of wizards; and he seemed to hear, even in the vaults and towers and remote chambers, the tread of feet that were hurrying on malign and secret errands. But oblivion was around him like the meshes of a sable net; and it closed in relentlessly upon his troubled mind, and drowned the alarms of his agitated senses.

When Gerard awoke at length, the tapers had burned to their sockets; and a sad and sunless daylight was filtering through the window. The staff was still in his hand; and though his senses were still dull with the strange slumber that had drugged them, he felt that he was unharmed. But peering between the curtains, he saw that Raoul was lying mortally pale and lifeless on the couch, with the air and look of an exhausted moribund.

He crossed the room, and stooped above the servant. There was a small red wound on Raoul's neck; and his pulses were slow and feeble, like those of one who has lost a great amount of blood. His very appearance was withered and vein-drawn. And a phantom spice arose from the couch —a lingering wraith of the perfume worn by the chatelaine Agathe.

Gerard succeeded at last in arousing the man; but Raoul was very weak and drowsy. He could remember nothing of what had happened during the night; and his horror was pitiful to behold when he realized the truth.

"It will be your turn next, Messire," he cried. "These vampires mean to hold us here amid their unhallowed necromancies till they have drained us of our last drop of blood. Their spells are like mandragora or the sleepy sirups of Cathay; and no man can keep awake in their despite."

Gerard was trying the door; and somewhat to his surprise he found it unlocked. The departing vampire had been careless, in the lethargy of her repletion. The castle was very still; and it seemed to Gerard that the animating spirit of evil was now quiescent; that the shadowy wings of horror and malignity, the feet that had sped on baleful errands, the summoning sorcerers, the responding familiars, were all lulled in a temporary slumber.

He opened the door, he tiptoed along the deserted hall, and knocked at the portal of the chamber allotted to Fleurette and her maid. Fleurette, fully dressed, answered his knock immediately; and he caught her in his arms without a word, searching her wan face with a tender anxiety. Over her shoulder he could see the maid Angelique, who was sitting listlessly on the bed with a mark on her white neck similar to the wound that had been suffered by Raoul. He knew, even before Fleurette began to speak, that the nocturnal experiences of the demoiselle and her maid had been identical with those of himself and the man-servant.

While he tried to comfort Fleurette and reassure her, his thoughts were now busy with a rather curious problem. No one was abroad in the castle; and it was more than probable that the Sieur du Malinbois and his lady were both asleep after the nocturnal feast which they had undoubtedly enjoyed. Gerard pictured to himself the place and the fashion of their slumber; and he grew even more reflective as certain possibilities occurred to him.

"Be of good cheer, sweetheart," he said to Fleurette. "It is in my mind that we may soon escape from this abominable mesh of enchantments. But I must leave you for a little and speak again with Raoul, whose help I shall require in a certain matter."

He went back to his own chamber. The man-servant was sitting on the couch and was crossing himself feebly and muttering prayers with a faint, hollow voice.

"Raoul," said the troubadour a little sternly, "you must gather all your strength and come with me. Amid the gloomy walls that surround us, the somber ancient halls, the high towers and the heavy bastions, there is but one thing that veritably exists; and all the rest is a fabric of illusion. We must find the reality whereof I speak, and deal with it like true and valiant Christians. Come, we will now search the castle ere the lord and chatelaine shall awaken from their vampire lethargy."

He led the way along the devious corridors with a swiftness that betokened much forethought. He had reconstructed in his mind the hoary pile of battlements and turrets as he had seen them on the previous day; and he felt that the great donjon, being the center and stronghold of the edifice, might well be the place which he sought. With the sharpened staff in his hand, with Raoul lagging bloodlessly at his heels, he passed the doors of many secret rooms, the many windows that gave on the blindness of an inner court, and came at last to the lower story of the donjon-keep.

It was a large, bare room, entirely built of stone, and illumined only by narrow slits high up in the wall, that had been designed for the use of archers. The place was very dim; but Gerard could see the glimmering outlines of an object not ordinarily to be looked for in such a situation, that arose from the middle of the floor. It was a tomb of marble; and stepping nearer, he saw that it was strangely weather-worn and was blotched by lichens of gray and yellow, such as flourish only within access of the sun. The slab that covered it was doubly broad and massive, and would require the full strength of two men to lift.

Raoul was staring stupidly at the tomb. "What now, Messire?" he queried.

"You and I, Raoul, are about to intrude upon the bed-chamber of our host and hostess."

At his direction, Raoul seized one end of the slab; and he himself took the other. With a mighty effort that strained their bones and sinews to the cracking-point, they sought to remove it; but the slab hardly stirred. At length, by grasping the same end in unison, they were able to tilt the slab; and it slid away and dropped to the floor with a thunderous crash. Within, there were two open coffins, one of which contained the Sieur Hugh du Malinbois and the other his lady Agathe. Both of them appeared to be slumbering peacefully as infants; a look of tranquil evil, of pacified malignity, was imprinted upon their features; and their lips were dyed with a fresher scarlet than before.

Without hesitation or delay, Gerard plunged the lance-like end of his staff into the bosom of the Sieur du Malinbois. The body crumbled as if it were wrought of ashes kneaded and painted to human semblance; and a slight odor as of age-old corruption arose to the nostrils of Gerard. Then the troubadour pierced in like manner the bosom of the chatelaine. And simultaneously with her dissolution, the walls and floor of the donjon seemed to dissolve like a sullen vapor, they rolled away on every side with a shock as of unheard thunder. With a sense of weird vertigo and confusion Gerard and Raoul saw that the whole chateau had vanished like the towers and battlements of a bygone storm; that the dead lake and its rotting shores no longer offered their malefical illusions to the eye. They were standing in a forest glade, in the full unshadowed light of the afternoon sun; and all that remained of the dismal castle was the lichen-mantled tomb that stood open beside them. Fleurette and her maid were a little distance away; and Gerard ran to the mercer's daughter and took her in his arms. She was dazed with wonderment, like one who emerges from the night-long labyrinth of an evil dream, and finds that all is well.

"I think, sweetheart," said Gerard, "that our next rendezvous will not be interrupted by the Sieur du Malinbois and his chatelaine."

But Fleurette was still bemused with wonder, and could only respond to his words with a kiss.

A NIGHT IN MALNÉANT

MY sojourn in the city of Malnéant occurred during a period of my life no less dim and dubious than that city itself and the misty regions lying thereabout. I have no precise recollection of its locality, nor can I remember exactly when and how I came to visit it. But I had heard vaguely that such a place was situated along my route; and when I came to the fog-enfolded river that flows beside its walls, and heard beyond the river the mortuary tolling of many bells, I surmised that I was approaching Malnéant.

On reaching the gray, colossal bridge that crosses the river, I could have continued at will on other roads leading to remoter cities: but it seemed to me that I might as well enter Malnéant as any other place. And so it was that I set foot on the bridge of shadowy arches, under which the black waters flowed in stealthy division and were joined again in a silence as of Styx and Acheron.

That period of my life, I have said, was dim and dubious: all the more so, mayhap, because of my need for forgetfulness, my persistent and at times partially rewarded search for oblivion. And that which I needed to forget above all was the death of the lady Mariel, and the fact that I myself had slain her as surely as if I had done the deed with my own hand. For she had loved me with an affection deeper and purer and more stable than mine; and my changeable temper, my fits of cruel indifference or ferocious irritability, had broken her gentle heart. So it was that she had sought the anodyne of a lethal poison; and after she was laid to rest in the somber vaults of her ancestors, I had become a wanderer, followed and forever tortured by a belated remorse. For months, or years, I am uncertain which, I roamed from old-world city to city, heeding little where I went if only wine and the other agents of oblivion where available. ... And thus I came, somewhile in my indefinite journeying, to the dim environs of Malnéant.

The sun (if ever there was a sun above this region) had been lost for I knew not how long in a sky of leaden vapors; the day was drear and sullen at best. But now, by the thickening of the shadows and the mist, I felt that evening must be near; and the bells I had heard, however heavy and sepulchral their tolling, gave at least the assurance of prospective shelter for the night. So I crossed the long bridge and entered the grimly yawning gate with a quickening of my footsteps even if with no alacrity of spirit.

The dusk had gathered behind the gray walls, but there were few lights in the city. Few people were abroad, and these went upon their way with a sort of solemn haste, as if on some funereal errand that would admit of no delay. The streets were narrow, the houses high, with overhanging balconies and heavily curtained or shuttered windows. All was very silent, except for the bells, which tolled recurrently, sometimes faint and far off, and sometimes with a loud and startling clangor that seemed to come almost from overhead.

As I plunged among the shadowy mansions, along the streets from which a visible twilight issued to envelop me, it seemed that I was going farther and farther away from my memories at every step. For this reason I did not at once inquire my way to a tavern but was content to lose myself more and more in the gray labyrinth of buildings, which grew vaguer and vaguer amid the ever-mounting darkness and fog, as if they were about to dissolve in oblivion.

I think that my soul would have been almost at peace with itself, if it had not been for the reiterant ringing of the bells, which were like all bells that toll for the repose of the dead, and therefore set me to remembering those that had rung for Mariel. But whenever they ceased, my thoughts would drift back with an indolent ease, a recovered security, to the all-surrounding vagueness. . . .

I have no idea how far I had gone in Malnéant, nor how long I had roamed among those houses that hardly seemed as if they could be peopled by any but the sleeping or the dead. At last, however, I became aware that I was very tired, and bethought me of food and wine and a lodging for the night. But nowhere in my wanderings had I noticed the sign-board of an inn; so I resolved to ask the next passer-by for the desired direction.

As I have said before, there were few people abroad. Now, when I made up my mind to address one of them, it appeared that there was no one at all; and I walked onward through street after street in my futile search for a living face.

At length I met two women, clothed in gray that was cold and dim as the folds of the fog, and veiled withal, who were hurrying along with the same funereal intentness I had perceived in all other denizens of that city. I made bold to accost them, asking if they could direct me to an inn.

Scarcely pausing or even turning their heads, they answered: "We cannot tell you. We are shroud-weavers, and we have been busy making a shroud for the lady Mariel."

Now, at that name, which of all names in the world was the one I should least have expected or cared to hear, an unspeakable chill invaded my heart, and a dreadful dismay smote me like the breath of the tomb. It was indeed strange that in this dim city, so far in time and space from all I had fled to escape, a woman should have recently died who was also named Mariel. The coincidence appeared so sinister, that an odd fear of the streets through which I had wandered was born suddenly in my soul. The name had evoked, with a more irrevocable fatality than the tolling of the bells, all that I had vainly wished to forget; and my memories were like living coals in my heart.

As I went onward, with paces that had become more hurried, more feverish than those of the people of Malnéant, I met two men, who were likewise dressed from head to foot in gray; and I asked of them the same question I had asked of the shroud-weavers.

"We cannot tell you," they replied. "We are coffin-makers, and we have been busy making a coffin for the lady Mariel."

As they spoke, and hastened on, the bells rang out again, this time very near at hand, with a more dismal and sepulchral menace in their leaden tolling. And everything about me, the tall and misty houses, the dark, indefinite streets, the rare and wraith-like figures, became as if part of the obscure confusion and fear and bafflement of a nightmare. Moment by moment, the coincidence on which I had stumbled appeared all too bizarre for belief, and I was troubled now by the monstrous and absurd idea that the Mariel I knew had only just died, and that this fantastic city was in some unsurmisable manner connected with her death. But this, of course, my reason rejected summarily, and I kept repeating to myself: "The Mariel of whom they speak is another Mariel." And it irritated me beyond all measure that a thought so enormous and ludicrous should return when my logic had dismissed it.

I met no more people of whom to inquire my way. But at length, as I fought with my shadowy perplexity and my burning memories, I found that I had paused beneath the weather-beaten sign of an inn, on which the lettering had been half effaced by time and the brown lichens. The building was obviously very old, like all the houses in Malnéant; its upper stories were lost in the swirling fog, except for a few furtive lights that glowed obscurely down; and a vague and musty odor of antiquity came forth to greet me as I mounted the steps and tried to open the ponderous door. But the door had been locked or bolted; so I began to pound upon it with my fists to attract the attention of those within.

After much delay, the door was opened slowly and grudgingly, and a cadaverous-looking individual peered forth, frowning with portentous gravity as he saw me.

"What do you desire?" he queried, in tones that were both brusk and solemn.

"A room for the night, and wine," I requested.

"We cannot accommodate you. All the rooms are occupied by people who have come to attend the obsequies of the lady Mariel; and all the wine in the house has been requisitioned for their use. You will have to go elsewhere."

He closed the door quickly upon me with the last words.

I turned to resume my wanderings, and all that had troubled me before was now intensified a hundredfold. The gray mists and the grayer houses were full of the menace of memory: they were like traitorous tombs from which the cadavers of dead hours poured forth to assail me with envenomed fangs and talons. I cursed the hour when I had entered Malnéant, for it seemed to me now that in so doing I had merely completed a funereal, sinister circle through time, and had returned to the day of Mariel's death. And certainly, all my recollections of Mariel, of her final agony and her entombment, had assumed the frightful vitality of present things. But my reason still maintained, of course, that the Mariel who lay dead somewhere in Malnéant, and for whom all these obsequial preparations were being made, was not the lady whom I had loved, but another.

After threading streets that were even darker and narrower than those before traversed, I found a second inn, bearing a similar weather-beaten sign, and in all other respects very much like the first. The door was barred, and I knocked thereon with trepidation and was in no manner surprised when a second individual with a cadaverous face informed me in tones of sepulchral solemnity:

"We cannot accommodate you. All the rooms have been taken by musicians and mourners who will serve at the obsequies of the lady Mariel; and all the wine has been reserved for their use."

Now I began to dread the city about me with a manifold fear: for apparently the whole business of the people in Malnéant consisted of preparations for the funeral of this lady Mariel. And it began to be obvious that I must walk the streets of the city all night because of these same preparations. All at once, an overwhelming weariness was mingled with my nightmare terror and perplexity.

I had not long continued my peregrinations, after leaving the second inn, when the bells were tolled once more. For the first time, I found it possible to identify their source: they were in the spires of a great cathedral which loomed immediately before me through the fog. Some people were entering the cathedral, and a curiosity, which I knew to be both morbid and perilous, prompted me to follow them. Here, I somehow felt, I should be able to learn more regarding the mystery that tormented me.

All was dim within, and the light of many tapers scarcely served to illumine the vast nave and altar. Masses were being said by priests in black whose faces I could not see distinctly; and to me, their chanting was like words in a dream; and I could hear nothing, and nothing was plainly visible in all the place, except a bier of opulent fabrics on which there lay a motionless form in white. Flowers of many hues had been strewn upon the bier, and their fragrance filled the air with a drowsy languor, with an anodyne that seemed to drug my heart and brain. Such flowers had been cast on the bier of Mariel; and even thus, at her funeral, I had been overcome by a momentary dulling of the senses because of their perfume.

Dimly I became aware that someone was at my elbow. With eyes still intent on the bier, I asked:

"Who is it that lies yonder, for whom these masses are being said and these bells are rung?" And a slow, sepulchral voice replied:

"It is the lady Mariel, who died yesterday and who will be interred tomorrow in the vaults of her ancestors. If you wish, you may go forward and gaze upon her."

So I went down the cathedral aisle, even to the side of the bier, whose opulent fabrics trailed on the cold flags. And the face of her who lay thereon, with a tranquil smile upon the lips, and tender shadows upon the shut eyelids, was the face of the Mariel I had loved and of none other. The tides of time were frozen in their flowing; and all that was or had been or could be, all of the world that existed aside from her, became as fading shadows; and even as once before (was it eons or instants ago?) my soul was locked in the marble hell of its supreme grief and regret. I could not move, I could not cry out nor even weep, for my very tears were turned to ice. And now I knew with a terrible certitude that this one event, the death of the lady Mariel, had drawn apart from all other happenings, had broken away from the sequences of time and had found for itself a setting of appropriate gloom and solemnity; or perhaps had even built around itself the whole enormous maze of that spectral city, in which to abide my destined return among the mists of a deceptive oblivion.

At length, with an awful effort of will, I turned my eyes away; and leaving the cathedral with steps that were both hurried and leaden, I sought to find an egress from the dismal labyrinth of Malnéant to the gate by which I had entered. But this was by no means easy, and I must have roamed for hours in alleys blind and stifling as tombs, and along the tortuous, self-reverting thoroughfares, ere I came to a familiar street and was able henceforward to direct my paces with something of surety. And a dull and sunless daylight was dawning behind the mists when I crossed the bridge and came again to the road that would lead me away from that fatal city.

Since then, I have wandered long and in many places. But never again have I cared to revisit those old-world realms of fog and mist, for fear that I should come once more to Malnéant, and find that its people are still busied with their preparations for the obsequies of the lady Mariel.

THE CITY OF THE SINGING FLAME

FOREWORD

WHEN Giles Angarth disappeared, nearly two years ago, we had been friends for a decade or more, and I knew him as well as anyone could purport to know him. Yet the thing was no less a mystery to me than to others at the time, and until now, it has remained a mystery.

Like the rest, I sometimes thought that he and Ebbonly had designed it all between them as a huge, insoluble hoax; that they were still alive, somewhere, and laughing at the world that was so sorely baffled by their disappearance. And, until I at last decided to visit Crater Ridge and find, if I could, the two boulders mentioned in Angarth's narrative, no one had uncovered any trace of the missing men or heard even the faintest rumour concerning them. The whole affair, it seemed then, was likely to remain a most singular and exasperating riddle.

Angarth, whose fame as a writer of fantastic fiction was already very considerable, had been spending that summer among the Sierras, and had been living alone until the artist, Felix Ebbonly, went to visit him. Ebbonly, whom I had never met, was well-known for his imaginative paintings and drawings, and had illustrated more than one of Angarth's novels.

When neighbouring campers became alarmed over the prolonged absence of the two men, and the cabin was searched for some possible clue, a package addressed to me was found lying on the table; and I received it in due course of time, after reading many newspaper speculations concerning the double vanishment. The package contained a small, leather-bound note-book, and Angarth had written on the fly-leaf:

Dear Hastane,

You can publish this journal sometime, if you like. People will think it the last and wildest of all my fictions—unless they take it for one of your own. In either case, it will be just as well. Good-bye.

Faithfully,
GILES ANGARTH.

Feeling that it would certainly meet with the reception he anticipated, and being unsure, myself, whether the tale was truth or fabrication, I delayed publishing his journal. Now, from my own experience, I have become satisfied of its reality; and am finally printing it, together with an account of my personal adventures. Perhaps the double publication, preceded as it is by Angarth's return to mundane surroundings, will help to ensure the acceptance of the whole story for more than mere fantasy.

Still, when I recall my own doubts, I wonder.... But let the reader decide for himself. And first, as to Giles Angarth's journal:

I. The Dimension Beyond

July 31st, 1938.—I have never acquired the diary-keeping habit—mainly, because of my uneventful mode of existence, in which there has seldom been anything to chronicle. But the thing which happened this morning is so extravagantly strange, so remote from mundane laws and parallels, that I feel impelled to write it down to the best of my understanding and ability. Also, I shall keep account of the possible repetition and continuation of my experience. It will be perfectly safe to do this, for no one who ever reads the record will be likely to believe it....

I had gone for a walk on Crater Ridge, which lies a mile or less to the north of my cabin near Summit. Though differing markedly in its character from the usual landscapes round about, it is one of my favourite places. It is exceptionally bare and desolate, with little more in the way of vegetation than mountain sunflowers, wild currant-bushes, and a few sturdy, wind-warped pines and supple tamaracks.

Geologists deny it a volcanic origin; yet its outcroppings of rough, nodular stone and enormous rubble-heaps have all the air of scoriac remains—at least, to my non-scientific eye. They look like the slag and refuse of Cyclopean furnaces, poured out in pre-human years, to cool and harden into shapes of limitless grotesquerie.

Among them are stones that suggest the fragments of primordial bas-reliefs, or small prehistoric idols and figurines; and others that seem to have been graven with lost letters of an indecipherable script. Unexpectedly, there is a little tarn lying on one end of the long, dry Ridge—a tarn that has never been fathomed. The hill is an odd interlude among the granite sheets and crags, and the fir-clothed ravines and valleys of this region.

It was a clear, windless morning, and I paused often to view the magnificent perspectives of varied scenery that were visible on every hand—the titan battlements of Castle Peak; the rude masses of Donner Peak, with its dividing pass of hemlocks; the remote, luminous blue of the Nevada Mountains, and the soft green of willows in the valley at my feet. It was an aloof, silent world, and I heard no sound other than the dry, crackling noise of cicadas among the currant-bushes.

I strolled on in a zigzag manner for some distance, and coming to one of the rubble-fields with which the Ridge is interstrewn, I began to search the ground closely, hoping to find a stone that was sufficiently quaint and grotesque in its form to be worth keeping as a curiosity: I had found several such in my previous wanderings. Suddenly, I came to a clear space amid the rubble, in which nothing grew—a space that was round as an artificial ring. In the centre were two isolated boulders, queerly alike in shape, and lying about five feet apart.

I paused to examine them. Their substance, a dull, greenish-grey stone, seemed to be different from anything else in the neighbourhood; and I conceived at once the weird, unwarrantable fancy that they might be the pedestals of vanished columns, worn away by incalculable years till there remained only these sunken ends. Certainly, the perfect roundness and uniformity of the boulders was peculiar, and though I possess a smattering of geology, I could not identify their smooth, soapy material.

My imagination was excited, and I began to indulge in some rather overheated fantasies. But the wildest of these was a homely commonplace in comparison with the thing that happened when I took a single step forward in the vacant space immediately between the two boulders. I shall try to describe it to the utmost of my ability; though human language is naturally wanting in words that are adequate for the delineation of events and sensations beyond the normal scope of human experience.

Nothing is more disconcerting than to miscalculate the degree of descent in taking a step. Imagine, then, what it was like to step forward on level, open ground, and find utter nothingness underfoot! I seemed to be going down into an empty gulf; and, at the same time, the landscape before me vanished in a swirl of broken images and everything went blind. There was a feeling of intense, hyperborean cold, and an indescribable sickness and vertigo possessed me, due, no doubt, to the profound disturbance of equilibrium. Either from the speed of my descent or for some other reason, I was, too, totally unable to draw breath.

My thoughts and feelings were unutterably confused, and

half the time it seemed to me that I was falling *upward* rather than downward, or was sliding horizontally or at some oblique angle. At last, I had the sensation of turning a complete somersault; and then I found myself standing erect on solid ground once more, without the least shock or jar of impact. The darkness cleared away from my vision, but I was still dizzy, and the optical images I received were altogether meaningless for some moments.

When, finally, I recovered the power of cognisance and was able to view my surroundings with a measure of perception, I experienced a mental confusion equivalent to that of a man who might find himself cast without warning on the shore of some foreign planet. There was the same sense of utter loss and alienation which would assuredly be felt in such a case; the same vertiginous, overwhelming bewilderment, the same ghastly sense of separation from all the familiar environmental details that give colour, form and definition to our lives and even determine our very personalities.

I was standing in the midst of a landscape which bore no degree or manner of resemblance to Crater Ridge. A long, gradual slope, covered with violet grass and studded at intervals with stones of monolithic size and shape, ran undulantly away beneath me to a broad plain with sinuous, open meadows and high, stately forests of an unknown vegetation whose predominant hues were purple and yellow. The plain seemed to end in a wall of impenetrable, golden-brownish mist, that rose with phantom pinnacles to dissolve on a sky of luminescent amber in which there was no sun.

In the foreground of this amazing scene, not more than two or three miles away, there loomed a city whose massive towers and mountainous ramparts of red stone were such as the Anakim of undiscovered worlds might build. Wall on beetling wall, spire on giant spire, it soared to confront the heavens, maintaining everywhere the severe and solemn lines of a rectilinear architecture. It seemed to overwhelm and crush down the beholder with its stern and crag-like imminence.

As I viewed this city, I forgot my initial sense of bewildering loss and alienage, in an awe with which something of actual terror was mingled; and, at the same time, I felt an obscure but profound allurement, the cryptic emanation of some enslaving spell. But after I had gazed awhile, the cosmic strangeness and bafflement of my unthinkable position returned upon me, and I felt only a wild desire to escape from the maddeningly oppressive bizarrerie of this region and regain my own world. In an effort to fight down my agitation, I tried to figure out, if possible, what had really happened.

I had read a number of transdimensional stories—in fact, I had written one or two myself; and I had often pondered the possibility of other worlds or material planes which may co-exist in the same space with ours, invisible and impalpable to human senses. Of course, I realised at once that I had fallen into some such dimension. Doubtless, when I took that step forward between the boulders, I had been precipitated into some sort of flaw or fissure in space, to emerge at the bottom in this alien sphere—in a totally different kind of space.

It sounded simple enough, in a way, but not simple enough to make the *modus operandi* anything but a brain-racking mystery, and in a further effort to collect myself, I studied my immediate surroundings with a close attention. This time, I was impressed by the arrangement of the monolithic stones I have spoken of, many of which were disposed at fairly regular intervals in two parallel lines running down the hill, as if to mark the course of some ancient road obliterated by the purple grass.

Turning to follow its ascent, I saw right behind me two columns, standing at precisely the same distance apart as the two odd boulders on Crater Ridge, and formed of the same soapy, greenish-grey stone. The pillars were perhaps nine feet high, and had been taller at one time, since the tops were splintered and broken away. Not far above them, the mounting slope vanished from view in a great bank of the same golden-brown mist that enveloped the remoter plain. But there were no more monoliths, and it seemed as if the road had ended with those pillars.

Inevitably, I began to speculate as to the relationship between the columns in this new dimension and the boulders in my own world. Surely, the resemblance could not be a matter of mere chance. If I stepped between the columns, could I return to the human sphere by a reversal of my precipitation therefrom? And if so, by what inconceivable beings from foreign time and space had the columns and boulders been established as the portals of a gateway between the two worlds? Who could have used the gateway, and for what purpose?

My brain reeled before the infinite vistas of surmise that were opened by such questions. However, what concerned me most was the problem of getting back to Crater Ridge. The weirdness of it all, the monstrous walls of the near-by town, the unnatural hues and forms of the outlandish scenery, were too much for human nerves, and I felt that I should go mad if forced to remain long in such a milieu. Also, there was no telling what hostile powers or entities I might encounter if I stayed.

The slope and plain were devoid of animate life, as far as I could see; but the great city was presumptive proof of its existence. Unlike the heroes in my own tales, who were wont to visit the Fifth Dimension or the worlds of Algol with perfect *sang froid,* I did not feel in the least adventurous, and

I shrank back with man's instinctive recoil before the unknown. With one fearful glance at the looming city and the wide plain with its lofty, gorgeous vegetation, I turned and stepped back between the columns.

There was the same instantaneous plunge into blind and freezing gulfs, the same indeterminate falling and twisting, which had marked my descent into this new dimension. At the end I found myself standing, very dizzy and shaken, on the same spot from which I had taken my forward step between the greenish-grey boulders. Crater Ridge was swirling and reeling about me as if in the throes of earthquake, and I had to sit down for a minute or two before I could recover my equilibrium.

I came back to the cabin like a man in a dream. The experience seemed, and still seems, incredible and unreal; and yet it has overshadowed everything else, and has coloured and dominated all my thoughts. Perhaps by writing it down I can shake it off a little. It has unsettled me more than any previous experience in my whole life, and the world about me seems hardly less improbable and nightmarish than the one which I have penetrated in a fashion so fortuitous.

August 2nd.—I have done a lot of thinking in the past few days, and the more I ponder and puzzle, the more mysterious it all becomes. Granting the flaw in space, which must be an absolute vacuum, impervious to air, ether, light and matter, how was it possible for me to fall into it? And having fallen in, how could I fall out—particularly into a sphere that has no certifiable relationship with ours?

But, after all, one process would be as easy as the other, in theory. The main objection is: how could one move in a vacuum, either up or down, or backward or forward? The whole thing would baffle the comprehension of an Einstein, and I cannot feel that I have even approached the true solution.

Also, I have been fighting the temptation to go back, if only to convince myself that the thing really occurred. But, after all, why shouldn't I go back? An opportunity has been vouchsafed to me such as no man may ever have been given before, and the wonders I shall see, the secrets I shall learn, are beyond imagining. My nervous trepidation is inexcusably childish under the circumstances. . . .

II. The Titan City

August 3rd.—I went back this morning, armed with a revolver. Somehow, without thinking that it might make a difference, I did not step in the very middle of the space between the boulders. Undoubtedly as a result of this, my descent was more prolonged and impetuous than before, and seemed to consist mainly of a series of spiral somersaults. It must have taken me several minutes to recover from the ensuing vertigo, and when I came to, I was lying on the violet grass.

This time, I went boldly down the slope, and keeping as much as I could in the shelter of that bizarre purple and yellow vegetation, I stole towards the looming city. All was very still; there was no breath of wind in those exotic trees, which appeared to imitate, in their lofty, upright boles and horizontal foliage, the severe architectural lines of the Cyclopean buildings.

I had not gone far when I came to a road in the forest—a road paved with stupendous blocks of stone at least twenty feet square. It ran towards the city. I thought for a while that it was wholly deserted, perhaps disused; and I even dared to walk upon it, till I heard a noise behind me and, turning, saw the approach of several singular entities. Terrified, I sprang back and hid myself in a thicket, from which I watched the passing of those creatures, wondering fearfully if they had seen me. Apparently, my fears were groundless, for they did not even glance at my hiding-place.

It is hard for me to describe or even visualise them now, for they were totally unlike anything that we are accustomed to think of as human or animal. They must have been ten feet tall, and they were moving along with colossal strides that took them from sight in a few instants, beyond a turn of the road. Their bodies were bright and shining, as if encased in some sort of armour, and their heads were equipped with high, curving appendages of opalescent hues which nodded above them like fantastic plumes, but may have been antennae or other sense-organs of a novel type.

Trembling with excitement and wonder, I continued my progress through the richly-coloured undergrowth. As I went on, I perceived for the first time that there were no shadows anywhere. The light came from all portions of the sunless, amber heaven, pervading everything with a soft, uniform luminosity. All was motionless and silent, as before; and there was no evidence of bird, insect or animal life in all this preternatural landscape.

But, when I had advanced to within a mile of the city— as well as I could judge the distance in a realm where the very proportions of objects were unfamiliar—I became aware of something which at first was recognisable as a vibration rather than a sound. There was a queer thrilling in my nerves; the disquieting sense of some unknown force or emanation flowing through my body. This was perceptible for some time before I heard the music, but having heard it, my auditory nerves identified it at once with the vibration.

It was faint and far-off, and seemed to emanate from the very heart of the Titan city. The melody was piercingly sweet, and resembled at times the singing of some voluptuous feminine voice. However, no human voice could have possessed that unearthly pitch, the shrill, perpetually sustained notes that somehow suggested the light of remote worlds and stars translated into sound.

Ordinarily, I am not very sensitive to music; I have even been reproached for not reacting more strongly to it. But I had not gone much farther when I realised the peculiar mental and emotional spell which the far-off sound was beginning to exert upon me. There was a siren-like allurement which drew me on, forgetful of the strangeness and potential perils of my situation; and I felt a slow, drug-like intoxication of brain and senses.

In some insidious manner, I know not how nor why, the music conveyed the ideas of vast but attainable space and altitude, of superhuman freedom and exultation; and it seemed to promise all the impossible splendours of which my imagination has vaguely dreamt. . . .

The forest continued almost to the city walls. Peering from behind the final boscage, I saw their overwhelming battlements in the sky above me, and noted the flawless jointure of their prodigious blocks. I was near the great road, which entered an open gate large enough to admit the passage of behemoths. There were no guards in sight, and several more of the tall, gleaming entities came striding along and went in as I watched.

From where I stood, I was unable to see inside the gate, for the wall was stupendously thick. The music poured from that mysterious entrance in an ever-strengthening flood, and sought to draw me on with its weird seduction, eager for unimaginable things. It was hard to resist; hard to rally my will-power and turn back. I tried to concentrate on the thought of danger—but the thought was tenuously unreal.

At last I tore myself away and retraced my footsteps, very

slowly and lingeringly, till I was beyond reach of the music. Even then, the spell persisted, like the effects of a drug; and all the way home I was tempted to return and follow those shining giants into the city.

August 5th.—I have visited the new dimension once more. I thought I could resist that summoning music, and I even took some cotton-wadding with which to stuff my ears if it should affect me too strongly. I began to hear the supernal melody at the same distance as before, and was drawn onward in the same manner. But, this time, I entered the open gate!

I wonder if I can describe that city? I felt like a crawling ant upon its mammoth pavements, amid the measureless Babel of its buildings, of its streets and arcades. Everywhere there were columns, obelisks, and the perpendicular pylons of fane-like structures that would have dwarfed those of Thebes and Heliopolis. And the people of the city! How is one to depict them, or give them a name!

I think that the gleaming entities I first saw are not the true inhabitants, but are only visitors, perhaps from some other world or dimension, like myself. The real people are giants, too; but they move slowly, with solemn, hieratic paces. Their bodies are nude and swart, and their limbs are those of caryatides—massive enough, it would seem, to uphold the roofs and lintels of their own buildings. I fear to describe them minutely, for human words would give the idea of something monstrous and uncouth, and these beings are not monstrous, but have merely developed in obedience to the laws of another evolution than ours; the environmental forces and conditions of a different world.

Somehow, I was not afraid when I saw them—perhaps the music had drugged me till I was beyond fear. There was a group of them just inside the gate, and they seemed to pay me no attention whatever as I passed them. The opaque, jet-like orbs of their huge eyes were impassive as the carven eyes of androsphinxes, and they uttered no sound from their heavy, straight, expressionless lips. Perhaps they lack the sense of hearing, for their strange, semi-rectangular heads were devoid of anything in the nature of external ears.

I followed the music, which was still remote and seemed to increase little in loudness. I was soon overtaken by several of those beings whom I had previously seen on the road outside the walls; and they passed me quickly and disappeared in the labyrinth of buildings. After them there came other beings of a less gigantic kind, and without the bright shards or armour worn by the first-comers. Then, overhead, two creatures with long, translucent, blood-coloured wings, intricately veined and ribbed, came flying side by side and vanished behind the others. Their faces, featured with organs of unsurmisable use, were not those of animals, and I felt sure that they were beings of a high order of development.

I saw hundreds of those slow-moving, sombre entities whom I have identified as the true inhabitants, but none of them appeared to notice me. Doubtless they were accustomed to seeing far weirder and more unusual kinds of life than humanity. As I went on, I was overtaken by dozens of improbable-looking creatures, all going in the same direction as myself, as if drawn by the same siren melody.

Deeper and deeper I went into the wilderness of colossal architecture, led by that remote, ethereal, opiate music. I soon noticed a sort of gradual ebb and flow in the sound, occupying an interval of ten minutes or more; but, by imperceptible degrees, it grew sweeter and nearer. I wondered how it could penetrate that manifold maze of builded stone and be heard outside the walls. . . .

I must have walked for miles, in the ceaseless gloom of those rectangular structures that hung above me, tier on tier, at an awful height in the amber zenith. Then, at length, I came to the core and secret of it all. Preceded and followed by a number of those chimerical entities, I emerged on a great square, in whose centre was a temple-like building more immense than the others. The music poured, imperiously shrill and loud, from its many-columned entrance.

I felt the thrill of one who approaches the sanctum of some hierarchal mystery, when I entered the halls of that building. People who must have come from many different worlds or dimensions went with me, and before me, along the titanic colonnades, whose pillars were graven with indecipherable runes and enigmatic bas-reliefs. The dark, colossal inhabitants of the town were standing or roaming about, intent, like all the others, on their own affairs. None of these beings spoke, either to me or to one another, and though several eyed me casually, my presence was evidently taken for granted.

There are no words to convey the incomprehensible wonder of it all. And the music? I have utterly failed to describe that, also. It was as if some marvellous elixir had been turned into sound-waves—an elixir conferring the gift of superhuman life, and the high, magnificent dreams which are dreamt by the Immortals. It mounted in my brain like a supernal drunkenness, as I approached the hidden source.

I do not know what obscure warning prompted me, now, to stuff my ears with cotton before I went any farther. Though I could still hear it, still feel its peculiar, penetrant vibration, the sound became muted when I had done this, and its influence was less powerful henceforth. There is little doubt that I owe my life to this simple and homely precaution.

The endless rows of columns grew dim for a while as the interior of a long, basaltic cavern; and then, some distance ahead, I perceived the glimmering of a soft light on the floor and pillars. The light soon became an over-flooding radiance, as if gigantic lamps were being lit in the temple's heart; and the vibrations of the hidden music pulsed more strongly in my nerves.

The hall ended in a chamber of immense, indefinite scope, whose walls and roof were doubtful with unremoving shadows. In the centre, amid the pavement of mammoth blocks, there was a circular pit, above which seemed to float a fountain of flame that soared in one perpetual, slowly lengthening jet. This flame was the sole illumination, and also, was the source of the wild, unearthly music. Even with my purposely deafened ears, I was wooed by the shrill and starry sweetness of its singing; and I felt the voluptuous lure and the high, vertiginous exaltation.

I knew immediately that the place was a shrine, and that the transdimensional beings who accompanied me were visiting pilgrims. There were scores of them—perhaps hundreds; but all were dwarfed in the cosmic immensity of that chamber. They were gathered before the flame in various attitudes of worship; they bowed their exotic heads, or made mysterious gestures of adoration with unhuman hands and members. And the voices of several, deep as booming drums, or sharp as the stridulation of giant insects, were audible amid the singing of the fountain.

Spellbound, I went forward and joined them. Enthralled by the music and by the vision of the soaring flame, I paid as little heed to my outlandish companions as they to me. The fountain rose and rose, until its light flickered on the limbs and features of throned, colossal statues behind it— of heroes, gods or demons from the earlier cycles of alien time, staring in stone from a dusk of illimitable mystery.

The fire was green and dazzling, pure as the central flame of a star; it blinded me, and when I turned my eyes away, the air was filled with webs of intricate colour, with swiftly changing arabesques whose numberless, unwonted hues and patterns were such as no mundane eye had ever beheld. And I felt a stimulating warmth that filled my very marrow with intenser life. . . .

III. *The Lure of the Flame*

The music mounted with the flame; and I understood, now, its recurrent ebb and flow. As I looked and listened, a mad thought was born in my mind—the thought of how marvellous and ecstatical it would be to run forward and leap headlong into the singing fire. The music seemed to tell me that I should find in that moment of flaring dissolution all the delight and triumph, all the splendour and exaltation it had promised from afar. It besought me; it pleaded with tones of supernal melody, and despite the wadding in my ears, the seduction was well-nigh irresistible.

However, it had not robbed me of all sanity. With a sudden start of terror, like one who has been tempted to fling himself from a high precipice, I drew back. Then I saw that the same dreadful impulse was shared by some of my companions. The two entities with scarlet wings, whom I have previously mentioned, were standing a little apart from the rest of us. Now, with a great fluttering, they rose and flew towards the flame like moths towards a candle. For a brief moment the light shone redly through their half-transparent wings, ere they disappeared in the leaping incandescence, which flared briefly and then burned as before.

Then, in rapid succession, a number of other beings, who represented the most divergent trends of biology, sprang forward and immolated themselves in the flame. There were creatures with translucent bodies, and some that shone with all the hues of the opal; there were winged colossi, and Titans who strode as with seven-league boots; and there was one being with useless, abortive wings, who crawled rather than ran, to seek the same glorious doom as the rest. But among them there were none of the city's people: these merely stood and looked on, impassive and statue-like as ever.

I saw that the fountain had now reached its greatest height, and was beginning to decline. It sank steadily, but slowly, to half its former elevation. During this interval, there were no more acts of self-sacrifice, and several of the beings beside me turned abruptly and went away, as if they had overcome the lethal spell.

One of the tall, armoured entities, as he left, addressed me in words that were like clarion-notes, with unmistakable accents of warning. By a mighty effort of will, in a turmoil of conflicting emotions, I followed him. At every step, the madness and delirium of the music warred with my instincts of self-preservation. More than once, I started to go back. My homeward journey was blurred and doubtful as the wanderings of a man in an opium-trance; and the music sang behind me, and told me of the rapture I had missed, of the flaming dissolution whose brief instant was better than aeons of mortal life. . . .

August 9th.—I have tried to go on with a new story, but have made no progress. Anything that I can imagine, or frame in language, seems flat and puerile beside the world of unsearchable mystery to which I have found admission. The temptation to return is more cogent than ever; the call of that remembered music is sweeter than the voice of a loved woman. And always I am tormented by the problem of it all, and tantalised by the little which I have perceived and understood.

What forces are these whose existence and working I have merely apprehended? Who are the inhabitants of the city? And who are the beings that visit the enshrined flame? What rumour or legend has drawn them from outland realms and ulterior planets to that place of inenarrable danger and destruction? And what is the fountain itself, what the secret of its lure and its deadly singing? These problems admit of infinite surmise, but no conceivable solution.

I am planning to go back once more . . . but not alone. Someone must go with me, this time, as a witness to the wonder and the peril. It is all too strange for credence: I must have human corroboration of what I have seen and felt and conjectured. Also, another might understand where I have failed to do more than apprehend.

Who shall I take? It will be necessary to invite someone here from the outer world—someone of high intellectual and aesthetic capacity. Shall I ask Philip Hastane, my fellow fiction-writer? He would be too busy, I fear. But there is the Californian artist, Felix Ebbonly, who has illustrated some of my fantastic novels. . . .

Ebbonly would be the man to see and appreciate the new dimension, if he can come. With his bent for the bizarre and unearthly, the spectacle of that plain and city, the Babelian buildings and arcades, and the Temple of the Flame, will simply enthrall him. I shall write immediately to his San Francisco address.

August 12th.—Ebbonly is here: the myterious hints in my letter, regarding some novel pictorial subjects along his own line, were too provocative for him to resist. Now, I have explained fully and given him a detailed account of my adventures. I can see that he is a little incredulous, for which I hardly blame him. But he will not remain incredulous very long, for tomorrow we shall visit together the City of the Singing Flame.

August 13th.—I must concentrate my disordered faculties, must choose my words and write with exceeding care. This will be the last entry in my journal, and the last writing I shall ever do. When I have finished, I shall wrap the journal up and address it to Philip Hastane, who can make such disposition of it as he sees fit.

I took Ebbonly into the other dimension today. He was impressed, even as I had been, by the two isolated boulders on Crater Ridge.

"They look like the guttered ends of columns established by pre-human gods," he remarked. "I begin to believe you now."

I told him to go first, and indicated the place where he should step. He obeyed without hesitation, and I had the singular experience of seeing a man melt into utter, instantaneous nothingness. One moment he was there—the next, there was only bare ground, and the far-off tamaracks whose view his body had obstructed. I followed, and found him standing, in speechless awe, on the violet grass.

"This," he said at last, "is the sort of thing whose existence I have hitherto merely suspected, and have never been able to hint at in my most imaginative drawings."

We spoke little as we followed the range of monolithic boulders towards the plain. Far in the distance, beyond those high and stately trees with their sumptuous foliage, the golden-brown vapours had parted, showing vistas of an immense horizon; and past the horizon were range on range of gleaming orbs and fiery, flying motes in the depth of that amber heaven. It was as if the veil of another universe than ours had been drawn back.

We crossed the plain, and came at length within earshot of the siren music. I warned Ebbonly to stuff his ears with cotton-wadding, but he refused.

"I don't want to deaden any new sensation I may experience," he observed.

We entered the city. My companion was in a veritable rhapsody of artistic delight when he beheld the enormous buildings and the people. I could see, too, that the music had taken hold upon him: his look soon became fixed and dreamy as that of an opium-eater.

At first, he made many comments on the architecture and the various beings who passed us, and called my attention to details which I had not perceived before. However, as we drew nearer the Temple of the Flame, his observational interest seemed to flag, and was replaced by more and more of an ecstatic inward absorption. His remarks became fewer and briefer, and he did not even seem to hear my questions. It was evident that the sound had wholly bemused and bewitched him.

Even as on my former visit, there were many pilgrims going towards the shrine—and few that were coming away from it. Most of them belonged to evolutionary types that I had seen before. Among those that were new to me, I recall one gorgeous creature with golden and cerulean wings like those of a giant lepidoptera, and scintillating, jewel-like eyes that must have been designed to mirror the glories of some Edenic world.

I felt, too, as before, the captious thraldom and bewitchment, the insidious, gradual perversion of thought and instinct, as if the music were working in my brain like a subtle alkaloid. Since I had taken my usual precaution, my subjection to the influence was less complete than that of Ebbonly; but, nevertheless, it was enough to make me forget a number of things—among them, the initial concern which I had felt when my companion refused to employ the same mode of protection as myself. I no longer thought of his danger, or my own, except as something very distant and immaterial.

The streets were like the prolonged and bewildering labyrinth of a nightmare. But the music led us forthrightly, and always there were other pilgrims. Like men in the grip of some powerful current, we were drawn to our destination.

As we passed along the hall of gigantic columns and neared the abode of the fiery fountain, a sense of our peril quickened momentarily in my brain, and I sought to warn Ebbonly once more. But all my protests and remonstrances were futile: he was deaf as a machine, and wholly impervious to anything but the lethal music. His expression and movements were those of a somnambulist. Even when I seized and shook him with such violence as I could muster, he remained oblivious of my presence.

The throng of worshippers was larger than upon my first visit. The jet of pure, incandescent flame was mounting steadily as we entered, and it sang with the pure ardour and ecstasy of a star alone in space. Again, with ineffable tones, it told me the rapture of a moth-like death in its lofty soaring, the exultation and triumph of a momentary union with its elemental essence.

The flame rose to its apex; and even for me, the mesmeric lure was well-nigh irresistible. Many of our companions succumbed, and the first to immolate himself was the giant lepidopterous being. Four others, of diverse evolutional types, followed in appallingly swift succession.

In my own partial subjection to the music, my own effort to resist that deadly enslavement, I had almost forgotten the very presence of Ebbonly. It was too late for me to even think of stopping him, when he ran forward in a series of leaps that were both solemn and frenzied, like the beginning of some sacerdotal dance, and hurled himself headlong into the flame. The fire enveloped him; it flared up for an instant with a more dazzling greenness, and that was all.

Slowly, as if from benumbed brain centres, a horror crept upon my conscious mind, and helped to annul the perilous mesmerism. I turned, while many others were following

Ebbonly's example, and fled from the shrine and from the city. But somehow the horror diminished as I went; more and more, I found myself envying my companion's fate, and wondering as to the sensations he had felt in that moment of fiery dissolution. . . .

Now, as I write this, I am wondering why I came back again to the human world. Words are futile to express what I have beheld and experienced, and the change that has come upon me, beneath the play of incalculable forces in a world of which no other mortal is even cognisant. Literature is nothing more than a shadow. Life, with its drawn-out length of monotonous, reiterative days, is unreal and without meaning, now, in comparison with the splendid death which I might have had—the glorious doom which is still in store.

I have no longer any will to fight the ever-insistent music which I hear in memory. And there seems to be no reason at all why I should fight it. . . . Tomorrow, I shall return to the city.

IV. *The Third Venturer*

Even when I, Philip Hastane, had read through the journal of my friend, Giles Angarth, so many times that I had almost learned it by heart, I was still doubtful as to whether the incidents related therein were fiction or verity. The transdimensional adventures of Angarth and Ebbonly; the City of the Flame, with its strange residents and pilgrims; the immolation of Ebbonly, and the hinted return of the narrator himself for a like purpose, in the last entry of the diary, were very much the sort of thing that Angarth might have imagined in one of the fantastic novels for which he had become so justly famous. Add to this the seemingly impossible and incredible nature of the whole tale, and my hesitancy in accepting it as veridical will easily be understood.

However, on the other hand, there was the unsolved and recalcitrant enigma offered by the disappearance of the two men. Both were well-known, one as a writer, the other as an artist; both were in flourishing circumstances, with no serious cares or troubles; and their vanishment, all things considered, was difficult to explain on the ground of any motive less unusual or extraordinary than the one assigned in the journal. At first, as I have mentioned in my foreword to the diary, I thought the whole affair might well have been devised as a somewhat elaborate practical joke; but this theory became less and less tenable as weeks and months went by, and linked themselves slowly into a year, without the reappearance of the presumptive jokers.

Now, at last, I can testify to the truth of all that Angarth wrote—and more. For I, too, have been in Ydmos, the City of Singing Flame, and have known also the supernal glories and raptures of the Inner Dimension. And of these I must tell, however falteringly and inadequately, with mere human words, before the vision fades. For these are things which neither I, nor any other, shall behold or experience again.

Ydmos itself is now a riven ruin; the Temple of the Flame has been blasted to its foundations in the basic rock, and the fountain of singing fire has been stricken at its source. The Inner Dimension has perished like a broken bubble, in the great war that was made upon Ydmos by the rulers of the Outer Lands. . . .

After having finally laid down Angarth's journal, I was unable to forget the peculiar and tantalising problems it raised. The vague, but infinitely suggestive vistas opened by the tale were such as to haunt my imagination recurrently with a hint of half-revealed mysteries. I was troubled by the possibility of some great and mystic meaning behind it all; some cosmic actuality of which the narrator had perceived merely the external veils and fringes. As time went on, I found myself pondering it perpetually, and becoming more and more possessed by an overwhelming wonder, and a sense of something which no mere fiction-weaver would have been likely to invent.

In the early summer of 1939, after finishing a new novel, I felt able for the first time to take the necessary leisure for the execution of a project that had often occurred to me. Putting all my affairs in order, and knitting all the loose ends of my literary labours and correspondence in case I should not return, I left my home in Auburn, ostensibly for a week's vacation. Actually, I went to Summit, with the idea of investigating closely the milieu in which Angarth and Ebbonly had disappeared from human ken.

With strange emotions, I visited the forsaken cabin south of Crater Ridge, that had been occupied by Angarth, and saw the rough table of pine boards upon which my friend had written his journal, and then left the sealed package containing it to be forwarded to me after his departure.

There was a weird and brooding loneliness about the place, as if the non-human infinitudes had already claimed it for their own. The unlocked door had sagged inward from the pressure of high-piled winter snows, and fir-needles had sifted across the sill to strew the unswept floor. Somehow, I know not why, the bizarre narrative became more real and more credible to me, while I stood there, as if an occult intimation of all that had happened to its author still lingered around the cabin.

This mysterious intimation grew stronger when I came to visit Crater Ridge itself, and to search amid its miles of pseudo-volcanic rubble for the two boulders so explicitly described by Angarth as having a likeness to the pedestals of ruined columns. Following the northward path which he must have taken from his cabin, and trying to retrace his wanderings on the long, barren hill, I combed it thoroughly from end to end and from side to side, since he had not specified the location of the boulders. And after two mornings spent in this manner, without result, I was almost ready to abandon the quest and dismiss the queer, soapy, greenish-grey column-ends as one of Angarth's most provocative and deceptive fictions.

It must have been the formless, haunting intuition to which I have referred, that made me renew the search on the third morning. This time, after crossing and re-crossing the hill-top for an hour or more, and weaving tortuously among the cicada-haunted wild-currant bushes and sun-flowers on the dusty slopes, I came at last to an open, circular, rock-surrounded space that was totally unfamiliar. I had somehow missed it in all my previous roamings. It was the place of which Angarth had told; and I saw, with an inexpressible thrill, the two rounded, worn-looking boulders that were situated in the centre of the ring.

I believe that I trembled a little with excitement, as I went forward to inspect the curious stones. Bending over, but not daring to enter the bare, pebbly space between them, I touched one of them with my hand, and received a sensation of preternatural smoothness, together with a coolness that was inexplicable, considering that the boulders and the soil about them must have lain unshaded from the sultry August sun for many hours.

From that moment, I became fully persuaded that Angarth's account was no mere fable. Just why I should have felt so certain of this, I am powerless to say. But it seemed to me that I stood on the threshold of an ultramundane mystery, on the brink of uncharted gulfs. I looked about at the familiar Sierran valleys and mountains, wondering that they still preserved their wonted outlines, and were still unchanged by the contiguity of alien worlds, still untouched by the luminous glories of arcanic dimensions.

Convinced that I had indeed found the gateway between

the worlds, I was prompted to strange reflections. What, and where, was this other sphere to which my friend had obtained entrance? Was it near at hand, like a secret room in the structure of space? Or was it, in reality, millions or trillions of light-years away, by the reckoning of astronomic distance, in a planet of some ulterior galaxy?

After all, we know little or nothing of the actual nature of space; and perhaps, in some way that we cannot imagine, the infinite is doubled upon itself in places, with dimensional folds and tucks, and short-cuts whereby the distance to Algenib or Aldebaran is but a step. Perhaps, also, there is more than one infinity. The spatial "flaw" into which Angarth had fallen might well be a sort of super-dimension, abridging the cosmic intervals and connecting universe with universe.

However, because of this very certitude that I had found the inter-spheric portals, and could follow Angarth and Ebbonly if I so desired, I hesitated before trying the experiment. I was mindful of the mystic danger and irrefragable lure that had overcome the others. I was consumed by imaginative curiosity, by an avid, well-nigh feverish longing to behold the wonders of this exotic realm; but I did not purpose to become a victim to the opiate power and fascination of the Singing Flame.

I stood for a long time, eyeing the odd boulders and the barren, pebble-littered spot that gave admission to the unknown. At length, I went away, deciding to defer my venture till the following morning. Visualising the weird doom to which the others had gone so voluntarily, and even gladly, I must confess that I was afraid. On the other hand, I was drawn by the fateful allurement that leads an explorer into far places . . . and, perhaps, by something more than this.

I slept badly that night, with nerves and brain excited by

formless, glowing premonitions, by intimations of half-conceived perils, and splendours and vastnesses. Early the next morning, while the sun was still hanging above the Nevada Mountains, I returned to Crater Ridge. I carried a strong hunting-knife and a Colt revolver, and wore a filled cartridge-belt, with a knapsack containing sandwiches and a thermos bottle of coffee.

Before starting, I had stuffed my ears tightly with cotton soaked in a new anaesthetic fluid, mild but efficacious, which would serve to deafen me completely for many hours. In this way, I felt that I should be immune to the demoralising music of the fiery fountain. I peered about at the rugged landscape with its far-flung vistas, wondering if I should ever see it again. Then, resolutely, but with the eerie thrilling and sinking of one who throws himself from a high cliff into some bottomless chasm, I stepped forward into the space between the greyish-green boulders.

My sensations, generally speaking, were similar to those described by Angarth in his diary. Blackness and illimitable emptiness seemed to wrap me round in a dizzy swirl as of rushing wind or milling water, and I went down and down in a spiral descent whose duration I have never been able to estimate. Intolerably stifled, and without even the power to gasp for breath, in the chill, airless vacuum that froze my very muscles and marrow, I felt that I should lose consciousness in another moment and descend into the greater gulf of death or oblivion.

Something seemed to arrest my fall, and I became aware that I was standing still, though I was troubled for some time by a queer doubt as to whether my position was vertical, horizontal, or upside-down in relation to the solid substance that my feet had encountered. Then the blackness lifted slowly like a dissolving cloud, and I saw the slope of violet grass, the rows of irregular monoliths running downwards from where I stood, and the grey-green columns near at hand. Beyond was the titan, perpendicular city of red stone that was dominant above the high and multi-coloured vegetation of the plain.

It was all very much as Angarth had depicted it; but somehow, even then, I became aware of differences that were not immediately or clearly definable, of scenic details and atmospheric elements for which his accounts had not prepared me. And, at the moment, I was too thoroughly disequilibrated and overpowered by the vision of it all to even speculate concerning the character of these differences.

As I gazed at the city, with its crowding tiers of battlements and its multitude of overlooming spires, I felt the invisible threads of a secret attraction, was seized by an imperative longing to know the mysteries hidden behind the massive walls and the myriad buildings. Then, a moment later, my gaze was drawn to the remote, opposite horizon of the plain, as if by some conflicting impulse whose nature and origin were undiscoverable.

It must have been because I had formed so clear and definite a picture of the scene from my friend's narrative, that I was surprised, and even a little disturbed as if by something wrong or irrelevant, when I saw in the far distance the shining towers of what seemed to be another city—a city of which Angarth had not written. The towers rose in serried lines, reaching for many miles in a curious arc-like formation, and were sharply defined against a blackish mass of cloud that had reared behind them and was spreading out on the luminous, amber sky in sullen webs and sinister, crawling filaments.

Subtle disquietude and repulsion seemed to emanate from the far-off, glittering spires, even as attraction emanated from those of the nearer city. I saw them quiver and pulse with an evil light, like living and moving things, through what I assumed to be some refractive trick of the atmosphere. Then, for an instant, the black cloud behind them glowed with dull, angry crimson throughout its whole mass, and even its questing webs and tendrils were turned into lurid threads of fire.

The crimson faded, leaving the cloud inert and lumpish as before; but from many of the vanward towers, lines of red and violet flame had leaped, like out-thrust lances, at the bosom of the plain beneath them. They were held thus for at least a minute, moving slowly across a wide area, before they vanished. In the spaces between the towers, I now perceived a multitude of gleaming, restless particles, like armies of militant atoms, and wondered if perchance they were living beings. If the idea had not appeared so fantastical, I could have sworn, even then, that the far city had already changed its position and was advancing towards the other on the plain.

V. *The Striding Doom*

Apart from the fulguration of the cloud, the flames that had sprung from the towers, and the quiverings which I deemed a refractive phenomenon, the whole landscape before and about me was unnaturally still. On the strange amber air, the Tyrian-tinted grasses, and the proud, opulent foliage of the unknown trees, there lay the dead calm that precedes the stupendous turmoil of typhonic storm or seismic cataclysm. The brooding sky was permeated with intuitions of cosmic menace, and weighed down by a dim, elemental despair.

Alarmed by this ominous atmosphere, I looked behind me at the two pillars which, according to Angarth, were the gateway of return to the human world. For an instant, I was tempted to go back. Then I turned once more to the near-by city, and the feelings I have mentioned were lost in an oversurging awesomeness and wonder. I felt the thrill of a deep, supernal exaltation before the magnitude of the mighty buildings; a compelling sorcery was laid upon me by the very lines of their construction, by the harmonies of a solemn architectural music. I forgot my impulse to return to Crater Ridge, and started down the slope towards the city.

Soon the boughs of the purple and yellow forest arched above me like the altitudes of Titan-builded aisles, with leaves that fretted the rich heaven in gorgeous arabesques. Beyond them, ever and anon, I caught glimpses of the piled ramparts of my destination; but looking back in the direction of that other city on the horizon, I found that its fulgurating towers were now lost to view.

I saw, however, that the masses of the great sombre cloud were rising steadily on the sky, and once again they flared to a swart, malignant red, as if with some unearthly form of sheet-lightning; and though I could hear nothing with my deadened ears, the ground beneath me trembled with long vibrations as of thunder. There was a queer quality in the vibrations, that seemed to tear my nerves and set my teeth on edge with its throbbing, lancinating discord, painful as broken glass or the torment of a tightened rack.

Like Angarth before me, I came to the paved Cyclopean highway. Following it, in the stillness after the unheard peals of thunder, I felt another and subtler vibration, which I knew to be that of the Singing Flame in the temple at the city's core. It seemed to soothe and exalt and bear me on, to erase with soft caresses the ache that still lingered in my nerves from the torturing pulsations of the thunder.

I met no one on the road, and was not passed by any of the trans-dimensional pilgrims such as had overtaken Angarth; and when the accumulated ramparts loomed above the highest trees and I came forth from the wood in their very shadow, I saw that the great gate of the city was closed, leaving no crevice through which a pygmy like myself might obtain entrance.

Feeling a profound and peculiar discomfiture, such as one would experience in a dream that had gone wrong, I stared at the grim, unrelenting blankness of the gate, which seemed to be wrought from one enormous sheet of sombre and lustreless metal. Then I peered upward at the sheerness of the wall, which rose above me like an alpine cliff, and saw that the battlements were seemingly deserted. Was the city forsaken by its people, by the guardians of the Flame? Was it no longer open to the pilgrims who came from outlying lands to worship the Flame and immolate themselves?

With a curious reluctance, after lingering there for many minutes in a sort of stupor, I turned away to retrace my steps. In the interim of my journey, the black cloud had drawn immeasurably nearer, and was now blotting out half the heaven with two portentous, wing-like formations. It was a sinister and terrible sight; and it lightened again with that ominous, wrathful flaming, with a detonation that beat upon my deaf ears like waves of disintegrative force, and seemed to lacerate the inmost fibres of my body.

I hesitated, fearing that the storm would burst upon me before I could reach the inter-dimensional portals, for I saw that I should be exposed to an elemental disturbance of unfamiliar character and supreme violence. Then, in mid-air before the imminent, ever-rising cloud, I perceived two flying creatures whom I can compare only to gigantic moths. With bright, luminous wings, upon the ebon forefront of the storm, they approached me in level but precipitate flight, and would have crashed headlong against the shut gate if they had not checked themselves with sudden, easy poise.

With hardly a flutter, they descended and paused on the

ground beside me, supporting themselves on queer, delicate legs that branched at the knee-joints in floating antennae and waving tentacles. Their wings were sumptuously mottled webs of pearl and madder, opal and orange; their heads were circled by a series of convex and concave eyes, and fringed with coiling, horn-like organs from whose hollow ends there hung aerial filaments. I was startled and amazed by their aspect; but somehow, by an obscure telepathy I felt assured that their intentions towards me were friendly.

I knew that they wished to enter the city, and also that they understood my predicament. Nevertheless, I was not prepared for what happened. With movements of utmost celerity and grace, one of the giant, moth-like beings stationed himself at my right hand, and the other at my left. Then, before I could even suspect their intention, they enfolded my limbs and body with their long tentacles, wrapping me round and round as if with powerful ropes; and carrying me between them as if my weight were a mere trifle, they rose in the air and soared at the mighty ramparts!

In that swift and effortless ascent, the wall seemed to flow downward beside and beneath us, like a wave of molten stone. Dizzily, I watched the falling away of the mammoth blocks in endless recession. Then we were level with the broad ramparts, were flying across the unguarded parapets and over a canyon-like space, towards the immense rectangular buildings and numberless square towers.

We had hardly crossed the walls when a weird, flickering glow was cast on the edifices before us by another lightening of the great cloud. The moth-like beings paid no apparent heed, and flew steadily on into the city with their strange faces towards an unseen goal. But, turning my head to peer backward at the storm, I beheld an astounding and appalling spectacle. Beyond the city ramparts, as if wrought by black magic or the toil of genii, another city had reared, and its high towers were moving swiftly forward beneath the rubescent dome of the burning cloud!

A second glance, and I perceived that the towers were identical with those I had beheld afar on the plain. In the interim of my passage through the woods, they had travelled over an expanse of many miles, by means of some unknown motive-power, and had closed in on the City of the Flame. Looking more closely, to determine the manner of their locomotion, I saw that they were not mounted on wheels, but on short, massy legs like jointed columns of metal, that gave them the stride of ungainly colossi. There were six or more of these legs to each tower, and near the tops of the towers were rows of huge eyelike openings, from which issued the bolts of red and violet flame I have mentioned before.

The many-coloured forest had been burned away by these flames in a league-wide swath of devastation, even to the walls, and there was nothing but a stretch of black, vapouring desert between the mobile towers and the city. Then, even as I gazed, the long, leaping beams began to assail the craggy ramparts, and the topmost parapets were melting like lava beneath them. It was a scene of utmost terror and grandeur; but, a moment later, it was blotted from my vision by the buildings among which we had now plunged.

The great lepidopterous creatures who bore me went on with the speed of eyrie-questing eagles. In the course of that flight, I was hardly capable of conscious thought or volition; I lived only in the breathless and giddy freedom of aerial movement, of dream-like levitation above the labyrinthine maze of stone immensities and marvels. I was without actual cognisance of much that I beheld in that stupendous Babel of architectural imageries, and only afterwards, in the more tranquil light of recollection, could I give coherent form and meaning to many of my impressions.

My senses were stunned by the vastness and strangeness

of it all; I realised but dimly the cataclysmic ruin that was being loosed upon the city behind us, and the doom from which we were fleeing. I knew that war was being made with unearthly weapons and engineries, by inimical powers that I could not imagine, for a purpose beyond my conception; but, to me, it all had the elemental confusion and vague, impersonal horror of some cosmic catastrophe.

We flew deeper and deeper into the city. Broad, platform roofs and terrace-like tiers of balconies flowed away beneath us, and the pavements raced like darkling streams at some enormous depth. Severe cubicular spires and square monoliths were all about and above us; and we saw on some of the roofs the dark, Atlantean people of the city, moving slowly and statuesquely, or standing in attitudes of cryptic resignation and despair, with their faces towards the flaming cloud. All were weaponless, and I saw no engineries anywhere such as might be used for purposes of military defence.

Swiftly as we flew, the climbing cloud was swifter, and the darkness of its intermittently glowing dome had overarched the town while its spidery filaments had meshed the further heavens and would soon attach themselves to the opposite horizon. The buildings darkened and lightened with the recurrent fulguration, and I felt in all my tissues the painful pulsing of the thunderous vibrations.

Dully and vaguely, I realised that the winged beings who carried me between them were pilgrims to the Temple of the Flame. More and more, I became aware of an influence that must have been that of the starry music emanating from the temple's heart. There were soft, soothing vibrations in the air, that seemed to absorb and nullify the tearing discords of the unheard thunder. I felt that we were entering a zone of mystic refuge, of sidereal and celestial security, and my troubled senses were both lulled and exalted.

The gorgeous wings of the giant lepidopters began to slant downward. Before and beneath us, at some distance, I perceived a mammoth pile which I knew at once for the Temple of the Flame. Down, still down we went, in the awesome space of the surrounding square; and then I was borne in through the lofty, ever-open entrance, and along the high hall with its thousand columns. Pregnant with strange balsams, the dim, mysterious dusk enfolded us, and we seemed to be entering realms of pre-mundane antiquity and trans-stellar immensity; to be following a pillared cavern that led to the core of some ultimate star.

It seemed that we were the last and only pilgrims, and also that the temple was deserted by its guardians, for we met no one in the whole extent of that column-crowded gloom. After a while, the dusk began to lighten, and we plunged into a widening beam of radiance, and then into the vast central chamber in which soared the fountain of green fire.

I remember only the impression of shadowy, flickering space, of a vault that was lost in the azure of infinity, of colossal and Memnonian statues that looked down from Himalaya-like altitudes; and, above all, the dazzling jet of flame that aspired from a pit in the pavement and rose into the air like the visible rapture of gods. But all this I saw for an instant only. Then I realised that the beings who bore me were flying straight towards the Flame on level wings, without the slightest pause or flutter of hesitation!

VI. *The Inner Sphere*

There was no room for fear, no time for alarm, in the dazed and chaotic turmoil of my sensations. I was stupified by all that I had experienced, and moreover, the drug-like spell of the Flame was upon me, even though I could not hear its fatal singing. I believe that I struggled a little, by some sort of mechanical muscular revulsion, against the tentacular arms that were wound about me. But the lepidopters gave no heed; it was plain that they were conscious of nothing but the mounting fire and its seductive music.

I remember, however, that there was no sensation of actual heat, such as might have been expected, when we neared the soaring column. Instead, I felt the most ineffable thrilling in all my fibres, as if I were being permeated by waves of celestial energy and demiurgic ecstasy. Then we entered the Flame. . . .

Like Angarth before me, I had taken it for granted that the fate of all those who flung themselves into the Flame was an instant though blissful destruction. I expected to undergo a briefly flaring dissolution, followed by the nothingness of utter annihilation. The thing which really happened was beyond the boldest reach of speculative thought, and to give even a meagre idea of my sensations would beggar the resources of language.

The Flame enfolded us like a green curtain, blotting from view the great chamber. Then it seemed to me that I was caught and carried to supercelestial heights, in an upward-rushing cataract of quintessential force and deific rapture, and an all-illuminating light. It seemed that I, and my companions, had achieved a god-like union with the Flame; that every atom of our bodies had undergone a transcendental expansion, and was winged with ethereal lightness.

It was as if we no longer existed, except as one divine, indivisible entity, soaring beyond the trammels of matter, beyond the limits of time and space, to attain undreamable shores. Unspeakable was the joy, and infinite the freedom of that ascent, in which we seemed to overpass the zenith of the highest star. Then, as if we had risen with the Flame to its culmination, had reached its very apex, we emerged and came to a pause.

My senses were faint with exaltation, my eyes blind with the glory of the fire; and the world on which I now gazed was a vast arabesque of unfamiliar forms and bewildering hues from another spectrum than the one to which our eyes are habituated. It swirled before my dizzy eyes like a labyrinth of gigantic jewels, with interweaving rays and tangled lustres, and only by slow degrees was I able to establish order and distinguish detail in the surging riot of my perceptions.

All about me were endless avenues of super-prismatic opal and jacinth; arches and pillars of ultra-violet gems, of transcendent sapphire, of unearthly ruby and amethyst, all suffused with a multi-tinted splendour. I appeared to be treading on jewels, and above me was a jewelled sky.

Presently, with recovered equilibrium, with eyes adjusted to a new range of cognition, I began to perceive the actual features of the landscape. With the two moth-like beings still beside me, I was standing on a million-flowered grass, among trees of a paradisal vegetation, with fruit, foliage, blossoms and trunks whose very forms were beyond the conception of tridimensional life. The grace of their drooping boughs, of their fretted fronds, was inexpressible in terms of earthly line and contour, and they seemed to be wrought of pure, ethereal substance, half-translucent to the empyrean light, with accounted for the gem-like impression I had first received.

I breathed a nectar-laden air, and the ground beneath me was ineffably soft and resilient, as if it were composed of some higher form of matter than ours. My physical sensations were those of the utmost buoyancy and well-being, with no trace of fatigue or nervousness, such as might have been looked for after the unparalleled and marvellous events in which I had played a part. I felt no sense of mental dislocation or confusion; and, apart from my ability to recognise unknown colours and non-Euclidean forms, I began to experience a queer alteration and extension of tactility, through which it seemed that I was able to touch remote objects.

The radiant sky was filled with many-coloured suns, like those that might shine on a world of some multiple solar system; but as I gazed, their glory became softer and dimmer, and the brilliant lustre of the trees and grass was gradually subdued, as if by encroaching twilight. I was beyond surprise, in the boundless marvel and mystery of it all, and nothing, perhaps, would have seemed incredible. But if anything could have amazed me or defied belief, it was the human face—the face of my vanished friend, Giles Angarth, which now emerged from among the waning jewels of the forest, followed by that of another man whom I recognised from photographs as Felix Ebbonly.

They came out from beneath the gorgeous boughs, and paused before me. Both were clad in lustrous fabrics, finer than Oriental silk, and of no earthly cut or pattern. Their look was both joyous and meditative, and their faces had taken on a hint of the same translucency that characterised the ethereal fruits and blossoms.

"We have been looking for you," said Angarth. "It occurred to me that, after reading my journal, you might be tempted to try the same experiment, if only to make sure whether the account was truth or fiction. This is Felix Ebbonly, whom I believe you have never met."

It surprised me when I found that I could hear his voice with perfect ease and clearness, and I wondered why the effect of the drug-soaked cotton should have died out so soon in my auditory nerves. Yet such details were trivial in the face of the astounding fact that I had found Angarth and Ebbonly; that they, as well as I, had survived the unearthly rapture of the Flame.

"Where are we?" I asked, after acknowledging his introduction. "I confess that I am totally at a loss to comprehend what has happened."

"We are now in what is called the Inner Dimension," explained Angarth. "It is a higher sphere of space and energy and matter than the one into which we were precipitated from Crater Ridge, and the only entrance is through the Singing Flame in the city of Ydmos. The Inner Dimension is born of the fiery fountain, and sustained by it; and those who fling themselves into the Flame are lifted thereby to this superior plane of vibration. For them, the Outer Worlds no longer exist. The nature of the Flame itself is not known, except that it is a fountain of pure energy springing from the central rock beneath Ydmos, and passing beyond mortal ken by virtue of its own ardency."

He paused, and seemed to be peering attentively at the winged entities, who still lingered at my side. Then he continued:

"I haven't been here long enough to learn very much, myself; but I have found out a few things, and Ebbonly and I have established a sort of telepathic communication with the other beings who have passed through the Flame. Many of them have no spoken language, nor organs of speech, and their very methods of thought are basically different from ours, because of their divergent lines of sense-development and the varying conditions of the worlds from which they come. But we are able to communicate a few images.

"The persons who came with you are trying to tell me something," he went on. "You and they, it seems, are the last pilgrims who will enter Ydmos and attain the Inner Dimension. War is being made on the Flame and its guardians by the rulers of the Outer Lands, because so many of their people have obeyed the lure of the singing fountain and vanished into the higher sphere. Even now, their armies have closed in upon Ydmos and are blasting the city's ramparts with the force-bolts of their moving towers."

I told him what I had seen, comprehending, now, much that had been obscure heretofore. He listened gravely, and then said:

"It has long been feared that such war would be made sooner or later. There are many legends in the Outer Lands concerning the Flame and the fate of those who succumb to its attraction, but the truth is not known, or is guessed only by a few. Many believe, as I did, that the end is destruction; and by some who suspect its existence, the Inner Dimension is hated as a thing that lures idle dreamers away from worldly reality. It is regarded as a lethal and pernicious chimera, as a mere poetic dream, or a sort of opium paradise.

"There are a thousand things to tell you regarding the Inner Sphere, and the laws and conditions of being to which we are now subject after the revibration of all our component atoms in the Flame. But at present there is no time to speak further, since it is highly probable that we are all in grave danger—that the very existence of the Inner Dimension, as well as our own, is threatened by the inimical forces that are destroying Ydmos.

"There are some who say that the Flame is impregnable, that its pure essence will defy the blasting of all inferior beams, and its source remain impenetrable to the lightnings of the Outer Lords. But most are fearful of disaster, and expect the failure of the fountain itself when Ydmos is riven to the central rock.

"Because of this imminent peril, we must not tarry longer. There is a way which affords egress from the Inner Sphere to another and remoter Cosmos in a second infinity—a Cosmos unconceived by mundane astronomers, or by the astronomers of the worlds about Ydmos. The majority of the pilgrims, after a term of sojourn here, have gone on to the worlds of this other universe; and Ebbonly and I have waited only for your coming before following them. We must make haste, and delay no more, or doom will overtake us."

Even as he spoke, the two moth-like entities, seeming to resign me to the care of my human friends, arose on the jewel-tinted air and sailed in long, level flight above the paradisal perspectives whose remoter avenues were lost in glory. Angarth and Ebbonly had now stationed themselves beside me, and one took me by the left arm, and the other by the right.

"Try to imagine that you are flying," said Angarth. "In this sphere, levitation and flight are possible through willpower, and you will soon acquire the ability. We shall support and guide you, however, till you have grown accustomed to the new conditions and are independent of such help."

I obeyed his injunction, and formed a mental image of myself in the act of flying. I was amazed by the clearness and verisimilitude of the thought-picture, and still more by the fact that the picture was becoming an actuality! With little sense of effort, but with exactly the same feeling that characterises a levitational dream, the three of us were soaring from the jewelled ground, slanting easily and swiftly upward through the glowing air.

Any attempt to describe the experience would be foredoomed to futility, since it seemed that a whole range of new senses had been opened up in me, together with corresponding thought-symbols for which there are no words in human speech. I was no longer Philip Hastane, but a larger, stronger and freer entity, differing as much from my former self as the personality developed beneath the influence of hashish or kava would differ. The dominant feeling was one of immense joy and liberation, coupled with a sense of imperative haste, of the need to escape into other realms where the joy would endure eternal and unthreatened.

My visual perceptions, as we flew above the burning, lucent woods, were marked by intense aesthetic pleasure. It was as far above the normal delight afforded by agreeable imagery as the forms and colours of this world were beyond the cognition of normal eyes. Every changing image was a source of veritable ecstasy; and the ecstasy mounted as the whole landscape began to brighten again and returned to the flashing, scintillating glory it had worn when I first beheld it.

VII. *The Destruction of Ydmos*

We soared at a lofty elevation, looking down on numberless miles of labyrinthine forest, on long, luxurious meadows, on voluptuously folded hills, on palatial buildings, and waters that were clear as the pristine lakes and rivers of Eden. It all seemed to quiver and pulsate like one living, effulgent, ethereal entity, and waves of radiant rapture passed from sun to sun in the splendour-crowded heaven.

As we went on, I noticed again, after an interval, that partial dimming of the light; that somnolent, dreamy saddening of the colours, to be followed by another period of ecstatic brightening. The slow tidal rhythm of this process appeared to correspond to the rising and falling of the Flame, as Angarth had described it in his journal, and I suspected immediately that there was some connection. No sooner had I formulated this thought, than I became aware that Angarth was speaking. And yet, I am not sure whether he spoke, or whether his worded thought was perceptible to me through another sense than that of physical audition. At any rate, I was cognisant of his comment:

"You are right. The waning and waxing of the fountain and its music is perceived in the Inner Dimension as a clouding and lightening of all visual images."

Our flight began to swiften, and I realised that my companions were employing all their psychic energies in an effort to redouble our speed. The lands below us blurred to a cataract of streaming colour, a sea of flowing luminosity; and we seemed to be hurtling onward like stars through the fiery air. The ecstasy of that endless soaring, the anxiety of that precipitate flight from an unknown doom, are incommunicable. But I shall never forget them, nor the state of ineffable communion and understanding that existed between the three of us. The memory of it all is housed in the deepest, most abiding cells of my brain.

Others were flying beside and above and beneath us, now, in the fluctuant glory: pilgrims of hidden worlds and occult dimensions, proceeding as we ourselves towards that other Cosmos of which the Inner Sphere was the antechamber. These beings were strange and outré beyond belief, in their corporeal forms and attributes; and yet I took no thought of their strangeness, but felt towards them the same conviction of fraternity that I felt towards Angarth and Ebbonly.

As we still went on, it appeared to me that my two companions were telling me many things; communicating, by what means I am not sure, much that they had learned in their new existence. With a grave urgency as if, perhaps, the time for imparting this information might well be brief, ideas were expressed and conveyed which I could never have understood amid terrestrial circumstances. Things that were inconceivable in terms of the five senses, or in abstract symbols of philosophic or mathematic thought, were made plain to me as the letters of the alphabet.

Certain of these data, however, are roughly conveyable or suggestible in language. I was told of the gradual process of initiation into the life of the new dimension, of the powers gained by the neophyte during his term of adaptation, of the various recondite, aesthetic joys experienced through a mingling and multiplying of all the perceptions, of the control acquired over natural forces and over matter itself, so that raiment could be woven and buildings reared solely through an act of volition.

I learned, also, of the laws that would control our passage to the further Cosmos, and the fact that such passage was difficult and dangerous for anyone who had not lived a certain length of time in the Inner Dimension. Likewise, I was told that no one could return to our present plane from the higher Cosmos, even as no one could go backward through the Flame into Ydmos.

Angarth and Ebbonly had dwelt long enough in the Inner Dimension, they said, to be eligible for entrance to the worlds beyond; and they thought that I, too, could escape through their assistance, even though I had not yet developed the faculty of spatial equilibrium necessary to sustain those who dared the interspheric path and its dreadful subjacent gulfs alone. There were boundless, unforeseeable realms, planet on planet, universe on universe, to which we might attain, and among whose prodigies and marvels we could dwell or wander indefinitely. In these worlds, our brains would be attuned to the comprehension of vaster and higher scientific laws, and states of entity beyond those of our present dimensional milieu.

I have no idea of the duration of our flight; since, like everything else, my sense of time was completely altered and transfigured. Relatively speaking, we may have gone on for hours; but it seemed to me that we had crossed an area of that supernal terrain for whose transit many years, or even centuries, might well have been required.

Even before we came within sight of it, a clear pictorial

image of our destination had arisen in my mind, doubtless through some sort of thought-transference. I seemed to envision a stupendous mountain range, with alp on celestial alp, higher than the summer cumuli of Earth; and above them all the horn of an ultra-violet peak whose head was enfolded in a hueless and spiral cloud, touched with the sense of invisible chromatic overtones, that seemed to come down upon it from skies beyond the zenith. I knew that the way to the Outer Cosmos was hidden in the high cloud. . . .

On and on we soared; and at length the mountain range appeared on the far horizon, and I saw the paramount peak of ultra-violet with its dazzling crown of cumulus. Nearer still we came, till the strange volutes of cloud were almost above us, towering to the heavens and vanishing among the vari-coloured suns; and we saw the gleaming forms of pilgrims who preceded us, as they entered the swirling folds.

At this moment, the sky and the landscape had flamed again to their culminating brilliance; they burned with a thousand hues and lustres, so that the sudden, unlooked-for eclipse which now occurred was all the more complete and terrible. Before I was conscious of anything amiss, I seemed to hear a despairing cry from my friends, who must have felt the oncoming calamity through a subtler sense than any of which I was yet capable. Then, beyond the high and luminescent alp of our destination, I saw the mounting of a wall of darkness, dreadful and instant, positive and palpable, that rose everywhere and toppled like some Atlantean wave upon the irised suns and the fiery-coloured vistas of the Inner Dimension.

We hung irresolute in the shadowed air, powerless and hopeless before the impending catastrophe, and saw that the darkness had surrounded the entire world and was rushing upon us from all sides. It ate the heavens, blotted the outer suns, and the vast perspectives over which we had flown appeared to shrink and shrivel like a fire-blackened paper. We seemed to wait alone, for one terrible instant, in a centre of dwindling light on which the cyclonic forces of night and destruction were impinging with torrential rapidity.

The centre shrank to a mere point—and then the darkness was upon us like an overwhelming maelstrom, like the falling and crashing of Cyclopean walls. I seemed to go down with the wreck of shattered worlds in a roaring sea of vortical space and force, to descend into some infra-stellar pit, some ultimate limbo to which the shards of forgotten suns and systems are flung. Then, after a measureless interval, there came the sensation of violent impact, as if I had fallen among these shards, at the bottom of the universal night. . . .

I struggled back to consciousness with slow, prodigious effort, as if I were crushed beneath some irremovable weight, beneath the lightless and inert débris of galaxies. It seemed to require the labours of a Titan to lift my lids, and my body and limbs were heavy, as if they had been turned to some denser element than human flesh, or had been subjected to the gravitation of a grosser planet than the Earth.

My mental processes were benumbed and painful, and confused to the last degree; but at length I realised that I was lying on a riven and tilted pavement, among gigantic blocks of fallen stone. Above me, the light of a livid heaven came down among over-turned and jagged walls that no longer supported their colossal dome. Close beside me, I saw a fuming pit from which a ragged rift extended through the floor, like the chasm wrought by an earthquake.

I could not recognise my surroundings for a time; but at last, with a toilsome groping of thought, I understood that

I was lying in the ruined temple of Ydmos, and that the pit whose grey and acrid vapours rose beside me was that from which the fountain of singing flame had issued. It was a scene of stupendous havoc and devastation: the wrath that had been visited upon Ydmos had left no wall nor pylon of the temple standing. I stared at the blighted heavens from an architectural ruin in which the remains of On and Angkor would have been mere rubble-heaps.

With herculean effort, I turned my head away from the smoking pit, whose thin, sluggish fumes curled upward in phantasmal coils where the green ardour of the Flame had soared and sung. Not until then did I perceive my companions. Angarth, still insensible, was lying near at hand, and just beyond him I saw the pale, contorted face of Ebbonly, whose lower limbs and body were pinned down by the rough and broken pediment of a fallen pillar.

Striving, as in some eternal nightmare, to throw off the leaden-clinging weight of my inertia, and able to bestir myself only with the most painful slowness and laboriousness, I got to my feet and went over to Ebbonly. Angarth, I saw at a glance, was uninjured and would presently regain consciousness, but Ebbonly, crushed by the monolithic mass of stone, was dying swiftly, and even with the help of a dozen men I could not have released him from his imprisonment; nor could I have done anything to palliate his agony.

He tried to smile, with gallant and piteous courage, as I stooped above him.

"It's no use—I'm going in a moment," he whispered. "Good-bye, Hastane—and tell Angarth good-bye for me, too."

His tortured lips relaxed, his eyelids dropped, and his head fell back on the temple pavement. With an unreal, dream-like horror, almost without emotion, I saw that he was dead. The exhaustion that still beset me was too profound to permit of thought or feeling; it was like the first reaction that follows the awakening from a drug-debauch. My nerves were like burnt-out wires, my muscles dead and unresponsive as clay; my brain was ashen and gutted, as if a great fire had burned within it and gone out.

Somehow, after an interval of whose length my memory is uncertain, I managed to revive Angarth, and he sat up dully and dazedly. When I told him that Ebbonly was dead, my words appeared to make no impression upon him, and I wondered for a while if he understood. Finally, rousing himself a little with evident difficulty, he peered at the body of our friend, and seemed to realise in some measure the horror of the situation. But I think he would have remained there for hours, or perhaps for all time, in his utter despair and lassitude, if I had not taken the initiative.

"Come," I said, with an attempt at firmness. "We must get out of this."

"Where to?" he queried, dully. "The Flame has failed at its source, and the Inner Dimension is no more. I wish I were dead, like Ebbonly—I might as well be, judging from the way I feel."

"We must find our way back to Crater Ridge," I said. "Surely we can do it, if the inter-dimensional portals have not been destroyed."

Angarth did not seem to hear me, but he followed obediently when I took him by the arm and began to seek an exit from the temple's heart, among the roofless halls and overturned columns. . . .

My recollections of our return are dim and confused, and full of the tediousness of some interminable delirium. I remember looking back at Ebbonly, lying white and still beneath the massive pillar that would serve as his eternal monument; and I recall the mountainous ruins of the city, in which it seemed that we were the only living beings. It was a wilderness of chaotic stone, of fused, obsidian-like blocks, where streams of molten lava still ran in the mighty chasms, or poured like torrents adown unfathomable pits that had opened in the ground. And I remember seeing, amid the wreckage, the charred bodies of those dark colossi who were the people of Ydmos and the warders of the Flame.

Like pygmies lost in some shattered fortalice of the giants, we stumbled onward, strangling in mephitic and metallic vapours, reeling with weariness, dizzy with the heat that emanated everywhere to surge upon us in buffeting waves. The way was blocked by overthrown buildings, by toppled towers and battlements, over which we climbed precariously and toilsomely; and often we were compelled to divagate from our direct course by enormous rifts that seemed to cleave the foundations of the world.

The moving towers of the wrathful Outer Lords had withdrawn; their armies had disappeared on the plain beyond Ydmos, when we staggered over the riven, shapeless and scoriac crags that had formed the city's ramparts. Before us was nothing but desolation—a fire-blackened and vapour-vaulted expanse in which no tree or blade of grass remained.

Across this waste we found our way to the slope of violet grass above the plain, which had lain beyond the path of the invader's bolts. There the guiding monoliths, reared by a people of whom we were never to learn even the name, still looked down upon the fuming desert and the mounded wrack of Ydmos. And there, at length, we came once more to the greyish-green columns that were the gateway between the worlds.

THE UNCHARTED ISLE

I DO not know how long I had been drifting in the boat. There are several days and nights that I remember only as alternate blanks of grayness and darkness; and, after these, there came a fantasmagoric eternity of delirium and an indeterminate lapse into pitch-black oblivion. The sea-water I had swallowed must have revived me; for when I came to myself, I was lying at the bottom of the boat with my head a little lifted in the stern, and six inches of brine lapping at my lips. I was gasping and strangling with the mouthfuls I had taken; the boat was tossing roughly, with more water coming over the sides at each toss; and I could hear the sound of breakers not far away.

I tried to sit up, and succeeded, after a prodigious effort. My thoughts and sensations were curiously confused, and I found it difficult to orient myself in any manner. The physical sensation of extreme thirst was dominant over all else—my mouth was lined with running, throbbing fire—and I felt light-headed, and the rest of my body was strangely limp and hollow. It was hard to remember just what had happened; and, for a moment, I was not even puzzled by the fact that I was alone in the boat. But, even to my dazed, uncertain senses, the roar of those breakers had conveyed a distinct warning of peril; and, sitting up, I reached for the oars.

The oars were gone; but, in my enfeebled state, it was not likely that I could have made much use of them anyway. I looked around, and saw that the boat was drifting rapidly in the wash of a shoreward current, between two low-lying darkish reefs half hidden by flying veils of foam. A steep and barren cliff loomed before me; but, as the boat neared it, the cliff seemed to divide miraculously, revealing a narrow chasm through which I floated into the mirror-like waters of a still lagoon. The passage from the rough sea without, to a realm of sheltered silence and seclusion, was no less abrupt than the transition of events or scenery which often occurs in a dream.

The lagoon was long and narrow, and ran sinuously away between level shores that were fringed with an ultra-tropical vegetation. There were many fern-palms, of a type I had never seen, and many stiff, gigantic cycads, and wide-leaved grasses taller than young trees. I wondered a little about them even then; though, as the boat drifted slowly toward the nearest beach, I was mainly preoccupied with the clarifying and assorting of my recollections. These gave me more trouble than one would think.

I must have been a trifle light-headed still; and the sea-water I had drunk couldn't have been very good for me, either, even though it had helped to revive me. I remembered, of course, that I was Mark Irwin, first mate of the freighter *Auckland*, plying between Callao and Wellington; and I recalled only too well the night when Captain Melville had wrenched me bodily from my bunk, from the dreamless under-sea of a dog-tired slumber, shouting that the ship was on fire. I recalled the roaring hell of flame and smoke through which we had fought our way to the deck, to find that the vessel was already past retrieving, since the fire had reached the oil that formed part of her cargo; and then the swift launching of boats in the lurid glare of the conflagration. Half the crew had been caught in the blazing forecastle; and those of us who escaped were compelled to put off without water or provisions. We had rowed for days in a dead calm, without sighting any vessel, and were suffering the tortures of the damned, when a storm had arisen. In this storm, two of the boats were lost; and the third, which was manned by Captain Melville, the second mate, the boatswain and myself, had alone survived. But some time during the storm, or during the days and nights of delirium that followed, my companions must have gone overboard.... This much I recalled; but all of it was somehow unreal and remote, and seemed to pertain only to another person than the one who was floating shoreward on the waters of a still lagoon. I felt very dreamy and detached; and even my thirst didn't trouble me half as much now as it had on awakening.

The boat touched a beach of fine, pearly sand, before I began to wonder where I was and to speculate concerning the shores I had reached. I knew that we had been hundreds of miles southwest of Easter Island on the night of the fire, in a part of the Pacific where there is no other land; and certainly this couldn't be Easter Island. What, then, could it be? I realized with a sort of shock that I must have found something not on any charted course or geological map. Of course, it was an isle of some kind; but I could form no idea of its possible extent; and I had no way of deciding offhand whether it was peopled or unpeopled. Except for the lush vegetation, and a few queer-looking birds and butterflies, and some equally queer-looking fish in the lagoon, there was no visible life anywhere.

I got out of the boat, feeling very weak and wobbly in the hot white sunshine that poured down upon everything like a motionless universal cataract. My first thought was to find fresh water; and I plunged at random among the mighty fern-trees, parting their enormous leaves with extreme effort, and sometimes reeling against their boles to save myself from falling. Twenty or thirty paces, however, and then I came to a tiny rill that sprang in shattered crystal from a low ledge, to collect in a placid pool where ten-inch mosses and broad, anemone-like blossoms mirrored themselves. The water was cool and sweet; I drank profoundly, and felt the benison of its freshness permeate all my parched tissues.

Now I began to look around for some sort of edible fruit. Close to the stream, I found a shrub that was trailing its burden of salmon-yellow drupes on the giant mosses. I couldn't identify the fruit; but its aspect was delicious, and I decided to take a chance. It was full of a sugary pulp; and strength returned to me even as I ate. My brain cleared, and I recovered many, if not all, of the faculties that had been in a state of partial abeyance.

I went back to the boat, and bailed out all the sea-water; then I tried to drag the boat as far up on the sand as I could, in case I might need it again at any future time. My strength was inadequate to the task; and still fearing that the tide might carry it away, I cut some of the high grasses with my clasp-knife and wove them into a long rope, with which I moored the boat to the nearest palm-tree.

Now, for the first time, I surveyed my situation with an analytic eye, and became aware of much that I had hitherto failed to observe or realize. A medley of queer impressions thronged upon me, some of which could not have arrived through the avenues of the known senses. To begin with, I saw more clearly the abnormal oddity of the plant-forms about me: they were not the palm-ferns, grasses and shrubs that are native to south-sea islands: their leaves, their stems, their frondage, were mainly of uncouth archaic types, such as might have existed in former eons, on the sea-lost littorals of Mu. They differed from anything I had seen in Australia or New Guinea, those asylums of a primeval flora; and, gazing upon them, I was overwhelmed with intimations of a dark and prehistoric antiquity. And the silence around me seemed to become the silence of dead ages and of things that have gone down beneath oblivion's tide. From that moment, I felt that there was something wrong about the island. But somehow I couldn't tell just what it was, or seize definitely upon everything that contributed to this impression.

Aside from the bizarre-looking vegetation, I noticed that there was a queerness about the very sun. It was too high in the heavens for any latitude to which I could conceivably have drifted; and it was too large anyway; and the sky was unnaturally bright, with a dazzling incandescence. There was a spell of perpetual quietude upon the air, and never the slightest rippling of leaves or water; and the whole landscape hung before me like a monstrous vision of unbelievable realms apart from time and space. According to all the maps, that island couldn't exist, anyhow.... More and more decisively, I knew that there was something wrong: I felt an eery confusion, a weird bewilderment, like one who has been cast away on the shores of an alien planet; and it seemed to me that I was separated from my former life, and from everything I had ever known, by an interval of distance more irremeable than all the blue leagues of sea and sky; that, like the island itself, I was lost to all possible reorientation. For a few instants, this feeling became a nervous panic, a paralyzing horror.

In an effort to overcome my agitation, I set off along the shore of the lagoon, pacing with feverish rapidity. It occurred to me that I might as well explore the island; and perhaps, after all, I might find some clue to the mystery, might stumble on something of explanation or reassurance.

After several serpent-like turns of the winding water, I reached the end of the lagoon. Here the country began to slope upward toward a high ridge, heavily wooded with the same vegetation I had already met, to which a long-leaved araucaria was now added. This ridge was apparently the crest of the island; and, after a half-hour of groping among the ferns, the stiff archaic shrubs and araucarias, I managed to surmount it.

Here, through a rift in the foliage, I looked down upon a scene no less incredible than unexpected. The farther shore of the island was visible below me; and all along the curving beach of a land-locked harbor were the stone roofs and towers of a town! Even at that distance, I could see that the architecture was of an unfamiliar type; and I was not sure at first glance whether the buildings were ancient ruins or the homes of a living people. Then, beyond the roofs, I saw that several strange-looking vessels were moored at a sort of mole, flaunting their orange sails in the sunlight.

My excitement was indescribable: at most (if the island were peopled at all) I had thought to find a few savage huts; and here below me were edifices that betokened a considerable degree of civilization! What they were, or who had built them, were problems beyond surmise; but, as I hastened down the slope toward the harbor, a very human eagerness was mingled with the dumfoundment and stupefaction I had been experiencing. At least, there were people on the island; and, at the realization of this, the horror that had been a part of my bewilderment was dissipated for the nonce.

When I drew nearer to the houses, I saw that they were indeed strange. But the strangeness was not wholly inherent in their architectural forms; nor was I able to trace its every source, or define it in any way, by word or image. The houses were built of a stone whose precise color I can not recall, since it was neither brown nor red nor gray, but a hue that seemed to combine, yet differ from, all these; and I remember only that the general type of construction was low and square, with square towers. The strangeness lay in more than this—in the sense of a remote and stupefying antiquity that emanated from them like an odor: I knew at once that they were old as the uncouth primordial trees and grasses, and, like these, were parcel of a long-forgotten world.

Then I saw the people—those people before whom not only my ethnic knowledge, but my very reason, were to own themselves baffled. There were scores of them in sight among the buildings, and all of them appeared to be intensely preoccupied with something or other. At first I couldn't make out what they were doing, or trying to do; but plainly they were very much in earnest about it. Some were looking at the sea or the sun, and then at long scrolls of a paper-like material which they held in their hands; and many were grouped on a stone platform around a large, intricate metal apparatus resembling an armillary. All of these people were dressed in tunic-like garments of unusual amber and azure and Tyrian shades, cut in a fashion that was unfamiliar to history; and when I came close, I saw that their faces were broad and flat, with a vague foreomening of the Mongolian in their oblique eyes. But, in an unspecifiable way, the character of their features was not that of any race that has seen the sun for a million years; and the low, liquid, many-vowelled words which they spoke to each other were not denotive of any recorded language.

None of them appeared to notice me; and I went up to a group of three who were studying one of the long scrolls I have mentioned, and addressed them. For all answer, they bent closer above the scroll; and even when I plucked one of them by the sleeve, it was evident that he did not observe me. Much amazed, I peered into their faces, and was struck by the mingling of supreme perplexity and monomaniacal intentness which their expression displayed. There was much of the madman, and more of the scientist absorbed in some irresoluble problem. Their eyes were fixed and fiery, their lips moved and mumbled in a fever of perpetual disquiet; and, following their gaze, I saw that the thing they were studying was a sort of chart or map, whose yellowing paper and faded inks were manifestly of past ages. The continents and seas and isles on this map were not those of the world I knew; and their names were written in heteroclitic runes of a lost alphabet. There was one immense continent in particular, with a tiny isle close to its southern shore; and ever and anon, one of the beings who pored above the map would touch this isle with his finger-tip, and then would stare toward the empty horizon, as if he were seeking to recover a vanished shoreline. I received a distinct impression that these people were as irretrievably lost as I myself; that they too were disturbed and baffled by a situation not to be solved or redeemed.

I went on toward the stone platform, which stood in a broad open space among the foremost houses. It was perhaps ten feet high, and access to it was given by a flight of winding steps. I mounted the steps, and tried to accost the people who were crowding about the armillary-like instrument. But they too were utterly oblivious of me, and intent upon the observations they were making. Some of them were turning the great sphere; some were consulting various geographical and celestial maps; and, from my nautical knowledge, I could see that certain of their companions were taking the height of the sun with a kind of astrolabe. All of them wore the same look of perplexity and savant-like preoccupation which I had observed in the others.

Seeing that my efforts to attract their attention were fruitless, I left the platform and wandered along the streets toward the harbor. The strangeness and inexplicability of it all were too much for me: more and more, I felt that I was being alienated from the realms of all rational experience or conjecture; that I had fallen into some unearthly limbo of confoundment and unreason, into the *cul-de-sac* of an ultra-terrestrial dimension. These beings were so palpably astray and bewildered; it was so obvious that they knew as well as I that there was something wrong with the geography, and perhaps with the chronology, of their island.

I spent the rest of the day roaming around; but nowhere could I find any one who was able to perceive my presence; and nowhere was there anything to reassure me, or resolve my ever-growing confusion of mind and spirit. Everywhere there were men, and also women; and though comparatively few of them were gray and wrinkled, they all conveyed to my apprehension a feeling of immemorial eld, of years and cycles beyond all record or computation. And all were troubled, all were feverously intent, and were perusing maps or reading ancient pells and volumes, or staring at the sea and sky, or studying the brazen tablets of astronomical parapegms along the streets, as if by so doing they could somehow find the flaw in their reckonings. There were men and women of mature years, and some with the fresh, unlined visages of youth; but in all the place I saw but one child; and the face of the child was no less perplexed and troubled than those of its elders. If any one ate or drank or carried on the normal occupations of life, it was not done within my scope of vision; and I conceived the idea that they had lived in this manner, obsessed with the same problem, through a period of time which would have been practically eternal in any other world than theirs.

I came to a large building, whose open door was dark with the shadows of the interior. Peering in, I found that it was a temple; for across the deserted twilight, heavy with the stale fumes of burnt-out incense, the slant eyes of a baleful and monstrous image glared upon me. The thing was seemingly of stone or wood, with gorilla-like arms and the malignant features of a subhuman race. From what little I could see in the gloom, it was not pleasant to look upon; and I left the temple, and continued my perambulations.

Now I came to the waterfront, where the vessels with

orange sails were moored at a stone mole. There were five or six of them in all: they were small galleys, with single banks of oars, and figureheads of metal that were graven with the likeness of primordial gods. They were indescribably worn by the waves of untold years; their sails were rotting rags; and no less than all else on the island, they bore the impress of a dread antiquity. It was easy to believe that their grotesquely carven prows had touched the eon-sunken wharves of Lemuria.

I returned to the town; and once again I sought to make my presence known to the inhabitants, but all in vain. And after awhile, as I trudged from street to street, the sun went down behind the island, and the stars came swiftly out in a heaven of purpureal velvet. The stars were large and lustrous and were innumerably thick: with the eye of a practised mariner, I studied them eagerly; but I could not trace the wonted constellations, though here and there I thought that I perceived a distortion or elongation of some familiar grouping. All was hopelessly askew, and disorder crept into my very brain, as I tried once more to orient myself, and noticed that the inhabitants of the town were still busied with a similar endeavor. . . .

I have no way of computing the length of my sojourn on that island. Time didn't seem to have any proper meaning there; and, even if it had, my mental state was not one to admit of precise reckoning. It was all so impossible and unreal, so much like an absurd and troublesome hallucination; and half the time, I thought that it was merely a continuation of my delirium—that probably I was still drifting in the boat. After all, this was the most reasonable supposition; and I don't wonder that those who have heard my story refuse to entertain any other. I'd agree with them, if it weren't for one or two quite material details. . . .

The manner in which I lived is pretty vague to me, also.

I remember sleeping under the stars, outside the town; I remember eating and drinking, and watching those people day after day, as they pursued their hopeless calculations. Sometimes I went into the houses and helped myself to food; and once or twice, if I remember rightly, I slept on a couch in one of them, without being disputed or heeded by the owners. There was nothing that could break the spell of their obsession or force them to notice me; and I soon gave up the attempt. And it semed to me, as time went on, that I myself was no less unreal, no less doubtful and insubstantial, than their disregard would appear to indicate.

In the midst of my bewilderment, however, I found myself wondering if it would be possible to get away from the island. I remembered my boat, and remembered also that I had no oars. And forthwith I made tentative preparations for departure. In broad daylight, before the eyes of the townspeople, I took two oars from one of the galleys in the harbor, and carried them across the ridge to where my boat was hidden. The oars were very heavy, their blades were broad as fans, and their handles were fretted with hieroglyphs of silver. Also, I appropriated from one of the houses two earthen jars, painted with barbaric figures, and bore them away to the lagoon, intending to fill them with fresh water when I left. And also I collected a supply of food. But somehow the brain-muddling mystery of it all had paralyzed my initiative; and even when everything was ready, I delayed my departure. I felt, too, that the inhabitants must have tried innumerable times to get away in their galleys, and had always failed. And so I lingered on, like a man in the grip of some ridiculous nightmare.

One evening, when those distorted stars had all come out, I became aware that unusual things were going on. The people were no longer standing about in groups, with their customary porings and discussions, but were all hastening toward the temple-like edifice. I followed them, and peered in at the door.

The place was lit with flaring torches that flung demoniac shadows on the crowd and on the idol before whom they were bowing. Perfumes were burnt, and chants were sung in the myriad-vowelled language with which my ear had become familiarized. They were invoking that frightful image with gorilla-like arms and half-human, half-animal face; and it was not hard for me to surmise the purpose of the invocation. Then the voices died to a sorrowful whisper, the smoke of the censers thinned, and the little child I had once seen was thrust forward in a vacant space between the congregation and the idol.

I had thought, of course, that the god was of wood or stone; but now, in a flash of terror and consternation, I wondered if I had been mistaken. For the oblique eyes opened more widely, and glowered upon the child, and the long arms, ending in knife-taloned fingers, lifted slowly and reached forward. And arrow-sharp fangs were displayed in the bestial grin of the leaning face. The child was still as a bird beneath the hypnotic eyes of a serpent; and there was no movement, and no longer even a whisper, from the waiting throng. . . .

I can not recall what happened then: whenever I try to recall it, there is a cloud of horror and darkness in my brain. I must have left the temple and fled across the island by starlight; but of this, too, I remember nothing. My first recollection is of rowing seaward through the narrow chasm by which I had entered the lagoon, and of trying to steer a course by the wried and twisted constellations. After that, there were days and days on a bland, unrippled sea, beneath a heaven of dazzling incandescence; and more nights below the crazy stars; till the days and nights became an eternity of tortured weariness; and my food and water were all consumed; and hunger and thirst and a feverous calenture with tossing, seething hallucinations, were all that I knew.

One night, I came to myself for a little while, and lay staring up at the sky. And once more the stars were those of the rightful heavens; and I gave thanks to God for my sight of the Southern Cross, ere I slid back into coma and delirium. And when I recovered consciousness again, I was lying in a ship's cabin, and the ship's doctor was bending over me.

They were all very kind to me on that ship. But when I tried to tell them my tale, they smiled pityingly; and after a few attempts, I learned to keep my silence. They were very curious about the two oars with silver-fretted handles, and the painted jars which they had found with me in the boat; but they were all too frank in refusing to accept my explanation. No such island and no such people could possibly exist, they said: it was contrary to all the maps that had ever been made, and gave the direct lie to all the ethnologists and geographers.

Often I wonder about it, myself, for there are so many things I can't explain. Is there a part of the Pacific that extends beyond time and space—an oceanic limbo into which, by some unknowable cataclysm, that island passed in a bygone period, even as Lemuria sank beneath the wave? And if so, by what abrogation of dimensional laws was I enabled to reach the island and depart from it? These things are beyond speculation. But often in my dreams, I see again the incognizably distorted stars, and share the confusion and bafflement of a lost people, as they pore above their useless charts, and take the altitude of a deviated sun.

JUDGMENTS AND DOOMS

THE SECOND INTERMENT

"WELL," said Guy Magbane, "I notice that you're still alive." His curtain-shadowed lips, as they shaped the words, took on a thin, ambiguous curve that might have been either smile or sneer. He came forward, peering a little obliquely at the sick man, and held out the glass of garnet-colored medicine.

Sir Uther Magbane, sitting amid the heavy pillows like a death's-head with tawny hair and blue eyes, made no answer and appeared to hesitate before accepting the glass. A dark, formless terror seemed to float upward in his pale gaze, like a drowned object that rises slowly in some autumnal weir. Finally he took the glass and drained its contents with a convulsive gulp, as if the act of swallowing were difficult.

"I'm pretty sick this time, Guy," he said, in a voice that some inner constriction had rendered harshly guttural and toneless. "But the worst fear is that I may not be sick enough—that the thing may happen again as it did before. My God! I can't think of anything else—can't imagine anything else but the black, suffocating agony, the blind, intolerable, stifling horror of it. Promise me—promise me again, Guy, that you'll defer my burial for at least a fortnight, for a month; and swear that when you do put me away you'll make sure that the push-button and electric wiring in my casket are in good order. Merciful God, supposing I should wake up in the tomb—and find that the alarm didn't work!"

"Don't worry; I'll attend to all that." The tone was soothing, a little contemptuous and, to the listener, touched with a sinister meaning. Guy Magbane turned to leave the room, and did not see that the floating fear in his brother's gaze had become for the moment a palpable, recognizable thing. He added over his shoulder, negligently and without looking back:

"That idea has grown to be a regular obsession with you. Just because the thing occurred once doesn't mean that it will ever occur again. If you die this time, you'll stay dead, in all likelihood. There won't be any more mistakes about it." With this equivocal and dubious reassurance, he went out and closed the door behind him.

Sir Uther Magbane leaned back among the pillows and stared at the somber oaken wainscoting. He felt—as he had felt ever since the beginning of his present illness—that the room was too cramped and narrow; that the walls were always threatening to close in upon him, the roof to descend above him, like the sides and lid of a coffin. He could never seem to draw a full breath. All he could do was to lie there, alone with his ghastly fear, his hideous memories and his even more hideous apprehensions. The visits of his younger brother, Guy, for some time past, had served merely to strengthen his feeling of sepulchral oppression—for Guy was now part of the fear.

He had always been afraid of death, even in his boyhood—that time when the specter should normally be dim and far away, if perceived at all. It had begun with the early death of his mother: ever since that black bereavement, a hovering vulturine shadow had seemed to taint and darken the things that were unspoiled for others. His imagination, morbidly acute, sick with suspicion of life itself, had seen everywhere the indwelling skeleton, the flower-shrouded corpse. The kisses of young love were flavored with mortality. The very sap of things was touched with putrefaction.

With heartfelt shudders, as he matured, he had nourished his charnel fancy on all that was macabre in art and literature. Like a seer who gazes into a black crystal, he foresaw with harrowing minuteness the physical and mental agonies of dissolution; he previsioned the activities of decay, the slow toil of the mordant worm, as clearly as if he had descended into the tomb's loathsome oblivion. But he had not imagined or feared the most poignant horror of all—that of premature burial—until he had himself experienced it.

The thing had come without warning, just after his succession to the estate, and his engagement to Alice Margreave, in whose love he had begun to forget a little his boyhood terrors. It was as if the haunting spectre had retired, only to strike in a more abhorrent and appalling shape.

Lying there now, the memory seemed to stop his very heart, to throttle his breathing, as it always did. Again, with hallucinatory distinctness, he recalled the first gradual attack of his mysterious malady. He recalled the beginning of his syncope, the lightless gulf into which he had gone down, by timeless degrees, as if through infinite empty space. Somewhere in that gulf, he had found oblivion—the black instant that might have been hours or ages—from which he had awakened in darkness, had tried to sit up, and had bruised his face against an adamantine obstruction that seemed to be only a few inches above him. He had struck out, blindly, in mad, insensate panic, trying to thresh about with hands and feet, and had met on all sides a hard, unyielding surface, more terrifying, because of its inexplicable *nearness*, than the walls of some nighted oubliette.

There was a period of nightmare confusion—and then he knew what had happened. By some ghastly mistake, he had been placed, still alive, in a casket; and the casket was in the old vaults of his family, below the chapel floor. He began to scream then, and his screams, with the dull, muffled repercussion of some underground explosion, were hurled back upon him appallingly in the narrow space. Already the air seemed to stifle him, thick with mortuary odors of wood and cloth.

Hysteria seized him, and he went quite mad, hurling himself against the lid in what seemed an eternity of cramped, hopeless struggle. He did not hear the sound of footsteps that came hurrying to his aid, and the blows of men with chisels and hammers on the heavy lid which mingled indistinguishably with his own cries and clamorings. Even when the lid was wrenched loose, he had become quite delirious with the horror of it all, and had fought against his rescuers, as if they too were part of the suffocating, constrictive nightmare.

Never was he able to believe that his experience had been a matter of a few minutes only—that he had awakened just after the depositing of the coffin in the vault and before the actual lowering of the slab and the departure of the pall bearers, whose horrified attention he had attracted by the muted sound of his cries and struggles. It seemed to him that he must have fought there for immeasurable cycles.

The shock had left him with shattered nerves that trembled uncontrollably; nerves that found a secret terror, a funereal alarm, in the most innocent, unshadowed things. Three years had gone by since then, but at no time had he been able to master his grisly obsession, to climb from the night-bound pit of his demoralization. His old fear of death was complicated by a new dread: that his illness, recurring, as it was likely to do, would again take the deceptive semblance of death, and again he would awaken in the tomb. With the ceaseless apprehension of a hypochondriac, he watched for the first repetition of the malady's preliminary symptoms, and felt himself irretrievably doomed from their beginning.

His fear had poisoned everything; had even parted him

from Alice Margreave. There had been no formal breaking of the engagement, merely a tacit falling apart of the self-preoccupied, self-tortured neurotic and the girl whose love had soon turned, perforce, to a bewildered and horror-mingled pity for him.

After that, he had abandoned himself more fully, if possible, to his monomania. He had read everything he could find on the subject of premature interment, he had collected clippings that told of known cases: people who had been rescued in time—or whose reanimation had been detected too late, perhaps had been surmised only from some change or contortion of posture noticed after many years in the removal of the body to a new burial place. Impelled by a shivering fascination, he delved without restraint in the full ghastliness of the abominable theme. And always, in the fate of others, he saw his own fate; and their sufferings, by some vicarious visitation, became his.

Fatally convinced that the insufferable horror would recur, he had made elaborate precautions, equipping the casket in which he was to be buried with an electrical device that would summon help. The least pressure of a button, within easy reach of his right hand, would set an alarm gong to ringing in the family chapel above, together with a second gong in the nearby manor house.

Even this, however, did little to assuage his fears. He was haunted by the idea that the push button might fail to work, or that no one would hear it, or that his rescuers might arrive too late, when he had undergone the full agonies of asphyxiation.

These apprehensions, growing more dolorous and more tyrannous daily, had accompanied the first stages of his second illness. Then, by vacillating degrees, he had begun to doubt his brother, to suspect that Guy, being next in the line of inheritance, might wish for his demise and have an interest in its consummation. Guy had always been a cynical, cold-blooded sort; and his half-concealed contempt and scant sympathy for Uther Magbane's obsession was readily translated into darker terms by a sick fantasy. Gradually, as he grew weaker, the invalid had come to fear that his brother would deliberately hasten the burial—might even disconnect the device for summoning aid, whose care had been confided to him.

Now, after Guy had gone out, the certainty of such treachery, like a black and noxious blossom, leaped full-grown in Sir Uther Magbane's mind. Swept by a cold, devastating panic, he resolved that he would speak, at the first opportunity, to someone else—would confide secretly to another person than Guy the responsibility of seeing that the electrical alarm was kept in good working order.

Hours went by in a shrouded file as he lay there with his poisonous and sepulchral thoughts. It was afternoon, and the sloping sun should have shone now through the leaded panes, but the yew-fringed sky beyond the window seemed to be overcast, and there was only a sodden glimmering. Twilight began to weave a gray web in the room; and Magbane remembered that it was almost time for the doctor to pay him his evening visit.

Could he dare confide in the doctor, he wondered? He did not know the man very well. The family physician had died some time ago, and this new doctor had been called in by Guy. Sir Uther had never cared much for his manner, which was both brisk and saturnine. He might be in league with Guy, might have an understanding as to the way in which the elder brother could be so conveniently disposed of, and his demise made certain. No, he could not speak to the doctor.

Who was there to help him, anyway? He had never made many friends, and even these seemed to have deserted him.

The manor house was in a lonely part of the country, and everything would facilitate the treachery that he apprehended. God! he was being smothered—buried alive! . . .

Someone opened the door quietly and came toward him. He felt so hopeless and helpless that he did not even try to turn. Presently the visitor stood before him, and he saw that it was Holton, the aged family butler, who had served three generations of the Magbanes. Probably he could trust Holton, and he would speak about the matter now.

He framed the words with which he would address the butler, and was horrified when his tongue and his lips refused to obey him. He had not noticed anything wrong heretofore: his brain and his senses had been preternaturally clear. But now an icy paralysis appeared to have seized his organs of articulation.

He tried to lift his pale, clawlike hand and beckon to Holton, but the hand lay moveless on the counterpane, in spite of the agonized and herculean effort of will which he exerted. Fully conscious, but powerless to stir by so much as the shifting of a finger or the drooping of an eyelid, he could only lie and watch the dawning concern in the old butler's rheumy eyes.

Holton came nearer, reaching out his tremulous hand. Magbane saw the hand approaching him, saw it hover above his body, and descend toward his heart, just below the direct focus of his vision. It seemed never to reach him—at least there was no sensation of contact. The room was dimming rapidly—strange that the darkness should have come so soon—and a faintness was creeping on all his senses, like an insidious mist.

With a start of familiar terror, and a feeling of some intolerable repetition, of doing what he had once before done under circumstances of dire fright, he felt that he was going down into a night-black abyss. Holton's face was fading to a remote star, was receding with awful velocity above unscalable pits at whose bottom nameless, inexorable doom awaited Magbane: a doom to which he had gone at some previous time, and which he had been predestined to meet from the beginning of cycles. Down, forever down he went; the star disappeared; there was no light anywhere—and his syncope was complete.

Magbane's reviving consciousness took the form of a fantastic dream. In this dream, he remembered his descent into the gulf; and he thought that the descent had been prolonged, after a dim interval, by some animate, malignant agency. Great demoniac hands had seemed to grasp him in the nadir-founded gloom, had lifted him, had carried him down immeasurable flights of inframundane stairs and along corridors that lay deeper than hell itself.

There was night everywhere. He could not see the forms of those who bore him, supporting him at feet and head, but he could hear their implacable, unceasing steps, echoing with hollow and sepulchral thunder in the black subterranes; and he could sense the funereal towering of their shapes, oppressing him from about and above in some ultra-tactual fashion, such as is possible only in dreams.

Somewhere in that nether night they laid him down, they left him and went away. In his dream he heard the departing rumble of their footsteps, with leaden reverberations, endless and ominous, through all the stairs and corridors by which they had come with their human burden. At last there was a prolonged clangor as of closing doors, somewhere in the upper profound, a clangor fraught with unutterable despair, like the knell of Titans. After its echoes had died away, the despair seemed to remain, stagnant and soundless, dwelling tyrannically, illimitably, in all the recesses of this sepulchral underworld.

Silence, dank, stifling, eonian silence prevailed, as if the whole universe had died, had gone down to some infraspatial burial. Magbane could neither move nor breathe; and he felt, by no physical sense, an infinity of dead things about him, lying hopeless of resurrection, like himself.

Then, within the dream, by no perceptible transition, another dream was intercalated. Magbane forgot the horror and hopelessness of his descent, as a new-born child might forget some former death. He thought that he was standing in a place of soft sunlight and blithe, many-tinted flowers. An April turf was deep and resilient beneath him; the heavens were those of some vernal paradise; and he was not alone in this Eden, for Alice Margreave, his former fiancée, stood lovely and smiling amid the nearer blossoms.

He stepped toward her, filled with ineffable happiness—and in the sward at his feet a black pit, shaped like the grave, opened and widened and deepened with awful rapidity. Powerless to avert his doom, he went down into the pit, falling, falling interminably; and the darkness closed above him, swooping from all sides on a dim pin-point of light which was all that remained of the April heavens. The light expired, and Magbane was lying once more among dead things, in vaults beneath the universe.

By slow, incalculably doubtful graduations, his dream began to merge into reality. At first, there had been no sense of time; only an ebon stagnation, in which eons and minutes were equally drowned. Then—through what channel of sense he knew not—there returned to Magbane the awareness of duration. The awareness sharpened, and he thought that he heard, at long, regular intervals, a remote and muffled sound. Insufferable doubt and bewilderment, associated with some horror which he could not recall, awoke and brooded noxiously in his dark mind.

Now he became aware of bodily discomfort. A dank chill, beginning as if in his very brain, crept downward through his body and limbs, till it reached his extremities and left them tingling. He felt, too, that he was intolerably cramped, was lying in some stiff, straitened position. With mounting terror, for which as yet he could find no name, he heard the remote muffled sound draw closer, till it was no longer a sound, but the palpable hammering of his heart against his side. With this clarifying of his sense-perceptions, he knew abruptly, as in a flash of black lightning, the thing of which he was afraid.

The terrible knowledge went through him in a lethal shock, leaving him frozen. It was like a tetanic rigor, oppressing all his members, constricting his throat and heart as with iron bands; inhibiting his breath, crushing him like some material incubus. He dared not, *could* not move to verify his fear.

Utterly unmanned by a conviction of atrocious doom, he fought to regain some nominal degree of composure. He must not give way to the horror, or he would go mad. Perhaps it was only a dream after all; perhaps he was lying awake in his own bed, in darkness, and if he reached out his hand, he would encounter free space—not the hideous nearness of a coffin lid.

In a sick vertigo of irresolution, he tried to summon courage and volition for the test. His sense of smell, awakening now, tended to confirm his despair; for there was a musty closeness, a dismal, sodden reek of wood and cloth—even as once before. It semed to grow heavier momently with confined impurities.

At first, he thought that he could not move his hand—that the strange paralysis of his malady had not yet left him. With the dread laboriousness of nightmare, he lifted it slowly, tediously, as if overcoming the obstruction of a viscid medium. When, finally, a few inches away, it met the cold, straight surface he had apprehended, he felt the iron tightening of his despair, but was not surprised. There had been no real room for hope: the thing was happening again, just as it had been ordained to happen. Every step he had taken since birth, every motion, every breath, every struggle —had led only to this.

Mad thoughts were milling in his brain, like crowded maggots in a corpse. Old memories and present fears were mingled in strange confusion, steeped with the same charnel blackness. He recalled, in that tumult of disconnected ideas, the push-button he had installed in the casket. At the same moment, his brother's face, callous, ironic, touched with a thin, ambiguous sneer, appeared like a hallucination from the darkness; and the newest of his fears came back upon him with sickening certitude. In a flash, he saw the face presiding above the entire process through which, by the illegal connivance of the doctor, he must have been hurried into the tomb without passing through an embalmer's hands. Fearing that he might revive at any moment, they had taken no chances—and had doomed him to this horror.

The mocking face, the cruel vision, seemed to disappear; and among his disordered, frenzy-driven thoughts there rose an irrational hope. Perhaps he had been wrong in his doubts of Guy. Perhaps the electrical device would work after all, and a light pressure would summon eager hands to loose him from his mortuary confinement. He forgot the ghastly chain of condemning logic.

Quickly, by an automatic impulse, he groped for the button. At first he did not find it, and a sick consternation filled him. Then, at last, his fingers touched it and he pressed the button again and again, listening desperately for the answering clang of the alarm gong in the chapel above. Surely he would hear it, even through the intervening wood and stone; and he tried insanely to believe that he *had* heard it—that he could even hear the sound of running footsteps somewhere above him. After seeming hours, with a hideous lapse into the most abominable despond, he realized that there was nothing—nothing but the stifled clamor of his own imprisoned heart.

For a while, he yielded to madness, as on that former occasion, beating obliviously against the sides of the casket, hurling himself blindly at the inexorable lid. He shrieked again and again, and the narrow space seemed to drown him with a volume of thick, demoniacally deep sound, which he did not recognize as his own voice or the voice of anything human. Exhaustion, and the wet, salty taste of blood in his mouth, flowing from his bruised face, brought him back at last to comparative calmness.

He perceived now that he was breathing with great difficulty—that his violent struggles and cries had served only to deplete the scant amount of air in the casket. In a moment of unnatural coolness, he recalled something that he had read, somewhere, about a method of shallow breathing by which men could survive protracted periods of inhumation. He must force himself to inhale lightly, must center all his faculties on the prolongation of life. Perhaps, even yet, if he could hold out, his rescuers would come. Perhaps the alarm *had* rung, and he had not been able to hear it. Men were hurrying to his aid, and he must not perish before they could lift the slab and break open the casket.

He wanted to live, as never before; he longed, with intolerable avidity, to breathe the open air once more, to know the unimaginable bliss of free movement and respiration. God! if someone would only come—if he could hear the ring of footsteps, the sullen grating of the slab, the hammers and chisels that would let in the blessed light, the pure air! Was this all that he could ever know, this dumb horror of living interment, this blind, cramped agony of slow suffocation?

He strove to breathe quietly, with no waste or effort, but his throat and chest seemed to constrict as with the inexorable tightening of some atrocious torture instrument. There was no relief, no escape, nothing but a ceaseless, relentless pressure, the strangling clutch of some monstrous garrote that compressed his lungs, his heart, his windpipe, his very brain.

The agony increased: there was a weight of piled monuments upon him, which he must lift if he were to breathe freely. He strove against the funereal burden. He seemed to hear, at the same time, the labored sound of some Cyclopean engine that sought to make headway in a subterranean passage beneath fallen masses of earth and mountainous stone. He did not know that the sound was his own tortured gasping. The engine seemed to pant, thunderous and stertorous, with earth-shaking vibrations, and upon it, he thought, the foundations of ruined worlds were descending slowly and steadily, to choke it into ultimate silence.

The last agonies of his asphyxiation were translated into a monstrous delirium, a phantasmagoria that seemed to prolong itself for cycles, with one implacable dream passing without transition into another.

He thought that he was lying captive in some Inquisitorial vault whose roof, floor and walls were closing upon him with appalling speed, were crushing him in their adamantine embrace.

For an instant, in a light that was not light, he strove to flee with leaden limbs from a formless, nameless juggernaut, taller than the stars, heavier than the world, that rolled upon him in black, iron silence, grinding him beneath it into the charnel dust of some nethermost limbo.

He was climbing eternal stairs, bearing in his arms the burden of some gigantic corpse, only to have the stairs crumble beneath him at each step, and to fall back with the corpse lying upon him and swelling to macrocosmic proportions.

Eyeless giants had stretched him prone on a granite plain and were building upon his chest, block by colossal block, through eons of slow toil, the black Babel of a sunless world.

An anaconda of black, living metal, huger than the Python of myth, coiling about him in the pit where he had fallen, constricted his body with its unimaginable folds. In a gray, livid flash, he saw its enormous mouth poised above him, sucking the last breath it had squeezed from his lungs.

With inconceivable swiftness, the head of the anaconda became that of his brother Guy. It mocked him with a vast sneer, it appeared to swell and expand, to lose all human semblance or proportion, to become a blank, dark mass that rushed upon him in cyclonic gloom, driving him down into the space beyond space.

Somewhere in that descent there came to him the unknown, incognizable mercy of nothingness. . . .

THE DOUBLE SHADOW

MY name is Pharpetron, among those who have known me in Poseidonis: but even I, the last and most forward pupil of the wise Avyctes, know not the name of that which I am fated to become ere tomorrow. Therefore, by the ebbing silver lamps, in my master's marble house above the loud sea, I write this tale with a hasty hand, scrawling an ink of wizard virtue on the gray, priceless, antique parchment of dragons. And having written, I shall enclose the pages in a sealed cylinder of orichalchum, and shall cast the cylinder from a high window into the sea, lest that which I am doomed to become should haply destroy the writing. And it may be that mariners from Lephara, passing to Umb and Pneor in their tall triremes, will find the cylinder; or fishers will draw it from the wave in their seines; and having read my story, men will learn the truth and take warning; and no man's feet, henceforward, will approach the pale and demon-haunted house of Avyctes.

For six years I have dwelt apart with the aged master, forgetting youth and its wonted desires in the study of arcanic things. We have delved more deeply than all others before us in an interdicted lore; we have called up the dwellers in sealed crypts, in fearful abysses beyond space. Few are the sons of mankind who have cared to seek us out among the bare, wind-worn crags; and many, but nameless, are the visitants who have come to us from further bourns of place and time.

Stern and white as a tomb is the mansion wherein we dwell. Far below, on black, naked reefs, the northern sea climbs and roars indomitably, or ebbs with a ceaseless murmur as of armies of baffled demons; and the house is filled evermore, like a hollow-sounding sepulcher, with the drear echo of its tumultuous voices; and the winds wail in dismal wrath around the high towers but shake them not. On the seaward side the mansion rises sheerly from the straight-falling cliff; but on the other sides there are narrow terraces, grown with dwarfish, crooked cedars that bow always beneath the gale. Giant marble monsters guard the landward portals; and huge marble women ward the strait porticos above the surf; and mighty statues and mummies stand everywhere in the chambers and along the halls. But, saving these, and the entities we have summoned, there is none to companion us; and liches and shadows have been the servitors of our daily needs.

Not without terror (since man is but mortal) did I, the neophyte, behold at first the abhorrent and tremendous faces of them that obeyed Avyctes. I shuddered at the black writhing of submundane things from the maney-volumed smoke of the braziers; I cried in horror at the gray foulnesses, colossal, without form, that crowded malignly about the drawn circle of seven colors, threatening unspeakable trespass on us that stood at the center. Not without revulsion did I drink wine that was poured by cadavers, and eat bread that was purveyed by phantoms. But use and custom dulled the strangeness, destroyed the fear; and in time I believed implicitly that Avyctes was the lord of all incantations and exorcisms, with infallible power to dismiss the beings he evoked.

Well had it been for Avyctes—and for me—if the master had contented himself with the lore preserved from Atlantis and Thule, or brought over from Mu. Surely this should have been enough: for in the ivory-sheeted books of Thule there were blood-writ runes that would call the demons of the fifth and seventh planets if spoken aloud at the hour of their ascent; and the sorcerers of Mu had left record of a process whereby the doors of far-future time could be unlocked; and our fathers, the Atlanteans, had known the road between the atoms and the path into far stars. But Avyctes thirsted for a darker knowledge, a deeper empery. . . . And into his hands, in the third year of my novitiate, there came the mirror-bright tablet of the lost serpent people.

At certain hours, when the tide had fallen from the steep rocks, we were wont to descend by cavern-hidden stairs to a cliff-walled crescent beach behind the promontory on which stood Avyctes' house. There, on the dun, wet sands, beyond the foamy tongues of the surf, would lie the worn and curious driftage of alien shores and trove the hurricanes had cast up from unsounded deeps. And there we had found the purple and sanguine volutes of great shells, and rude lumps of ambergris, and white flowers of perpetually blooming coral; and once, the barbaric idol of green brass that had been the figurehead of a galley from far hyperborean isles. . . .

There had been a great storm, such as must have riven the sea to its last profound; but the tempest had gone by with morning, and the heavens were cloudless on that fatal day; and the demon winds were hushed among the black crags and chasms; and the sea lisped with a low whisper, like the rustle of gowns of samite trailed by fleeing maidens on the sand. And just beyond the ebbing wave, in a tangle of russet sea-weed, we descried a thing that glittered with blinding sun-like brilliance.

And running forward, I plucked it from the wrack before the wave's return, and bore it to Avyctes.

The tablet was wrought of some nameless metal, like never-rusting iron, but heavier. It had the form of a triangle and was broader at the widest than a man's heart. On one side it was wholly blank, like a mirror. On the other side many rows of small crooked ciphers were incised deeply in the metal, as if by the action of some mordant acid; and these ciphers were not the hieroglyphs or alphabetic characters of any language known to the master or to me.

Of the tablet's age and origin we could form no conjecture; and our erudition was wholly baffled. For many days thereafter we studied the writing and held argument that came to no issue. And night by night, in a high chamber closed against the perennial winds, we pondered over the dazzling triangle by the tall straight flames of silver lamps. For Avyctes deemed that knowledge of rare value, some secret of an alien or elder magic, was held by the clueless crooked ciphers. Then, since all our scholarship was in vain, the master sought another divination, and had recourse to wizardry and necromancy. But at first, among all the devils and phantoms that answered our interrogation, none could tell us aught concerning the tablet. And any other than Avyctes would have despaired in the end . . . and well would it have been if he had despaired, and had sought no longer to decipher the writing.

The months and years went by with a slow thundering of seas on the dark rocks, and a headlong clamor of winds around the white towers. Still we continued our delving and evocations; and farther, always farther we went into lampless realms of space and spirit; learning, perchance, to unlock the hithermost of the manifold infinities. And at whiles Avyctes would resume his pondering of the sea-found tablet, or would question some visitant regarding its interpretation.

At length, by the use of a chance formula, in idle experiment, he summoned up the dim, tenuous ghost of a sorcerer from prehistoric years; and the ghost, in a thin whisper of uncouth, forgotten speech, informed us that the letters on the tablet were those of a language of the serpent-men, whose primal continent had sunk eons before the lifting of

Hyperborea from the ooze. But the ghost could tell us naught of their significance; for, even in his time, the serpent-people had become a dubious legend; and their deep, antehuman lore and sorcery were things irretrievable by man.

Now, in all the books of conjuration owned by Avyctes, there was no spell whereby we could call the lost serpent-men from their fabulous epoch. But there was an old Lemurian formula, recondite and uncertain, by which the shadow of a dead man could be sent into years posterior to those of his own lifetime, and could be recalled after an interim by the wizard. And the shade, being wholly insubstantial, would suffer no harm from the temporal transition, and would remember, for the information of the wizard, that which he had been instructed to learn during the journey.

So, having called again the ghost of the prehistoric sorcerer, whose name was Ybith, Avyctes made a singular use of several very ancient gums and combustible fragments of fossil wood; and he and I, reciting the responses of the formula, sent the thin spirit of Ybith into the far ages of the serpent-men.

And after a time which the master deemed sufficient, we performed the curious rites of incantation that would recall Ybith. And the rites were successful; and Ybith stood before us again, like a blown vapor that is nigh to vanishing. And in words faint as the last echo of perishing memories, the specter told us the key to the meaning of the letters, which he had learned in the prehuman past. And after this, we questioned Ybith no more but suffered him to return unto slumber and oblivion.

Then, knowing the import of the tiny, twisted ciphers, we read the tablet's writing and made thereof a transliteration, though not without labor and difficulty, since the very phonetics of the serpent tongue, and the symbols and ideas, were somewhat alien to those of mankind. And when we had mastered the inscription, we found that it contained the formula for a certain evocation which, no doubt, had been used by the serpent sorcerers. But the object of the evocation was not named; nor was there any clue to the nature or identity of that which would come in answer to the rites. And, moreover, there was no corresponding rite of exorcism nor spell of dismissal.

Great was Avyctes' jubilation, deeming that we had learned a lore beyond the memory or prevision of man. And though I sought to dissuade him, he resolved to employ the evocation, arguing that our discovery was no chance thing but was fatefully predestined from the beginning. And he seemed to think lightly of the menace that might be brought upon us by the conjuration of things whose nativity and attributes were wholly obscure. "For," said Avyctes, "I have called up, in all the years of my sorcery, no god or devil, no demon or lich or shadow which I could not control and dismiss at will. And I am loath to believe that any spirit or power beyond the subversion of my spells could have been summoned by a race of serpents, whatever their skill in necromancy and demonism."

So, seeing that he was obstinate, and acknowledging him for my master in all ways, I agreed to aid Avyctes in the experiment, though not without misgivings. And then we gathered together, in the chamber of conjuration, at the specified hour and configuration of the stars, the equivalents of sundry rare materials that the tablet had instructed us to use in the ritual.

Of much that we did, and of certain agents that we employed, it were better not to tell; nor shall I record the shrill, sibilant words, difficult for beings not born of serpents to articulate, whose intonation formed a signal part of the ceremony. Toward the last, we drew a triangle on the marble floor with the fresh blood of birds; and Avyctes stood at one angle, and I at another; and the gaunt umber mummy of an Atlantean warrior, whose name had been Oigos, was stationed at the third angle. And standing thus, Avyctes and I held tapers of corpse-tallow in our hands, till the tapers had burned down between our fingers as into a socket. And in the outstretched palms of the mummy of Oigos, as if in shallow thuribles, talc and asbestos burned, ignited by a strange fire whereof we knew the secret. At one side we had traced on the floor an infrangible ellipse, made by an endless linked repetition of the twelve unspeakable Signs of Oumor, to which we could retire if the visitant should prove inimical or rebellious. We waited while the pole-circling stars went over, as had been prescribed. Then, when the tapers had gone out between our seared fingers, and the talc and asbestos were wholly consumed in the mummy's eaten palms, Avyctes uttered a single word whose sense was obscure to us; and Oigos, being animated by sorcery and subject to our will, repeated the word after a given interval, in tones that were hollow as a tomb-born echo; and I, in my turn, also repeated it.

Now, in the chamber of evocation, before beginning the ritual, we had opened a small window giving upon the sea, and had likewise left open a high door on the hall to landward, lest that which came in answer to us should require a spatial mode of entrance. And during the ceremony, the sea became still and there was no wind, and it seemed that all things were hushed in expectation of the nameless visitor. But after all was done, and the last word had been repeated by Oigos and me, we stood and waited vainly for a visible sign or other manifestation. The lamps burned stilly; and no shadows fell, other than were cast by ourselves and Oigos and by the great marble women along the walls.

And in the magic mirrors we had placed cunningly, to reflect those that were otherwise unseen, we beheld no breath or trace of any image.

At this, after a given interim, Avyctes was sorely disappointed, deeming that the evocation had failed of its purpose; and I, having the same thought, was secretly relieved. We questioned the mummy of Oigos, to learn if he had perceived in the room, with such senses as are peculiar to the dead, the sure token or doubtful proof of a presence undescried by us the living. And the mummy gave a necromantic answer, saying that there was nothing.

"Verily," said Avyctes, "it were useless to wait longer. For surely in some way we have misunderstood the purport of the writing, or have failed to duplicate the matters used in the evocation, or the correct intonement of the words. Or it may be that in the lapse of so many eons, the thing that was formerly wont to respond has long ceased to exist, or has altered in its attributes, so that the spell is now void and valueless."

To this I assented readily, hoping that the matter was at an end. And afterward we resumed our habitual studies, but made no mention to each other of the strange tablet or the vain formula.

Even as before, our days went on; and the sea climbed and roared in white fury on the cliffs; and the winds wailed by in their unseen, sullen wrath, bowing the dark cedars as witches are bowed by the breath of Taaran, god of Evil. Almost, in the marvel of new tests and cantraips, I forgot the ineffectual conjuration; and I deemed that Avyctes had forgotten it.

All things were as of yore, to our sorcerous perception; and there was naught to trouble us in our wisdom and power and serenity, which we deemed secure above the sovereignty of kings. Reading the horoscopic stars, we found no future ill in their aspect; nor was any shadow of bale foreshown to us through geomancy, or such other modes of divination as we employed. And our familiars, though grisly and dreadful to mortal gaze, were wholly obedient to us the masters.

Then, on a clear summer afternoon, we walked, as was often our custom, on the marble terrace behind the house. In robes of ocean-purple, we paced among the windy trees with their blown crooked shadows; and there, following us, I saw the blue shadow of Avyctes and my own shadow on the marble; and between them, an adumbration that was not wrought by any of the cedars. And I was greatly startled, but spoke not of the matter to Avyctes, and observed the unknown shadow with covert care.

I saw that it followed closely the master's shadow, keeping ever the same distance. And it fluttered not in the wind, but moved with a flowing as of some heavy, thick and purulent liquid; and its color was not blue nor purple nor black, nor any other hue to which man's eyes are habituated, but a hue as of some darker putrescence than that of death; and its form was altogether monstrous, seeming to move as if cast by one that trod erect, but having the squat head and long, undulant body of things that should creep rather than walk.

Avyctes heeded not the shadow, and still I feared to speak, though I thought it an ill thing for the master to be companioned thus. And I moved closer to him, in order to detect by touch or other perception the invisible presence that had cast the adumbration. But the air was void to sunward of the shadow; and I found nothing opposite the sun nor in any oblique direction, though I searched closely, knowing that certain beings cast their shadows in such wise.

After a while, at the customary hour, we returned by the coiling stairs and monster-flanked portals into the house.

And I saw that the strange adumbration moved ever behind the shadow of Avyctes, falling horrible and unbroken on the steps and passing clearly separate and distinct amid the long umbrage of the towering monsters. And in the dim halls beyond the sun, where shadows should not have been, I beheld with terror the loathly, distorted blot, having a pestilential hue without name, that followed Avyctes as if in lieu of his own extinguished shadow. And all that day, everywhere that we went, at the table served by spectres, or in the mummy-warded room of volumes and books, the thing pursued Avyctes, clinging to him even as leprosy to the leper. And still the master had perceived it not; and still I forbore to warn him, hoping that the visitant would withdraw in its own time, going obscurely as it had come.

But at midnight, when we sat together by the silver lamps, pondering the blood-writ runes of Hyperborea, I saw that the shadow had drawn closer to the shadow of Avyctes, towering behind his chair on the wall. And the thing was a streaming ooze of charnel pollution, a foulness beyond the black leprosies of hell; and I could bear it no more; and I cried out in my fear and loathing, and informed the master of its presence.

Beholding now the shadow, Avyctes considered it closely; and there was neither fear nor awe nor abhorrence in the deep-graven wrinkles of his visage. And he said to me at last: "This thing is a mystery beyond my lore: but never, in all the practise of my art, has any shadow come to me unbidden. And since all others of our evocations have found answer ere this, I must deem that the shadow is a very entity, or the shade or sign of an entity, that has come in belated response to the formula of the serpent-sorcerers, which we thought powerless and void. And I think it well that we should now repair to the chamber of conjuration, and interrogate the shadow in such manner as we may."

We went forthwith into the chamber of conjuration, and made such preparations as were both needful and possible. And when we were prepared to question it, the unknown shadow had drawn closer still to the shadow of Avyctes, so that the clear space between the two was no wider than the thickness of a necromancer's rod.

Now, in all feasible ways, we interrogated the shadow, speaking through our own lips and the lips of mummies and statues. But there was no answer; and calling certain of the devils and phantoms that were our familiars, we made question through the mouths of these, but without result. And all the while, our mirrors were void of any presence that might have cast the shadow; and they that had been our spokesmen could detect nothing in the room. And there was no spell, it seemed, that had power upon the visitant. So Avyctes became troubled; and drawing on the floor with blood and ashes the ellipse of Oumor, wherein no demon nor spirit may intrude, he retired to its center. But still, within the ellipse, like a flowing taint of liquid corruption, the shadow followed his shadow; and the space between the two was no wider than the thickness of a wizard's pen.

On the face of Avyctes, horror had graved new wrinkles; and his brow was beaded with a deathly sweat. For he knew, even as I, that this was a thing beyond all laws, and foreboding naught but untold disaster and evil. And he cried to me in a shaken voice, and said:

"I have no knowledge of this thing nor its intention toward me, and no power to stay its progress. Go forth and leave me now: for I would not that any man should witness the defeat of my sorcery and the doom that may follow thereupon. Also, it were well to depart while there is yet time, lest you too should become the quarry of the shadow. . . ."

Though terror had fastened upon my inmost soul, I was loath to leave Avyctes. But I had sworn to obey his will at all times and in every respect; and moreover I knew myself doubly powerless against the adumbration, since Avyctes himself was impotent.

So, bidding him farewell, I went forth with trembling limbs from the haunted chamber; and peering back from the threshold, I saw that the alien umbrage, creeping like a noisome blotch on the floor, had touched the shadow of Avyctes. And at that moment the master shrieked aloud like one in nightmare; and his face was no longer the face of Avyctes but was convulsed and contorted like that of some helpless madman who wrestles with an unseen incubus. And I looked no more, but fled along the dim outer hall and through the portals giving upon the terrace.

A red moon, ominous and gibbous, had declined above the crags; and the shadows of the cedars were elongated in the moon; and they wavered in the gale like the blown cloaks of enchanters. And stooping against the gale, I fled across the terrace toward the outer stairs that led to a steep path in the waste of rocks and chasms lying behind Avyctes' house. I neared the terrace-edge, running with the speed of fear; but I could not reach the topmost outer stair: for at every step the marble flowed beneath me, fleeing like a pale horizon before the seeker. And though I raced and panted without pause, I could draw no nearer to the terrace-edge.

At length I desisted, seeing that an unknown spell had altered the very space around the house of Avyctes, so that none could escape therefrom. So, resigning myself to whatever might befall, I returned toward the house. And climbing the white stairs in the low, level beams of the crag-caught moon, I saw a figure that awaited me in the portals. And I knew by the trailing robe of sea-purple, but by no other token, that the figure was Avyctes. For the face was no longer in its entirety the face of man, but was become a loathly fluid amalgam of human features with a thing not to be identified on earth. The transfiguration was ghastlier than death or decay; and the face was already hued with the nameless, corrupt and purulent color of the strange shadow; and its outlines had assumed a partial likeness to the squat profile of the shadow. The hands of the figure were not those of any terrene being; and the shape beneath the robe had lengthened with a nauseous undulant pliancy; and the face and fingers seemed to drip in the moonlight with a deliquescent corruption. And the pursuing umbrage, like a thickly flowing blight, had corroded and distorted the very shadow of Avyctes, which was now double in a manner not to be narrated here.

Fain would I have cried or spoken aloud: but horror had dried up the font of speech. And the thing that had been Avyctes beckoned me in silence, uttering no word from its living and putrescent lips. And with eyes that were no longer eyes but an oozing abomination, it peered steadily upon me. And it clutched my shoulder closely with the soft leprosy of its fingers, and led me half swooning with revulsion along the hall, and into that room where the mummy of Oigos, who had assisted us in the threefold incantation of the serpent-men, was stationed with several of his fellows.

By the lamps which illumed the chamber, burning with pale, still, perpetual flames, I saw that the mummies stood erect along the wall in their exanimate repose, each in his wonted place, with his tall shadow beside him. But the great, gaunt shadow of Oigos on the wall was companioned by an adumbration similar in all respects to the evil thing that had followed the master and was now incorporate with him. I remembered that Oigos had performed his share of the ritual, and had repeated an unknown stated word in turn after Avyctes; and so I knew that the horror had come to Oigos in turn and would wreak itself upon the dead even as upon the living. For the foul, anonymous thing that we had called in our presumption could manifest itself to mortal ken in no other way than this. We had drawn it from fathomless deeps of time and space, using ignorantly a dire formula; and the thing had come at its own chosen hour, to stamp itself in abomination uttermost on the evocators.

Since then, the night has ebbed away, and a second day has gone by like a sluggish ooze of horror. . . . I have seen the complete identification of the shadow with the flesh and the shadow of Avyctes . . . and also I have seen the slow encroachment of that other umbrage, mingling itself with the lank shadow and the sere, bituminous body of Oigos, and turning them to a similitude of the thing which Avyctes has become. And I have heard the mummy cry out like a living man in great pain and fear, as with the throes of a second dissolution, at the impingement of the shadow. And long since it has grown silent, like the other horror, and I know not its thoughts or its intent. . . . And verily I know not if the thing that has come to us be one or several; nor if its avatar will rest complete with the three that summoned it forth into time, or be extended to others.

But these things, and much else, I shall soon know: for now, in turn, there is a shadow that follows mine, drawing ever closer. The air congeals and curdles with unknown fear; and they that were our familiars have fled from the mansion; and the great marble women seem to tremble visibly where they stand along the walls. But the horror that was Avyctes, and the second horror that was Oigos, have left me not, and neither do they tremble. With eyes that are not eyes, they seem to brood and watch, waiting till I too shall become as they. And their stillness is more terrible than if they had rended me limb from limb. And there are strange voices in the wind, and alien roarings upon the sea; and the walls quiver like a thin veil in the black breath of remote abysses.

So, knowing that the time is brief, I have shut myself in the room of volumes and books and have written this account. And I have taken the bright triangular tablet, whose solution was our undoing, and have cast it from the window into the sea, hoping that none will find it after us. And now I must make an end, and enclose this writing in the sealed cylinder of orichalchum, and fling it forth to drift upon the sea-wave. For the space between my shadow and the shadow of the horror is straitened momently . . . and the space is no wider than the thickness of a wizard's pen.

THE CHAIN OF AFORGOMON

IT is indeed strange that John Milwarp and his writings should have fallen so speedily into semi-oblivion. His books, treating of Oriental life in a somewhat flowery, romantic style, were popular a few months ago. But now, in spite of their range and penetration, their pervasive verbal sorcery, they are seldom mentioned; and they seem to have vanished unaccountably from the shelves of bookstores and libraries.

Even the mystery of Milwarp's death, baffling to both law and science, has evoked but a passing interest, an excitement quickly lulled and forgotten.

I was well acquainted with Milwarp over a term of years. But my recollection of the man is becoming strangely blurred, like an image in a misted mirror. His dark, half-alien personality, his preoccupation with the occult, his immense knowledge of Eastern life and lore, are things I remember with such effort and vagueness as attends the recovery of a dream. Sometimes I almost doubt that he ever existed. It is as if the man, and all that pertains to him, were being erased from human record by some mysterious acceleration of the common process of obliteration.

In his will, he appointed me his executor. I have vainly tried to interest publishers in the novel he left among his papers: a novel surely not inferior to anything he ever wrote. They say that his vogue has passed. Now I am publishing as a magazine story the contents of the diary kept by Milwarp for a period preceding his demise.

Perhaps, for the open-minded, this diary will explain the enigma of his death. It would seem that the circumstances of that death are virtually forgotten, and I repeat them here as part of my endeavor to revive and perpetuate Milwarp's memory.

Milwarp had returned to his house in San Francisco after a long sojourn in Indo-China. We who knew him gathered that he had gone into places seldom visited by Occidentals. At the time of his demise he had just finished correcting the typescript of a novel which dealt with the more romantic and mysterious aspects of Burma.

On the morning of April 2nd, 1933, his housekeeper, a middle-aged woman, was startled by a glare of brilliant light which issued from the half-open door of Milwarp's study. It was as if the whole room were in flames. Horrified, the woman hastened to investigate. Entering the study, she saw her master sitting in an armchair at the table, wearing the rich, somber robes of Chinese brocade which he affected as a dressing-gown. He sat stiffly erect, a pen clutched unmoving in his fingers on the open pages of a manuscript volume. About him, in a sort of nimbus, glowed and flickered the strange light; and her only thought was that his garments were on fire.

She ran toward him, crying out a warning. At that moment the weird nimbus brightened intolerably, and the wan early dayshine, the electric bulbs that still burned to attest the night's labor, were alike blotted out. It seemed to the housekeeper that something had gone wrong with the room itself; for the walls and table vanished, and a great, luminous gulf opened before her; and on the verge of the gulf, in a seat that was not his cushioned armchair but a huge and rough-hewn seat of stone, she beheld her master stark and rigid. His heavy brocaded robes were gone, and about him, from head to foot, were blinding coils of pure white fire, in the form of linked chains. She could not endure the brilliance of the chains, and cowering back, she shielded her eyes with her hands. When she dared to look again, the weird glowing had faded, the room was as usual; and Milwarp's motionless figure was seated at the table in the posture of writing.

Shaken and terrified as she was, the woman found courage to approach her master. A hideous smell of burnt flesh arose from beneath his garments, which were wholly intact and without visible trace of fire. He was dead, his fingers clenched on the pen and his features frozen in a stare of tetanic agony. His neck and wrists were completely encircled by frightful burns that had charred them deeply. The coroner, in his examination, found that these burns, preserving an outline as of heavy links, were extended in long unbroken spirals around the arms and legs and torso. The burning was apparently the cause of Milwarp's death: it was as if iron chains, heated to incandescence, had been wrapped about him.

Small credit was given to the housekeeper's story of what she had seen. No one, however, could suggest an acceptable explanation of the bizzare mystery. There was, at the time, much aimless discussion; but, as I have hinted, people soon turned to other matters. The efforts made to solve the riddle were somewhat perfunctory. Chemists tried to determine the nature of a queer drug, in the form of a gray powder with pearly granules, to whose use Milwarp had become addicted. But their tests merely revealed the presence of an alkaloid whose source and attributes were obscure to Western science.

Day by day, the whole incredible business lapsed from public attention; and those who had known Milwarp began to display the forgetfulness that was no less unaccountable than his weird doom. The housekeeper, who had held stedfastly in the beginning to her story, came at length to share the common dubiety. Her account, with repetition, became vague and contradictory; detail by detail, she seemed to forget the abnormal circumstances that she had witnessed with overwhelming horror.

The manuscript volume, in which Milwarp had apparently been writing at the time of death, was given into my charge with his other papers. It proved to be a diary, its last entry breaking off abruptly. Since reading the diary, I have hastened to transcribe it in my own hand, because, for some mysterious reason, the ink of the original is already fading and has become almost illegible in places.

The reader will note certain lacunae, due to passages written in an alphabet which neither I nor any scholar of my acquaintance can transliterate. These passages seem to form an integral part of the narrative, and they occur mainly toward the end, as if the writer had turned more and more to a language remembered from his ancient avatar. To the same mental reversion one must attribute the singular dating, in which Milwarp, still employing English script, appears to pass from our contemporary notation to that of some premundane world.

I give hereunder the entire diary, which begins with an undated footnote:

This book, unless I have been misinformed concerning the qualities of the drug *souvara*, will be the record of my former life in a lost cycle. I have had the drug in my possession for seven months, but fear has prevented me from using it. Now, by certain tokens, I perceive that the longing for knowledge will soon overcome the fear.

Ever since my earliest childhood I have been troubled by intimations, dim, unplaceable, that seemed to argue a forgotten existence. These intimations partook of the nature of feelings rather than ideas or images: they were like the wraiths of dead memories. In the background of my mind there has lurked a sentiment of formless, melancholy desire for some nameless beauty long perished out of time. And, coincidentally, I have been haunted by an equally formless dread, an apprehension as of some bygone but still imminent doom.

Such feelings have persisted, undiminished, throughout my youth and maturity, but nowhere have I found any clue to their causation. My travels in the mystic Orient, my delvings into occultism have merely convinced me that these shadowy intuitions pertain to some incarnation buried under the wreck of remotest cycles.

Many times, in my wanderings through Buddhistic lands, I had heard of the drug *souvara*, which is believed to restore, even for the uninitiate, the memory of other lives. And at last, after many vain efforts, I managed to procure a supply of the drug. The manner in which I obtained it is a tale sufficiently remarkable in itself, but of no special relevance here. So far—perhaps because of that apprehension which I have hinted—I have not dared to use the drug.

March 9th, 1933. This morning I took *souvara* for the first time, dissolving the proper amount in pure distilled water as I had been instructed to do. Afterward I leaned back easily in my chair, breathing with a slow, regular rhythm. I had no preconceived idea of the sensations that would mark the drug's initial effect, since these were said to vary prodigiously with the temperament of the users; but I composed myself to await them with tranquillity, after formulating clearly in my mind the purpose of the experiment. For a while there was no change in my awareness. I noticed a slight quickening of the pulse, and modulated my breathing in conformity with this. Then, by slow degrees, I experienced a sharpening of visual perception. The Chinese rugs on the floor, the backs of the serried volumes in my bookcases, the very wood of chairs, table and shelves, began to exhibit new and unimagined colors. At the same time there were curious alterations of outline, every object seeming to extend itself in a hitherto unsuspected fashion.

Following this, my surroundings became semi-transparent, like molded shapes of mist. I found that I could see through the marbled cover the illustrations in a volume of John Martin's edition of *Paradise Lost*, which lay before me on the table.

All this, I knew, was a mere extension of ordinary physical vision. It was only a prelude to those apperceptions of occult realms which I sought through *souvara*. Fixing my mind once more on the goal of the experiment, I became aware that the misty walls had vanished like a drawn arras. About me, like reflections in rippled water, dim sceneries wavered and shifted, erasing one another from instant to instant. I seemed to hear a vague but ever-present sound, more musical than the murmurs of air, water or fire, which was a property of the unknown element that environed me.

With a sense of troublous familiarity, I beheld the blurred unstable pictures which flowed past me upon this never-resting medium. Orient temples, flashing with sun-struck bronze and gold; the sharp, crowded gables and spires of medieval cities; tropic and northern forests; the costumes and physiognomies of the Levant, of Persia, of old Rome and Carthage, went by like blown, flying mirages. Each succeeding tableau belonged to a more ancient period than the one before it—and I knew that each was a scene from some former existence of my own.

Still tethered, as it were, to my present self, I reviewed these visible memories, which took on tri-dimensional depth and clarity. I saw myself as warrior and troubadour, as noble and merchant and mendicant. I trembled with dead fears, I thrilled with lost hopes and raptures, and was drawn by ties that death and Lethe had broken. Yet never did I fully identify myself with those other avatars: for I knew well that the memory I sought pertained to some incarnation of older epochs.

Still the fantasmagoria streamed on, and I turned giddy

with vertigo ineffable before the vastness and diuturnity of the cycles of being. It seemed that I, the watcher, was lost in a gray land where the homeless ghosts of all dead ages went fleeing from oblivion to oblivion.

The walls of Nineveh, the columns and towers of unnamed cities, rose before me and were swept away. I saw the luxuriant plains that are now the Gobi desert. The sea-lost capitals of Atlantis were drawn to the light in unquenched glory. I gazed on lush and cloudy scenes from the first continents of Earth. Briefly I relived the beginnings of terrestrial man—and knew that the secret I would learn was ancienter even than these.

My visions faded into black voidness—and yet, in that void, through fathomless eons, it seemed that I existed still like a blind atom in the space between the worlds. About me was the darkness and repose of that night which antedated the Earth's creation. Time flowed backward with the silence of dreamless sleep. . . .

The illumination, when it came, was instant and complete. I stood in the full, fervid blaze of day amid royally towering blossoms in a deep garden, beyond whose lofty, vine-clad walls I heard the confused murmuring of the great city called Kalood. Above me, at their vernal zenith, were the four small suns that illumed the planet Hestan. Jewel-colored insects fluttered about me, lighting without fear on the rich habiliments of gold and black, enwrought with astronomic symbols, in which I was attired. Beside me was a dial-shaped altar of zoned agate, carved with the same symbols, which were those of the dreadful omnipotent time-god, Aforgomon, whom I served as a priest.

I had not even the slightest memory of myself as John Milwarp, and the long pageant of my terrestrial lives was as something that had never been—or was yet to be. Sorrow and desolation choked my heart as ashes fill some urn consecrated to the dead; and all the hues and perfumes of the garden about me were redolent only of the bitterness of death. Gazing darkly upon the altar, I muttered blasphemy against Aforgomon, who, in his inexorable course, had taken away my beloved and had sent no solace for my grief. Separately I cursed the signs upon the altar: the stars, the worlds, the suns, the moons, that meted and fulfilled the processes of time. Belthoris, my betrothed, had died at the end of the previous autumn: and so, with double maledictions, I cursed the stars and planets presiding over that season.

I became aware that a shadow had fallen beside my own on the altar, and knew that the dark sage and sorcerer Atmox had obeyed my summons. Fearfully but not without hope I turned toward him, noting first of all that he bore under his arm a heavy, sinister-looking volume with covers of black steel and hasps of adamant. Only when I had made sure of this did I lift my eyes to his face, which was little less somber and forbidding than the tome he carried.

"Greeting, O Calaspa," he said harshly. "I have come against my own will and judgment. The lore that you request is in this volume; and since you saved me in former years from the inquisitorial wrath of the time-god's priests, I cannot refuse to share it with you. But understand well that even I, who have called upon names that are dreadful to utter, and have evoked forbidden presences, shall never dare to assist you in this conjuration. Gladly would I help you to hold converse with the shadow of Belthoris, or to animate her still unwithered body and draw it forth from the tomb. But that which you purpose is another matter. You alone must perform the ordained rites, must speak the necessary words: for the consequences of this thing will be direr than you deem."

"I care not for the consequences," I replied eagerly, "if it be possible to bring back the lost hours which I shared with Belthoris. Think you that I could content myself with her shadow, wandering thinly back from the Borderland? Or that I could take pleasure in the fair clay that the breath of necromancy has troubled and has made to arise and walk without mind or soul? Nay, the Belthoris I would summon is she on whom the shadow of death has never yet fallen!"

It seemed that Atmox, the master of doubtful arts, the vassal of umbrageous powers, recoiled and blenched before my vehement declaration.

"Bethink you," he said with minatory sternness, "that this thing will constitute a breath of the sacred logic of time and a blasphemy against Aforgomon, god of the minutes and the cycles. Moreover, there is little to be gained: for not in its entirety may you bring back the season of your love, but only one single hour, torn with infinite violence from its rightful period in time. . . . Refrain, I adjure you, and content yourself with a lesser sorcery."

"Give me the book," I demanded. "My service to Aforgomon is forfeit. With due reverence and devotion I have worshipped the time-god, and have done in his honor the rites ordained from eternity; and for all this the god has betrayed me."

Then, in that high-climbing, luxuriant garden beneath the four suns, Atmox opened the adamantine clasps of the steel-bound volume; and, turning to a certain page, he laid the book reluctantly in my hands. The page, like its fellows, was of some unholy parchment streaked with musty discolorations and blackening at the margin with sheer antiquity; but upon it shone unquenchably the dread characters a primal archimage had written with an ink bright as the new-shed ichor of demons. Above this page I bent in my madness, conning it over and over till I was dazzled by the fiery runes; and, shutting my eyes, I saw them burn on a red darkness, still legible, and writhing like hellish worms.

Hollowly, like the sound of a far bell, I heard the voice of Atmox: "You have learned, O Calaspa, the unutterable name of that One whose assistance can alone restore the fled hours. And you have learned the incantation that will rouse that hidden power, and the sacrifice needed for its propitiation. Knowing these things, is your heart still strong and your purpose firm?"

The name I had read in the wizard volume was that of the chief cosmic power antagonistic to Aforgomon; the incantation and the required offering were those of a foul demonolatry. Nevertheless, I did not hesitate, but gave resolute affirmative answer to the somber query of Atmox.

Perceiving that I was inflexible, he bowed his head, trying no more to dissuade me. Then, as the flame-runed volume had bade me do, I defiled the altar of Aforgomon, blotting certain of its prime symbols with dust and spittle. While Atmox looked on in silence, I wounded my right arm to its deepest vein on the sharp-tipped gnomon of the dial; and, letting the blood drip from zone to zone, from orb to orb on the graven agate, I made unlawful sacrifice, and intoned aloud, in the name of the Lurking Chaos, Xexanoth, an abominable ritual composed by a backward repetition and jumbling of litanies sacred to the time-god.

Even as I chanted the incantation, it seemed that webs of shadow were woven foully athwart the suns; and the ground shook a little, as if colossal demons trod the world's rim, striding stupendously from abysses beyond. The garden walls and trees wavered like a wind-blown reflection in a pool; and I grew faint with the loss of that life-blood I had poured out in demonolatrous offering. Then, in my flesh and in my brain, I felt the intolerable racking of a vibration like the long-drawn shock of cities riven by earthquake, and coasts crumbling before some chaotic sea; and my flesh was torn and harrowed, and my brain shuddered with the toneless discords sweeping through me from deep to deep.

I faltered, and confusion gnawed at my inmost being. Dimly I heard the prompting of Atmox, and dimmer still was the sound of my own voice that made answer to Xexanoth, naming the impious necromancy which was to be effected only through its power. Madly I implored from Xexanoth, in despite of time and its ordered seasons, one hour of that bygone autumn which I had shared with Belthoris; and imploring this, I named no special hour: for all, in memory, had seemed of an equal joy and gladness.

As the words ceased upon my lips, I thought that darkness fluttered in the air like a great wing; and the four suns went out, and my heart was stilled as if in death. Then the light returned, falling obliquely from suns mellow with full-tided autumn; and nowhere beside me was there any shadow of Atmox; and the altar of zoned agate was bloodless and undefiled. I, the lover of Belthoris, witting not of the doom and sorrow to come, stood happily with my beloved before the altar, and saw her young hands crown its ancient dial with the flowers we had plucked from the garden.

Dreadful beyond all fathoming are the mysteries of time. Even I, the priest and initiate, though wise in the secret doctrines of Aforgomon, know little enough of that elusive, ineluctable process whereby the present becomes the past and the future resolves itself into the present. All men have pondered the riddles of duration and transience; have wondered, vainly, to what bourn the lost days and the sped cycles are consigned. Some have dreamt that the past abides unchanged, becoming eternity as it slips from our mortal ken; and others have deemed that time is a stairway whose steps crumble one by one behind the climber, falling into a gulf of nothing.

Howsoever this may be, I know that she who stood beside me was the Belthoris on whom no shadow of mortality had yet descended. The hour was one new-born in a golden season; and the minutes to come were pregnant with all wonder and surprise belonging to the untried future.

Taller was my beloved than the frail, unbowed lilies of the garden. In her eyes was the sapphire of moonless evenings sown with small golden stars. Her lips were strangely curved, but only blitheness and joy had gone to their shaping. She and I had been betrothed from our childhood, and the time of the marriage-rites was now approaching. Our intercourse was wholly free, according to the custom of that world. Often she came to walk with me in my garden and to decorate the altar of that god whose revolving moons and suns would soon bring the season of our felicity.

The moths that flew about us, winged with aerial cloth-of-gold, were no lighter than our hearts. Making blithe holiday, we fanned our frolic mood to a high flame of rapture. We were akin to the full-hued, climbing flowers, the swift-darting insects, and our spirits blended and soared with the perfumes that were drawn skyward in the warm air. Unheard by us was the loud murmuring of the mighty city of Kalood lying beyond my garden walls; for us the many-peopled planet known as Hestan no longer existed; and we dwelt alone in a universe of light, in a blossomed heaven. Exalted by love in the high harmony of those moments, we seemed to touch eternity; and even I, the priest of Aforgomon, forgot the blossom-fretting days, the system-devouring cycles.

In the sublime folly of passion, I swore then that death or discord could never mar the perfect communion of our hearts. After we had wreathed the altar, I sought the rarest, the most delectable flowers: frail-curving cups of wine-washed pearl, of moony azure and white with scrolled purple lips; and these I twined, between kisses and laughter, in the black maze of Belthoris' hair; saying that another shrine than that of time should receive its due offering.

Tenderly, with a lover's delay, I lingered over the wreathing; and, ere I had finished, there fluttered to the ground beside us a great, crimson-spotted moth whose wing had somehow been broken in its airy voyaging through the garden. And Belthoris, ever tender of heart and pitiful, turned from me and took up the moth in her hands; and some of the bright blossoms dropped from her hair unheeded. Tears welled from her deep blue eyes; and seeing that the moth was sorely hurt and would never fly again, she refused to be comforted; and no longer would she respond to my passionate wooing. I, who grieved less for the moth than she, was somewhat vexed; and between her sadness and my vexation, there grew between us some tiny, temporary rift. . . .

Then, ere love had mended the misunderstanding; then, while we stood before the dread altar of time with sundered hands, with eyes averted from each other, it seemed that a shroud of darkness descended upon the garden. I heard the crash and crumbling of shattered worlds, and a black flowing of ruinous things that went past me through the darkness. The dead leaves of winter were blown about me, and there was a falling of tears or rain. . . . Then the vernal suns came back, high-stationed in cruel splendor; and with them came the knowledge of all that had been, of Belthoris' death and my sorrow, and the madness that had led to forbidden sorcery. Vain now, like all other hours, was the resummoned hour; and doubly irredeemable was my loss. My blood dripped heavily on the dishallowed altar, my faintness grew deathly, and I saw through murky mist the face of Atmox beside me; and the face was like that of some comminatory demon. . . .

March 13th. I, John Milwarp, write this date and my name with an odd dubiety. My visionary experience under the drug *souvara* ended with that rilling of my blood on the symboled dial, that glimpse of the terror-distorted face of

Atmox. All this was in another world, in a life removed from the present by births and deaths without number; and yet, it seems, not wholly have I returned from the twice-ancient past. Memories, broken but strangely vivid and living, press upon me from the existence of which my vision was a fragment; and portions of the lore of Hestan, and scraps of its history, and words from its lost language, arise unbidden in my mind.

Above all, my heart is still shadowed by the sorrow of Calaspa. His desperate necromancy, which would seem to others no more than a dream within a dream, is stamped as with fire on the black page of recollection. I know the awfulness of the god he had blasphemed; and the foulness of the demonolatry he had done, and the sense of guilt and despair under which he swooned. It is this that I have striven all my life to remember, this which I have been doomed to re-experience. And I fear with a great fear the further knowledge which a second experiment with the drug will reveal to me.

The next entry of Milwarp's diary begins with a strange dating in English script: "The second day of the moon Occalat, in the thousand-and-ninth year of the Red Eon." This dating, perhaps, is repeated in the language of Hestan: for, directly beneath it, a line of unknown ciphers is set apart. Several lines of the subsequent text are in the alien tongue; and then, as if by an unconscious reversion, Milwarp continues the diary in English. There is no reference to another experiment with *souvara:* but apparently such had been made, with a continued revival of his lost memories.

... What genius of the nadir gulf had tempted me to this thing and had caused me to overlook the consequences? Verily, when I called up for myself and Belthoris an hour of former autumn, with all that was attendant upon the hour, *that bygone interim was likewise evoked and repeated for the whole world Hestan, and the four suns of Hestan.* From the full midst of spring, all men had stepped backward into autumn, keeping only the memory of things prior to the hour thus resurrected, and knowing not the events future to the hour. But, returning to the present, they recalled with amazement the unnatural necromancy; and fear and bewilderment were upon them; and none could interpret the meaning.

For a brief period, the dead had lived again; the fallen leaves had returned to the bough; the heavenly bodies had stood at a long-abandoned station; the flower had gone back into the seed, the plant into the root. Then, with eternal disorder set among all its cycles, time had resumed its delayed course.

No movement of any cosmic body, no year or instant of the future, would be precisely as it should have been. The error and discrepancy I had wrought would bear fruit in ways innumerable. The suns would find themselves at fault; the worlds and atoms would go always a little astray from their appointed bourns.

It was of these matters that Atmox spoke, warning me, after he had staunched my bleeding wound. For he too, in that relumined hour, had gone back and had lived again through a past happening. For him the hour was one in which he had descended into the nether vaults of his house. There, standing in a many-pentacled circle, with burning of unholy incense and uttering of accurst formulae, he had called upon a malign spirit from the bowels of Hestan and had questioned it concerning the future. But the spirit, black and voluminous as the fumes of pitch, refused to answer him directly and pressed furiously with its clawed members against the confines of the circle. It said only: "Thou hast summoned me at thy peril. Potent are the spells thou hast used, and strong is the circle to withstand me, and

I am restrained by time and space from the wreaking of my anger upon thee. *But haply thou shalt summon me again, albeit in the same hour of the same autumn;* and in that summoning the laws of time shall be broken, and a rift shall be made in space; and through the rift, though with some delay and divagation, I will yet win to thee."

Saying no more, it prowled restlessly about the circle; and its eyes burned down upon Atmox like embers in a high-lifted sooty brazier; and ever and anon its fanged mouth was flattened on the spell-defended air. And in the end he could dismiss it only after a double repetition of the form of exorcism.

As he told me this tale in the garden, Atmox trembled; and his eyes searched the narrow shadows wrought by the high suns; and he seemed to listen for the noise of some evil thing that burrowed toward him beneath the earth.

Fourth day of the moon Occalat. Stricken with terrors beyond those of Atmox, I kept apart in my mansion amid the city of Kalood. I was still weak with the loss of blood I had yielded to Xexanoth; my senses were full of strange shadows; my servitors, coming and going about me, were as phantoms, and scarcely I heeded the pale fear in their eyes or heard the dreadful things they whispered. . . . Madness and chaos, they told me, were abroad in Kalood; the divinity of Aforgomon was angered. All men thought that some baleful doom impended because of that unnatural confusion which had been wrought among the hours of time.

This afternoon they brought me the story of Atmox's death. In bated tones they told me how his neophytes had heard a roaring as of a loosed tempest in the chamber where he sat alone with his wizard volumes and paraphernalia. Above the roaring, for a little, human screams had sounded, together with a clashing as of hurled censers and braziers, a crashing as of overthrown tables and tomes. Blood rilled from under the shut door of the chamber, and, rilling, it took from instant to instant the form of dire ciphers that spelt an unspeakable name. After the noises had ceased, the neophytes waited a long while ere they dared to open the door. Entering at last, they saw the floor and the walls heavily bespattered with blood, and rags of the sorcerer's raiment mingled everywhere with the sheets of his torn volumes of magic, and the shreds and manglings of his flesh strewn amid broken furniture, and his brains daubed in a horrible paste on the high ceiling.

Hearing this tale, I knew that the earthly demon feared by Atmox had found him somehow and had wreaked its wrath upon him. In ways unguessable, it had reached him through the chasm made in ordered time and space by one hour repeated through necromancy. And because of that lawless chasm, the magician's power and lore had utterly failed to defend him from the demon. . . .

Fifth day of the moon Occalat. Atmox, I am sure, had not betrayed me: for in so doing, he must have betrayed his own implicit share in my crime. . . . Howbeit, this evening the priests came to my house ere the setting of the westernmost sun: silent, grim, with eyes averted as if from a foulness innominable. Me, their fellow, they enjoined with loth gestures to accompany them. . . .

Thus they took me from my house and along the thoroughfares of Kalood toward the lowering suns. The streets were empty of all other passers, and it seemed that no man desired to meet or behold the blasphemer. . . .

Down the avenue of gnomon-shaped pillars, I was led to the portals of Aforgomon's fane: those awfully gaping portals arched in the likeness of some devouring chimera's mouth. . . .

Sixth day of the moon Occalat. They had thrust me into an oubliette beneath the temple, dark, noisome and soundless except for the maddening, measured drip of water beside me. There I lay and knew not when the night passed and the morning came. Light was admitted only when my captors opened the iron door, coming to lead me before the tribunal. . . .

. . . Thus the priests condemned me, speaking with one voice in whose dreadful volume the tones of all were indistinguishably blended. Then the aged high-priest Helpenor called aloud upon Aforgomon, offering himself as a mouthpiece to the god, and asking the god to pronounce through him the doom that was adequate for such enormities as those of which I had been judged guilty by my fellows.

Instantly, it seemed, the god descended into Helpenor; and the figure of the high-priest appeared to dilate prodigiously beneath his mufflings; and the accents that issued from his mouth were like thunders of the upper heaven:

"O Calaspa, thou hast set disorder amid all future hours and eons through this evil necromancy. Thereby, moreover, thou hast wrought thine own doom: fettered art thou for ever to the hour thus unlawfully repeated, apart from its due place in time. According to hieratic rule, thou shalt meet the death of the fiery chains: but deem not that this death is more than the symbol of thy true punishment. Thou shalt pass hereafter through other lives in Hestan, and shalt climb midway in the cycles of the world subsequent to Hestan in time and space. But through all thine incarnations the chaos thou hast invoked will attend thee, widening ever like a rift. And always, in all thy lives, the rift will bar thee from reunion with the soul of Belthoris; and always, though merely by an hour, thou shalt miss the love that should otherwise have been oftentimes regained.

"At last, when the chasm has widened overmuch, thy soul shall fare no farther in the onward cycles of incarnation. At that time it shall be given thee to remember clearly thine ancient sin; and remembering, thou shalt perish out of time. Upon the body of that latter life shall be found the charred imprint of the chains, as the final token of thy bondage. But they that knew thee will soon forget, and thou shalt belong wholly to the cycles limited for thee by thy sin."

March 29th. I write this date with infinite desperation, trying to convince myself that there is a John Milwarp who exists on Earth, in the Twentieth Century. For two days running, I have not taken the drug *souvara:* and yet I have returned twice to that oubliette of Aforgomon's temple, in which the priest Calaspa awaits his doom. Twice I have been immersed in its stagnant darkness, hearing the slow drip of water beside me, like a clepsydra that tells the black ages of the damned.

Even as I write this at my library table, it seems that an ancient midnight plucks at the lamp. The bookcases turn to walls of oozing, nighted stone. There is no longer a table ... nor one who writes ... and I breathe the noisome dankness of a dungeon lying unfathomed by any sun, in a lost world.

Eighteenth day of the moon Occalat. Today, for the last time, they took me from my prison. Helpenor, together with three others, came and led me to the adytum of the god. Far beneath the outer temple we went, through spacious crypts unknown to the common worshippers. There was no word spoken, no glance exchanged between the others and me; and it seemed that they already regarded me as one cast out from time and claimed by oblivion.

We came ultimately to that sheer-falling gulf in which the spirit of Aforgomon is said to dwell. Lights, feeble and far-scattered, shone around it like stars on the rim of cosmic vastness, shedding no ray into the depths. There, in a seat of hewn stone overhanging the frightful verge, I was placed by the executioners; and a ponderous chain of black unrusted metal, stapled in the solid rock, was wound about and about me, circling my naked body and separate limbs, from head to foot.

To this doom, others had been condemned for heresy or impiety . . . though never for a sin such as mine. After the chaining of the victim, he was left for a stated interim, to ponder his crime—and haply to confront the dark divinity of Aforgomon. At length, from the abyss into which his position forced him to peer, a light would dawn, and a bolt of strange flame would leap upward, striking the many-coiled chain about him and heating it instantly to the whiteness of candescent iron. The source and nature of the flame were mysterious, and many ascribed it to the god himself rather than to mortal agency. . . .

Even thus they have left me, and have gone away. Long since the burden of the massy links, cutting deeper and deeper into my flesh, has become an agony. I am dizzy from gazing downward into the abyss—and yet I cannot fall. Beneath, immeasurably beneath, at recurrent intervals, I hear a hollow and solemn sound. Perhaps it is the sigh of sunken waters . . . of cavern-straying winds . . . or the respiration of One that abides in the darkness, meting with his breath the slow minutes, the hours, the days, the ages. . . . My terror has become heavier than the chain, my vertigo is born of a two-fold gulf. . . .

Eons have passed by and all the worlds have ebbed into nothingness, like wreckage borne on a chasm-falling stream, taking with them the lost face of Belthoris. I am poised above the gaping maw of the Shadow. . . . Somehow, in another world, an exile phantom has written these words

... a phantom who must fade utterly from time and place, even as I, the doomed priest Calaspa. I cannot remember the name of the phantom.

Beneath me, in the black depths, there is an awful brightening. ...

THE DARK EIDOLON

Thasaidon, lord of seven hells
Wherein the single Serpent dwells,
With volumes drawn from pit to pit
Through fire and darkness infinite—
Thasaidon, sun of nether skies,
Thine ancient evil never dies,
For aye thy somber fulgors flame
On sunken worlds that have no name,
Man's heart enthrones thee, still supreme,
Though the false sorcerers blaspheme.
  —*The Song of Xeethra.*

ON Zothique, the last continent of Earth, the sun no longer shone with the whiteness of its prime, but was dim and tarnished as if with a vapor of blood. New stars without number had declared themselves in the heavens, and the shadows of the infinite had fallen closer. And out of the shadows, the older gods had returned to man: the gods forgotten since Hyperborea, since Mu and Poseidonis, bearing other names but the same attributes. And the elder demons had also returned, battening on the fumes of evil sacrifice, and fostering again the primordial sorceries.

Many were the necromancers and magicians of Zothique, and the infamy and marvel of their doings were legended everywhere in the latter days. But among them all there was none greater than Namirrha, who imposed his black yoke on the cities of Xylac, and later, in a proud delirium, deemed himself the veritable peer of Thasaidon, lord of Evil.

Namirrha had built his abode in Ummaos, the chief town of Xylac, to which he came from the desert realm of Tasuun with the dark renown of his thaumaturgies like a cloud of desert storm behind him. And no man knew that in coming to Ummaos he returned to the city of his birth; for all deemed him a native of Tasuun. Indeed, none could have dreamt that the great sorcerer was one with the beggar-boy, Narthos, an orphan of questionable parentage, who had begged his daily bread in the streets and bazars of Ummaos. Wretchedly had he lived, alone and despised; and a hatred of the cruel, opulent city grew in his heart like a smothered flame that feeds in secret, biding the time when it shall become a conflagration consuming all things.

Bitterer always, through his boyhood and early youth, was the spleen and rancor of Narthos toward men. And one day the prince Zotulla, a boy but little older than he, riding a restive palfrey, came upon him in the square before the imperial palace; and Narthos implored an alms. But Zotulla, scorning his plea, rode arrogantly forward, spurring the palfrey; and Narthos was ridden down and trampled under its hooves. And afterward, nigh to death from the trampling, he lay senseless for many hours, while the people passed him by unheeding. And at last, regaining his senses, he dragged himself to his hovel; but he limped a little thereafter all his days, and the mark of one hoof remained like a brand on his body, fading never. Later, he left Ummaos and was forgotten quickly by its people. Going southward into Tasuun, he lost his way in the great desert, and was near to perishing. But finally he came to a small oasis, where dwelt the wizard Ouphaloc, a hermit who preferred the company of honest jackals and hyenas to that of men. And Ouphaloc, seeing the great craft and evil in the starveling boy, gave succor to Narthos and sheltered him. He dwelt for years with Ouphaloc, becoming the wizard's pupil and the heir of his demon-wrested lore. Strange things he learned in that hermitage, being fed on fruits and grain that had sprung not from the watered earth, and wine that was not the juice of terrene grapes. And like Ouphaloc, he became a master in devildom and drove his own bond with the archfiend Thasaidon. When Ouphaloc died, he took the name of

Namirrha, and went forth as a mighty sorcerer among the wandering peoples and the deep-buried mummies of Tasuun. But never could he forget the miseries of his boyhood in Ummaos and the wrong he had endured from Zotulla; and year by year he spun over in his thoughts the black web of revenge. And his fame grew ever darker and vaster, and men feared him in remote lands beyond Tasuun. With bated whispers they spoke of his deeds in the cities of Yoros, and in Zul-Bha-Sair, the abode of the ghoulish deity Mordiggian. And long before the coming of Namirrha himself, the people of Ummaos knew him as a fabled scourge that was direr than simoom or pestilence.

Now, in the years that followed the going-forth of the boy Narthos from Ummaos, Pithaim, the father of Prince Zotulla, was slain by the sting of a small adder that had crept into his bed for warmth on an autumn night. Some said that the adder had been purveyed by Zotulla, but this was a thing that no man could verily affirm. After the death of Pithaim, Zotulla, being his only son, was emperor of Xylac, and ruled evilly from his throne in Ummaos. Indolent he was, and tyrannic, and full of strange luxuries and cruelties; but the people, who were also evil, acclaimed him in his turpitude. So he prospered, and the lords of hell and heaven smote him not. And the red suns and ashen moons went westward over Xylac, falling into that seldom-voyaged sea, which, if the mariners' tales were true, poured evermore like a swiftening river past the infamous isle of Naat, and fell in a worldwide cataract upon nether space from the far, sheer edge of Earth.

Grosser still he grew, and his sins were as overswollen fruits that ripen above a deep abyss. But the winds of time blew softly; and the fruits fell not. And Zotulla laughed amid his fools and his eunuchs and his lemans; and the tale of his luxuries was borne afar, and was told by dim outland peoples, as a twin marvel with the bruited necromancies of Namirrha.

It came to pass, in the year of the Hyena and the month of the star Canicule, that a great feast was given by Zotulla to the inhabitants of Ummaos. Meats that had been cooked in exotic spices from Sotar, isle of the east, were spread everywhere; and the ardent wines of Yoros and Xylac, filled as with subterranean fires, were poured inexhaustibly from huge urns for all. The wines awoke a furious mirth and a royal madness; and afterward they brought a slumber no less profound than the Lethe of the tomb. And one by one, as they drank, the revellers fell down in the streets, the houses and gardens, as if a plague had struck them; and Zotulla slept in his banquet-hall of gold and ebony, with his odalisques and chamberlains about him. So, in all Ummaos, there was no man or woman wakeful at the hour when Sirius began to fall toward the west.

Thus it was that none saw or heard the coming of Namirrha. But awakening heavily in the latter forenoon, the emperor Zotulla heard a confused babble, a troublous clamor of voices from such of his eunuchs and women as had awakened before him. Inquiring the cause, he was told that a strange prodigy had occurred during the night; but, being still bemused with wine and slumber, he comprehended little enough of its nature, till his favorite concubine, Obexah, led him to the eastern portico of the palace, from which he could behold the marvel with his own eyes.

Now the palace stood alone at the center of Ummaos, and to north, west and south, for wide intervals of distance, there stretched the imperial gardens, full of superbly arching palms and loftily spiring fountains. But to eastward was a broad open area, used as a sort of common, between the palace and the mansions of high optimates. And in this space, which had lain wholly vacant at eve, a building towered colossal and lordly beneath the full-risen sun, with domes like monstrous fungi of stone that had come up in the night. And the domes, rearing level with those of Zotulla, were builded of death-white marble; and the huge façade, with multi-columned porticoes and deep balconies, was wrought in alternate zones of night-black onyx and porphyry hued as with dragons'-blood. And Zotulla swore lewdly, calling with hoarse blasphemies on the gods and devils of Xylac; and great was his dumfoundment, deeming the marvel a work of wizardry. The women gathered about him, crying out with shrill cries of awe and terror; and more and more of his courtiers, awakening, came to swell the hub-bub; and the fat castradoes diddered in their cloth-of-gold like immense black jellies in golden basins. But Zotulla, mindful of his dominion as emperor of all Xylac, sought to conceal his own trepidation, saying:

"Now who is this that has presumed to enter Ummaos like a jackal in the dark, and has made his impious den in proximity and counterview with my palace? Go forth, and inquire the miscreant's name; but, ere you go, instruct the headsman to make sharp his double-handed sword."

Then, fearing the emperor's wrath if they tarried, certain of the chamberlains went forth unwillingly and approached the portals of the strange edifice. It seemed that the portals were deserted till they drew near, and then, on the threshold, there appeared a titanic skeleton, taller than any man of earth; and it strode forward to meet them with ell-long strides. The skeleton was swathed in a loin-cloth of scarlet silk with a buckle of jet, and it wore a black turban, starred with diamonds, whose topmost foldings nearly touched the high lintel. Eyes like flickering marsh-fires burned in its deep eye-sockets; and a blackened tongue like that of a long-dead man protruded between its teeth; but otherwise it was clean of flesh, and the bones glittered whitely in the sun as it came onward.

The chamberlains were mute before it, and there was no sound except the golden creaking of their girdles, the shrill rustling of their silks, as they shook and trembled. And the foot-bones of the skeleton clicked sharply on the pavement of black onyx as it paused; and the putrefying tongue began to quiver between its teeth; and it uttered these words in an unctuous, nauseous voice:

"Return, and tell the emperor Zotulla that Namirrha, seer and magician, has come to dwell beside him."

Hearing the skeleton speak as if it had been a living man, and hearing the dread name of Namirrha as men hear the tocsin of doom in some fallen city, the chamberlains could stand before it no longer, and they fled with ungainly swiftness and bore the message to Zotulla.

Now, learning who it was that had come to neighbor with him in Ummaos, the emperor's wrath died out like a feeble and blustering flame on which the wind of darkness has blown; and the vinous purple of his cheeks was mottled with a strange pallor; and he said nothing, but his lips mumbled loosely as if in prayer or malediction. And the news of Namirrha's coming passed like the flight of evil night-birds through all the palace and throughout the city, leaving a noisome terror that abode in Ummaos thereafter till the end. For Namirrha, through the black renown of his thaumaturgies and the frightful entities who served him, had become a power that no secular sovereign dared dispute; and men feared him everywhere, even as they feared the gigantic, shadowy lords of hell and of outer space. And in Ummaos, people said that he had come on the desert wind from Tasuun with his underlings, even as the pestilence comes, and had reared his house in an hour with the aid of devils beside Zotulla's palace. And they said that the foundations of the house were laid on the adamantine cope of hell; and in its floors were pits at whose bottom burned the nether fires, or stars could be seen as they passed under in lowermost night. And the followers of Namirrha were the dead of strange kingdoms, the demons of sky and earth and the abyss, and mad, impious, hybrid things that the sorcerer himself had created from forbidden unions.

Men shunned the neighborhood of his lordly house; and in the palace of Zotulla few cared to approach the windows and balconies that gave thereon; and the emperor himself spoke not of Namirrha, pretending to ignore the intruder; and the women of the harem babbled evermore with an evil gossip concerning Namirrha and his concubines. But the sorcerer himself was not beheld by the people of the city, though some believed that he walked forth at will, clad with invisibility. His servitors likewise were not seen; but a howling as of the damned was sometimes heard to issue from his portals; and sometimes there came a stony cachinnation, as if some adamantine image had laughed aloud; and sometimes there was a chuckling like the sound of shattered ice in a frozen hell. Dim shadows moved in the porticoes when there was neither sunlight nor lamp to cast them; and red, eery lights appeared and vanished in the windows at eve, like a blinking of demoniac eyes. And slowly the ember-colored suns went over Xylac, and were quenched in far seas; and the ashy moons were blackened as they fell nightly toward the hidden gulf. Then, seeing that the wizard had wrought no open evil, and that none had endured palpable harm from his presence, the people took heart; and Zotulla drank deeply, and feasted in oblivious luxury as before; and dark Thasaidon, prince of all turpitudes, was the true but never-acknowledged lord of Xylac. And in time the men of Ummaos bragged a little of

Namirrha and his dread thaumaturgies, even as they had boasted of the purple sins of Zotulla.

But Namirrha, still unbeheld by living men and living women, sat in the inner halls of that house which his devils had reared for him, and spun over and over in his thoughts the black web of revenge. And in all Ummaos there was none, even among his fellow-beggars, who recalled the beggar-boy Narthos. And the wrong done by Zotulla to Narthos in old time was the least of those cruelties which the emperor had forgotten.

Now, when the fears of Zotulla were somewhat lulled, and his women gossiped less often of the neighboring wizard, there occurred a new wonder and a fresh terror. For, sitting one eve at his banquet-table with his courtiers about him, the emperor heard a noise as of myriad iron-shod hooves that came trampling through the palace-gardens. And the courtiers also heard the sound, and were startled amid their mounting drunkenness; and the emperor was angered, and he sent certain of his guards to examine into the cause of the trampling. But peering forth upon the moon-bright lawns and parterres, the guards beheld no visible shape, though the loud sounds of trampling still went to and fro. It seemed as if a rout of wild stallions passed and re-passed before the façade of the palace with tumultuous gallopings and capricoles. And a fear came upon the guards as they looked and listened; and they dared not venture forth, but returned to Zotulla. And the emperor himself grew sober when he heard their tale; and he went forth with high blusterings to view the prodigy. And all night the unseen hooves rang out sonorously on the pavements of onyx, and ran with deep thuddings over the grasses and flowers. The palm-fronds waved on the windless air as if parted by racing steeds; and visibly the tall-stemmed lilies and broad-petaled exotic blossoms were trodden under. And rage and terror nested together in Zotulla's heart as he stood in a balcony above the garden, hearing the spectral tumult, and beholding the harm done to his rarest flower-beds. The women, the courtiers and eunuchs cowered behind him, and there was no slumber for any occupant of the palace; but toward dawn the clamor of hooves departed, going toward Namirrha's house.

When the dawn was full-grown above Ummaos, the emperor walked forth with his guards about him, and saw that the crushed grasses and broken-down stems were blackened as if by fire where the hooves had fallen. Plainly were the marks imprinted, like the tracks of a great company of horses, in all the lawns and parterres; but they ceased at the verge of the gardens. And though every one believed that the visitation had come from Namirrha, there was no proof of this in the grounds that fronted the sorcerer's abode; for here the turf was untrodden.

"A pox upon Namirrha, if he has done this!" cried Zotulla. "For what harm have I ever done to him? Verily, I shall set my heel on the dog's neck; and the torture-wheel shall serve him even as these horses from hell have served my blood-red lilies of Sotar and my vein-colored irises of Naat and my orchids from Uccastrog which were purple as the bruises of love. Yea, though he stand the viceroy of Thasaidon above Earth, and overlord of ten thousand devils, my wheel shall break him, and fires shall heat the wheel white-hot in its turning, till he withers black as the seared blossoms." Thus did Zotulla make his brag; but he issued no orders for the execution of the threat; and no man stirred from the palace toward Namirrha's house. And from the portals of the wizard none came forth; or if any came, there was no visible sign or sound.

So the day went over, and the night rose, bringing later a moon that was slightly darkened at the rim. And the night was silent; and Zotulla, sitting long at the banquet-table, drained his wine-cup often and wrathfully, muttering new threats against Namirrha. And the night wore on, and it seemed that the visitation would not be repeated. But at midnight, lying in his chamber with Obexah, and fathom-deep in slumber from his wine, Zotulla was awakened by a monstrous clangor of hooves that raced and capered in the palace porticoes and in the long balconies. All night the hooves thundered back and forth, echoing awfully in the vaulted stone, while Zotulla and Obexah, listening, huddled close amid their cushions and coverlets; and all the occupants of the palace, wakeful and fearful, heard the noise but stirred not from their chambers. A little before dawn the hooves departed suddenly; and afterward, by day, their marks were found on the marble flags of the porches and balconies; and the marks were countless, deep-graven, and black as if branded there by flame.

Like mottled marble were the emperor's cheeks when he saw the hoof-printed floors; and terror stayed with him hence-forward, following him to the depths of his inebriety, since he knew not where the haunting would cease. His women murmured and some wished to flee from Ummaos, and it seemed that the revels of the day and evening were shadowed by ill wings that left their umbrage in the yellow wine and bedimmed the aureate lamps. And again, toward midnight, the slumber of Zotulla was broken by the hooves, which came galloping and pacing on the palace-roof and through all the corridors and halls. Thereafter, till dawn, the hooves filled the palace with their iron clatterings, and they rang hollowly on the topmost domes, as if the coursers of gods had trodden there, passing from heaven to heaven in tumultuous cavalcade.

Zotulla and Obexah, lying together while the terrible hooves went to and fro in the hall outside their chamber, had no heart or thought for sin, nor could they find any comfort in their nearness. In the gray hour before dawn they heard a great thundering high on the barred brazen door of the room, as if some mighty stallion, rearing, had drummed there with his forefeet. And soon after this, the hooves went away, leaving a silence like an interlude in some gathering storm of doom. Later, the marks of the hooves were found everywhere in the halls, marring the bright mosaics. Black holes were burnt in the golden-threaded rugs and the rugs of silver and scarlet; and the high white domes were pitted pox-wise with the marks; and far up on the brazen door of Zotulla's chamber the prints of a horse's forefeet were incised deeply.

Now, in Ummaos, and throughout Xylac, the tale of this haunting became known, and the thing was deemed an ominous prodigy, though people differed in their interpretations. Some held that the sending came from Namirrha, and was meant as a token of his supremacy above all kings and emperors; and some thought that it came from a new wizard who had risen in Tinarath, far to the east, and who wished to supplant Namirrha. And the priests of the gods of Xylac held that their various deities had dispatched the haunting, as a sign that more sacrifices were required in the temples.

Then, in his hall of audience, whose floor of sard and jasper had been grievously pocked by the unseen hooves, Zotulla called together many priests and magicians and soothsayers, and asked them to declare the cause of the sending and devise a mode of exorcism. But, seeing that there was no agreement among them, Zotulla provided the several priestly sects with the wherewithal of sacrifice to their sundry gods, and sent them away; and the wizards and prophets, under threat of decapitation if they refused, were enjoined to visit Namirrha in his mansion of sorcery and learn his will, if haply the sending were his and not the work of another.

Loth were the wizards and the soothsayers, fearing Namirrha, and caring not to intrude upon the frightful mysteries of his obscure mansion. But the swordsmen of the emperor drave them forth, lifting great crescent blades against them when they tarried; so one by one, in a straggling order, the delegation went toward Namirrha's portals and vanished into the devil-built house.

Pale, muttering and distraught, like men who have looked upon hell and have seen their doom, they returned before sunset to the emperor. And they said that Namirrha had received them courteously and had sent them back with this message:

"Be it known to Zotulla that the haunting is a sign of that which he has long forgotten; and the reason of the haunting will be revealed to him at the hour prepared and set apart by destiny. And the hour draws near: for Namirrha bids the emperor and all his court to a great feast on the afternoon of the morrow."

Having delivered this message, to the wonder and consternation of Zotulla, the delegation begged his leave to depart. And though the emperor questioned them minutely, they seemed unwilling to relate the circumstances of their visit to Namirrha; nor would they describe the sorcerer's fabled house, except in a vague manner, each contradicting the other as to what he had seen. So, after a little, Zotulla bade them go, and when they had gone he sat musing for a long while on the invitation of Namirrha, which was a thing that he cared not to accept but feared to decline. That evening he drank even more liberally than was his wont; and he slept a Lethean slumber, nor was there any noise of trampling hooves about the palace to awaken him. And silently, during the night, the prophets and the magicians passed like furtive shadows from Ummaos; and no man saw them depart; and at morning they were gone from Xylac into other lands, never to return. . . .

Now, on that same evening, in the great hall of his house, Namirrha sat alone, having dismissed the familiars who attended him ordinarily. Before him, on an altar of jet, was the dark, gigantic statue of Thasaidon which a devil-begotten sculptor had wrought in ancient days for an evil king of Tasuun, called Pharnoc. The archdemon was depicted in the guise of a full-armored warrior, lifting a spiky mace as if in heroic battle. Long had the statue lain in the desert-sunken palace of Pharnoc, whose very site was disputed by the nomads; and Namirrha, by his divination, had found it and had reared up the infernal image to abide with him always thereafter. And often, through the mouth of the statue, Thasaidon would utter oracles to Namirrha, or would answer interrogations.

Before the black-armored image there hung seven silver lamps, wrought in the form of horses' skulls, with flames issuing changeably in blue and purple and crimson from their eye-sockets. Wild and lurid was their light, and the face of the demon, peering from under his crested helmet, was filled with malign, equivocal shadows that shifted and changed eternally. And sitting in his serpent-carven chair, Namirrha regarded the statue grimly, with a deep-furrowed frown between his eyes: for he had asked a certain thing of Thasaidon, and the fiend, replying through the statue, had refused him. And rebellion was in the heart of Namirrha, grown mad with pride, and deeming himself the lord of all sorcerers and a ruler by his own right among the princes of devildom. So, after long pondering, he repeated his request in a bold and haughty voice, like one who addresses an equal rather than the all-formidable suzerain to whom he has sworn a fatal fealty.

"I have helped you heretofore in all things," said the image, with stony and sonorous accents that were echoed metallically in the seven silver lamps. "Yea, the undying worms of fire and darkness have come forth like an army at your summons, and the wings of nether genii have risen to occlude the sun when you called them. But, verily, I will not aid you in this vengeance you have planned: for the emperor Zotulla has done me no wrong and has served me well though unwittingly; and the people of Xylac, by reason of their turpitudes, are not the least of my terrestrial worshippers. Therefore, Namirrha, it were well for you to live in peace with Zotulla, and well to forget this olden wrong that was done to the beggar-boy Narthos. For the ways of destiny are strange, and the workings of its laws are sometimes hidden; and truly, if the hooves of Zotulla's palfrey had not spurned you and trodden you under, your life had been otherwise, and the name and renown of Namirrha had still slept in oblivion as a dream undreamed. Yea, you would tarry still as a beggar in Ummaos, content with a beggar's guerdon, and would never have fared forth to become the pupil of the wise and learned Ouphaloc; and I, Thasaidon, would have lost the lordliest of all necromancers who have accepted my service and my bond. Think well, Namirrha, and ponder these matters: for both of us, it would seem, are indebted to Zotulla in all gratitude for the trampling that he gave you."

"Yea, there is a debt," Namirrha growled implacably. "And truly, I will pay the debt tomorrow, even as I have planned. . . . There are Those who will aid me, Those who will answer my summoning in your despite."

"It is an ill thing to affront me," said the image, after an interval. "And also, it is not well to call upon Those that you designate. However, I perceive clearly that such is your intent. You are proud and stubborn and revengeful. Do, then, as you will, but blame me not for the outcome."

So, after this, there was silence in the hall where Namirrha sate before the eidolon; and the flames burned darkly, with changeable colors, in the skull-shapen lamps; and the shadows fled and returned, unresting, on the face of the statue and the face of Namirrha. Then, toward midnight, the necromancer rose and went upward by many spiral stairs to a high dome of his house in which was a single small round window that looked forth on the constellations. The window was set in the top of the dome; but Namirrha had contrived, by means of his magic, that one entering by the last spiral of the stairs would suddenly seem to descend rather than climb, and, reaching the final step, would peer *downward* through the window while stars passed under him in a giddying gulf. There, kneeling, Namirrha touched a secret spring in the marble, and the circular pane slid back without sound. Then, lying prone on the curved interior of the dome, with his face over the abyss, and his long beard trailing stiffly into space, he whispered a prehuman rune, and held speech with certain entities who belonged neither to hell nor the mundane elements, and were more fearsome to invoke than the infernal genii or the devils of earth, air, water and flame. With them he made his compact, defying Thasaidon's will, while the air curdled about him with their voices, and rime gathered palely on his sable beard from the cold that was wrought by their breathing as they leaned earthward.

Laggard and loth was the awakening of Zotulla from his wine; and quickly, ere he opened his eyes, the daylight was poisoned for him by the thought of that invitation which he feared to accept or decline. But he spoke to Obexah, saying:

"Who, after all, is this wizardly dog, that I should obey his summons like a beggar called in from the street by some haughty lord?"

Obexah, a golden-skinned and oblique-eyed girl from Uccastrog, Isle of the Torturers, eyed the emperor subtly, and said:

"O Zotulla, it is yours to accept or refuse, as you deem fitting. And truly, it is a small matter for the lord of Ummaos and all Xylac, whether to go or stay, since naught can impugn your sovereignty. Therefore, were it not as well to go?" For Obexah, though fearful of the wizard, was curious regarding that devil-built house of which so little was known; and likewise, in the manner of women, she wished to behold the famed Namirrha, whose mien and appearance were still but a far-brought legend in Ummaos.

"There is something in what you say," admitted Zotulla. "But an emperor, in his conduct, must always consider the public good; and there are matters of state involved, which a woman can scarcely be expected to understand."

So, later in the forenoon, after an ample and well-irrigated breakfast, he called his chamberlains and courtiers about him and took counsel with them. And some advised him to ignore the invitation of Namirrha; and others held that the invitation should be accepted, lest a graver evil than the trampling of ghostly hooves should be sent upon the palace and the city.

Then Zotulla called the many priesthoods before him in a body, and sought to resummon those wizards and soothsayers who had fled privily in the night. Among all the latter, there was none who answered the crying of his name through Ummaos; and this aroused a certain wonder. But the priests came in greater number than before, and thronged the hall of audience so that the paunches of the foremost were straitened against the imperial dais and the buttocks of the hindmost were flattened on the rear walls and pillars. And Zotulla debated with them the matter of acceptance or refusal. And the priests argued, as before, that Namirrha was nowise concerned with the sending; and his invitation, they said, portended no harm nor bale to the emperor; and it was plain, from the terms of the message, that an oracle would be imparted to Zotulla by the wizard; and this oracle, if Namirrha were a true archimage, would confirm their own holy wisdom and reestablish the divine source of the sending; and the gods of Xylac would again be glorified.

Then, having heard the pronouncement of the priests, the emperor instructed his treasurers to load them down with new offerings; and, calling unctuously upon Zotulla and all his household the vicarious blessings of their several gods, the priests departed. And the day wore on, and the sun passed its meridian, falling slowly beyond Ummaos through the spaces of afternoon that were floored with sea-ending deserts. And still Zotulla was irresolute; and he called his wine-bearers, bidding them pour for him the strongest and most magistral of their vintages; but in the wine he found neither certitude nor decision.

Sitting still on his throne in the hall of audience, he heard, toward middle afternoon, a mighty and clamorous outcry that arose at the palace-portals. There were deep wailings of men and the shrillings of eunuchs and women, as if terror passed from tongue to tongue, invading the halls and apartments. And the fearful clamor spread throughout all the palace, and Zotulla, rousing from the lethargy of wine, was about to send his attendants to inquire the cause.

Then, into the hall, there filed an array of tall mummies, clad in royal cerements of purple and scarlet, and wearing gold crowns on their withered craniums. And after them, like servitors, came gigantic skeletons who wore loin-cloths of nacarat orange and about whose upper skulls, from brow to crown, live serpents of banded saffron and ebon had wrapped themselves for head-dresses. And the mummies bowed before Zotulla, saying with thin, sere voices:

"We, who were kings of the wide realm of Tasuun aforetime, have been sent as a guard of honor for the emperor Zotulla, to attend him as is befitting when he goes forth to the feast prepared by Namirrha."

Then, with dry clickings of their teeth, and whistlings as of air through screens of fretted ivory, the skeletons spoke:

"We, who were giant warriors of a race forgotten, have also been sent by Namirrha, so that the emperor's household, following him to the feast, should be guarded from all peril and should fare forth in such pageantry as is meet and proper."

Witnessing these prodigies, the wine-bearers and other attendants cowered about the imperial dais or hid behind the pillars, while Zotulla, with pupils swimming starkly in a bloodshot white, with face bloated and ghastly pale, sat frozen on his throne and could utter no word in reply to the ministers of Namirrha.

Then, coming forward, the mummies said in dusty accents: "All is made ready, and the feast awaits the arrival of Zotulla." And the cerements of the mummies stirred and fell open at the bosom, and small rodent monsters, brown as bitumen, eyed as with accursed rubies, reared forth from the eaten hearts of the mummies like rats from their holes and chittered shrilly in human speech, repeating the words. The skeletons in turn took up the solemn sentence; and the black and saffron serpents hissed it from their skulls; and the words were repeated lastly in baleful rumblings by certain furry creatures of dubious form, hitherto unseen by Zotulla, who sat behind the ribs of the skeletons as if in cages of white wicker.

Like a dreamer who obeys the doom of dreams, the emperor rose from his throne and went forward, and the mummies surrounded him like an escort. And each of the skeletons drew from the reddish-yellow folds of his loin-cloth a curiously pierced archaic flute of silver; and all began a sweet and evil and deathly fluting as the emperor went out through the halls of the palace. A fatal spell was in the music: for the chamberlains, the women, the guards, the eunuchs, and all members of Zotulla's household even to the cooks and scullions, were drawn like a procession of night-walkers from the rooms and alcoves in which they had vainly hidden themselves; and, marshaled by the flutists, they followed after Zotulla. A strange thing it was to behold this mighty company of people, going forth in the slanted sunlight toward Namirrha's house, with a cortège of dead kings about them, and the blown breath of skeletons thrilling eldritchly in the silver flutes. And little was Zotulla comforted when he found the girl Obexah at his side, moving, as he, in a thralldom of involitient horror, with the rest of his women close behind.

Coming to the open portals of Namirrha's house, the emperor saw that they were guarded by great crimson-wattled things, half dragon, half man, who bowed before him, sweeping their wattles like bloody besoms on the flags of dark onyx. And the emperor passed with Obexah between the louting monsters, with the mummies, the skeletons and his own people behind him in strange pageant, and entered a vast and multicolumned hall, where the daylight, following timidly, was drowned by the baleful arrogant blaze of a thousand lamps.

Even amid his horror, Zotulla marvelled at the vastness of the chamber, which he could hardly reconcile with the mansion's outer length and height and breadth, though these indeed were of most palatial amplitude. For it seemed that he gazed down great avenues of topless pillars, and vistas of tables laden with piled-up viands and thronged urns of wine, that stretched away before him into luminous distance and gloom as of starless night.

In the wide intervals between the tables, the familiars of Namirrha and his other servants went to and fro incessantly, as if a fantasmagoria of ill dreams were embodied before the emperor. Kingly cadavers in robes of time-rotten brocade, with worms seething in their eye-pits, poured a blood-like wine into cups of the opalescent horn of unicorns. Lamias, trident-tailed, and four-breasted chimeras, came in with fuming platters lifted high by their brazen claws. Dog-headed devils, tongued with lolling flames, ran forward to offer themselves as ushers for the company. And before Zotulla and Obexah, there appeared a curious being with the full-fleshed lower limbs and hips of a great black woman and the clean-picked bones of some titanic ape from there-upward. And this monster signified by certain indescribable becks of its finger-bones that the emperor and his odalisque were to follow it.

Verily, it seemed to Zotulla that they had gone a long way into some malignly litten cavern of hell, when they came to the end of that perspective of tables and columns down which the monster had led them. Here, at the room's end, apart from the rest, was a table at which Namirrha sat alone, with the flames of the seven horse-skull lamps burning restlessly behind him, and the mailed black image of Thasaidon towering from the altar of jet at his right hand. And a little aside from the altar, a diamond mirror was upborne by the claws of iron basilisks.

Namirrha rose to greet them, observing a solemn and funereal courtesy. His eyes were bleak and cold as distant stars in the hollows wrought by strange fearful vigils. His lips were like a pale-red seal on a shut parchment of doom. His beard flowed stiffly in black-anointed banded locks across the bosom of his vermilion robe, like a mass of straight black serpents. Zotulla felt the blood pause and thicken about his heart, as if congealing into ice. And Obexah, peering beneath lowered lids, was abashed and frightened by the visible horror that invested this man and hung upon him even as royalty upon a king. But amid her fear, she found room to wonder what manner of man he was in his intercourse with women.

"I bid you welcome, O Zotulla, to such hospitality as is mine to offer," said Namirrha, with the iron ringing of some hidden funereal bell deep down in his hollow voice. "Prithee, be seated at my table."

Zotulla saw that a chair of ebony had been placed for him opposite Namirrha; and another chair, less stately and imperial, had been placed at the left hand for Obexah. And the twain seated themselves; and Zotulla saw that his people were sitting likewise at other tables throughout the huge hall, with the frightful servitors of Namirrha waiting upon them busily, like devils attending the damned.

Then Zotulla perceived that a dark and corpse-like hand was pouring wine for him in a crystal cup; and upon the hand was the signet-ring of the emperors of Xylac, set with a monstrous fire-opal in the mouth of a golden bat: even such a ring as Zotulla himself wore perpetually on his index-finger. And, turning, he beheld at his right hand a figure that bore the likeness of his father, Pithaim, after the poison of the adder, spreading through all his limbs, had left behind it the purple bloating of death. And Zotulla, who had caused the adder to be placed in the bed of Pithaim, cowered in his seat and trembled with a guilty fear. And the thing that wore the similitude of Pithaim, whether corpse or ghost or an image wrought by Namirrha's enchantment, came and went at Zotulla's elbow, waiting upon him with stark, black, swollen fingers that never fumbled. Horribly he was aware of its bulging, unregarding eyes, and its livid purple mouth that was locked in a rigor of mortal silence, and the spotted adder that peered at intervals with chill orbs from its heavy-folded sleeve as it leaned beside him to replenish his cup or to serve him with meat. And dimly, through the icy mist of his terror, the emperor beheld the shadowy-armored shape, like a moving replica of the still, grim statue of Thasaidon, which Namirrha had reared up in his blasphemy to perform the same office for himself. And vaguely, without comprehension, he saw the dreadful ministrant that hovered beside Obexah: a flayed and eyeless corpse in the image of her first lover, a boy from Cyntrom who had been cast ashore in shipwreck on the Isle of the Torturers. There Obexah had found him, lying beyond the ebbing wave; and reviving the boy, she had hidden him awhile in a secret cave for her own pleasure, and had brought him food and drink. Later, wearying, she had betrayed him to the Torturers, and had taken a new delight in the various pangs and ordeals inflicted upon him before death by that cruel, pernicious people.

"Drink," said Namirrha, quaffing a strange wine that was red and dark as if with disastrous sunsets of lost years. And Zotulla and Obexah drank the wine, feeling no warmth in their veins thereafter, but a chill as of hemlock mounting slowly toward the heart.

"Verily, 'tis a good wine," said Namirrha, "and a proper one in which to toast the furthering of our acquaintance: for it was buried long ago with the royal dead, in amphorae of somber jasper shapen like funeral urns; and my ghouls found it, whenas they came to dig in Tasuun."

Now it seemed that the tongue of Zotulla froze in his mouth, as a mandrake freezes in the rime-bound soil of winter; and he found no reply to Namirrha's courtesy.

"Prithee, make trial of this meat," quoth Namirrha, "for it is very choice, being the flesh of that boar which the Torturers of Uccastrog are wont to pasture on the well-minced leavings of their wheels and racks; and, moreover, my cooks have spiced it with the powerful balsams of the tomb, and have farced it with the hearts of adders and the tongues of black cobras."

Naught could the emperor say; and even Obexah was silent, being sorely troubled in her turpitude by the presence of that flayed and piteous thing which had the likeness of her lover from Cyntrom. And her dread of the necromancer grew prodigiously; for his knowledge of this old, forgotten crime, and the raising of the fantasm, appeared to her a more baleful magic than all else.

"Now, I fear," said Namirrha, "that you find the meat devoid of savor, and the wine without fire. So, to enliven our feasting, I shall call forth my singers and my musicians."

He spoke a word unknown to Zotulla or Obexah, which sounded throughout the mighty hall as if a thousand voices in turn had taken it up and prolonged it. Anon there appeared the singers, who were she-ghouls with shaven bodies and hairy shanks, and long yellow tushes full of shredded carrion curving across their chaps from mouths that fawned hyena-wise on the company. Behind them entered the musicians, some of whom were male devils pacing erect on the hind-quarters of sable stallions and plucking with the fingers of white apes at lyres of the bone and sinew of cannibals from Naat; and others were pied satyrs puffing their goatish cheeks at hautboys made from the femora of young witches, or bagpipes formed from the bosom-skin of negro queens and the horn of rhinoceri.

They bowed before Namirrha with grotesque ceremony. Then, without delay, the she-ghouls began a most dolorous and execrable howling, as of jackals that have sniffed their carrion; and the satyrs and devils played a lament that was like the moaning of desert-born winds through forsaken palace harems. And Zotulla shivered, for the singing filled his marrow with ice, and the music left in his heart a desolation as of empires fallen and trod under by the iron-shod hooves of time. Ever, amid that evil music, he seemed to hear the sifting of sand across withered gardens, and the windy rustling of rotted silks upon couches of bygone luxury, and the hissing of coiled serpents from the low fusts of shattered columns. And the glory that had been Ummaos seemed to pass away like the blown pillars of the simoom.

"Now that was a brave tune," said Namirrha when the music ceased and the she-ghouls no longer howled. "But verily I fear that you find my entertainment somewhat dull. Therefore, my dancers shall dance for you."

He turned toward the great hall, and described in the air an enigmatic sign with the fingers of his right hand. In answer to the sign, a hueless mist came down from the high roof and hid the room like a fallen curtain for a brief interim. There was a babel of sounds, confused and muffled, beyond the curtain, and a crying of voices faint as if with distance.

Then, dreadfully, the vapor rolled away, and Zotulla saw that the laden tables were gone. In the wide interspaces of the columns, his palace-inmates, the chamberlains, the eunuchs, the courtiers and odalisques and all the others, lay trussed with thongs on the floor, like so many fowls of gorgeous plumage. Above them, in time to a music made by the lyrists and flutists of the necromancer, a troupe of skeletons pirouetted with light clickings of their toe-bones; and a rout of mummies bounded stiffly; and others of Namirrha's creatures moved with monstrous caperings. To and fro they leapt on the bodies of the emperor's people, in the paces of an evil saraband. At every step they grew taller and heavier, till the saltant mummies were as the mummies of Anakim, and the skeletons were boned like colossi; and louder the music rose, drowning the faint cries of Zotulla's people. And huger still became the dancers, towering far into vaulted shadow among the vast columns, with thudding feet that wrought thunder in the room; and those whereon they danced were as grapes trampled for a vintage in autumn; and the floor ran deep with a sanguine must.

As a man drowning in a noisome, night-bound fen, the emperor heard the voice of Namirrha:

"It would seem that my dancers please you not. So now I shall present you a most royal spectacle. Arise and follow me, for the spectacle is one that requires an empire for its stage."

Zotulla and Obexah rose from their chairs in the fashion of night-walkers. Giving no backward glance at their ministering phantoms, or the hall where the dancers bounded, they followed Namirrha to an alcove beyond the altar of Thasaidon. Thence, by the upward-coiling stairways, they came at length to a broad high balcony that faced Zotulla's palace and looked forth above the city roofs toward the bourn of sunset.

It seemed that several hours had gone by in that hellish feasting and entertainment; for the day was near to its close, and the sun, which had fallen from sight behind the imperial palace, was barring the vast heavens with bloody rays.

"Behold," said Namirrha, adding a strange vocable to which the stone of the edifice resounded like a beaten gong.

The balcony pitched a little, and Zotulla, looking over the balustrade, beheld the roofs of Ummaos lessen and sink beneath him. It seemed that the balcony flew skyward to a prodigious height, and he peered down across the domes of his own palace, upon the houses, the tilled fields and the desert beyond, and the huge sun brought low on the desert's verge. And Zotulla grew giddy; and the chill airs of the upper heavens blew upon him. But Namirrha spoke another word, and the balcony ceased to ascend.

"Look well," said the necromancer, "on the empire that was yours, but shall be yours no longer." Then, with arms outstretched toward the sunset, and the gulfs beyond the sunset, he called aloud the twelve names that were perdition to utter, and after them the tremendous invocation: *Gna padambis devompra thungis furidor avoragomon.*

Instantly, it seemed that great ebon clouds of thunder beetled against the sun. Lining the horizon, the clouds took the form of colossal monsters with heads and members somewhat resembling those of stallions. Rearing terribly, they trod down the sun like an extinguished ember; and racing as in some hippodrome of Titans, they rose higher and vaster, coming toward Ummaos. Deep, calamitous rumblings preceded them, and the earth shook visibly, till Zotulla saw that these were not immaterial clouds, but actual living forms that had come forth to tread the world in macrocosmic vastness. Throwing their shadows for many leagues before them, the coursers charged as if devil-ridden into Xylac, and their feet descended like falling mountain crags upon far oases and towns of the outer waste.

Like a many-turreted storm they came, and it seemed that the world sank gulfward, tilting beneath the weight. Still as a man enchanted into marble, Zotulla stood and beheld the ruining that was wrought on his empire. And closer drew the gigantic stallions, racing with inconceivable speed, and louder was the thundering of their footfalls, that now began to blot the green fields and fruited orchards lying for many miles to the west of Ummaos. And the shadow of the stallions climbed like an evil gloom of eclipse, till it covered Ummaos; and looking up, the emperor saw their eyes halfway between earth and zenith, like baleful suns that glare down from soaring cumuli.

Then, in the thickening gloom, above that insupportable thunder, he heard the voice of Namirrha, crying in mad triumph:

"Know, Zotulla, that I have called up the coursers of

Thamogorgos, lord of the abyss. And the coursers will tread your empire down, even as your palfrey trod and trampled in former time a beggar-boy named Narthos. And learn also that I, Namirrha, was that boy." And the eyes of Namirrha, filled with a vain-glory of madness and bale, burned like malign, disastrous stars at the hour of their culmination.

To Zotulla, wholly mazed with the horror and tumult, the necromancer's words were no more than shrill, shrieked overtones of the tempest of doom; and he understood them not. Tremendously, with a rending of staunch-built roofs, and an instant cleavage and crumbling down of mighty masonries, the hooves descended upon Ummaos. Fair temple-domes were pashed like shells of the haliotis, and haughty mansions were broken and stamped into the ground even as gourds; and house by house the city was trampled flat with a crashing as of worlds beaten into chaos. Far below, in the darkened streets, men and camels fled like scurrying emmets but could not escape. And implacably the hooves rose and fell, till ruin was upon half the city, and night was over all. The palace of Zotulla was trodden under, and now the forelegs of the coursers loomed level with Namirrha's balcony, and their heads towered awfully above. It seemed that they would rear and trample down the necromancer's house; but at that moment they parted to left and right, and a dolorous glimmering came from the low sunset; and the coursers went on, treading under them that portion of Ummaos which lay to the eastward. And Zotulla and Obexah and Namirrha looked down on the city's fragments as on a shard-strewn midden, and heard the cataclysmic clamor of the hooves departing toward eastern Xylac.

"Now that was a goodly spectacle," quoth Namirrha. Then, turning to the emperor, he added malignly: "Think not that I have done with thee, however, or that doom is yet consummate."

It seemed that the balcony had fallen to its former elevation, which was still a lofty vantage above the sharded ruins. And Namirrha plucked the emperor by the arm and led him from the balcony to an inner chamber, while Obexah followed mutely. The emperor's heart was crushed within him by the trampling of such calamities, and despair weighed upon him like a foul incubus on the shoulders of a man lost in some land of accursed night. And he knew not that he had been parted from Obexah on the threshold of the chamber, and that certain of Namirrha's creatures, appearing like shadows, had compelled the girl to go downward with them by the stairs, and had stifled her outcries with their rotten cerements as they went.

The chamber was one that Namirrha used for his most unhallowed rites and alchemies. The rays of the lamps that illumed it were saffron-red like the spilt ichor of devils, and they flowed on aludels and crucibles and black athanors and alembics whereof the purpose was hardly to be named by mortal man. The sorcerer heated in one of the alembics a dark liquid full of star-cold lights, while Zotulla looked on unheeding. And when the liquid bubbled and sent forth a spiral vapor, Namirrha distilled it into goblets of gold-rimmed iron, and gave one of the goblets to Zotulla and retained the other himself. And he said to Zotulla with a stern imperative voice: "I bid thee quaff this liquor."

Zotulla, fearing that the draft was poison, hesitated. And the necromancer regarded him with a lethal gaze, and cried loudly: "Fearest thou to do as I?" and therewith he set the goblet to his lips.

So the emperor drank the draft, constrained as if by the bidding of some angel of death, and a darkness fell upon his senses. But, ere the darkness grew complete, he saw that Namirrha had drained his own goblet. Then, with unspeakable agonies, it seemed that the emperor died; and his soul floated free; and again he saw the chamber, though with bodiless eyes. And discarnate he stood in the saffron-crimson light, with his body lying as if dead on the floor beside him, and near it the prone body of Namirrha and the two fallen goblets.

Standing thus, he beheld a strange thing: for anon his own body stirred and arose, while that of the necromancer remained still as death. And Zotulla looked on his own lineaments and his figure in its short cloak of azure samite sewn with black pearls and balas-rubies; and the body lived before him, though with eyes that held a darker fire and a deeper evil than was their wont. Then, without corporeal ears, Zotulla heard the figure speak, and the voice was the strong, arrogant voice of Namirrha, saying:

"Follow me, O houseless phantom, and do in all things as I enjoin thee."

Like an unseen shadow, Zotulla followed the wizard, and the twain went downward by the stairs to the great banquet hall. They came to the altar of Thasaidon and the mailed image, with the seven horse-skull lamps burning before it as formerly. Upon the altar, Zotulla's beloved leman Obexah, who alone of women had power to stir his sated heart, was lying bound with thongs at Thasaidon's feet. But the hall beyond was deserted, and nothing remained of that Saturnalia of doom except the fruit of the treading, which had flowed together in dark pools among the columns.

Namirrha, using the emperor's body in all ways for his own, paused before the dark eidolon; and he said to the spirit of Zotulla: "Be imprisoned in this image, without power to free thyself or to stir in any wise."

Being wholly obedient to the will of the necromancer, the soul of Zotulla was embodied in the statue, and he felt its cold, gigantic armor about him like a strait sarcophagus, and he peered forth immovably from the bleak eyes that were overhung by its carven helmet.

Gazing thus, he beheld the change that had come on his

own body through the sorcerous possession of Namirrha: for below the short azure cloak, the legs had turned suddenly to the hind legs of a black stallion, with hooves that glowed redly as if heated by infernal fires. And even as Zotulla watched this prodigy, the hooves glowed white and incandescent, and fumes mounted from the floor beneath them.

Then, on the black altar, the hybrid abomination came pacing haughtily toward Obexah, and smoking hoofprints appeared behind it as it came. Pausing beside the girl, who lay supine and helpless regarding it with eyes that were pools of frozen horror, it raised one glowing hoof and set the hoof on her naked bosom between the small breast-cups of golden filigree begemmed with rubies. And the girl screamed beneath that atrocious treading as the soul of one newly damned might scream in hell; and the hoof glared with intolerable brilliance, as if freshly plucked from a furnace wherein the weapons of demons were forged.

At that moment, in the cowed and crushed and sodden shade of the emperor Zotulla, close-locked within the adamantine image, there awoke the manhood that had slumbered unaroused before the ruining of his empire and the trampling under of his retinue. Immediately a great abhorrence and a high wrath were alive in his soul, and mightily he longed for his own right arm to serve him, and a sword in his right hand.

Then it seemed that a voice spoke within him, chill and bleak and awful, and as if uttered inwardly by the statue itself. And the voice said: "I am Thasaidon, lord of the seven hells beneath the earth, and the hells of man's heart above the earth, which are seven times seven. For the moment, O Zotulla, my power is become thine for the sake of a mutual vengeance. Be one in all ways with the statue that has my likeness, even as the soul is one with the flesh. Behold!

there is a mace of adamant in thy right hand. Lift up the mace, and smite."

Zotulla was aware of a great power within him, and giant thews about him that thrilled with the power and responded agilely to his will. He felt in his mailed right hand the haft of the huge spiky-headed mace; and though the mace was beyond the lifting of any man in mortal flesh, it seemed no more than a goodly weight to Zotulla. Then, rearing the mace like a warrior in battle, he struck down with one crashing blow the impious thing that wore his own rightful flesh united with the legs and hooves of a demon courser. And the thing crumpled swiftly down and lay with the brain spreading pulpily from its shattered skull on the shining jet. And the legs twitched a little and then grew still; and the hooves glowed from a fiery, blinding white to the redness of red-hot iron, cooling slowly.

For a space there was no sound, other than the shrill screaming of the girl Obexah, mad with pain and the terror of those prodigies which she had beheld. Then, in the soul of Zotulla, grown sick with that screaming, the chill, awful voice of Thasaidon spoke again:

"Go free, for there is nothing more for thee to do." So the spirit of Zotulla passed from the image of Thasaidon and found in the wide air the freedom of nothingness and oblivion.

But the end was not yet for Namirrha, whose mad, arrogant soul had been loosened from Zotulla's body by the blow, and had returned darkly, not in the manner planned by the magician, to its own body lying in the room of accursed rites and forbidden transmigrations. There Namirrha woke anon, with a dire confusion in his mind, and a partial forgetfulness: for the curse of Thasaidon was upon him now because of his blasphemies.

Nothing was clear in his thought except a malign, exorbitant longing for revenge; but the reason thereof, and the object, were as doubtful shadows. And still prompted by that obscure animus, he arose; and girding to his side an enchanted sword with runic sapphires and opals in its hilt, he descended the stairs and came again to the altar of Thasaidon, where the mailed statue stood impassive as before, with the poised mace in its immovable right hand, and below it, on the altar, the double sacrifice.

A veil of weird darkness was upon the senses of Namirrha, and he saw not the stallion-legged horror that lay dead with slowly blackening hooves; and he heard not the moaning of the girl Obexah, who still lived beside it. But his eyes were drawn by the diamond mirror that was upheld in the claws of black iron basilisks beyond the altar; and going to the mirror, he saw therein a face that he knew no longer for his own. And because his eyes were shadowed and his brain filled with shifting webs of delusion, he took the face for that of the emperor Zotulla. Insatiable as hell's own flame, his old hatred rose within him; and he drew the enchanted sword and began to hew therewith at the reflection. Sometimes, because of the curse laid upon him, and the impious transmigration which he had performed, he thought himself Zotulla warring with the necromancer; and again, in the shiftings of his madness, he was Namirrha smiting at the emperor; and then, without name, he fought a nameless foe. And soon the sorcerous blade, though tempered with formidable spells, was broken close to the hilt, and Namirrha beheld the image still unharmed. Then, howling aloud the half-forgotten runes of a most tremendous curse, made invalid through his forgettings, he hammered still with the heavy sword-hilt on the mirror, till the runic sapphires and opals cracked in the hilt and fell away at his feet in little fragments.

Obexah, dying on the altar, saw Namirrha battling with

his image, and the spectacle moved her to mad laughter like the pealing of bells of ruined crystal. And above her laughter, and above the cursings of Namirrha, there came anon like a rumbling of swift-risen storm the thunder made by the macrocosmic stallions of Thamogorgos, returning gulfward through Xylac over Ummaos, to trample down the one house that they had spared aforetime.

THE LAST HIEROGLYPH

The world itself, in the end, shall be turned to a round cipher.
— *Old prophecy of Zothique*

NUSHAIN the astrologer had studied the circling orbs of night from many far-separated regions, and had cast, with such skill as he was able to command, the horoscopes of a myriad men, women and children. From city to city, from realm to realm he had gone, abiding briefly in any place: for often the local magistrates had banished him as a common charlatan; or elsewise, in due time, his consultants had discovered the error of his predictions and had fallen away from him. Sometimes he went hungry and shabby; and small honor was paid to him anywhere. The sole companions of his precarious fortunes were a wretched mongrel dog that had somehow attached itself to him in the desert town of Zul-Bha-Sair, and a mute, one-eyed negro whom he had bought very cheaply in Yoros. He had named the dog Ansarath, after the canine star, and had called the negro Mouzda, which was a word signifying darkness.

In the course of his prolonged itinerations, the astrologer came to Xylac and made his abode in its capital, Ummaos, which had been built above the shards of an elder city of the same name, long since destroyed by a sorcerer's wrath. Here Nushain lodged with Ansarath and Mouzda in a half-ruinous attic of a rotting tenement; and from the tenement's roof, Nushain was wont to observe the positions and movements of the sidereal bodies on evenings not obscured by the fumes of the city. At intervals some housewife or jade, some porter or huckster or petty merchant, would climb the decaying stairs to his chamber, and would pay him a small sum for the nativity which he plotted with immense care by the aid of his tattered books of astrological science.

When, as often occurred, he found himself still at a loss regarding the significance of some heavenly conjunction or opposition after poring over his books, he would consult Ansarath, and would draw profound auguries from the variable motions of the dog's mangy tail or his actions in searching for fleas. Certain of these divinations were fulfilled, to the considerable benefit of Nushain's renown in Ummaos. People came to him more freely and frequently, hearing that he was a soothsayer of some note; and, moreover, he was immune from prosecution, owing to the liberal laws of Xylac, which permitted all the sorcerous and mantic arts.

It seemed, for the first time, that the dark planets of his fate were yielding to auspicious stars. For this fortune, and the coins which accrued thereby to his purse, he gave thanks to Vergama who, throughout the whole continent of Zothique, was deemed the most powerful and mysterious of the genii, and was thought to rule over the heavens as well as the earth.

On a summer night, when the stars were strewn thickly like a fiery sand on the black azure vault, Nushain went up to the roof of his lodging-place. As was often his custom, he took with him the negro Mouzda, whose one eye possessed a miraculous sharpness and had served well, on many occasions, to supplement the astrologer's own rather near-sighted vision. Through a well-codified system of signs and gestures, the mute was able to communicate the result of his observations to Nushain.

On this night the constellation of the Great Dog, which had presided over Nushain's birth, was ascendant in the east. Regarding it closely, the dim eyes of the astrologer were troubled by a sense of something unfamiliar in its configuration. He could not determine the precise character of the change till Mouzda, who evinced much excitement, called his attention to three new stars of the second magnitude which had appeared in close proximity to the Dog's hindquarters. These remarkable novae, which Nushain could discern only as three reddish blurs, formed a small equilateral triangle. Nushain and Mouzda were both certain that they had not been visible on any previous evening.

"By Vergama, this is a strange thing," swore the astrologer, filled with amazement and dumbfoundment. He began to compute the problematic influence of the novae on his future reading of the heavens, and perceived at once that they would exert, according to the law of astral emanations, a modifying effect on his own destiny, which had been so largely controlled by the Dog.

He could not, however, without consulting his books and tables, decide the particular trend and import of this supervening influence; though he felt sure that it was most momentous, whether for his bale or welfare. Leaving Mouzda to watch the heavens for other prodigies, he descended at once to his attic. There, after collating the opinions of several old-time astrologers on the power exerted by novae, he began to re-cast his own horoscope. Painfully and with much agitation he labored throughout the night, and did not finish his figurings till the dawn came to mix a deathly grayness with the yellow light of the candles.

There was, it seemed, but one possible interpretation of the altered heavens. The appearance of the triangle of novae in conjunction with the Dog signified clearly that Nushain was to start ere long on an unpremeditated journey which would involve the transit of no less than three elements. Mouzda and Ansarath were to accompany him; and three guides, appearing successively, at the proper times, would lead him toward a destined goal. So much his calculations had revealed, but no more: there was nothing to foretell whether the journey would prove auspicious or disastrous, nothing to indicate its bourn, purpose or direction.

The astrologer was much disturbed by this somewhat singular and equivocal augury. He was ill pleased by the prospect of an imminent journey, for he did not wish to leave Ummaos, among whose credulous people he had begun to establish himself not without success. Moreover, a strong apprehension was roused within him by the oddly manifold nature and veiled outcome of the journey. All this, he felt, was suggestive of the workings of some occult and perhaps sinister providence; and surely it was no common traveling which would take him through three elements and would require a triple guidance.

During the nights that followed, he and Mouzda watched the mysterious novae as they went over toward the west behind the bright-flaming Dog. And he puzzled interminably over his charts and volumes hoping to discover some error in the reading he had made. But always, in the end, he was compelled to the same interpretation.

More and more, as time went on, he was troubled by the thought of that unwelcome and mysterious journey which he must make. He continued to prosper in Ummaos, and it seemed that there was no conceivable reason for his departure from that city. He was as one who awaited a dark and secret summons, not knowing whence it would come, nor at what hour. Throughout the days, he scanned with fearful anxiety the faces of his visitors, deeming that the first of the three star-predicted guides might arrive unheralded and unrecognized among them.

Mouzda and the dog Ansarath, with the intuition of dumb things, were sensible of the weird uneasiness felt by their master. They shared it palpably, the negro showing his apprehension by wild and demoniac grimaces, and the dog crouching under the astrologer's table or prowling restlessly to and fro with his half-hairless tail between his legs. Such behavior, in its turn, served to reconfirm the inquietude of Nushain, who deemed it a bad omen.

On a certain evening, Nushain pored for the fiftieth time over his horoscope, which he had drawn with sundry-colored inks on a sheet of papyrus. He was much startled when, on the blank lower margin of the sheet, he saw a curious character which was no part of his own scribbling. The character was a hieroglyph written in dark bituminous brown, and seeming to represent a mummy whose shroudings were loosened about the legs and whose feet were set in the posture of a long stride. It was facing toward that quarter of the chart where stood the sign indicating the Great Dog, which, in Zothique, was a House of the zodiac.

Nushain's surprise turned to a sort of trepidation as he studied the hieroglyph. He knew that the margin of the chart had been wholly clear on the previous night; and during the past day he had not left the attic at any time. Mouzda, he felt sure, would never have dared to touch the chart; and, moreover, the negro was little skilled in writing. Among the various inks employed by Nushain, there was none that resembled the sullen brown of the character, which seemed to stand out in a sad relief on the white papyrus.

Nushain felt the alarm of one who confronts a sinister and unexplainable apparition. No human hand, surely, had inscribed the mummy-shapen character, like the sign of a strange outer planet about to invade the Houses of his horoscope. Here, as in the advent of the three novae, an occult agency was suggested. Vainly, for many hours, he sought to unriddle the mystery: but in all his books there was naught to enlighten him; for this thing, it seemed, was wholly without precedent in astrology.

During the next day he was busied from morn till eve

with the plotting of those destinies ordained by the heavens for certain people of Ummaos. After completing the calculations with his usual toilsome care, he unrolled his own chart once more, albeit with trembling fingers. An eeriness that was nigh to panic seized him when he saw that the brown hieroglyph no longer stood on the margin, but was now placed like a striding figure in one of the lower Houses, where it still fronted toward the Dog, as if advancing on that ascendant sign.

Henceforth the astrologer was fevered with the awe and curiosity of one who watches a fatal but inscrutable portent. Never, during the hours that he pondered above it, was there any change in the intruding character; and yet, on each successive evening when he took out the chart, he saw that the mummy had strode upward into a higher House, drawing always nearer to the House of the Dog. . . .

There came a time when the figure stood on the Dog's threshold. Portentous with mystery and menace that were still beyond the astrologer's divining, it seemed to wait while the night wore on and was shot through with the gray wefting of dawn. Then, overworn with his prolonged studies and vigils, Nushain slept in his chair. Without the troubling of any dream he slept; and Mouzda was careful not to disturb him; and no visitors came to the attic on that day. So the morn and the noon and the afternoon went over, and their going was unheeded by Nushain.

He was awakened at eve by the loud and dolorous howling of Ansarath, which appeared to issue from the room's farthest corner. Confusedly, ere he opened his eyes, he became aware of an odor of bitter spices and piercing natron. Then, with the dim webs of sleep not wholly swept from his vision, he beheld, by the yellowy tapers that Mouzda had lighted, a tall, mummy-like form that waited in silence beside him. The head, arms and body of the shape were wound closely with bitumen-colored cerements; but the folds were loosened from the hips downward, and the figure stood like a walker, with one brown, withered foot in advance of its fellow.

Terror quickened in Nushain's heart, and it came to him that the shrouded shape, whether lich or phantom, resembled the weird, invasive hieroglyph that had passed from House to House through the chart of his destiny. Then, from the thick swathings of the apparition, a voice issued indistinctly, saying: "Prepare yourself, O Nushain, for I am the first guide of that journey which was foretold to you by the stars."

Ansarath, cowering beneath the astrologer's bed, was still howling his fear of the visitant; and Nushain saw that Mouzda had tried to conceal himself in company with the dog. Though a chill as of imminent death was upon him, and he deemed the apparition to be death itself, Nushain arose from his chair with that dignity proper to an astrologer, which he had maintained through all the vicissitudes of his lifetime. He called Mouzda and Ansarath from their hiding-place, and the two obeyed him, though with many cringings before the dark, muffled mummy.

With the comrades of his fortune behind him, Nushain turned to the visitant. "I am ready," he said, in a voice whose quavering was almost imperceptible. "But I would take with me certain of my belongings."

The mummy shook his mobled head. "It were well to take with you nothing but your horoscope: for this alone shall you retain in the end."

Nushain stooped above the table on which he had left his nativity. Before he began to roll the open papyrus, he noticed that the hieroglyph of the mummy had vanished. It was as if the written symbol, after moving athwart his horoscope, had materialized itself in the figure that now attended him. But on the chart's nether margin, in remote opposition to the Dog, was the sea-blue hieroglyph of a quaint merman with carp-like tail and head half human, half apish; and behind the merman was the black hieroglyph of a small barge.

Nushain's fear, for a moment, was subdued by wonder. But he rolled the chart carefully, and stood holding it in his right hand.

"Come," said the guide. "Your time is brief, and you must pass through the three elements that guard the dwelling-place of Vergama from unseasonable intrusion."

These words, in a measure, confirmed the astrologer's divinations. But the mystery of his future fate was in no wise lightened by the intimation that he must enter, presumably at the journey's end, the dim House of that being called Vergama, whom some considered the most secret of all the gods, and others, the most cryptical of demons. In all the lands of Zothique, there were rumors and fables regarding Vergama; but these were wholly diverse and contradictory, except in their common attribution of almost omnipotent powers to this entity. No man knew the situation of his abode; but it was believed that vast multitudes of people had entered it during the centuries and millenniums, and that none had returned therefrom.

Ofttimes had Nushain called upon the name of Vergama, swearing or protesting thereby as men are wont to do by the cognomens of their shrouded lords. But now, hearing the name from the lips of his macabre visitor, he was filled with the darkest and most eery apprehensions. He sought to subdue these feelings, and to resign himself to the manifest will of the stars. With Mouzda and Ansarath at his heels, he followed the striding mummy, which seemed little hampered, if at all, by its trailing cerements.

With one regretful backward glance at his littered books

and papers, he passed from the attic room and down the tenement stairs. A wannish light seemed to cling about the swathings of the mummy; but, apart from this, there was no illumination; and Nushain thought that the house was strangely dark and silent, as if all its occupants had died or had gone away. He heard no sound from the evening city; nor could he see aught but close-encroaching darkness beyond the windows that should have gazed on a little street. Also, it seemed that the stairs had changed and lengthened, giving no more on the courtyard of the tenement, but plunging deviously into an unsuspected region of stifling vaults and foul, dismal, nitrous corridors.

Here the air was pregnant with death, and the heart of Nushain failed him. Everywhere, in the shadow-curtained crypts and deep-shelved recesses, he felt the innumerable presence of the dead. He thought that there was a sad sighing of stirred cerements, a breath exhaled by long-stiffened cadavers, a dry clicking of lipless teeth beside him as he went. But darkness walled his vision, and he saw nothing save the luminous form of his guide, who stalked onward as if through a natal realm.

It semed to Nushain that he passed through boundless catacombs in which were housed the mortality and corruption of all the ages. Behind him still he heard the shuffling of Mouzda, and at whiles the low, frightened whine of Ansarath; so he knew that the twain were faithful to him. But upon him, with a chill of lethal damps, there grew the horror of his surroundings; and he shrank with all the repulsion of living flesh from the shrouded thing that he followed, and those other things that moldered round about in the fathomless gloom.

Half thinking to hearten himself by the sound of his own voice, he began to question the guide; though his tongue clove to his mouth as if palsied. "Is it indeed Vergama, and none other, who has summoned me forth upon this journey? For what purpose has he called me? And in what land is his dwelling?"

"Your fate has summoned you," said the mummy. "In the end, at the time appointed and no sooner, you shall learn the purpose. As to your third question, you would be no wiser if I should name the region in which the house of Vergama is hidden from mortal trespass: for the land is not listed on any terrene chart, nor map of the starry heavens."

These answers seemed equivocal and disquieting to Nushain, who was possessed by frightful forebodings as he went deeper into the subterranean charnels. Dark, indeed, he thought, must be the goal of a journey whose first stage had led him so far amid the empire of death and corruption; and dubious, surely, was the being who had called him forth and had sent to him as the first guide a sere and shrunken mummy clad in the tomb's habiliments.

Now, as he pondered these matters almost to frenzy, the shelfy walls of the catacomb before him were outlined by a dismal light, and he came after the mummy into a chamber where tall candles of black pitch in sockets of tarnished silver burned about an immense and solitary sarcophagus. Upon the blank lid and sides of the sarcophagus, as Nushain neared it, he could see neither runes nor sculptures nor hieroglyphs engraven; but it seemed, from the proportions, that a giant must lie within.

The mummy passed athwart the chamber without pausing. But Nushain, seeing that the vaults beyond were full of darkness, drew back with a reluctance that he could not conquer; and though the stars had decreed his journey, it seemed to him that human flesh could go no farther. Prompted by a sudden impulse, he seized one of the heavy yard-long tapers that burned stilly about the sarcophagus; and, holding it in his left hand, with his horoscope still firmly clutched in the right, he fled with Mouzda and Ansarath on the way he had come, hoping to retrace his footsteps through the gloomy caverns and return to Ummaos by the taper's light.

He heard no sound of pursuit from the mummy. But ever, as he fled, the pitch candle, flaring wildly, revealed to him the horrors that darkness had curtained from his eyes. He saw the bones of men that were piled in repugnant confusion with those of fell monsters, and the riven sarcophagi from which protruded the half-decayed members of innominate beings; members which were neither heads nor hands nor feet. And soon the catacomb divided and redivided before him, so that he must choose his way at random, not knowing whether it would lead him back to Ummaos or into the untrod depths.

Presently he came to the huge, browless skull of an uncouth creature, which reposed on the ground with upward-gazing orbits; and beyond the skull was the monster's moldy skeleton, wholly blocking the passage. Its ribs were cramped by the narrowing walls, as if it had crept there and had died in the darkness, unable to withdraw or go forward. White spiders, demon-headed and large as monkeys, had woven their webs in the hollow arches of the bones; and they swarmed out interminably as Nushain approached; and the skeleton seemed to stir and quiver as they seethed over it abhorrently and dropped to the ground before the astrologer. Behind them others poured in a countless army, crowding and mantling every ossicle. Nushain fled with his companions; and running back to the forking of the caverns, he followed another passage.

Here he was not pursued by the demon spiders. But, hurrying on lest they or the mummy overtake him, he was soon halted by the rim of a great pit which filled the catacomb from wall to wall and was overwide for the leaping of man. The dog Ansarath, sniffing certain odors that arose from the pit, recoiled with a mad howling; and Nushain, holding the taper outstretched above it, discerned far down a glimmer of ripples spreading circle-wise on some unctuous black fluid; and two blood-red spots appeared to swim with a weaving motion at the center. Then he heard a hissing as of some great cauldron heated by wizard fires; and it seemed that the blackness boiled upward, mounting swiftly and evilly to overflow the pit; and the red spots, as they neared him, were like luminous eyes that gazed malignantly into his own. . . .

So Nushain turned away in haste; and, returning upon his steps, he found the mummy awaiting him at the junction of the catacombs.

"It would seem, O Nushain, that you have doubted your own horoscope," said the guide, with a certain irony. "However, even a bad astrologer, on occasion, may read the heavens aright. Obey, then, the stars that decreed your journey."

Henceforward, Nushain followed the mummy without recalcitrance. Returning to the chamber in which stood the immense sarcophagus, he was enjoined by his guide to replace in its socket the black taper he had stolen. Without other light than the phosphorescence of the mummy's cerements, he threaded the foul gloom of those profounder ossuaries which lay beyond. At last, through caverns where a dull dawning intruded upon the shadows, he came out beneath shrouded heavens, on the shore of a wild sea that clamored in mist and cloud and spindrift. As if recoiling from the harsh air and light, the mummy drew back into the subterrane, and it said:

"Here my dominion ends, and I must leave you to await the second guide."

Standing with the poignant sea-salt in his nostrils, with

his hair and garments outblown on the gale, Nushain heard a metallic clangor, and saw that a door of rusty bronze had closed in the cavern-entrance. The beach was walled by unscalable cliffs that ran sheerly to the wave on each hand. So perforce the astrologer waited; and from the torn surf he beheld erelong the emergence of a sea-blue merman whose head was half human, half apish; and behind the merman there hove a small black barge that was not steered or rowed by any visible being. At this, Nushain recalled the hieroglyphs of the sea-creature and the boat which had appeared on the margin of his nativity; and unrolling the papyrus, he saw with wonderment that the figures were both gone; and he doubted not that they had passed, like the mummy's hieroglyph, through all the zodiacal Houses, even to that House which presided over his destiny; and thence, mayhap, they had emerged into material being. But in their stead now was the burning hieroglyph of a fire-colored salamander, set opposite to the Great Dog.

The merman beckoned to him with antic gestures, grinning deeply, and showing the white serrations of his shark-like teeth. Nushain went forward and entered the barge in obedience to the signs made by the sea-creature; and Mouzda and Ansarath, in faithfulness to their master, accompanied him. Thereupon the merman swam away through the boiling surf; and the barge, as if oared and ruddered by mere enchantment, swung about forthwith, and warring smoothly against wind and wave, was drawn straightly over that dim, unnamable ocean.

Half seen amid rushing foam and mist, the merman swam steadily on before. Time and space were surely outpassed during that voyage; and as if he had gone beyond mortal existence, Nushain experienced neither thirst nor hunger. But it seemed that his soul drifted upon seas of strange doubt and direst alienation; and he feared the misty chaos about him even as he had feared the nighted catacombs. Often he tried to question the mer-creature concerning their destination, but received no answer. And the wind blowing from shores unguessed, and the tide flowing to unknown gulfs, were alike filled with whispers of awe and terror.

Nushain pondered the mysteries of his journey almost to madness; and the thought came to him that, after passing through the region of death, he was now traversing the gray limbo of uncreated things; and, thinking this, he was loth to surmise the third stage of his journey; and he dared not reflect upon the nature of its goal.

Anon, suddenly, the mists were riven, and a cataract of golden rays poured down from a high-seated sun. Near at hand, to the lee of the driving barge, a tall island hove with verdurous trees and light, shell-shaped domes, and blossomy gardens hanging far up in the dazzlement of noon. There, with a sleepy purling, the surf was lulled on a low, grassy shore that had not known the anger of storm; and fruited vines and full-blown flowers were pendent above the water. It seemed that a spell of oblivion and slumber was shed from the island, and that any who landed thereon would dwell inviolable for ever in sun-bright dreams. Nushain was seized with a longing for its green, bowery refuge; and he wished to voyage no farther into the dreadful nothingness of the mist-bound ocean. And between his longing and his terror, he quite forgot the terms of that destiny which had been ordained for him by the stars.

There was no halting nor swerving of the barge; but it drew still nearer to the isle in its coasting; and Nushain saw that the intervening water was clear and shallow, so that a tall man might easily wade to the beach. He sprang into the sea, holding his horoscope aloft, and began to walk toward the island; and Mouzda and Ansarath followed him, swimming side by side.

Though hampered somewhat by his long wet robes, the astrologer thought to reach that alluring shore; nor was there any movement on the part of the merman to intercept him. The water was midway between his waist and his armpits; and now it lapped at his girdle; and now at the knee-folds of his garment; and the island vines and blossoms drooped fragrantly above him.

Then, being but a step from that enchanted beach, he heard a great hissing, and saw that the vines, the boughs, the flowers, the very grasses, were intertwined and mingled with a million serpents, writhing endlessly to and fro in hideous agitation. From all parts of that lofty island the hissing came, and the serpents, with foully mottled volumes, coiled, crept and slithered upon it everywhere; and no single yard of its surface was free from their defilement, or clear for human treading.

Turning seaward in his revulsion, Nushain found the merman and the barge waiting close at hand. Hopelessly he reentered the barge with his followers, and the magically driven boat resumed its course. And now, for the first time, the merman spoke, saying over his shoulder in a harsh, half-articulate voice, not without irony: "It would seem, O Nushain, that you lack faith in your own divinations. However, even the poorest of astrologers may sometimes cast a horoscope correctly. Cease, then, to rebel against that which the stars have written."

The barge drove on, and the mists closed heavily about it, and the noon-bright island was lost to view. After a vague interim the muffled sun went down behind inchoate waters and clouds; and a darkness as of primal night lay everywhere. Presently, through the torn rack, Nushain beheld a strange heaven whose signs and planets he could not recognize; and at this there came upon him the black horror of utmost dereliction. Then the mists and clouds returned, veiling that unknown sky from his scrutiny. And he could discern nothing but the merman, who was visible by a wan phosphor that clung always about him in his swimming.

Still the barge drove on; and in time it seemed that a red morning rose stifled and conflagrant behind the mists. The boat entered the broadening light, and Nushain, who had thought to behold the sun once more, was dazzled by a strange shore where flames towered in a high unbroken wall, feeding perpetually, to all appearance, on bare sand and rock. With a mighty leaping and a roar as of blown surf the flames went up, and a heat like that of many furnaces smote far on the sea. Swiftly the barge neared the shore; and the merman, with uncouth gestures of farewell, dived and disappeared under the waters.

Nushain could scarcely regard the flames or endure their heat. But the barge touched the strait tongue of land lying between them and the sea; and before Nushain, from the wall of fire, a blazing salamander emerged, having the form and hue of that hieroglyph which had last appeared on his horoscope. And he knew, with ineffable consternation, that this was the third guide of his threefold journey.

"Come with me," said the salamander, in a voice like the crackling of fagots. Nushain stepped from the barge to that strand which was hot as an oven beneath his feet; and behind him, though with palpable reluctance, Mouzda and Ansarath still followed. But, approaching the flames behind the salamander, and half swooning from their ardor, he was overcome by the weakness of mortal flesh; and seeking again to evade his destiny, he fled along the narrow scroll of beach between the fire and the water. But he had gone only a few paces when the salamander, with a great fiery roaring and racing, intercepted him; and it drove him straight toward the fire with terrible flailings of its dragon-like tail, from which showers of sparks were emitted. He could not face the salamander, and he thought the flames would consume him like paper as he entered them: but in the wall there appeared a sort of opening, and the fires arched themselves into an arcade, and he passed through with his followers, herded by the salamander, into an ashen land where all things were veiled with low-hanging smoke and steam. Here the salamander observed with a kind of irony: "Not wrongly, O Nushain, have you interpreted the stars of your horoscope. And now your journey draws to an end, and you will need no longer the services of a guide." So saying, it left him, going out like a quenched fire on the smoky air.

Nushain, standing irresolute, beheld before him a white stairway that mounted amid the veering vapors. Behind him the flames rose unbroken, like a topless rampart; and on either hand, from instant to instant, the smoke shaped itself into demon forms and faces that menaced him. He began to climb the stairs, and the shapes gathered below and about, frightful as a wizard's familiars, and keeping pace with him as he went upward, so that he dared not pause or retreat. Far up he climbed in the fumy dimness, and came unaware to the open portals of a house of gray stone rearing to unguessed height and amplitude.

Unwillingly, but driven by the thronging of the smoky shapes, he passed through the portals with his companions. The house was a place of long, empty halls, tortuous as the folds of a sea-conch. There were no windows, no lamps; but it seemed that bright suns of silver had been dissolved and diffused in the air. Fleeing from the hellish wraiths that pursued him, the astrologer followed the winding halls and emerged ultimately in an inner chamber where space itself was immured. At the room's center a cowled and muffled figure of colossal proportions sat upright on a marble chair, silent, unstirring. Before the figure, on a sort of table, a vast volume lay open.

Nushain felt the awe of one who approaches the presence of some high demon or deity. Seeing that the phantoms had vanished, he paused on the room's threshold: for its immensity made him giddy, like the void interval that lies between the worlds. He wished to withdraw; but a voice issued from the cowled being, speaking softly as the voice of his own inmost mind:

"I am Vergama, whose other name is Destiny; Vergama, on whom you have called so ignorantly and idly, as men are wont to call on their hidden lords; Vergama, who has summoned you on the journey which all men must make at one time or another, in one way or another way. Come forward, O Nushain, and read a little in my book."

The astrologer was drawn as by an unseen hand to the table. Leaning above it, he saw that the huge volume stood open at its middle pages, which were covered with a myriad signs written in inks of various colors, and representing men, gods, fishes, birds, monsters, animals, constellations, and many other things. At the end of the last column of the right-hand page, where little space was left for other inscriptions, Nushain beheld the hieroglyphs of an equal-sided triangle of stars, such as had lately appeared in proximity to the Dog; and, following these, the hieroglyphs of a mummy, a merman, a barge and a salamander, resembling the figures that had come and gone on his horoscope, and those that had guided him to the house of Vergama.

"In my book," said the cowled figure, "the characters of all things are written and preserved. All visible forms, in the beginning, were but symbols written by me; and at the last they shall exist only as the writing of my book. For a season they issue forth, taking to themselves that which is known as substance. . . . It was I, O Nushain, who set in the heavens the stars that foretold your journey; I, who sent the three guides. And these things, having served their purpose, are now but infoliate ciphers, as before."

Vergama paused, and an infinite silence returned to the room, and a measureless wonder was upon the mind of Nushain. Then the cowled being continued:

"Among men, for a while, there was that person called Nushain the astrologer, together with the dog Ansarath and the negro Mouzda, who followed his fortunes. . . . But now, very shortly, I must turn the page, and before turning it, must finish the writing that belongs thereon."

Nushain thought that a wind arose in the chamber, moving lightly with a weird sigh, though he felt not the actual breath of its passing. But he saw that the fur of Ansarath, cowering close beside him, was ruffled by the wind. Then, beneath his marveling eyes, the dog began to dwindle and wither, as if seared by a lethal magic; and he lessened to the size of a rat, and thence to the smallness of a mouse and the lightness of an insect, though preserving still his original form. After that, the tiny thing was caught up by the sighing air, and it flew past Nushain as a gnat might fly; and, following it, he saw that the hieroglyph of a dog was inscribed suddenly beside that of the salamander, at the bottom of the right-hand page. But, apart from this, there remained no trace of Ansarath.

Again a wind breathed in the room, touching not the astrologer, but fluttering the ragged raiment of Mouzda, who crouched near to his master, as if appealing for protection, and the mute became shrunken and shriveled, turning at the last to a thing light and thin as the black, tattered wing-shard of a beetle, which the air bore aloft. And Nushain saw that the hieroglyph of a one-eyed negro was inscribed following that of the dog; but, aside from this, there was no sign of Mouzda.

Now, perceiving clearly the doom that was designed for him, Nushain would have fled from the presence of Vergama. He turned from the outspread volume and ran toward the chamber door, his worn, tawdry robes of an astrologer flapping about his thin shanks. But softly in his ear, as he went, there sounded the voice of Vergama:

"Vainly do men seek to resist or evade that destiny which turns them to ciphers in the end. In my book, O Nushain, there is room even for a bad astrologer."

Once more the weird sighing arose, and a cold air played upon Nushain as he ran; and he paused midway in the vast room as if a wall had arrested him. Gently the air breathed on his lean, gaunt figure, and it lifted his graying locks and beard, and it plucked softly at the roll of papyrus which he still held in his hand. To his dim eyes, the room seemed to reel and swell, expanding infinitely. Borne upward, around and around, in a swift vertiginous swirling, he beheld the seated shape as it loomed ever higher above him in cosmic vastness. Then the god was lost in light; and Nushain was a weightless and exile thing, the withered skeleton of a lost leaf, rising and falling on the bright whirlwind.

In the book of Vergama, at the end of the last column of the right-hand page, there stood the hieroglyph of a gaunt astrologer, carrying a furled nativity.

Vergama leaned forward from his chair, and turned the page.

SADASTOR

LISTEN, for this is the tale that was told to a fair lamia by the demon Charnadis as they sat together on the top of Mophi, above the sources of the Nile, in those years when the sphinx was young. Now the lamia was vexed, for her beauty was grown an evil legend in both Thebais and Elephantine; so that men were become fearful of her lips and cautious of her embrace, and she had no lover for almost a fortnight. She lashed her serpentine tail on the ground, and moaned softly, and wept those mythical tears which a serpent weeps. And the demon told this tale for her comforting:

Long, long ago, in the red cycles of my youth (said Charnadis), I was like all young demons, and was prone to use the agility of my wings in fantastic flights; to hover and poise like a gier-eagle above Tartarus and the pits of Python; or to lift the broad blackness of my vans on the orbit of stars. I have followed the moon from evening twilight to morning twilight; and I have gazed on the secrets of that Medusean face which she averts eternally from the earth. I have read through filming ice the ithyphallic runes on columns yet extant in her deserts; and I know the hieroglyphs which solve forgotten riddles, or hint eonian histories, on the walls of her cities taken by ineluctable snow. I have flown through the triple ring of Saturn, and have mated with lovely basilisks, on isles towering league-high from stupendous oceans where each wave is like the rise and fall of Himalayas. I have dared the clouds of Jupiter, and the black and freezing abysses of Neptune, which are crowned with eternal starlight; and I have sailed beyond to incommensurable suns, compared with which the sun that thou knowest is a corpse-candle in a stinted vault. There, in tremendous planets, I have furled my flight on the terraced mountains, large as fallen asteroids, where, with a thousand names and a thousand images, undreamt-of Evil is served and worshipt in unsurmisable ways. Or, perched in the flesh-colored lips of columnar blossoms, whose perfume was an ecstasy of incommunicable dreams, I have mocked the wiving monsters, and have lured their females, that sang and fawned at the base of my hiding-place.

Now, in my indefatigable questing among the remoter galaxies, I came one day to that forgotten and dying planet which in the language of its unrecorded peoples was called Sadastor. Immense and drear and gray beneath a waning sun, far-fissured with enormous chasms, and covered from pole to pole with the never-ebbing tides of the desert sand, it hung in space without moon or satellite, an abomination and a token of doom to fairer and younger worlds. Checking the speed of my interstellar flight, I followed its equator with a poised and level wing, above the peaks of cyclopean volcanoes, and bare, terrific ridges of elder hills, and deserts pale with the ghastliness of salt, that were manifestly the beds of former oceans.

In the very center of one of these ocean-beds, beyond sight of the mountains that formed its primeval shoreline, and leagues below their level, I found a vast and winding valley that plunged even deeplier into the abysses of this dreadful world. It was walled with perpendicular cliffs and buttresses and pinnacles of a rusty-red stone, that were fretted into a million bizarrely sinister forms by the sinking of the olden seas. I flew slowly among these cliffs as they wound ever downward in tortuous spirals for mile on mile of utter and irredeemable desolation, and the light grew dimmer above me as ledge on ledge and battlement on battlement of that strange red stone upreared themselves between my wings and the heavens. Here, when I rounded a sudden turn of the precipice, in the profoundest depth where the rays of the sun fell only for a brief while at noon, and the rocks were purple with everlasting shadow, I found a pool of dark-green water—the last remnant of the former ocean, ebbing still amid steep, insuperable walls. And from this pool there cried a voice, in accents that were subtly sweet as the mortal wine of mandragora, and faint as the murmuring of shells. And the voice said:

"Pause and remain, I pray, and tell me who thou art, who comest thus to the accursed solitude wherein I die."

Then, pausing on the brink of the pool, I peered into its gulf of shadow, and saw the pallid glimmering of a female form that upreared itself from the waters. And the form was that of a siren, with hair the color of ocean-kelp, and berylline eyes, and a dolphin-shapen tail. And I said to her:

"I am the demon Charnadis. But who art thou, who lingerest thus in this ultimate pit of abomination, in the depth of a dying world?"

She answered: "I am a siren, and my name is Lyspial. Of the seas wherein I swam and sported at leisure many centuries ago, and whose gallant mariners I drew to an enchanted death on the shores of my disastrous isle, there remains only this fallen pool. Alas! For the pools dwindles daily, and when it is wholly gone I too must perish."

She began to weep, and her briny tears fell down and were added to the briny waters.

Fain would I have comforted her, and I said:

"Weep not, for I will lift thee upon my wings and bear thee to some newer world, where the sky-blue waters of abounding seas are shattered to intricate webs of wannest foam, on low shores that are green and aureate with pristine spring. There, perchance for eons, thou shalt have thine abode, and galleys with painted oars and great barges purpureal-sailed shall be drawn upon thy rocks in the red light of sunsets domed with storm, and shall mingle the crash of their figured prows with the sweet sorcery of thy mortal singing."

But still she wept, and would not be comforted, crying:

"Thou art kind, but this would avail me not, for I was born of the waters of this world, and with its waters I must die. Alas! my lovely seas, that ran in unbroken sapphire from shores of perennial blossoms to shores of everlasting snow! Alas! the sea-winds, with their mingled perfumes of brine and weed, and scents of ocean flowers and flowers of the land, and far-blown exotic balsams! Alas! the quinquiremes of cycle-ended wars, and the heavy-laden argosies with sails and cordage of byssus, that plied between barbaric isles with their cargoes of topaz or garnet-colored wines and jade and ivory idols, in the antique summers that now are less than legend! Alas! the dead captains, the beautiful dead sailors that were borne by the ebbing tide to my couches of amber seaweed, in my caverns underneath a cedared promontory! Alas! the kisses that I laid on their cold and hueless lips, on their sealed marmorean eyelids!"

And sorrow and pity seized me at her words, for I knew that she spoke the lamentable truth, that her doom was in the lessening of the bitter waters. So, after many proffered condolences, no less vague than vain, I bade her a melancholy farewell and flew heavily away between the spiral cliffs where I had come, and clomb the somber skies till the world Sadastor was only a darkling mote far down in space. But the tragic shadow of the siren's fate, and her sorrow, lay grievously upon me for hours, and only in the kisses of a beautiful fierce vampire, in a far-off and young and exuberant world, was I able to forget it. And I tell thee now the tale thereof, that haply thou mayest be consoled by the contemplation of a plight that was infinitely more dolorous and irremediable than thine own.

THE DEATH OF ILALOTHA

Black Lord of bale and fear, master of all confusion!
By thee, thy prophet saith,
New power is given to wizards after death,
And witches in corruption draw forbidden breath
And weave such wild enchantment and illusion
As none but lamiae may use;
And through thy grace the charneled corpses lose
Their horror, and nefandous loves are lighted
In noisome vaults long nighted;
And vampires make their sacrifice to thee—
Disgorging blood as if great urns had poured
Their bright vermilion hoard
About the washed and weltering sarcophagi.
  —*Ludar's Litany to Thasaidon.*

ACCORDING to the custom in old Tasuun, the obsequies of Ilalotha, lady-in-waiting to the self-widowed Queen Xantlicha, had formed an occasion of much merrymaking and prolonged festivity. For three days, on a bier of diverse-colored silks from the Orient, under a rose-hued canopy that might well have domed some nuptial couch, she had lain clad with gala garments amid the great feasting-hall of the royal palace in Miraab. About her, from morning dusk to sunset, from cool even to torridly glaring dawn, the feverish tide of the funeral orgies had surged and eddied without slackening. Nobles, court officials, guardsmen, scullions, astrologers, eunuchs, and all the high ladies, waiting-women and female slaves of Xantlicha, had taken part in that prodigal debauchery which was believed to honor most fitly the deceased. Mad songs and obscene ditties were sung, and dancers whirled in vertiginous frenzy to the lascivious pleading of untirable lutes. Wines and liquors were poured torrentially from monstrous amphoras; the tables fumed with spicy meats piled in huge hummocks and forever replenished. The drinkers offered libation to Ilalotha, till the fabrics of her bier were stained to darker hues by the split vintages. On all sides around her, in attitudes of disorder or prone abandonment, lay those who had yielded to amorous license of the fullness of their potations. With half-shut eyes and lips slightly parted, in the rosy shadow cast by the catafalque, she bore no aspect of death but seemed a sleeping empress who ruled impartially over the living and the dead. This appearance, together with a strange heightening of her natural beauty, was remarked by many: and some said that she seemed to await a lover's kiss rather than the kisses of the worm.

On the third evening, when the many-tongued brazen lamps were lit and the rites drew to their end, there returned to court the Lord Thulos, acknowledged lover of Queen Xantlicha, who had gone a week previous to visit his domain on the western border and had heard nothing of Ilalotha's death. Still unaware, he came into the hall at that hour when the saturnalia began to flag and the fallen revelers to outnumber those who still moved and drank and made riot.

He viewed the disordered hall with little surprise, for such scenes were familiar to him from childhood. Then, approaching the bier, he recognized its occupant with a certain startlement. Among the numerous ladies of Miraab who had drawn his libertine affections, Ilalotha had held sway longer than most; and, it was said, she had grieved more passionately over his defection than any other. She had been superseded a month before by Xantlicha, who had shown favor to Thulos in no ambiguous manner; and Thulos, perhaps, had abandoned her not without regret: for the role of lover to the queen, though advantageous and not wholly disagreeable, was somewhat precarious. Xantlicha, it was universally believed, had rid herself of the late King Archain by means of a tomb-discovered vial of poison that owed its peculiar subtlety and virulence to the art of ancient sorcerers. Following this act of disposal, she had taken many lovers, and those who failed to please her came invariably to ends no less violent than that of Archain. She was exigent, exorbitant, demanding a strict fidelity somewhat irksome to Thulos; who, pleading urgent affairs on his remote estate, had been glad enough of a week away from court.

Now, as he stood beside the dead woman, Thulos forgot the queen and bethought him of certain summer nights that had been honeyed by the fragrance of jasmine and the jasmine-white beauty of Ilalotha. Even less than the others could he believe her dead: for her present aspect differed in no wise from that which she had often assumed during their old intercourse. To please his whim, she had feigned the inertness and complaisance of slumber or death; and at such times he had loved her with an ardor undismayed by the pantherine vehemence with which, at other whiles, she was wont to reciprocate or invite his caresses.

Moment by moment, as if through the working of some powerful necromancy, there grew upon him a curious hallucination, and it seemed that he was again the lover of those lost nights, and had entered that bower in the palace gardens where Ilalotha waited him on a couch strewn with overblown petals, lying with bosom quiet as her face and hands. No longer was he aware of the crowded hall: the high-flaring lights, the wine-flushed faces, had become a moonbright parterre of drowsily nodding blossoms, and the voices of the courtiers were no more than a faint suspiration of wind amid cypress and jasmine. The warm, aphrodisiac perfumes of the June night welled about him; and again, as of old, it seemed that they arose from the person of Ilalotha no less than from the flowers. Prompted by intense desire, he stooped over and felt her cool arm stir involuntarily beneath his kiss.

Then, with the bewilderment of a sleep-walker awakened rudely, he heard a voice that hissed in his ear with soft venom: "Hast forgotten thyself, my Lord Thulos? Indeed I wonder little, for many of my bawcocks deem that she is fairer in death than in life." And, turning from Ilalotha, while the weird spell dissolved from his senses, he found Xantlicha at his side. Her garments were disarrayed, her hair was unbound and disheveled, and she reeled slightly, clutching him by the shoulder with sharp-nailed fingers. Her full, poppy-crimson lips were curled by a vixenish fury, and in her long-lidded yellow eyes there blazed the jealousy of an amorous cat.

Thulos, overwhelmed by a strange confusion, remembered but partially the enchantment to which he had succumbed; and he was unsure whether or not he had actually kissed Ilalotha and had felt her flesh quiver to his mouth. Verily, he thought, this thing could not have been, and a waking dream had momentarily seized him. But he was troubled by the words of Xantlicha and her anger, and by the half-furtive drunken laughters and ribald whispers that he heard passing among the people about the hall.

"Beware, my Thulos," the queen murmured, her strange anger seeming to subside; "for men say that she was a witch."

"How did she die?" queried Thulos.

"From no other fever than that of love, it is rumored."

"Then, surely, she was no witch," Thulos argued with a lightness that was far from his thoughts and feelings; "for true sorcery should have found the cure."

"It was from love of thee," said Xantlicha darkly; "and as all women know, thy heart is blacker and harder than black adamant. No witchcraft, however potent, could prevail thereon." Her mood, as she spoke, appeared to soften suddenly. "Thy absence has been long, my lord. Come to me at midnight: I will wait for thee in the south pavilion."

Then, eyeing him sultrily for an instant from underdrooped lids, and pinching his arm in such a manner that her nails pierced through cloth and skin like a cat's talons, she turned from Thulos to hail certain of the harem-eunuchs.

Thulos, when the queen's attention was disengaged from him, ventured to look again at Ilalotha; pondering, meanwhile, the curious remarks of Xantlicha. He knew that Ilalotha, like many of the court-ladies, had dabbled in spells and philtres; but her witchcraft had never concerned him, since he felt no interest in other charms or enchantments than those with which nature had endowed the bodies of women. And it was quite impossible for him to believe that Ilalotha had died from a fatal passion: since, in his experience, passion was never fatal.

Indeed, as he regarded her with confused emotions, he was again beset by the impression that she had not died at all. There was no repetition of the weird, half-remembered hallucination of other time and place; but it seemed to him that she had stirred from her former position on the wine-stained bier, turning her face toward him a little, as a woman turns to an expected lover; that the arm he had kissed (either in dream or reality) was outstretched a little farther from her side.

Thulos bent nearer, fascinated by the mystery and drawn by a stranger attraction that he could not have named. Again, surely, he had dreamt or had been mistaken. But even as the doubt grew, it seemed that the bosom of Ilalotha stirred in faint respiration, and he heard an almost inaudible but thrilling whisper: "Come to me at midnight. I will wait for thee . . . in the tomb."

At this instant there appeared beside the catafalque certain people in the sober and rusty raiment of sextons, who had entered the hall silently, unperceived by Thulos or by any of the company. They carried among them a thin-walled sarcophagus of newly welded and burnished bronze. It was their office to remove the dead woman and bear her to the sepulchral vaults of her family, which were situated in the old necropolis lying somewhat to northward of the palace-gardens.

Thulos would have cried out to restrain them from their purpose; but his tongue clove tightly; nor could he move any of his members. Not knowing whether he slept or woke, he watched the people of the cemetery as they placed Ilalotha in the sarcophagus and bore her quickly from the hall, unfollowed and still unheeded by the drowsy bacchanalians. Only when the somber cortège had departed was he able to stir from his position by the empty bier. His thoughts were sluggish, and full of darkness and indecision. Smitten by an immense fatigue that was not unnatural after his day-long journey, he withdrew to his apartments and fell instantly into death-deep slumber.

Freeing itself gradually from the cypress-boughs, as if from the long, stretched fingers of witches, a waning and misshapen moon glared horizontally through the eastern window when Thulos awoke. By this token, he knew that the hour drew toward midnight, and recalled the assignation which Queen Xanthlicha had made with him: an assignation which he could hardly break without incurring the queen's deadly displeasure. Also, with singular clearness, he recalled another rendezvous . . . at the same time but in a different place. Those incidents and impressions of Ilalotha's funeral, which, at the time, had seemed so dubitable and dream-like, returned to him with a profound conviction of reality, as if etched on his mind by some mordant chemistry of sleep . . . or the strengthening of some sorcerous charm. He felt that Ilalotha had indeed stirred on her bier and spoken to him; that the sextons had borne her still living to the tomb. Perhaps her supposed demise had been merely a sort of catalepsy; or else she had deliberately feigned death in a last effort to revive his passion. These thoughts awoke within him a raging fever of curiosity and desire; and he saw before him her pale, inert, luxurious beauty, presented as if by enchantment.

Direly distraught, he went down by the lampless stairs and hallways to the moonlit labyrinth of the gardens. He cursed the untimely exigence of Xantlicha. However, as he told himself, it was more than likely that the queen, continuing to imbibe the liquors of Tasuun, had long since reached a condition in which she would neither keep nor recall her appointment. This thought reassured him: in his queerly bemused mind, it soon became a certainty; and he did not hasten toward the south pavilion but strolled vaguely amid the wan and somber boscage.

More and more it seemed unlikely that any but himself was abroad: for the long, unlit wings of the palace sprawled as in vacant stupor; and in the gardens there were only dead shadows, and pools of still fragrance in which the winds had drowned. And over all, like a pale, monstrous poppy, the moon distilled her death-white slumber.

Thulos, no longer mindful of his rendezvous with Xantlicha, yielded without further reluctance to the urgence that drove him toward another goal. . . . Truly, it was no less than obligatory that he should visit the vaults and learn whether or not he had been deceived in his belief concerning Ilalotha. Perhaps, if he did not go, she would stifle in the shut sarcophagus, and her pretended death would quickly become an actuality. Again, as if spoken in the moonlight before him, he heard the words she had whispered, or seemed to whisper, from the bier: "Come to me at midnight . . . I will wait for thee . . . in the tomb."

With the quickening steps and pulses of one who fares

to the warm, petal-sweet couch of an adored mistress, he left the palace-grounds by an unguarded northern postern and crossed the weedy common between the royal gardens and the old cemetery. Unchilled and undismayed, he entered those always-open portals of death, where ghoul-headed monsters of black marble, glaring with hideously pitted eyes, maintained their charnel postures before the crumbling pylons.

The very stillness of the low-bosomed graves, the rigor and pallor of the tall shafts, the deepness of bedded cypress shadows, the inviolacy of death by which all things were invested, served to heighten the singular excitement that had fired Thulos' blood. It was as if he had drunk a philtre spiced with mummia. All around him the mortuary silence seemed to burn and quiver with a thousand memories of Ilalotha, together with those expectations to which he had given as yet no formal image. . . .

Once, with Ilalotha, he had visited the subterranean tomb of her ancestors; and, recalling its situation clearly, he came without indirection to the low-arched and cedar-darkened entrance. Rank nettles and fetid fumitories, growing thickly about the seldom-used adit, were crushed down by the tread of those who had entered there before Thulos; and the rusty, iron-wrought door sagged heavily inward on its loose hinges. At his feet there lay an extinguished flambeau, dropped, no doubt, by one of the departing sextons. Seeing it, he realized that he had brought with him neither candle nor lantern for the exploration of the vaults, and found in that providential torch an auspicious omen.

Bearing the lit flambeau, he began his investigation. He gave no heed to the piled and dusty sarcophagi in the first reaches of the subterrane: for, during their past visit, Ilalotha had shown to him a niche at the innermost extreme, where, in due time, she herself would find sepulture among the members of that decaying line. Strangely, insidiously, like the breath of some vernal garden, the languid and luscious odor of jasmine swam to meet him through the musty air, amid the tiered presence of the dead; and it drew him to the sarcophagus that stood open between others tightly lidded. There he beheld Ilalotha lying in the gay garments of her funeral, with half-shut eyes and half-parted lips; and upon her was the same weird and radiant beauty, the same voluptuous pallor and stillness, that had drawn Thulos with a necromantic charm.

"I knew that thou wouldst come, O Thulos," she murmured, stirring a little, as if involuntarily, beneath the deepening ardor of his kisses that passed quickly from throat to bosom. . . .

The torch that had fallen from Thulos' hand expired in the thick dust. . . .

Xantlicha, retiring to her chamber betimes, had slept illy. Perhaps she had drunk too much or too little of the dark, ardent vintages; perhaps her blood was fevered by the return of Thulos, and her jealousy still troubled by the hot kiss which he had laid on Ilalotha's arm during the obsequies. A restlessness was upon her; and she rose well before the hour of her meeting with Thulos, and stood at her chamber window seeking such coolness as the night air might afford.

The air, however, seemed heated as by the burning of hidden furnaces; her heart appeared to swell in her bosom and stifle her; and her unrest and agitation were increased rather than diminished by the spectacle of the moon-lulled gardens. She would have hurried forth to the tryst in the pavilion; but, despite her impatience, she thought it well to keep Thulos waiting. Leaning thus from her sill, she beheld Thulos when he passed amid the parterres and arbors below. She was struck by the unusual haste and intentness of his steps, and she wondered at their direction, which could bring him only to places remote from the rendezvous she had named. He disappeared from her sight in the cypress-lined alley that led to the north garden-gate; and her wonderment was soon mingled with alarm and anger when he did not return.

It was incomprehensible to Xantlicha that Thulos, or any man, would dare to forget the tryst in his normal senses; and seeking an explanation, she surmised that the working of some baleful and potent sorcery was probably involved. Nor, in the light of certain incidents that she had observed, and much else that had been rumored, was it hard for her to identify the possible sorceress. Ilalotha, the queen knew, had loved Thulos to the point of frenzy, and had grieved inconsolably after his desertion of her. People said that she had wrought various ineffectual spells to bring him back; that she had vainly invoked demons and sacrificed to them, and had made futile invultuations and death-charms against Xantlicha. In the end, she had died of sheer chagrin and despair, or perhaps had slain herself with some undetected poison. . . . But, as was commonly believed in Tasuun, a witch dying thus, with unslaked desires and frustrate cantraips, could turn herself into a lamia or vampire and procure thereby the consummation of all her sorceries. . . .

The queen shuddered, remembering these things; and remembering also the hideous and malign transformation that was said to accompany the achievement of such ends: for those who used in this manner the power of hell must take on the very character and the actual semblance of infernal beings. Too well she surmised the destination of Thulos, and the danger to which he had gone forth if her suspicions were true. And, knowing that she might face an equal danger, Xantlicha determined to follow him.

She made little preparation, for there was no time to

waste; but took from beneath her silken bed-cushion a small, straight-bladed dagger that she kept always within reach. The dagger had been anointed from point to hilt with such venom as was believed efficacious against either the living or the dead. Bearing it in her right hand, and carrying in the other a slot-eyed lantern that she might require later, Xantlicha stole swiftly from the palace.

The last lees of the evening's wine ebbed wholly from her brain, and dim, ghastly fears awoke, warning her like the voices of ancestral phantoms. But, firm in her determination, she followed the path taken by Thulos; the path taken earlier by those sextons who had borne Ilalotha to her place of sepulture. Hovering from tree to tree, the moon accompanied her like a worm-hollowed visage. The soft, quick patter of her cothurns, breaking the white silence, seemed to tear the filmy cobweb pall that withheld from her a world of spectral abominations. And more and more she recalled, of those legendries that concerned such beings as Ilalotha; and her heart was shaken within her: for she knew that she would meet no mortal woman but a thing raised up and inspirited by the seventh hell. But amid the chill of these horrors, the thought of Thulos in the lamia's arms was like a red brand that seared her bosom.

Now the necropolis yawned before Xantlicha, and her path entered the cavernous gloom of far-vaulted funereal trees, as if passing into monstrous and shadowy mouths that were tusked with white monuments. The air grew dank and noisome, as if filled with the breathings of open crypts. Here the queen faltered, for it seemed that black, unseen cacodemons rose all about her from the graveyard ground, towering higher than the shafts and boles, and standing in readiness to assail her if she went farther. Nevertheless, she came anon to the dark adit that she sought. Tremulously she lit the wick of the slot-eyed lantern; and, piercing the gross underground darkness before her with its bladed beam, she passed with ill-subdued terror and repugnance into that abode of the dead . . . and perchance of the Undead.

However, as she followed the first turnings of the catacomb, it seemed that she was to encounter nothing more abhorrent than charnel mold and century-sifted dust; nothing more formidable than the serried sarcophagi that lined the deeply hewn shelves of stone; sarcophagi that had stood silent and undisturbed ever since the time of their deposition. Here, surely the slumber of all the dead was unbroken, and the nullity of death was inviolate.

Almost the queen doubted that Thulos had preceded her there; till, turning her light on the ground, she discerned the print of his poulaines, long-tipped and slender in the deep dust amid those foot-marks left by the rudely shod sextons. And she saw that footprints of Thulos pointed only in one direction, while those of the others plainly went and returned.

Then, at an undetermined distance in the shadows ahead, Xantlicha heard a sound in which the sick moaning of some amorous woman was blent with a snarling as of jackals over their meat. Her blood returned frozen upon her heart as she went onward step by slow step, clutching her dagger in a hand drawn sharply back, and holding the light high in advance. The sound grew louder and more distinct; and there came to her now a perfume as of flowers in some warm June night; but, as she still advanced, the perfume was mixed with more and more of a smothering foulness such as she had never heretofore known, and was touched with the reeking of blood.

A few paces more, and Xantlicha stood as if a demon's arm had arrested her: for her lantern's light had found the inverted face and upper body of Thulos, hanging from the end of a burnished, new-wrought sarcophagus that occupied a scant interval between others green with rust. One of Thulos' hands clutched rigidly the rim of the sarcophagus, while the other hand, moving feebly, seemed to caress a dim shape that leaned above him with arms showing jasmine-white in the narrow beam, and dark fingers plunging into his bosom. His head and body seemed but an empty hull, and his hand hung skeleton-thin on the bronze rim, and his whole aspect was vein-drawn, as if he had lost more blood than was evident on his torn throat and face, and in his sodden raiment and dripping hair.

From the thing stooping above Thulos, there came ceaselessly that sound which was half moan and half snarl. And as Xantlicha stood in petrific fear and loathing, she seemed to hear from Thulos' lips an indistinct murmur, more of ecstasy than pain. The murmur ceased, and his head hung slacklier than before, so that the queen deemed him verily dead. At this she found such wrathful courage as enabled her to step nearer and raise the lantern higher: for, even amid her extreme panic, it came to her that by means of the wizard-poisoned dagger she might still haply slay the thing that had slain Thulos.

Waveringly the light crept aloft, disclosing inch by inch that infamy which Thulos had caressed in the darkness.... It crept even to the crimson-smeared wattles, and the fanged and ruddled orifice that was half mouth and half beak ... till Xantlicha knew why the body of Thulos was a mere shrunken hull.... In what the queen saw, there remained nothing of Ilalotha except the white, voluptuous arms, and a vague outline of human breasts melting momently into breasts that were not human, like clay molded by a demon sculptor. The arms too began to change and darken; and, as they changed, the dying hand of Thulos stirred again and fumbled with a caressing movement toward the horror.

And the thing seemed to heed him not but withdrew its fingers from his bosom, and reached across him with members stretching enormously, as if to claw the queen or fondle her with its dribbling talons.

It was then that Xantlicha let fall the lantern and the dagger, and ran with shrill, endless shriekings and laughters of immitigable madness from the vault.

THE RETURN OF THE SORCERER

I HAD been out of work for several months, and my savings were perilously near the vanishing point. Therefore I was naturally elated when I received from John Carnby a favorable answer inviting me to present my qualifications in person. Carnby had advertised for a secretary, stipulating that all applicants must offer a preliminary statement of their capacities by letter; and I had written in response to the advertisement.

Carnby, no doubt, was a scholarly recluse who felt averse to contact with a long waiting-list of strangers; and he had chosen this manner of weeding out beforehand many, if not all, of those who were ineligible. He had specified his requirements fully and succinctly, and these were of such nature as to bar even the average well-educated person. A knowledge of Arabic was necessary, among other things; and luckily I had acquired a certain degree of scholarship in this unusual tongue.

I found the address, of whose location I had formed only a vague idea, at the end of a hilltop avenue in the suburbs of Oakland. It was a large, two-story house, overshaded by ancient oaks and dark with a mantling of unchecked ivy, among hedges of unpruned privet and shrubbery that had gone wild for many years. It was separated from its neighbors by a vacant, weed-grown lot on one side and a tangle of vines and trees on the other, surrounding the black ruins of a burnt mansion.

Even apart from its air of long neglect, there was something drear and dismal about the place—something that inhered in the ivy-blurred outlines of the house, in the furtive, shadowy windows, and the very forms of the misshapen oaks and oddly sprawling shrubbery. Somehow, my elation became a trifle less exuberant, as I entered the grounds and followed an unswept path to the front door.

When I found myself in the presence of John Carnby, my jubilation was still somewhat further diminished; though I could not have given a tangible reason for the premonitory chill, the dull, somber feeling of alarm that I experienced, and the leaden sinking of my spirits. Perhaps it was the dark library in which he received me as much as the man himself—a room whose musty shadows could never have been wholly dissipated by sun or lamplight. Indeed, it must have been this; for John Carnby himself was very much the sort of person I had pictured him to be.

He had all the earmarks of the lonely scholar who has devoted patient years to some line of erudite research. He was thin and bent, with a massive forehead and a mane of grizzled hair; and the pallor of the library was on his hollow, clean-shaven cheeks. But coupled with this, there was a nerve-shattered air, a fearful shrinking that was more than the normal shyness of a recluse, and an unceasing apprehensiveness that betrayed itself in every glance of his dark-ringed, feverish eyes and every movement of his bony hands. In all likelihood his health had been seriously impaired by over-application; and I could not help but wonder at the nature of the studies that had made him a tremulous wreck. But there was something about him—perhaps the width of his bowed shoulders and the bold aquilinity of his facial outlines—which gave the impression of great former strength and a vigor not yet wholly exhausted.

His voice was unexpectedly deep and sonorous.

"I think you will do, Mr. Ogden," he said, after a few formal questions, most of which related to my linguistic knowledge, and in particular my mastery of Arabic. "Your labors will not be very heavy; but I want someone who can be on hand at any time required. Therefore you must live with me. I can give you a comfortable room, and I guarantee that my cooking will not poison you. I often work at night; and I hope you will not find the irregular hours too disagreeable."

No doubt I should have been overjoyed at this assurance that the secretarial position was to be mine. Instead, I was aware of a dim, unreasoning reluctance and an obscure forewarning of evil as I thanked John Carnby and told him that I was ready to move in whenever he desired.

He appeared to be greatly pleased; and the queer apprehensiveness went out of his manner for a moment.

"Come immediately—this very afternoon, if you can," he said. "I shall be very glad to have you, and the sooner the better. I have been living entirely alone for some time; and I must confess that the solitude is beginning to pall upon me. Also, I have been retarded in my labors for lack of the proper help. My brother used to live with me and assist me, but he has gone away on a long trip."

I returned to my downtown lodgings, paid my rent with the last few dollars that remained to me, packed my belongings, and in less than an hour was back at my new employer's home. He assigned me a room on the second floor, which, though unaired and dusty, was more than luxurious in comparison with the hall-bedroom that failing funds had compelled me to inhabit for some time past. Then he took me to his own study, which was on the same floor, at the further end of the hall. Here, he explained to me, most of my future work would be done.

I could hardly restrain an exclamation of suprise as I viewed the interior of this chamber. It was very much as I should have imagined the den of some old sorcerer to be. There were tables strewn with archaic instruments of doubtful use, with astrological charts, with skulls and alembics and crystals, with censers such as are used in the Catholic

Church, and volumes bound in worm-eaten leather with verdigris-mottled clasps. In one corner stood the skeleton of a large ape; in another, a human skeleton; and overhead a stuffed crocodile was suspended.

There were cases overpiled with books, and even a cursory glance at the titles showed me that they formed a singularly comprehensive collection of ancient and modern works on demonology and the black arts. There were some weird paintings and etchings on the walls, dealing with kindred themes; and the whole atmosphere of the room exhaled a medley of half-forgotten superstitions. Ordinarily I would have smiled if confronted with such things; but somehow, in this lonely, dismal house, beside the neurotic, hag-ridden Carnby, it was difficult for me to repress an actual shudder.

On one of the tables, contrasting incongruously with this mélange of medievalism and Satanism, there stood a typewriter, surrounded with piles of disorderly manuscript. At one end of the room there was a small, curtained alcove with a bed in which Carnby slept. At the end opposite the alcove, between the human and simian skeletons, I perceived a locked cupboard that was set in the wall.

Carnby had noted my surprise, and was watching me with a keen, analytic expression which I found impossible to fathom. He began to speak, in explanatory tones.

"I have made a life-study of demonism and sorcery," he declared. "It is a fascinating field, and one that is singularly neglected. I am now preparing a monograph, in which I am trying to correlate the magical practices and demon-worship of every known age and people. Your labors, at least for a while, will consist in typing and arranging the voluminous preliminary notes which I have made, and in helping me to track down other references and correspondences. Your knowledge of Arabic will be invaluable to me, for I am none too well-grounded in this language myself, and I am depending for certain essential data on a copy of the Necronomicon in the original Arabic text. I have reason to think that there are certain omissions and erroneous renderings in the Latin version of Olaus Wormius."

I had heard of this rare, well-nigh fabulous volume, but had never seen it. The book was supposed to contain the ultimate secrets of evil and forbidden knowledge; and, moreover, the original text, written by the mad Arab, Abdul Alhazred, was said to be unprocurable. I wondered how it had come into Carnby's possession.

"I'll show you the volume after dinner," Carnby went on. "You will doubtless be able to elucidate one or two passages that have long puzzled me."

The evening meal, cooked and served by my employer himself, was a welcome change from cheap restaurant fare. Carnby seemed to have lost a good deal of his nervousness. He was very talkative, and even began to exhibit a certain scholarly gaiety after we had shared a bottle of mellow Sauterne. Still, with no manifest reason, I was troubled by intimations and forebodings which I could neither analyze nor trace to their rightful source.

We returned to the study, and Carnby brought out from a locked drawer the volume of which he had spoken. It was enormously old, and was bound in ebony covers arabesqued with silver and set with darkly glowing garnets. When I opened the yellowing pages, I drew back with involuntary revulsion at the odor which arose from them—an odor that was more than suggestive of physical decay, as if the book had lain among corpses in some forgotten graveyard and had taken on the taint of dissolution.

Carnby's eyes were burning with a fevered light as he took the old manuscript from my hands and turned to a page near the middle. He indicated a certain passage with his lean forefinger.

"Tell me what you make of this," he said, in a tense, excited whisper.

I deciphered the paragraph, slowly and with some difficulty, and wrote down a rough English version with the pad and pencil which Carnby offered me. Then, at his request, I read it aloud:

"It is verily known by few, but is nevertheless an attestable fact, that the will of a dead sorcerer hath power upon his own body and can raise it up from the tomb and perform therewith whatever action was unfulfilled in life. And such resurrections are invariably for the doing of malevolent deeds and for the detriment of others. Most readily can the corpse be animated if all its members have remained intact; and yet there are cases in which the excelling will of the wizard hath reared up from death the sundered pieces of a body hewn in many fragments, and hath caused them to serve his end, either separately or in a temporary reunion. But in every instance, after the action hath been completed, the body lapseth into its former state."

Of course, all this was errant gibberish. Probably it was the strange, unhealthy look of utter absorption with which my employer listened, more than that damnable passage from the Necronomicon, which caused my nervousness and made me start violently when, toward the end of my reading, I heard an indescribable slithering noise in the hall outside. But when I finished the paragraph and looked up at Carnby, I was more than startled by the expression of stark, staring fear which his features had assumed—an expression as of one who is haunted by some hellish phantom. Somehow, I got the feeling that he was listening to that odd noise in the hallway rather than to my translation of Abdul Alhazred.

"The house is full of rats," he explained, as he caught my inquiring glance. "I have never been able to get rid of them, with all my efforts."

The noise, which still continued, was that which a rat might make in dragging some object slowly along the floor. It seemed to draw closer, to approach the door of Carnby's room, and then, after an intermission, it began to move again and receded. My employer's agitation was marked; he listened with fearful intentness and seemed to follow the progress of the sound with a terror that mounted as it drew near and decreased a little with its recession.

"I am very nervous," he said. "I have worked too hard lately, and this is the result. Even a little noise upsets me."

The sound had now died away somewhere in the house. Carnby appeared to recover himself in a measure.

"Will you please re-read your translation?" he requested. "I want to follow it very carefully, word by word."

I obeyed. He listened with the same look of unholy absorption as before, and this time we were not interrupted by any noises in the hallway. Carnby's face grew paler, as if the last remnant of blood had been drained from it, when I read the final sentences; and the fire in his hollow eyes was like phosphorescence in a deep vault.

"That is a most remarkable passage," he commented. "I was doubtful about its meaning, with my imperfect Arabic; and I have found that the passage is wholly omitted in the Latin of Olaus Wormius. Thank you for your scholarly rendering. You have certainly cleared it up for me."

His tone was dry and formal, as if he were repressing himself and holding back a world of unsurmisable thoughts and emotions. Somehow I felt that Carnby was more nervous and upset than ever, and also that my rendering from the Necronomicon had in some mysterious manner contributed to his perturbation. He wore a ghastly brooding expression, as if his mind were busy with some unwelcome and forbidden theme.

However, seeming to collect himself, he asked me to

translate another passage. This turned out to be a singular incantatory formula for the exorcism of the dead, with a ritual that involved the use of rare Arabian spices and the proper intoning of at least a hundred names of ghouls and demons. I copied it all out for Carnby, who studied it for a long time with a rapt eagerness that was more than scholarly.

"That, too," he observed, "is not in Olaus Wormius." After perusing it again, he folded the paper carefully and put it away in the same drawer from which he had taken the Necronomicon.

That evening was one of the strangest I have ever spent. As we sat for hour after hour discussing renditions from that unhallowed volume, I came to know more and more definitely that my employer was mortally afraid of something; that he dreaded being alone and was keeping me with him on this account rather than for any other reason. Always he seemed to be waiting and listening with a painful, tortured expectation, and I saw that he gave only a mechanical awareness to much that was said. Among the weird appurtenances of the room, in that atmosphere of unmanifested evil, of untold horror, the rational part of my mind began to succumb slowly to a recrudescence of dark ancestral fears. A scorner of such things in my normal moments, I was now ready to believe in the most baleful creations of superstitious fancy. No doubt, by some process of mental contagion, I had caught the hidden terror from which Carnby suffered.

By no word or syllable, however, did the man admit the actual feelings that were evident in his demeanor, but he spoke repeatedly of a nervous ailment. More than once, during our discussion, he sought to imply that his interest in the supernatural and the Satanic was wholly intellectual, that he, like myself, was without personal belief in such things. Yet I knew infallibly that his implications were false;

that he was driven and obsessed by a real faith in all that he pretended to view with scientific detachment, and had doubtless fallen a victim to some imaginary horror entailed by his occult researches. But my intuition afforded me no clue to the actual nature of this horror.

There was no repetition of the sounds that had been so disturbing to my employer. We must have sat till after midnight with the writings of the mad Arab open before us. At last Carnby seemed to realize the lateness of the hour.

"I fear I have kept you up too long," he said apologetically. "You must go and get some sleep. I am selfish, and I forget that such hours are not habitual to others, as they are to me."

I made the formal denial of his self-impeachment which courtesy required, said good night, and sought my own chamber with a feeling of intense relief. It seemed to me that I would leave behind me in Carnby's room all the shadowy fear and oppression to which I had been subjected.

Only one light was burning in the long passage. It was near Carnby's door; and my own door at the further end, close to the stair-head, was in deep shadow. As I groped for the knob, I heard a noise behind me, and turned to see in the gloom a small, indistinct body that sprang from the hall-landing to the top stair, disappearing from view. I was horribly startled; for even in that vague, fleeting glimpse, the thing was much too pale for a rat and its form was not at all suggestive of an animal. I could not have sworn what it was, but the outlines had seemed unmentionably monstrous. I stood trembling violently in every limb, and heard on the stairs a singular bumping sound like the fall of an object rolling downward from step to step. The sound was repeated at regular intervals, and finally ceased.

If the safety of the soul and body had depended upon it, I could not have turned on the stair-light; nor could I have gone to the top steps to ascertain the agency of that unnatural bumping. Anyone else, it might seem, would have done this. Instead, after a moment of virtual petrification, I entered my room, locked the door, and went to bed in a turmoil of unresolved doubt and equivocal terror. I left the light burning; and I lay awake for hours, expecting momentarily a recurrence of that abominable sound. But the house was as silent as a morgue, and I heard nothing. At length, in spite of my anticipations to the contrary, I fell asleep and did not awaken till after many sodden, dreamless hours.

It was ten o'clock, as my watch informed me. I wondered whether my employer had left me undisturbed through thoughtfulness, or had not arisen himself. I dressed and went downstairs, to find him waiting at the breakfast table. He was paler and more tremulous than ever, as if he had slept badly.

"I hope the rats didn't annoy you too much," he remarked, after a preliminary greeting. "Something really must be done about them."

"I didn't notice them at all," I replied. Somehow, it was utterly impossible for me to mention the queer, ambiguous thing which I had seen and heard on retiring the night before. Doubtless I had been mistaken; doubtless it had been merely a rat after all, dragging something down the stairs. I tried to forget the hideously repeated noise and the momentary flash of unthinkable outlines in the gloom.

My employer eyed me with uncanny sharpness, as if he sought to penetrate my inmost mind. Breakfast was a dismal affair; and the day that followed was no less dreary. Carnby isolated himself till the middle of the afternoon, and I was left to my own devices in the well-supplied but conventional library downstairs. What Carnby was doing alone in his room I could not surmise; but I thought more than once that I heard the faint, monotonous intonations of a solemn voice. Horror-breeding hints and noisome intuitions invaded my brain. More and more the atmosphere of that house enveloped and stifled me with poisonous, miasmal mystery; and I felt everywhere the invisible brooding of malignant incubi.

It was almost a relief when my employer summoned me to his study. Entering, I noticed that the air was full of a pungent, aromatic smell and was touched by the vanishing coils of a blue vapor, as if from the burning of Oriental gums and spices in the church censers. An Ispahan rug had been moved from its position near the wall to the center of the room, but was not sufficient to cover entirely a curving violet mark that suggested the drawing of a magic circle on the floor. No doubt Carnby had been performing some sort of incantation; and I thought of the awesome formula I had translated at his request.

However, he did not offer any explanation of what he had been doing. His manner had changed remarkably and was more controlled and confident than at any former time. In a fashion almost business-like he laid before me a pile of manuscript which he wanted me to type for him. The familiar click of the keys aided me somewhat in dismissing my apprehensions of vague evil, and I could almost smile at the recherché and terrific information comprised in my employer's notes, which dealt mainly with formulae for the acquisition of unlawful power. But still, beneath my reassurance, there was a vague, lingering disquietude.

Evening came; and after our meal we returned again to the study. There was a tenseness in Carnby's manner now, as if he were eagerly awaiting the result of some hidden test. I went on with my work; but some of his emotion communicated itself to me, and ever and anon I caught myself in an attitude of strained listening.

At last, above the click of the keys, I heard the peculiar

slithering in the hall. Carnby had heard it, too, and his confident look had utterly vanished, giving place to the most pitiable fear.

The sound drew nearer and was followed by a dull, dragging noise, and then by more sounds of an unidentifiable slithering and scuttling nature that varied in loudness. The hall was seemingly full of them, as if a whole army of rats were hauling some carrion booty along the floor. And yet no rodent or number of rodents could have made such sounds, or could have moved anything so heavy as the object which came behind the rest. There was something in the character of those noises, something without name or definition, which caused a slowly creeping chill to invade my spine.

"Good Lord! What is all that racket?" I cried.

"The rats! I tell you it is only the rats!" Carnby's voice was a high, hysterical shriek.

A moment later, there came an unmistakable knocking on the door, near the sill. At the same time I heard a heavy thudding in the locked cupboard at the further end of the room. Carnby had been standing erect, but now he sank limply into a chair. His features were ashen, and his look was almost maniacal with fright.

The nightmare doubt and tension became unbearable and I ran to the door and flung it open, in spite of a frantic remonstrance from my employer. I had no idea what I should find as I stepped across the sill into the dim-lit hall.

When I looked down and saw the thing on which I had almost trodden, my feeling was one of sick amazement and actual nausea. It was a human hand which had been severed at the wrist—a bony, bluish hand like that of a week-old corpse, with garden-mold on the fingers and under the long nails. *The damnable thing had moved!* It had drawn back to avoid me, and was crawling along the passage somewhat in the manner of a crab! And following it with my gaze, I saw that there were other things beyond it, one of which I recognized as a man's foot and another as a forearm. I dared not look at the rest. All were moving slowly, hideously away in a charnel procession, and I cannot describe the fashion in which they moved. Their individual vitality was horrifying beyond endurance. It was more than the vitality of life, yet the air was laden with a carrion taint. I averted my eyes and stepped back into Carnby's room, closing the door behind me with a shaking hand. Carnby was at my side with the key, which he turned in the lock with palsy-stricken fingers that had become as feeble as those of an old man.

"You saw them?" he asked in a dry, quavering whisper.

"In God's name, what does it all mean?" I cried.

Carnby went back to his chair, tottering a little with weakness. His lineaments were agonized by the gnawing of some inward horror, and he shook visibly like an ague patient. I sat down in a chair beside him, and he began to stammer forth his unbelievable confession, half incoherently, with inconsequential mouthings and many breaks and pauses:

"He is stronger than I am—even in death, even with his body dismembered by the surgeon's knife and saw that I used. I thought he could not return after that—after I had buried the portions in a dozen different places, in the cellar, beneath the shrubs, at the foot of the ivy-vines. But the Necronomicon is right . . . and Helman Carnby knew it. He warned me before I killed him, he told me he could return—*even in that condition.*

"But I did not believe him. I hated Helman, and he hated me, too. He had attained to higher power and knowledge and was more favored by the Dark Ones than I. That was why I killed him—my own twin-brother, and my brother in the service of Satan and of Those who were before Satan. We had studied together for many years. We had celebrated the Black Mass together and we were attended by the same familiars. But Helman Carnby had gone deeper into the occult, into the forbidden, where I could not follow him. I feared him, and I could not endure his supremacy.

"It is more than a week—it is ten days since I did the deed. But Helman—or some part of him—has returned every night.... God! His accursed hands crawling on the floor! His feet, his arms, the segments of his legs, climbing the stairs in some unmentionable way to haunt me!... Christ! His awful, bloody torso lying in wait! I tell you, his hands have come even by day to tap and fumble at my door . . . and I have stumbled over his arms in the dark.

"Oh, God! I shall go mad with the awfulness of it. But he wants me to go mad, he wants to torture me till my brain gives way. That is why he haunts me in this piece-meal fashion. He could end it all at any time, with the demoniacal power that is his. He could re-knit his sundered limbs and body and slay me as I slew him.

"How carefully I buried the parts, with what infinite forethought! And how useless it was! I buried the saw and knife, too, at the farther end of the garden, as far away as possible from his evil, itching hands. But I did not bury the head with the other pieces—I kept it in that cupboard at the end of my room. Sometimes I have heard it moving there, as you heard it a little while ago.... But he does not need the head, his will is elsewhere, and can work intelligently through all his members.

"Of course, I locked all the doors and windows at night when I found that he was coming back.... But it made no difference. And I have tried to exorcise him with the appropriate incantations—with all those that I knew. Today I tried that sovereign formula from the Necronomicon which you translated for me. I got you here to translate it. Also, I could no longer bear to be alone and I thought that it might help if there were someone else in the house. That formula was my last hope. I thought it would hold him—it is a most ancient and most dreadful incantation. But, as you have seen, it is useless. . . ."

His voice trailed off in a broken mumble, and he sat staring before him with sightless, intolerable eyes in which I saw the beginning flare of madness. I could say nothing—the confession he had made was so ineffably atrocious. The moral shock, and the ghastly supernatural horror, had almost stupefied me. My sensibilities were stunned; and it was not till I had begun to recover myself that I felt the irresistible surge of a flood of loathing for the man beside me.

I rose to my feet. The house had grown very silent, as if the macabre and charnel army of beleaguerment had now retired to its various graves. Carnby had left the key in the lock; and I went to the door and turned it quickly.

"Are you leaving? Don't go," Carnby begged in a voice that was tremulous with alarm, as I stood with my hand on the door-knob.

"Yes, I am going," I said coldly. "I am resigning my position right now; and I intend to pack my belongings and leave your house with as little delay as possible."

I opened the door and went out, refusing to listen to the arguments and pleadings and protestations he had begun to babble. For the nonce, I preferred to face whatever might lurk in the gloomy passage, no matter how loathsome and terrifying, rather than endure any longer the society of John Carnby.

The hall was empty; but I shuddered with repulsion at the memory of what I had seen, as I hastened to my room.

I think I should have screamed aloud at the least sound or movement in the shadows.

I began to pack my valise with a feeling of the most frantic urgency and compulsion. It seemed to me that I could not escape soon enough from that house of abominable secrets, over which hung an atmosphere of smothering menace. I made mistakes in my haste, I stumbled over chairs, and my brain and fingers grew numb with a paralyzing dread.

I had almost finished my task, when I heard the sound of slow measured footsteps coming up the stairs. I knew that it was not Carnby, for he had locked himself immediately in his room when I had left; and I felt sure that nothing could have tempted him to emerge. Anyway, he could hardly have gone downstairs without my hearing him.

The footsteps came to the top landing and went past my door along the hall, with that same dead monotonous repetition, regular as the movement of a machine. Certainly it was not the soft, nervous tread of John Carnby.

Who, then, could it be? My blood stood still in my veins; I dared not finish the speculation that arose in my mind.

The steps paused; and I knew that they had reached the door of Carnby's room. There followed an interval in which I could scarcely breathe; and then I heard an awful crashing and shattering noise, and above it the soaring scream of a man in the uttermost extremity of fear.

I was powerless to move, as if an unseen iron hand had reached forth to restrain me; and I have no idea how long I waited and listened. The scream had fallen away in a swift silence; and I heard nothing now, except a low, peculiar, recurrent sound which my brain refused to identify.

It was not my own volition, but a stronger will than mine,

which drew me forth at last and impelled me down the hall to Carnby's study. I felt the presence of that will as an overpowering, superhuman thing—a demoniac force, a malign mesmerism.

The door of the study had been broken in and was hanging by one hinge. It was splintered as by the impact of more than mortal strength. A light was still burning in the room, and the unmentionable sound I had been hearing ceased as I neared the threshold. It was followed by an evil, utter stillness.

Again I paused, and could go no further. But, this time, it was something other than the hellish, all-pervading magnetism that petrified my limbs and arrested me before the sill. Peering into the room, in the narrow space that was framed by the doorway and lit by an unseen lamp, I saw one end of the Oriental rug, and the gruesome outlines of a monstrous, unmoving shadow that fell beyond it on the floor. Huge, elongated, misshapen, the shadow was seemingly cast by the arms and torso of a naked man who stooped forward with a surgeon's saw in his hand. Its monstrosity lay in this: though the shoulders, chest, abdomen and arms were all clearly distinguishable, the shadow was headless and appeared to terminate in an abruptly severed neck. It was impossible, considering the relative position, for the head to have been concealed from sight through any manner of foreshortening.

I waited, powerless to enter or withdraw. The blood had flowed back upon my heart in an ice-thick tide, and thought was frozen in my brain. An interval of termless horror, and then, from the hidden end of Carnby's room, from the direction of the locked cupboard, there came a fearsome and violent crash, and the sound of splintering wood and whining hinges, followed by the sinister, dismal thud of an unknown object striking the floor.

Again there was silence—a silence as of consummated Evil brooding above its unnamable triumph. The shadow had not stirred. There was a hideous contemplation in its attitude, and the saw was still held in its poising hand, as if above a completed task.

Another interval, and then, without warning, I witnessed the awful and unexplainable *disintegration* of the shadow, which seemed to break gently and easily into many different shadows ere it faded from view. I hesitate to describe the manner, or specify the places, in which this singular disruption, this manifold cleavage, occurred. Simultaneously, I heard the muffled clatter of a metallic implement on the Persian rug, and a sound that was not that of a single body but of many bodies falling.

Once more there was silence—a silence as of some nocturnal cemetery, when grave-diggers and ghouls are done with their macabre toil, and the dead alone remain.

Drawn by that baleful mesmerism, like a somnambulist led by an unseen demon, I entered the room. I knew with a loathly prescience the sight that awaited me beyond the sill—the *double* heap of human segments, some of them fresh and bloody, and others already blue with beginning putrefaction and marked with earth-stains, that were mingled in abhorrent confusion on the rug.

A reddened knife and saw were protruding from the pile; and a little to one side, between the rug and the open cupboard with its shattered door, there reposed a human head that was fronting the other remnants in an upright posture. It was in the same condition of incipient decay as the body to which it had belonged; but I swear that I saw the fading of a malignant exultation from its features as I entered. Even with the marks of corruption upon them, the lineaments bore a manifest likeness to those of John Carnby, and plainly they could belong only to a twin brother.

The frightful inferences that smothered my brain with their black and clammy cloud are not to be written here. The horror which I beheld—and the greater horror which I surmised—would have put to shame hell's foulest enormities in their frozen pits. There was but one mitigation and one mercy: I was compelled to gaze only for a few instants on that intolerable scene. Then, all at once, I felt that something had withdrawn from the room; the malign spell was broken, the overpowering volition that had held me captive was gone. It had released me now, even as it had released the dismembered corpse of Helman Carnby. I was free to go; and I fled from the ghastly chamber and ran headlong through an unlit house and into the outer darkness of the night.

HYPERBOREAN GROTESQUES

THE TESTAMENT OF ATHAMMAUS

IT has become needful for me, who am no wielder of the stylus of bronze or the pen of calamus, and whose only proper tool is the long, double-handed sword, to indite this account of the curious and lamentable happenings which foreran the desertion of Commoriom by its king and its people. This I am well fitted to do, for I played a signal part in these happenings; and I left the city only when all the others had gone.

Now Commoriom, as every one knows, was aforetime the resplendent, high-built capital, and the marble and granite crown of all Hyperborea. But concerning the cause of its abandonment there are now so many warring legends and so many tales of a false and fabulous character, that I, who am old in years and triply old in honors, I, who have grown weary with no less than eleven lustrums of public service, am compelled to write this record of the truth ere it fade utterly from the tongues and memories of men. And this I do, though the telling thereof will include a confession of my one defeat, my one failure in the dutiful administration of a committed task.

For those who will read the narrative in future years, and haply in future lands, I shall now introduce myself. I am Athammaus, the chief headsman of Uzuldaroum, who held formerly the same office in Commoriom. My father, Manghai Thal, was headsman before me; and the sires of my father, even to the mythic generations of the primal kings, have wielded the great copper sword of justice on the block of *eighon*-wood.

Forgive an aged man if he seem to dwell, as is the habit of the old, among the youthful recollections that have gathered to themselves the kingly purple of removed horizons and the strange glory that illumines irretrievable things. Lo! I am made young again when I recall Commoriom, when in this gray city of the sunken years I behold in retrospect her walls that looked mountainously down upon the jungle, and the alabastrine multitude of her heaven-fretting spires. Opulent among cities, and superb and magisterial, and paramount over all was Commoriom, to whom tribute was given from the shores of the Atlantean sea to that sea in which is the immense continent of Mu; to whom the traders came from utmost Thulan that is walled on the north with unknown ice, and from the southern realm of Tscho Vulpanomi which ends in a lake of boiling asphaltum. Ah! proud and lordly was Commoriom, and her humblest dwellings were more than the palaces of other cities. And it was not, as men fable nowadays, because of that maundering prophecy once uttered by the white sybil from the isle of snow which is named Polarion, that her splendor and spaciousness were delivered over to the spotted vines of the jungle and the spotted snakes. Nay, it was because of a direr thing than this, and a tangible horror against which the law of kings, the wisdom of hierophants and the sharpness of swords were alike impotent. Ah! not lightly was she overcome, not easily were her defenders driven forth. And though others forget, or haply deem her no more than a vain and dubitable tale, I shall never cease to lament Commoriom.

My sinews have dwindled grievously now; and Time has drunken stealthily from my veins; and has touched my hair with the ashes of suns extinct. But in the days whereof I tell, there was no braver and more stalwart headsman than I in the whole of Hyperborea; and my name was a red menace, a loudly spoken warning to the evil-doers of the forest and the town, and the savage robbers of uncouth outland tribes. Wearing the blood-bright purple of my office, I stood each morning in the public square where all might attend and behold, and performed for the edification of all men my allotted task. And each day the tough, golden-ruddy copper of the huge crescent blade was darkened not once but many times with a rich and wine-like sanguine. And because of my never-faltering arm, my infallible eye, and the clean blow which there was never any necessity to repeat, I was much honored by the King Loquamethros and by the populace of Commoriom.

I remember well, on account of their unique atrocity, the earliest rumors that came to me in my active life regarding the outlaw Knygathin Zhaum. This person belonged to an obscure and highly unpleasant people called the Voormis, who dwelt in the black Eiglophian Mountains at a full day's journey from Commoriom, and inhabited according to their tribal custom the caves of ferine animals less savage than themselves, which they had slain or otherwise dispossessed. They were generally looked upon as more beast-like than human, because of their excessive hairiness and the vile, ungodly rites and usages to which they were addicted. It was mainly from among these beings that the notorious Knygathin Zhaum had recruited his formidable band, who were terrorizing the hills subjacent to the Eiglophian Mountains with daily deeds of the most infamous and iniquitous rapine. Wholesale robbery was the least of their crimes; and mere anthropophagism was far from being the worst.

It will readily be seen, from this, that the Voormis were a somewhat aboriginal race, with an ethnic heritage of the darkest and most revolting type. And it was commonly said that Knyghathin Zhaum himself possessed an even murkier strain of ancestry than the others, being related on the maternal side to that queer, non-anthropomorphic god, Tsathoggua, who was worshipped so widely during the sub-human cycles. And there were those who whispered of even stranger blood (if one could properly call it blood) and a monstrous linkage with the swart, Protean spawn that had come down with Tsathoggua from elder worlds and exterior dimensions where physiology and geometry had both assumed an altogether inverse trend of development. And, because of this mingling of ultra-cosmic strains, it was said that the body of Knygathin Zhaum, unlike his shaggy, umber-colored fellow-tribesmen, was hairless from crown to heel and was pied with great spots of black and yellow; and moreover he himself was reputed to exceed all others in his cruelty and cunning.

For a long time this execrable outlaw was no more to me than an horrific name; but inevitably I thought of him with a certain professional interest. There were many who believed him invulnerable by any weapon, and who told of his having escaped in a manner which none could elucidate from more than one dungeon whose walls were not to be scaled or pierced by mortal beings. But of course I discounted all such tales, for my official experience had never yet included any one with properties or abilities of a like sort. And I knew well the superstitiousness of the vulgar multitude.

From day to day new reports reached me amid the preoccupations of never-slighted duty. This noxious marauder was not content with the seemingly ample sphere of operations afforded by his native mountains and the outlying hill-regions with their fertile valleys and well-peopled towns. His forays became bolder and more extensive; till one night he descended on a village so near Commoriom that it was usually classed as a suburb. Here he and his filthy crew committed numerous deeds of an unspecifiable enormity; and bearing with them many of the villagers for purposes even less designable, they retired to their caves in the glassy-walled Eiglophian peaks ere the ministers of justice could overtake them.

It was this audaciously offensive act which prompted the law to exert its full power and vigilance against Knygathin Zhaum. Before that, he and his men had been left to the local officers of the countryside; but now his misdeeds were such as to demand the rigorous attention of the constabulary of Commoriom. Henceforth all his movements were followed as closely as possible; the towns where he might descend were strictly guarded; and traps were set everywhere.

Even thus, Knygathin Zhaum contrived to evade capture for month after month; and all the while he repeated his far-flung raids with an embarrassing frequency. It was almost by chance, or through his own foolhardiness, that he was eventually taken in broad daylight on the highway near the city's outskirts. Contrary to all expectation, in view of his renowned ferocity, he made no resistance whatever; but finding himself surrounded by mailed archers and bill-bearers, he yielded to them at once with an oblique, enigmatic smile—a smile that troubled for many nights thereafter the dreams of all who were present.

For reasons which were never explained, he was altogether alone when taken; and none of his fellows were captured either coincidentally or subsequently. Nevertheless, there was much excitement and jubilation in Commoriom, and every one was curious to behold the dreaded outlaw. More even than others, perhaps, I felt the stirrings of interest; for upon me, in due course, the proper decapitation of Knygathin Zhaum would devolve.

From hearing the hideous rumors and legends whose nature I have already outlined, I was prepared for something out of the ordinary in the way of criminal personality. But even at first sight, when I watched him as he was borne to prison through a moiling crowd, Knygathin Zhaum surpassed the most sinister and disagreeable anticipations. He was naked to the waist, and wore the fulvous hide of some long-haired animal which hung in filthy tatters to his knees. Such details, however, contributed little to those elements in his appearance which revolted and even shocked me. His limbs, his body, his lineaments were outwardly formed like those of aboriginal man; and one might even have allowed for his utter hairlessness, in which there was a remote and blasphemously caricatural suggestion of the shaven priest; and even the broad, formless mottling of his skin, like that of a huge boa, might somehow have been glossed over as a rather extravagant peculiarity of pigmentation. It was something else, it was the unctuous, verminous ease, the undulant litheness and fluidity of his every movement, seeming to hint at an inner structure and vertebration that were less than human—or, one might almost have said, a sub-ophidian lack of all bony framework—which made me view the captive, and also my incumbent task, with an unaccustomed distaste. He seemed to slither rather than walk; and the very fashion of his jointure, the placing of knees, hips, elbows and shoulders, appeared arbitrary and factitious. One felt that the outward semblance of humanity was a mere concession to anatomical convention; and that his corporeal formation might easily have assumed—and might still assume at any instant—the unheard-of outlines and concept-defying dimensions that prevail in trans-galactic worlds. Indeed, I could now believe the outrageous tales concerning his ancestry. And with equal horror and curiosity I wondered what the stroke of justice would reveal, and what noisome, mephitic ichor would befoul the impartial sword in lieu of honest blood.

It is needless to record in circumstantial detail the process by which Knygathin Zhaum was tried and condemned for his manifold enormities. The workings of the law were implacably swift and sure, and their equity permitted of no quibbling or delay. The captive was confined in an oubliette below the main dungeons—a cell hewn in the basic, Archean gneiss at a profound depth, with no entrance other than a hole through which he was lowered and drawn up by means of a long rope and windlass. This hole was lidded with a huge block and was guarded day and night by a dozen men-at-arms. However, there was no attempt to escape on the part of Knygathin Zhaum: indeed, he seemed unnaturally resigned to his prospective doom.

To me, who have always been possessed of a strain of prophetic intuition, there was something overtly ominous in this unlooked-for resignation. Also, I did not like the demeanor of the prisoner during his trial. The silence which he had preserved at all times following his capture and incarceration was still maintained before his judges. Though interpreters who knew the harsh, sibilant Eiglophian dialect were provided, he would make no answer to questions; and he offered no defense. Least of all did I like the unabashed and unblinking manner in which he received the final pronouncement of death which was uttered in the high court of Commoriom by eight judges in turn and solemnly reaffirmed at the end by King Loquamethros. After that, I looked well to the sharpening of my sword, and promised myself that I would concentrate all the resources of a brawny arm and a flawless manual artistry upon the forthcoming execution.

My task was not long deferred, for the usual interval of a fortnight between condemnation and decapitation had been shortened to three days in view of the suspicious peculiarities of Knygathin Zhaum and the heinous magnitude of his proven crimes.

On the morning appointed, after a night that had been rendered dismal by a long-drawn succession of the most abominable dreams, I went with my unfailing punctuality to the block of *eighon*-wood, which was situated with geometrical exactness in the center of the main square. Here a huge crowd had already gathered; and the clear amber sun blazed royally down on the silver and nacarat of court dignitaries, the hodden of merchants and artizans, and the rough pelts that were worn by outland people.

With a like punctuality, Knygathin Zhaum soon appeared amid his entourage of guards, who surrounded him with a bristling hedge of billhooks and lances and tridents. At the same time, all the outer avenues of the city, as well as the entrances to the square, were guarded by massed soldiery, for it was feared that the uncaught members of the desperate outlaw band might make an effort to rescue their infamous chief at the last moment.

Amid the unremitting vigilance of his warders, Knygathin Zhaum came forward, fixing upon me the intent but inexpressive gaze of his lidless, ocher-yellow eyes, in which a face-to-face scrutiny could discern no pupils. He knelt down beside the block, presenting his mottled nape without a tremor. As I looked upon him with a calculating eye, and made ready for the lethal stroke, I was impressed more powerfully and more disagreeably than ever by the feeling of a loathsome, underlying plasticity, an invertebrate structure, nauseous and non-terrestrial, beneath his impious mockery of human form. And I could not help perceiving also the air of abnormal coolness, of abstract, impenetrable cynicism, that was maintained by all his parts and members. He was like a torpid snake, or some huge liana of the jungle, that is wholly unconscious of the shearing ax.

I was well aware that I might be dealing with things which were beyond the ordinary province of a public headsman; but nathless I lifted the great sword in a clean, symmetrically flashing arc, and brought it down on the piebald nape with all of my customary force and address.

Necks differ in the sensations which they afford to one's hand beneath the penetrating blade. In this case, I can only say that the sensation was not such as I have grown to associate with the cleaving of any known animal substance. But I saw with relief that the blow had been successful: the head of Knygathin Zhaum lay cleanly severed on the porous block, and his body sprawled on the pavement without even a single quiver of departing animation. As I had expected, there was no blood—only a black, tarry, fetid exudation, far from copious, which ceased in a few minutes and vanished utterly from my sword and from the *eighon*-wood. Also, the inner anatomy which the blade had revealed was devoid of all legitimate vertebration. But to all appearance Knygathin Zhaum had yielded up his obscene life; and the sentence of King Loquamethros and the eight judges of Commoriom had been fulfilled with a legal precision.

Proudly but modestly I received the applause of the waiting multitudes, who bore willing witness to the consummation of my official task and were loudly jubilant over the dead scourge. After seeing that the remains of Knygathin Zhaum were given into the hands of the public grave-diggers, who always disposed of such offal, I left the square and returned to my home, since no other decapitations had been set for that day. My conscience was serene, and I felt that I had acquitted myself worthily in the performance of a far from pleasant duty.

Knygathin Zhaum, as was the custom in dealing with the bodies of the most nefarious criminals, was interred with contumelious haste in a barren field outside the city where people cast their orts and rubbish. He was left in an unmarked and unmounded grave between two middens. The power of the law had now been amply vindicated; and every one was satisfied, from Lòquamethros himself to the villagers that had suffered from the depredations of the deceased outlaw.

I retired that night, after a bounteous meal of *suvana*-fruit and *djongua*-beans, well irrigated with *foum*-wine. From a moral standpoint, I had every reason to sleep the sleep of the virtuous; but, even as on the preceding night, I was made the victim of one cacodemoniacal dream after another. Of these dreams, I recall only their pervading, unifying consciousness of insufferable suspense, of monotonously cumulative horror without shape or name; and the ever-torturing sentiment of vain repetition and dark, hopeless toil and frustration. Also, there is a half-memory, which refuses to assume any approach to visual form, of things that were never intended for human perception or human cognition; and the aforesaid sentiment, and all the horror, were dimly but indissolubly bound up with these.

Awaking unrefreshed and weary from what seemed an eon of thankless endeavor, of treadmill bafflement, I could only impute my nocturnal sufferings to the *djongua*-beans; and decided that I must have eaten all too liberally of these nutritious viands. Mercifully, I did not suspect in my dreams the dark, portentous symbolism that was soon to declare itself.

Now must I write the things that are formidable unto Earth and the dwellers of Earth; the things that exceed all human or terrene regimen; that subvert reason; that mock the dimensions and defy biology. Dire is the tale; and, after seven lustrums, the tremor of an olden fear still agitates my hand as I write.

But of such things I was still oblivious when I sallied forth that morning to the place of execution, where three criminals of a quite average sort, whose very cephalic contours I have forgotten along with their offenses, were to meet their well-deserved doom beneath my capable arm. Howbeit, I had not gone far when I heard an unconscionable uproar that was spreading swiftly from street to street, from alley to alley throughout Commoriom. I distinguished myriad cries of rage, horror, fear and lamentation that were seemingly caught up and repeated by every one who chanced to be abroad at that hour. Meeting some of the citizenry, who were plainly in a state of the most excessive agitation and were still continuing their outcries, I inquired the reason of all this clamor. And thereupon I learned from them that Knygathin Zhaum, whose illicit career was presumably at an end, had now reappeared and had signalized the unholy miracle of his return by the commission of a most appalling act on the main avenue before the very eyes of early passers! He had seized a respectable seller of *djongua*-beans, and had proceeded instantly to devour his victim *alive*, without heeding the blows, bricks, arrows, javelins, cobblestones and curses that were rained upon him by the gathering throng and by the police. It was only when he had satisfied his atrocious appetite that he suffered the police to lead him away, leaving little more than the bones and raiment of the *djongua*-seller to mark the spot of this outrageous happening. Since the case was without legal parallel, Knygathin Zhaum had been thrown once more into the oubliette below the city dungeons, to await the will of Loquamethros and the eight judges.

The exceeding discomfiture, the profound embarrassment felt by myself, as well as by the people and the magistracy of Commoriom, can well be imagined. As every one bore witness, Knygathin Zhaum had been efficiently beheaded and buried according to the customary ritual; and his resurrection was not only against nature but involved a most contumelious and highly mystifying breach of the law. In fact, the legal aspects of the case were such as to render necessary the immediate passage of a special statute, calling for rejudgment, and allowing re-execution, of such malefactors as might thus return from their lawful graves. Apart from all this, there was general consternation; and even at that early date, the more ignorant and more religious among the townsfolk where prone to regard the matter as an omen of some impending civic calamity.

As for me, my scientific turn of mind, which repudiated the supernatural, led me to seek an explanation of the problem in the non-terrestrial side of Knygathin Zhaum's ancestry. I felt sure that the forces of an alien biology, the properties of a trans-stellar life-substance, were somehow involved.

With the spirit of the true investigator, I summoned the grave-diggers who had interred Knygathin Zhaum and bade them lead me to his place of sepulture in the refuse-grounds. Here a most singular condition disclosed itself. The earth had not been disturbed, apart from a deep hole at one end of the grave, such as might have been made by a large rodent. No body of human size, or, at least, of human form, could possibly have emerged from this hole. At my command, the diggers removed all the loose soil, mingled with potsherds and other rubbish, which they had heaped upon the beheaded outlaw. When they reached the bottom, nothing was found but a slight stickiness where the corpse had lain; and this, along with an odor of ineffable foulness which was its concomitant, soon dissipated itself in the open air.

Baffled, and more mystified than ever, but still sure that the enigma would permit of some natural solution, I awaited the new trial. This time, the course of justice was even quicker and less given to quibbling than before. The prisoner was again condemned, and the time of decapitation was delayed only till the following morn. A proviso concerning burial was added to the sentence: the remains were to be sealed in a strong wooden sarcophagus, the sarcophagus was to be inhumed in a deep pit in the solid stone, and the pit filled with massy boulders. These measures, it was felt, should serve amply to restrain the unwholesome and irregular inclinations of this obnoxious miscreant.

When Knygathin Zhaum was again brought before me, amid a redoubled guard and a throng that overflowed the square and all of the outlying avenues, I viewed him with profound concern and with more than my former repulsion. Having a good memory for anatomic details, I noticed some odd changes in his physique. The huge splotches of dull black and sickly yellow that had covered him from head to heel were now somewhat differently distributed. The shifting of the facial blotches around the eyes and mouth had given him an expression that was both grim and sardonic to an unbearable degree. Also, there was a perceptible *shortening* of his neck, though the place of cleavage and reunion, midway between head and shoulders, had left no mark whatever. And looking at his limbs, I discerned other and more subtle changes. Despite my acumen in physical matters, I found myself unwilling to speculate regarding the processes that might underlie these alterations; still less did I wish to surmise the problematic results of their continuation, if such should ensue. Hoping fervently that Knygathin Zhaum and the vile, flagitious properties of his unhallowed carcass would now be brought to a permanent end, I raised the sword of justice high in air and smote with heroic might.

Once again, as far as mortal eyes were able to determine, the effects of the shearing blow were all that could be desired. The head rolled forward on the *eighon*-wood, and the torso and its members fell and lay supinely on the maculated flags. From a legal viewpoint, this doubly nefarious malefactor was now twice-dead.

Howbeit, this time I superintended in person the disposal of the remains, and saw to the bolting of the fine sarcophagus of *apha*-wood in which they were laid, and the filling with chosen boulders of the ten-foot pit into which the sarcophagus was lowered. It required three men to lift even the least of these boulders. We all felt that the irrepressible Knygathin Zhaum was due for a quietus.

Alas for the vanity of earthly hopes and labors! The morrow came with its unspeakable, incredible tale of renewed outrage: once more the weird, semi-human offender was abroad, once more his anthropophagic lust had taken toll from among the honorable denizens of Commoriom. He had eaten no less a personage than one of the eight judges; and, not satisfied with picking the bones of this rather obese individual, had devoured by way of dessert the more outstanding facial features of one of the police who had tried to deter him from finishing his main course. All this, as before, was done amid the frantic protests of a great throng. After a final nibbling at the scant vestiges of the unfortunate constable's left ear, Knygathin Zhaum had seemed to experience a feeling of repletion and had suffered himself to be led docilely away by the jailers.

I and the others who had helped me in the arduous toils of entombment were more than astounded when we heard the news. And the effect on the general public was indeed deplorable. The more superstitious and timid began leaving the city forthwith; and there was much revival of forgotten prophecies; and much talk among the various priesthoods anent the necessity of placating with liberal sacrifice their mystically angered gods and eidolons. Such nonsense I was wholly able to disregard; but, under the circumstances, the persistent return of Knygathin Zhaum was no less alarming to science than to religion.

We examined the tomb, if only as a matter of form; and found that certain of the superincumbent boulders had been displaced in such a manner as to admit the outward passage of a body with the lateral dimensions of some large snake or muskrat. The sarcophagus, with its metal bolts, was bursten at one end; and we shuddered to think of the immeasurable force that must have been employed in its disruption.

Because of the way in which the case overpassed all known biologic laws, the formalities of civil law were now waived; and I, Athammaus, was called upon that same day before the sun had reached its meridian, and was solemnly charged with the office of re-beheading Knygathin Zhaum at once. The interment or other disposal of the remains was left to my discretion; and the local soldiery and constabulary were all placed at my command, if I should require them.

Deeply conscious of the honor thus implied, and sorely perplexed but undaunted, I went forth to the scene of my labors. When the criminal reappeared, it was obvious to every one that his physical personality, in achieving this new recrudescence, had undergone a most salient change. His mottling had developed more than a suggestion of some startling and repulsive pattern; and his human characteristics had yielded to the inroads of an unearthly distortion. The head was now joined to the shoulders almost without the intermediation of a neck; the eyes were set diagonally in a face with oblique bulgings and flattenings; the nose and mouth were showing a tendency to displace each other; and there were still further alterations which I shall not specify, since they involved an abhorrent degradation of man's noblest and most distinctive corporeal members. I shall, however, mention the strange, pendulous formations, like annulated dewlaps or wattles, into which his kneecaps had now evolved. Nathless, it was Knygathin Zhaum himself who stood (if one could dignify the fashion of his carriage by that word) before the block of justice.

Because of the virtual non-existence of a nape, the third beheading called for a precision of eye and a nicety of hand which, in all likelihood, no other headsman than myself could have shown. I rejoice to stay that my skill was adequate to the demand made upon it; and once again the culprit was shorn of his vile cephaloid appendage. But if the blade had gone even a little to either side, the dismemberment entailed would have been technically of another sort than decapitation.

The laborious care with which I and my assistants conducted the third inhumation was indeed deserving of success. We laid the body in a strong sarcophagus of bronze, and the head in a second but smaller sarcophagus of the same material. The lids were then soldered down with molten metal; and after this the two sarcophagi were conveyed to opposite parts of Commoriom. The one containing the body was buried at a great depth beneath monumental masses of stone; but that which enclosed the head I left uninterred, proposing to watch over it all night in company with a guard of armed men. I also appointed a numerous guard to keep vigil above the burial-place of the body.

Night came; and with seven trusty trident-bearers I went forth to the place where we had left the smaller of the two sarcophagi. This was in the courtyard of a deserted mansion amid the suburbs, far from the haunts of the populace. For weapons, I myself wore a short falchion and carried a great bill. We took along a plentiful supply of torches, so that we might not lack for light in our gruesome vigil; and we lit several of them at once and stuck them in crevices between the flagstones of the court in such wise that they formed a circle of lurid flames about the sarcophagus.

We had also brought with us an abundance of the crimson *foum*-wine in leathern bottles, and dice of mammoth-ivory with which to beguile the black nocturnal hours; and eyeing our charge with a casual but careful vigilance, we applied ourselves discreetly to the wine and began to play for small sums of no more than five *pazoors,* as is the wont of good gamblers till they have taken their opponents' measure.

The darkness deepened apace; and in the square of sapphire overhead, to which the illumination of our torches had given a jetty tinge, we saw Polaris and the red planets that looked down for the last time upon Commoriom in her glory. But we dreamed not of the nearness of disaster, but jested bravely and drank in ribald mockery to the monstrous head that was now so securely coffined and so remotely sundered from its odious body. And the wine passed and re-passed among us; and its rosy spirit mounted in our brains; and we played for bolder stakes; and the game quickened to a goodly frenzy.

I know not how many stars had gone over us in the smoky heavens, nor how many times I had availed myself of the ever-circling bottles. But I remember well that I had won no less than ninety *pazoors* from the trident-bearers, who were all swearing lustily and loudly as they strove in vain to stem the tide of my victory. I, as well as the others, had wholly forgotten the object of our vigil.

The sarcophagus containing the head was one that had been primarily designed for the reception of a small child. Its present use, one might have argued, was a sinful and sacrilegious waste of fine bronze; but nothing else of proper size and adequate strength was available at the time. In the mounting fervor of the game, as I have hinted, we had all ceased to watch this receptacle; and I shudder to think how long there may have been something visibly or even audibly amiss before the unwonted and terrifying behavior of the sarcophagus was forced upon our attention. It was the sudden, loud, metallic clangor, like that of a smitten gong or shield, which made us realize that all things were not as they should have been; and turning unanimously in the direction of the sound, we saw that the sarcophagus was heaving and pitching in a most unseemly fashion amid its ring of flaring torches. First on one end or corner, then on another, it danced and pirouetted, clanging resonantly all the while on the granite pavement.

The true horror of the situation had scarcely seeped into our brains, ere a new and even more ghastly development occurred. We saw that the casket was bulging ominously at top and sides and bottom, and was rapidly losing all similitude to its rightful form. Its rectangular outlines swelled and curved and were horribly erased as in the changes of a nightmare, till the thing became a slightly oblong sphere; and then, with a most appalling noise, it began to split at the welded edges of the lid, and burst violently asunder. Through the long, ragged rift there poured in hellish ebullition a dark, ever-swelling mass of incognizable matter, frothing as with the venomous foam of a million serpents, hissing as with the yeast of fermenting wine, and putting forth here and there great sooty-looking bubbles that were large as pig-bladders. Overturning several of the torches, it rolled in an inundating wave across the flagstones and we all sprang back in the most abominable fright and stupefaction to avoid it.

Cowering against the rear wall of the courtyard, while the overthrown torches flickered wildly and smokily, we watched the remarkable actions of the mass, which had paused as if to collect itself, and was now subsiding like a sort of infernal dough. It shrank, it fell in, till after awhile its dimensions began to re-approach those of the encoffined head, though they still lacked any true semblance of its shape. The thing became a round, blackish ball, on whose palpitating surface the nascent outlines of random features were limned with the flatness of a drawing. There was one lidless eye, tawny, pupilless and phosphoric, that stared upon us from the center of the ball while the thing appeared to be making up its mind. It lay still for more than a minute; then, with a catapulting bound, it sprang past us toward the open entrance of the courtyard, and disappeared from our ken on the midnight streets.

Despite our amazement and disconcertion, we were able to note the general direction in which it had gone. This, to our further terror and confoundment, was toward the suburb of Commoriom in which the body of Knygathin Zhaum had been entombed. We dared not conjecture the meaning of it all, and the probable outcome. But, though there were a million fears and apprehensions to deter us, we seized our weapons and followed on the path of that unholy head with all the immediacy and all the forthrightness of motion which a goodly cargo of *foum*-wine would permit.

No one other than ourselves was abroad at an hour when even the most dissolute revellers had either gone home or had succumbed to their potations under tavern tables. The streets were dark, and were somehow drear and cheerless; and the stars above them were half stifled as by the invading mist of a pestilential miasma. We went on, following a main street, and the pavements echoed to our tread in the stillness with a hollow sound, as if the solid stone beneath them had been honeycombed with mausolean vaults in the interim of our weird vigil.

In all our wanderings, we found no sign of that supremely noxious and execrable thing which had issued from the riven sarcophagus. Nor, to our relief, and contrary to all our fears, did we encounter anything of an allied or analogous nature, such as might be abroad if our surmises were correct. But, near the central square of Commoriom, we met with a number of men, carrying bills and tridents and torches, who proved to be the guards I had posted that evening above the tomb of Knygathin Zhaum's body. These men were in a state of pitiable agitation; and they told us a fearsome tale, of how the deep-hewn tomb and the monumental blocks piled within it had heaved as with the throes of earthquake; and of how a python-shaped mass of frothing and hissing matter had poured forth from amid the blocks and had vanished into the darkness toward Commoriom. In return, we told them of that which had happened during our vigil in the courtyard; and we all agreed that a great foulness, a thing more baneful than beast or serpent, was again loose and ravening in the night. And we spoke only in shocked whispers of what the morrow might declare.

Uniting our forces, we searched the city, combing cautiously its alleys and its thoroughfares and dreading with the dread of brave men the dark, iniquitous spawn on which the light of our torches might fall at any turn or in any nook or portal. But the search was vain; and the stars grew faint above us in a livid sky; and the dawn came in among the marble spires with a glimmering of ghostly silver; and a thin, fantasmal amber was sifted on walls and pavements.

Soon there were footsteps other than ours that echoed through the town; and one by one the familiar clangors and clamors of life awoke. Early passers appeared; and the sellers of fruits and milk and legumes came in from the countryside. But of that which we sought there was still no trace.

We went on, while the city continued to resume its matutinal activities around us. Then, abruptly, with no warning, and under circumstances that would have startled the most robust and affrayed the most valorous, we came upon our quarry. We were entering the square in which was the *eighon*-block whereon so many thousand miscreants had laid their piacular necks, when we heard an outcry of mortal dread and agony such as only one thing in the world could have occasioned. Hurrying on, we saw that two wayfarers, who had been crossing the square near the block of justice, were struggling and writhing in the clutch of an unequalled monster which both natural history and fable would have repudiated.

In spite of the baffling, ambiguous oddities which the thing displayed, we identified it as Knygathin Zhaum when we drew closer. The head, in its third reunion with that detestable torso, had attached itself in a semi-flattened manner to the region of the lower chest and diaphragm; and during the process of this novel coalescence, one eye had slipped away from all relation with its fellow or the head and was now occupying the navel, just below the embossment of the chin. Other and even more shocking alterations had occurred: the arms had lengthened into tentacles, with fingers that were like knots of writhing vipers; and where the head would normally have been, the shoulders had reared themselves to a cone-shaped eminence that ended in a cup-like mouth. Most fabulous and impossible of all, however, were the changes in the nether limbs: at each knee and hip, they had re-bifurcated into long, lithe proboscides that were lined with throated suckers. By making a combined use of its various mouths and members, the abnormality was devouring both of the hapless persons whom it had seized.

Drawn by the outcries, a crowd gathered behind us as we neared this atrocious tableau. The whole city seemed to fill with a well-nigh instantaneous clamor, an ever-swelling hubbub, in which the dominant note was one of supreme, all-devastating terror.

I shall not speak of our feelings as officers and men. It

was plain to us that the ultra-mundane factors in Knygathin Zhaum's ancestry had asserted themselves with a hideously accelerative ratio, following his latest resurrection. But, despite this, and the wholly stupendous enormity of the miscreation before us, we were still prepared to fulfil our duty and defend as best we could the helpless populace. I boast not of the heroism required: we were simple men, and should have done only that which we were visibly called upon to do.

We surrounded the monster, and would have assailed it immediately with our bills and tridents. But here an embarrassing difficulty disclosed itself: the creature before us had entwined itself so tortuously and inextricably with its prey, and the whole group was writhing and tossing so violently, that we could not use our weapons without grave danger of impaling or otherwise injuring our two fellow-citizens. At length, however, the strugglings and heavings grew less vehement, as the substance and life-blood of the men were consumed; and the loathsome mass of devourer and devoured became gradually quiescent.

Now, if ever, was our opportunity; and I am sure we should all have rallied to the attack, useless and vain as it would certainly have been. But plainly the monster had grown weary of all such trifling and would no longer submit himself to the petty annoyance of human molestation. As we raised our weapons and made ready to strike, the thing drew back, still carrying its vein-drawn, flaccid victims, and climbed upon the *eighon*-block. Here, before the eyes of all assembled, it began to swell in every part, in every member, as if it were inflating itself with a superhuman rancor and malignity. The rate at which the swelling progressed, and the proportions which the thing attained as it covered the block from sight and lapsed down on every side with undulating, inundating folds, would have been enough to daunt the heroes of remotest myth. The bloating of the main torso, I might add, was more lateral than vertical.

When the abnormality began to present dimensions that were beyond those of any creature of this world, and to bulge aggressively toward us with a slow, interminable stretching of boa-like arms, my valiant and redoubtable companions were scarcely to be censured for retreating. And even less can I blame the general population, who were now evacuating Commoriom in torrential multitudes, with shrill cries and wailings. Their flight was no doubt accelerated by the vocal sounds, which, for the first time during our observation, were being emitted by the monster. These sounds partook of the character of hissings more than anything else; but their volume was overpowering, their timbre was a torment and a nausea to the ear; and, worst of all, they were issuing not only from the diaphragmic mouth but from each of the various other oral openings or suckers which the horror had developed. Even I, Athammaus, drew back from those hissings and stood well beyond reach of the coiling serpentine fingers.

I am proud to say, however, that I lingered on the edge of the empty square for some time, with more than one backward and regretful glance. The thing that had been Knygathin Zhaum was seemingly content with its triumph; and it brooded supine and mountainous above the vanquished *eighon*-block. Its myriad hisses sank to a slow, minor sibilation such as might issue from a family of somnolent pythons; and it made no overt attempt to assail or even approach me. But seeing at last that the professional problem which it offered was quite insoluble; and divining moreover that Commoriom was by now entirely without a king, a judicial system, a constabulary or a people, I finally abandoned the doomed city and followed the others.

THE WEIRD OF AVOOSL WUTHOQQUAN

"GIVE, give, O magnanimous and liberal lord of the poor," cried the beggar.

Avoosl Wuthoqquan, the richest and most avaricious money-lender in all Commoriom, and, by that token, in the whole of Hyperborea, was startled from his train of revery by the sharp, eery, cicada-like voice. He eyed the supplicant with acidulous disfavor. His meditations, as he walked homeward that evening, had been splendidly replete with the shining of costly metals, with coins and ingots and gold-work and argentry, and the flaming or sparkling of many-tinted gems in rills, rivers and cascades, all flowing toward the coffers of Avoosl Wuthoqquan. Now the vision had flown; and this untimely and obstreperous voice was imploring him for alms.

"I have nothing for you." His tones were like the grating of a shut clasp.

"Only two *pazoors*, O generous one, and I will prophesy."

Avoosl Wuthoqquan gave the beggar a second glance. He had never seen so disreputable a specimen of the mendicant class in all his wayfarings through Commoriom. The man was preposterously old, and his mummy-brown skin, wherever visible, was webbed with wrinkles that were like the heavy weaving of some giant jungle spider. His rags were no less than fabulous; and the beard that hung down and mingled with them was hoary as the moss of a primeval juniper.

"I do not require your prophecies."

"One *pazoor* then."

"No."

The eyes of the beggar became evil and malignant in their hollow sockets, like the heads of two poisonous little pit-vipers in their holes.

"Then, O Avoosl Wuthoqquan," he hissed, "I will prophesy gratis. Harken to your weird: the godless and exceeding love which you bear to all material things, and your lust therefor, shall lead you on a strange quest and bring you to a doom whereof the stars and the sun will alike be ignorant. The hidden opulence of earth shall allure you and ensnare you; and earth itself shall devour you at the last."

"Begone," said Avoosl Wuthoqquan. "The weird is more than a trifle cryptic in its earlier clauses; and the final clause is somewhat platitudinous. I do not need a beggar to tell me the common fate of mortality."

It was many moons later, in that year which became known to pre-glacial historians as the year of the Black Tiger.

Avoosl Wuthoqquan sat in a lower chamber of his house, which was also his place of business. The room was obliquely shafted by the brief, aerial gold of the reddening sunset, which fell through a crystal window, lighting a serpentine line of irised sparks in the jewel-studded lamp that hung from copper chains, and touching to fiery life the tortuous threads of silver and similor in the dark arrases. Avoosl Wuthoqquan, seated in an umber shadow beyond the aisle of light, peered with an austere and ironic mien at his client, whose swarthy face and somber mantle were gilded by the passing glory.

The man was a stranger; possibly a travelling merchant from outland realms, the usurer thought—or else an outlander of more dubious occupation. His narrow, slanting, beryl-green eyes, his bluish, unkempt beard, and the uncouth cut of his sad raiment, were sufficient proof of his alienage in Commoriom.

"Three hundred *djals* is a large sum," said the money-lender thoughtfully. "Moreover, I do not know you. What security have you to offer?"

The visitor produced from the bosom of his garment a small bag of tiger-skin, tied at the mouth with sinew, and opening the bag with a deft movement, poured on the table before Avoosl Wuthoqquan two uncut emeralds of immense size and flawless purity. They flamed at the heart with a cold and ice-green fire as they caught the slanting sunset; and a greedy spark was kindled in the eyes of the usurer. But he spoke coolly and indifferently.

"It may be that I can loan you one hundred and fifty *djals*. Emeralds are hard to dispose of; and if you should not return to claim the gems and repay me the money, I might have reason to repent my generosity. But I will take the hazard."

"The loan I ask is a mere tithe of their value," protested the stranger. "Give me two hundred and fifty *djals*. . . . There are other money-lenders in Commoriom, I am told."

"Two hundred *djals* is the most I can offer. It is true that the gems are not without value. But you may have stolen them. How am I to know? It is not my habit to ask indiscreet questions."

"Take them," said the stranger, hastily. He accepted the silver coins which Avoosl Wuthoqquan counted out, and offered no further protest. The usurer watched him with a sardonic smile as he departed, and drew his own inferences. He felt sure that the jewels had been stolen, but was in no wise perturbed or disquieted by this fact. No matter whom they had belonged to, or what their history, they would form a welcome and valuable addition to the coffers of Avoosl Wuthoqquan. Even the smaller of the two emeralds would have been absurdly cheap at three hundred *djals*; but the usurer felt no apprehension that the stranger would return to claim them at any time. . . . No, the man was plainly a thief, and had been glad to rid himself of the evidence of his guilt. As to the rightful ownership of the gems—that was hardly a matter to arouse the concern or the curiosity of the money-lender. They were his own property now, by virtue of the sum in silver which had been tacitly regarded by himself and the stranger as a price rather than a mere loan.

The sunset faded swiftly from the room and a brown twilight began to dull the metal broideries of the curtains and the colored eyes of the gems. Avoosl Wuthoqquan lit the fretted lamp; and then, opening a small brazen strong-box, he poured from it a flashing rill of jewels on the table beside the emeralds. There were pale and ice-clear topazes from Mhu Thulan, and gorgeous crystals of tourmaline from Tscho Vulpanomi; there were chill and furtive sapphires of the north, and arctic carnelians like frozen blood, and diamonds that were hearted with white stars. Red, unblinking rubies glared from the coruscating pile, chatoyants shone like the eyes of tigers, garnets and alabraundines gave their somber flames to the lamplight amid the restless hues of opals. Also, there were other emeralds, but none so large and flawless as the two that he had acquired that evening.

Avoosl Wuthoqquan sorted out the gems in gleaming rows and circles, as he had done so many times before; and he set apart all the emeralds with his new acquisitions at one end, like captains leading a file. He was well pleased with his bargain, well satisfied with his overflowing caskets. He regarded the jewels with an avaricious love, a miserly complacence; and one might have thought that his eyes were little beads of jasper, set in his leathery face as in the smoky parchment cover of some olden book of doubtful magic. Money and precious gems—these things alone, he thought, were immutable and non-volatile in a world of never-ceasing change and fugacity.

His reflections, at this point, were interrupted by a singular occurrence. Suddenly and without warning—for he had not touched or disturbed them in any manner—the two large emeralds started to roll away from their companions on the smooth, level table of black *ogga*-wood; and before the startled money-lender could put out his hand to stop them, they had vanished over the opposite edge and had fallen with a muffled rattling on the carpeted floor.

Such behavior was highly eccentric and peculiar, not to say unaccountable; but the usurer leapt to his feet with no other thought save to retrieve the jewels. He rounded the table in time to see that they had continued their mysterious rolling and were slipping through the outer door, which the stranger in departing had left slightly ajar. This door gave on a courtyard; and the courtyard, in turn, opened on the streets of Commoriom.

Avoosl Wuthoqquan was deeply alarmed, but was more concerned by the prospect of losing the emeralds than by the eeriness and mystery of their departure. He gave chase with an agility of which few would have believed him capable, and throwing open the door, he saw the fugitive emeralds gliding with an uncanny smoothness and swiftness across the rough, irregular flags of the courtyard. The twilight was deepening to a nocturnal blue; but the jewels seemed to wink derisively with a strange phosphoric luster as he followed them. Clearly visible in the gloom, they passed through the unbarred gate that gave on a principal avenue, and disappeared.

It began to occur to Avoosl Wuthoqquan that the jewels were bewitched; but not even in the face of an unknown sorcery was he willing to relinquish anything for which he had paid the munificent sum of two hundred *djals*. He gained the open street with a running leap, and paused only to make sure of the direction in which his emeralds had gone.

The dim avenue was almost entirely deserted; for the worthy citizens of Commoriom, at that hour, were preoccupied with the consumption of their evening meal. The jewels, gaining momentum, and skimming the ground lightly in their flight, were speeding away on the left toward the less reputable suburbs and the wild, luxuriant jungle beyond. Avoosl Wuthoqquan saw that he must redouble his pursuit if he were to overtake them.

Panting and wheezing valiantly with the unfamiliar exertion, he renewed the chase; but in spite of all his efforts, the jewels ran always at the same distance before him, with a maddening ease and eery volitation, tinkling musically at whiles on the pavement. The frantic and bewildered usurer was soon out of breath; and being compelled to slacken his speed, he feared to lose sight of the eloping gems; but strangely, thereafterward, they ran with a slowness that corresponded to his own, maintaining ever the same interval.

The money-lender grew desperate. The flight of the emeralds was leading him into an outlying quarter of Commoriom where thieves and murderers and beggars dwelt. Here he met a few passers, all of dubious character, who stared in stupefaction at the fleeing stones, but made no effort to stop them. Then the foul tenements among which he ran became smaller, with wider spaces between; and soon there were only sparse huts, where furtive lights gleamed out in the full-grown darkness, beneath the lowering frondage of high palms.

Still plainly visible, and shining with a mocking phosphorescence, the jewels fled before him on the dark road. It seemed to him, however, that he was gaining upon them a little. His flabby limbs and pursy body were faint with fatigue, and he was grievously winded; but he went on in renewed hope, gasping with eager avarice. A full moon, large and amber-tinted, rose beyond the jungle and began to light his way.

Commoriom was far behind him now; and there were no more huts on the lonely forest road, nor any other wayfarers. He shivered a little—either with fear or the chill night air; but he did not relax his pursuit. He was closing in on the emeralds, very gradually but surely; and he felt that he would recapture them soon. So engrossed was he in the weird chase, with his eyes on the ever-rolling gems, that he failed to perceive that he was no longer following an open highway. Somehow, somewhere, he had taken a narrow path that wound among monstrous trees whose foliage turned the moonlight to a mesh of quick-silver with heavy, fantastic raddlings of ebony. Crouching in grotesque menace, like giant retiarii, they seemed to close in upon him from all sides. But the money-lender was oblivious of their shadowy threats, and heeded not the sinister strangeness and solitude of the jungle path, nor the dank odors that lingered beneath the trees like unseen pools.

Nearer and nearer he came to the fleeting gems, till they ran and flickered tantalizingly a little beyond his reach, and seemed to look back at him like two greenish, glowing eyes, filled with allurement and mockery. Then, as he was about to fling himself forward in a last and supreme effort to secure them, they vanished abruptly from view, as if they had been swallowed by the forest shadows that lay like sable pythons athwart the moonlit way.

Baffled and disconcerted, Avoosl Wuthoqquan paused and peered in bewilderment at the place where they had disappeared. He saw that the path ended in a cavern-mouth yawning blackly and silently before him, and leading to unknown subterranean depths. It was a doubtful and suspicious-looking cavern, fanged with sharp stones and bearded with queer grasses; and Avoosl Wuthoqquan, in his cooler moments, would have hesitated a long while before entering it. But just then he was capable of no other impulse than the fervor of the chase and the prompting of avarice.

The cavern that had swallowed his emeralds in a fashion so nefarious was a steep incline running swiftly down into darkness. It was low and narrow, and slippery with noisome oozings; but the money-lender was heartened as he went on by a glimpse of the glowing jewels, which seemed to float beneath him in the black air, as if to illuminate his way. The incline led to a level, winding passage, in which Avoosl Wuthoqquan began to overtake his elusive property once more; and hope flared high in his panting bosom.

The emeralds were almost within reach; then, with sleightful suddenness, they slipped from his ken beyond an abrupt angle of the passage; and following them, he paused in wonder, as if halted by an irresistible hand. He was half blinded for some moments by the pale, mysterious, bluish light that poured from the roof and walls of the huge cavern into which he had emerged; and he was more than dazzled by the multi-tinted splendor that flamed and glowed and glistened and sparkled at his very feet.

He stood on a narrow ledge of stone; and the whole chamber before and beneath him, almost to the level of this ledge, was filled with jewels even as a granary is filled with grain! It was as if all the rubies, opals, beryls, diamonds, amethysts, emeralds, chrysolites and sapphires of the world had been gathered together and poured into an immense pit. He thought that he saw his own emeralds, lying tranquilly and decorously in a nearer mound of the undulant mass; but there were so many others of like size and flawlessness that he could not be sure of them.

For awhile, he could hardly believe the ineffable vision. Then, with a single cry of ecstasy, he leapt forward from the ledge, sinking almost to his knees in the shifting and tinkling and billowing gems. In great double handfuls, he lifted the flaming and scintillating stones and let them sift between his fingers, slowly and voluptuously, to fall with a light clash on the monstrous heap. Blinking joyously, he watched the royal lights and colors run in spreading or narrowing ripples; he saw them burn like steadfast coals and secret stars, or leap out in blazing eyes that seemed to catch fire from each other.

In his most audacious dreams, the usurer had never even suspected the existence of such riches. He babbled aloud in a rhapsody of delight, as he played with the numberless gems; and he failed to perceive that he was sinking deeper with every movement into the unfathomable pit. The jewels had risen above his knees, were engulfing his pudgy thighs, before his avaricious rapture was touched by any thought of peril.

Then, startled by the realization that he was sinking into his new-found wealth as into some treacherous quicksand, he sought to extricate himself and return to the safety of the ledge. He floundered helplessly; for the moving gems gave way beneath him, and he made no progress but went deeper still, till the bright, unstable heap had risen to his waist.

Avoosl Wuthoqquan began to feel a frantic terror amid the intolerable irony of his plight. He cried out; and as if in answer, there came a loud, unctuous, evil chuckle from the cavern behind him. Twisting his fat neck with painful effort, so that he could peer over his shoulder, he saw a most peculiar entity that was couching on a sort of shelf above the pit of jewels. The entity was wholly and outrageously unhuman; and neither did it resemble any species of animal, or any known god or demon of Hyperborea. Its aspect was not such as to lessen the alarm and panic of the money-lender; for it was very large and pale and squat, with a toad-like face and a swollen, squidgy body and numerous cuttlefish limbs or appendages. It lay flat on the shelf, with its chinless head and long slit-like mouth overhanging the pit, and its cold, lidless eyes peering obliquely at Avoosl Wuthoqquan. The usurer was not reassured when it began to speak in a thick and loathsome voice, like the molten tallow of corpses dripping from a wizard's kettle.

"Ho! what have we here?" it said. "By the black altar of Tsathoggua, 'tis a fat money-lender, wallowing in my jewels like a lost pig in a quagmire!"

"Help me!" cried Avoosl Wuthoqquan. "See you not that I am sinking?"

The entity gave its oleaginous chuckle. "Yes, I see your predicament, of course. . . . What are you doing here?"

"I came in search of my emeralds—two fine and flawless stones for which I have just paid the sum of two hundred *djals.*"

"*Your* emeralds?" said the entity. "I fear that I must contradict you. The jewels are mine. They were stolen not long ago from this cavern, in which I have been wont to gather and guard my subterranean wealth for many ages. The thief was frightened away . . . when he saw me . . . and I suffered him to go. He had taken only the two emeralds; and I knew that they would return to me—as my jewels always return—whenever I choose to call them. The thief was lean and bony, and I did well to let him go; for now, in his place, there is a plump and well-fed usurer."

Avoosl Wuthoqquan, in his mounting terror, was barely

able to comprehend the words or to grasp their implications. He had sunk slowly but steadily into the yielding pile; and green, yellow, red and violet gems were blinking gorgeously about his bosom and sifting with a light tinkle beneath his armpits.

"Help! help!" he wailed. "I shall be engulfed!"

Grinning sardonically, and showing the cloven tip of a fat white tongue, the singular entity slid from the shelf with boneless ease; and spreading its flat body on the pool of gems, into which it hardly sank, it slithered forward to a position from which it could reach the frantic usurer with its octopus-like members. It dragged him free with a single motion of incredible celerity. Then, without pause or preamble or further comment, in a leisurely and methodical fashion, it began to devour him.

UBBO-SATHLA

> ... *For Ubbo-Sathla is the source and the end. Before the coming of Zhothaqquah or Yok-Zothoth or Kthulhut from the stars, Ubbo-Sathla dwelt in the steaming fens of the new-made Earth: a mass without head or members, spawning the gray, formless efts of the prime and the grisly prototypes of terrene life.... And all earthly life, it is told, shall go back at last through the great circle of time to Ubbo-Sathla.*
> —*The Book of Eibon.*

PAUL TREGARDIS found the milky crystal in a litter of oddments from many lands and eras. He had entered the shop of the curio-dealer through an aimless impulse, with no object in mind, other than the idle distraction of eyeing and fingering a miscellany of far-gathered things. Looking desultorily about, his attention had been drawn by a dull glimmering on one of the tables; and he had extricated the queer orb-like stone from its shadowy, crowded position between an ugly little Aztec idol, the fossil egg of a dinornis, and an obscene fetish of black wood from the Niger.

The thing was about the size of a small orange and was slightly flattened at the ends, like a planet at its poles. It puzzled Tregardis, for it was not like an ordinary crystal, being cloudy and changeable, with an intermittent glowing in its heart, as if it were alternately illumed and darkened from within. Holding it to the wintry window, he studied it for awhile without being able to determine the secret of this singular and regular alternation. His puzzlement was soon complicated by a dawning sense of vague and irrecognizable familiarity, as if he had seen the thing before under circumstances that were now wholly forgotten.

He appealed to the curio-dealer, a dwarfish Hebrew with

an air of dusty antiquity, who gave the impression of being lost to commercial considerations in some web of cabalistic revery.

"Can you tell me anything about this?"

The dealer gave an indescribable, simultaneous shrug of his shoulders and his eyebrows.

"It is very old—palaegean, one might say. I can not tell you much, for little is known. A geologist found it in Greenland, beneath glacial ice, in the Miocene strata. Who knows? It may have belonged to some sorcerer of primeval Thule. Greenland was a warm, fertile region beneath the sun of Miocene times. No doubt it is a magic crystal; and a man might behold strange visions in its heart, if he looked long enough."

Tregardis was quite startled; for the dealer's apparently fantastic suggestion had brought to mind his own delvings in a branch of obscure lore; and, in particular, had recalled *The Book of Eibon,* that strangest and rarest of occult forgotten volumes, which is said to have come down through a series of manifold translations from a prehistoric original written in the lost language of Hyperborea. Tregardis, with much difficulty, had obtained the mediaeval French version —a copy that had been owned by many generations of sorcerers and Satanists—but had never been able to find the Greek manuscript from which the version was derived.

The remote, fabulous original was supposed to have been the work of a great Hyperborean wizard, from whom it had taken its name. It was a collection of dark and baleful myths, of liturgies, rituals and incantations both evil and esoteric. Not without shudders, in the course of studies that the average person would have considered more than singular, Tregardis had collated the French volume with the frightful *Necronomicon* of the mad Arab, Abdul Alhazred. He had found many correspondences of the blackest and most appalling significance, together with much forbidden data that was either unknown to the Arab or omitted by him . . . or by his translators.

Was this what he had been trying to recall, Tregardis wondered—the brief, casual reference, in *The Book of Eibon*, to a cloudy crystal that had been owned by the wizard Zon Mezzamalech, in Mhu Thulan? Of course, it was all too fantastic, too hypothetic, too incredible—but Mhu Thulan, that northern portion of ancient Hyperborea, was supposed to have corresponded roughly with modern Greenland, which had formerly been joined as a peninsula to the main continent. Could the stone in his hand, by some fabulous fortuity, be the crystal of Zon Mezzamalech?

Tregardis smiled at himself with inward irony for even conceiving the absurd notion. Such things did not occur— at least, not in present-day London; and in all likelihood, *The Book of Eibon* was sheer superstitious fantasy, anyway. Nevertheless, there was something about the crystal that continued to tease and inveigle him. He ended by purchasing it, at a fairly moderate price. The sum was named by the seller and paid by the buyer without bargaining.

With the crystal in his pocket, Paul Tregardis hastened back to his lodgings instead of resuming his leisurely saunter. He installed the milky globe on his writing-table, where it stood firmly enough on one of its oblate ends. Then, still smiling at his own absurdity, he took down the yellow parchment manuscript of *The Book of Eibon* from its place in a somewhat inclusive collection of recherché literature. He opened the vermiculated leather cover with hasps of tarnished steel, and read over to himself, translating from the archaic French as he read, the paragraph that referred to Zon Mezzamalech:

"This wizard, who was mighty among sorcerers, had found a cloudy stone, orb-like and somewhat flattened at the ends, in which

he could behold many visions of the terrene past, even to the Earth's beginning, when Ubbo-Sathla, the unbegotten source, lay vast and swollen and yeasty amid the vaporing slime. . . . But of that which he beheld, Zon Mezzamalech left little record; and people say that he vanished presently, in a way that is not known; and after him the cloudy crystal was lost."

Paul Trègardis laid the manuscript aside. Again there was something that tantalized and beguiled him, like a lost dream or a memory forfeit to oblivion. Impelled by a feeling which he did not scrutinize or question, he sat down before the table and began to stare intently into the cold, nebulous orb. He felt an expectation which, somehow, was so familiar, so permeative a part of his consciousness, that he did not even name it to himself.

Minute by minute he sat, and watched the alternate glimmering and fading of the mysterious light in the heart of the crystal. By imperceptible degrees, there stole upon him a sense of dream-like duality, both in respect to his person and his surroundings. He was still Paul Tregardis— and yet he was some one else; the room was his London apartment—and a chamber in some foreign but well-known place. And in both milieus he peered steadfastly into the same crystal.

After an interim, without surprize on the part of Tregardis, the process of re-identification became complete. He knew that he was Zon Mezzamalech, a sorcerer of Mhu Thulan, and a student of all lore anterior to his own epoch. Wise with dreadful secrets that were not known to Paul Tregardis, amateur of anthropology and the occult sciences in latter-day London, he sought by means of the milky crystal to attain an even older and more fearful knowledge.

He had acquired the stone in dubitable ways, from a more than sinister source. It was unique and without fellow in any land or time. In its depths, all former years, all things that had ever been, were supposedly mirrored, and would reveal themselves to the patient visionary. And through the crystal, Zon Mezzamalech had dreamt to recover the wisdom of the gods who died before the Earth was born. They had passed to the lightless void, leaving their lore inscribed upon tablets of ultra-stellar stone; and the tablets were guarded in the primal mire by the formless, idiotic demiurge, Ubbo-Sathla. Only by means of the crystal could he hope to find and read the tablets.

For the first time, he was making trial of the globe's reputed virtues. About him an ivory-panelled chamber, filled with his magic books and paraphernalia, was fading slowly from his consciousness. Before him, on a table of some dark Hyperborean wood that had been graven with grotesque ciphers, the crystal appeared to swell and deepen, and in its filmy depth he beheld a swift and broken swirling of dim scenes, fleeting like the bubbles of a millrace. As if he looked upon an actual world, cities, forests, mountains, seas and meadows flowed beneath him, lightening and darkening as with the passage of days and nights in some weirdly accelerated stream of time.

Zon Mezzamalech had forgotten Paul Tregardis—had lost the remembrance of his own entity and his own surroundings in Mhu Thulan. Moment by moment, the flowing vision in the crystal became more definite and distinct, and the orb itself deepened till he grew giddy, as if he were peering from an insecure height into some never-fathomed abyss. He knew that time was racing backward in the crystal, was unrolling for him the pageant of all past days; but a strange alarm had seized him, and he feared to gaze longer. Like one who has nearly fallen from a precipice, he caught himself with a violent start and drew back from the mystic orb.

Again, to his gaze, the enormous whirling world into which he had peered was a small and cloudy crystal on his rune-wrought table in Mhu Thulan. Then, by degrees, it seemed that the great room with sculptured panels of mammoth ivory was narrowing to another and dingier place; and Zon Mezzamalech, losing his preternatural wisdom and sorcerous power, went back by a weird regression into Paul Tregardis.

And yet not wholly, it seemed, was he able to return. Tregardis, dazed and wondering, found himself before the writing-table on which he had set the oblate sphere. He felt the confusion of one who has dreamt and has not yet fully awakened from the dream. The room puzzled him vaguely, as if something were wrong with its size and furnishings; and his remembrance of purchasing the crystal from a curio-dealer was oddly and discrepantly mingled with an impression that he had acquired it in a very different manner.

He felt that something very strange had happened to him when he peered into the crystal; but just what it was he could not seem to recollect. It had left him in the sort of psychic muddlement that follows a debauch of hashish. He assured himself that he was Paul Tregardis, that he lived on a certain street in London, that the year was 1933; but such commonplace verities had somehow lost their meaning and their validity; and everything about him was shadow-like and insubstantial. The very walls seemed to waver like smoke; the people in the streets were phantoms of phantoms; and he himself was a lost shadow, a wandering echo of something long forgot.

He resolved that he would not repeat his experiment of crystal-gazing. The effects were too unpleasant and equivocal. But the very next day, by an unreasoning impulse to which he yielded almost mechanically, without reluctation, he found himself seated before the misty orb. Again he became the sorcerer Zon Mezzamalech in Mhu Thulan; again he dreamt to retrieve the wisdom of the antemundane gods; again he drew back from the deepening crystal with the terror of one who fears to fall; and once more—but doubtfully and dimly, like a failing wraith—he was Paul Tregardis.

Three times did Tregardis repeat the experience on successive days; and each time his own person and the world about him became more tenuous and confused than before. His sensations were those of a dreamer who is on the verge of waking; and London itself was unreal as the lands that slip from the dreamer's ken, receding in filmy mist and cloudy light. Beyond it all, he felt the looming and crowding of vast imageries, alien but half familiar. It was as if the fantasmagoria of time and space were dissolving about him, to reveal some veritable reality—or another dream of space and time.

There came, at last, the day when he sat down before the crystal—and did not return as Paul Tregardis. It was the day when Zon Mezzamalech, boldly disregarding certain evil and portentous warnings, resolved to overcome his curious fear of falling bodily into the visionary world that he beheld—a fear that had hitherto prevented him from following the backward stream of time for any distance. He must, he assured himself, conquer his fear if he were ever to see and read the lost tablets of the gods. He had beheld nothing more than a few fragments of the years of Mhu Thulan immediately posterior to the present —the years of his own lifetime; and there were inestimable cycles between these years and the Beginning.

Again, to his gaze, the crystal deepened immeasurably, with scenes and happenings that flowed in a retrograde stream. Again the magic ciphers of the dark table faded from his ken, and the sorcerously carven walls of his chamber melted into less than dream. Once more he grew giddy with an awful vertigo as he bent above the swirling and milling of the terrible gulfs of time in the world-like orb. Fearfully, in spite of his resolution, he would have drawn away; but he had looked and leaned too long. There was a sense of abysmal falling, a suction as of ineluctable winds, of maelstroms that bore him down through fleet unstable visions of his own past life into antenatal years and dimensions. He seemed to endure the pangs of an inverse dissolution; and then he was no longer Zon Mezzamalech, the wise and learned watcher of the crystal, but an actual part of the weirdly racing stream that ran back to reattain the Beginning.

He seemed to live unnumbered lives, to die myriad deaths, forgetting each time the death and life that had gone before. He fought as a warrior in half-legendary battles; he was a child playing in the ruins of some olden city of Mhu Thulan; he was the king who had reigned when the city was in its prime, the prophet who had foretold its building and its doom. A woman, he wept for the bygone dead in necropoli long-crumbled; an antique wizard, he muttered the rude spells of earlier sorcery; a priest of some pre-human god, he wielded the sacrificial knife in cave-temples of pillared basalt. Life by life, era by era, he retraced the long and groping cycles through which Hyperborea had risen from savagery to a high civilization.

He became a barbarian of some troglodytic tribe, fleeing from the slow, turreted ice of a former glacial age into lands illumed by the ruddy flare of perpetual volcanoes. Then, after incomputable years, he was no longer man but a man-like beast, roving in forests of giant fern and calamite, or building an uncouth nest in the boughs of mighty cycads.

Through eons of anterior sensation, of crude lust and hunger, of aboriginal terror and madness, there was someone—or something—that went ever backward in time. Death became birth, and birth was death. In a slow vision of reverse change, the earth appeared to melt away, to slough off the hills and mountains of its latter strata. Always the sun grew larger and hotter above the fuming swamps that teemed with a crasser life, with a more fulsome vegetation. And the thing that had been Paul Tregardis, that had been Zon Mezzamalech, was a part of all the monstrous devolution. It flew with the claw-tipped wings of a pterodactyl, it swam in tepid seas with the vast, winding bulk of an ichthyosaurus, it bellowed uncouthly with the armored throat of some forgotten behemoth to the huge moon that burned through Liassic mists.

At length, after eons of immemorial brutehood, it became one of the lost serpent-men who reared their cities of black gneiss and fought their venomous wars in the world's first continent. It walked undulously in ante-human streets, in strange crooked vaults; it peered at primeval stars from high, Babelian towers; it bowed with hissing litanies to great serpent-idols. Through years and ages of the ophidian era it returned, and was a thing that crawled in the ooze, that had not yet learned to think and dream and build. And the time came when there was no longer a continent, but only a vast, chaotic marsh, a sea of slime, without limit or horizon, that seethed with a blind writhing of amorphous vapors.

There, in the gray beginning of Earth, the formless mass that was Ubbo-Sathla reposed amid the slime and the vapors. Headless, without organs or members, it sloughed from its oozy sides, in a slow, ceaseless wave, the amebic forms that were the archetypes of earthly life. Horrible it was, if there had been aught to apprehend the horror; and loathsome, if there had been any to feel loathing. About it, prone or tilted in the mire, there lay the mighty tablets of star-quarried stone that were writ with the inconceivable wisdom of the premundane gods.

And there, to the goal of a forgotten search, was drawn the thing that had been—or would sometime be—Paul Tregardis and Zon Mezzamalech. Becoming a shapeless eft of the prime, it crawled sluggishly and obliviously across the fallen tablets of the gods, and fought and ravened blindly with the other spawn of Ubbo-Sathla.

Of Zon Mezzamalech and his vanishing, there is no mention anywhere, save the brief passage in *The Book of Eibon*. Concerning Paul Tregardis, who also disappeared, there was a curt notice in several London papers. No one seems to have known anything about him: he is gone as if he had never been; and the crystal, presumably, is gone too. At least, no one has found it.

INTERPLANETARIES

THE MONSTER OF THE PROPHECY

A DISMAL, fog-dank afternoon was turning into a murky twilight when Theophilus Alvor paused on Brooklyn Bridge to peer down at the dim river with a shudder of sinister surmise. He was wondering how it would feel to cast himself into the chill, turbid waters, and whether he could summon up the necessary courage for an act which, he persuaded himself, was now becoming inevitable as well as laudable. He felt that he was too weary, sick and disheartened to go on with the evil dream of existence.

From any human standpoint, there was doubtless abundant reason for Alvor's depression. Young, and full of unquenched visions and desires, he had come to Brooklyn from an up-state village three months before, hoping to find a publisher for his writings; but his old-fashioned classic verses, in spite (or because) of their high imaginative fire, had been unanimously rejected both by magazines and book-firms. Though Alvor had lived frugally and had chosen lodgings so humble as almost to constitute the proverbial poetic garret, the small sum of his savings was now exhausted. He was not only quite penniless, but his clothes were so worn as to be no longer presentable in editorial offices, and the soles of his shoes were becoming rapidly non-existent from the tramping he had done. He had not eaten for days, and his last meal, like the several preceding ones, had been at the expense of his soft-hearted Irish landlady.

For more reasons than one, Alvor would have preferred another death than that of drowning. The foul and icy waters were not inviting from an esthetic viewpoint; and in spite of all he had heard to the contrary, he did not believe that such a death could be anything but disagreeable and painful. By choice he would have selected a sovereign Oriental opiate, whose insidious slumber would have led through a realm of gorgeous dreams to the gentle night of an ultimate oblivion; or, failing this, a deadly poison of merciful swiftness. But such Lethean media are not readily obtainable by a man with an empty purse.

Damning his own lack of forethought in not reserving enough money for such an eventuation, Alvor shuddered on the twilight bridge, and looked at the dismal waters, and then at the no less dismal fog through which the troubled lights of the city had begun to break. And then, through the instinctive habit of a country-bred person who is also imaginative and beauty-seeking, he looked at the heavens above the city to see if any stars were visible. He thought of his recent *Ode to Antares*, which, unlike his earlier productions, was written in *vers libre* and had a strong modernistic irony mingled with its planturous lyricism. It had, however, proved as unsalable as the rest of his poems. Now, with a sense of irony far more bitter than that which he had put into his ode, he looked for the ruddy spark of Antares itself, but was unable to find it in the sodden sky. His gaze and his thoughts returned to the river.

"There is no need for that, my young friend," said a voice at his elbow. Alvor was startled not only by the words and by the clairvoyance they betrayed, but also by something that was unanalyzably strange in the tones of the voice that uttered them. The tones were both refined and authoritative; but in them there was a quality which, for lack of more precise words or imagery, he could think of only as metallic and unhuman. While his mind wrestled with swift-born unseizable fantasies, he turned to look at the stranger who had accosted him.

The man was neither uncommonly nor disproportionately tall; and he was modishly dressed, with a long overcoat and top hat. His features were not unusual, from what could be seen of them in the dusk, except for his full-lidded and burning eyes, like those of some nyctalopic animal. But from him there emanated a palpable sense of things that were inconceivably strange and outre and remote—a sense that was more patent, more insistent than any impression of mere form and odor and sound could have been, and which was well-nigh tactual in its intensity.

"I repeat," continued the man, "that there is no necessity for you to drown yourself in that river. A vastly different fate can be yours, if you choose. . . . In the meanwhile, I shall be honored and delighted if you will accompany me to my house, which is not far away."

In a daze of astonishment preclusive of all analytical thought, or even of any clear cognizance of where he was going or what was happening, Alvor followed the stranger for several blocks in the swirling fog. Hardly knowing how he had come there, he found himself in the library of an old house which must in its time have had considerable pretensions to aristocratic dignity, for the paneling, carpet and furniture were all antique and were both rare and luxurious.

The poet was left alone for a few minutes in the library. Then his host reappeared and led him to a dining-room where an excellent meal for two had been brought in from a neighboring restaurant. Alvor, who was faint with inanition, ate with no attempt to conceal his ravening appetite, but noticed that the stranger made scarcely even a pretense of touching his own food. With a manner preoccupied and distrait, the man sat opposite Alvor, giving no more ostensible heed to his guest than the ordinary courtesies of a host required.

"We will talk now," said the stranger, when Alvor had finished. The poet, whose energies and mental faculties had been revived by the food, became bold enough to survey his host with a frank attempt at appraisal. He saw a man of indefinite age, whose lineaments and complexion were Caucasian, but whose nationality he was unable to determine. The eyes had lost something of their weird luminosity beneath the electric light, but nevertheless they were most remarkable, and from them there poured a sense of unearthly knowledge and power and strangeness not to be formulated by human thought or conveyed in human speech. Under his scrutiny, vague, dazzling, intricate unshapable images rose on the dim borders of the poet's mind and fell back into oblivion ere he could envisage them. Apparently without rime or reason, some lines of his *Ode to Antares* returned to him, and he found that he was repeating them over and over beneath his breath:

> "*Star of strange hope,*
> *Pharos beyond our desperate mire,*
> *Lord of unscalable gulfs,*
> *Lamp of unknowable life.*"

The hopeless, half-satiric yearning for another sphere which he had expressed in this poem, haunted his thoughts with a weird insistence.

"Of course, you have no idea who or what I am," said the stranger, "though your poetic intuitions are groping darkly toward the secret of my identity. On my part, there is no need for me to ask you anything, since I have already learned all that there is to learn about your life, your personality, and the dismal predicament from which I am now able to offer you a means of escape. Your name is Theophilus Alvor, and you are a poet whose classic style and romantic genius are not likely to win adequate recognition in this age and land. With an inspiration more prophetic than you dream, you have written, among other masterpieces, a quite admirable *Ode to Antares*."

"How do you know all this?" cried Alvor.

"To those who have the sensory apparatus with which to perceive them, thoughts are no less audible than spoken words. I can hear your thoughts, so you will readily understand that there is nothing surprizing in my possession of more or less knowledge concerning you."

"But who are you?" exclaimed Alvor. "I have heard of people who could read the minds of others; but I did not believe that there was any human being who actually possessed such powers."

"I am not a human being," rejoined the stranger, "even though I have found it convenient to don the semblance of one for a while, just as you or another of your race might wear a masquerade costume. Permit me to introduce myself: my name, as nearly as can be conveyed in the phonetics of your world, is Vizaphmal, and I have come from a planet of the far-off mighty sun that is known to you as Antares. In my own world, I am a scientist, though the more ignorant classes look upon me as a wizard. In the course of profound experiments and researches, I have invented a device which enables me at will to visit other planets, no matter how remote in space. I have sojourned for varying intervals in more than one solar system; and I have found your world and its inhabitants so quaint and curious and monstrous that I have lingered here a little longer than I intended, because of my taste for the bizarre —a taste which is ineradicable, though no doubt reprehensible. It is now time for me to return: urgent duties call me, and I can not tarry. But there are reasons why I should like to take with me to my world a member of your race; and when I saw you on the bridge tonight, it occurred to me that you might be willing to undertake such an adventure. You are, I believe, utterly weary of the sphere in which you find yourself, since a little while ago you were ready to depart from it into the unknown dimension that you call death. I can offer you something much more agreeable and diversified than death, with a scope of sensation, a potentiality of experience beyond anything of which you have had even the faintest intimation in the poetic reveries looked upon as extravagant by your fellows."

Again and again, while listening to this long and singular address, Alvor seemed to catch in the tones of the voice that uttered it a supervening resonance, a vibration of overtones beyond the compass of a mortal throat. Though perfectly clear and correct in all details of enunciation, there was a hint of vowels and consonants not to be found in any terrestrial alphabet. However, the logical part of his mind refused to accept entirely these intimations of the supermundane; and he was now seized by the idea that the man before him was some new type of lunatic.

"Your thought is natural enough, considering the limitations of your experience," observed the stranger calmly. "However, I can easily convince you of its error by revealing myself to you in my true shape."

He made the gesture of one who throws off a garment. Alvor was blinded by an insufferable blaze of light, whose white glare, emanating in huge beams from an orb-like center, filled the entire room and seemed to pass illimitably beyond through dissolving walls. When his eyes became accustomed to the light, he saw before him a being who had no conceivable likeness to his host. This being was more than seven feet in height, and had no less than five intricately jointed arms and three legs that were equally elaborate. His head, on a long, swan-like neck, was equipped not only with visual, auditory, nasal and oral organs of unfamiliar types, but had several appendages whose use was not readily to be determined. His three eyes, obliquely set and with oval pupils, rayed forth a green phosphorescence; the mouth, or what appeared to be such, was very small and had the lines of a downward-curving crescent; the nose was rudimentary, though with finely wrought nostrils; in lieu of eyebrows, he had a triple series of semi-circular markings on his forehead, each of a different hue; and above his intellectually shapen head, above the tiny drooping ears with their complex lobes, there towered a gorgeous comb of crimson, not dissimilar in form to the crest on the helmet of a Grecian warrior. The head, the limbs and the whole body were mottled with interchanging lunes and moons of opalescent colors, never the same for a moment in their unresting flux and reflux.

Alvor had the sensation of standing on the rim of prodigious gulfs, on a new earth beneath new heavens; and the vistas of illimitable horizons, fraught with the multitudinous terror and manifold beauty of an imagery no human eye had ever seen, hovered and wavered and flashed upon him with the same unstable fluorescence as the lunar variegations of the body at which he stared with such stupefaction. Then, in a little while, the strange light seemed to withdraw upon itself, retracting all its beams to a common center, and faded in a whirl of darkness. When this darkness had cleared away, he saw once more the form of his host, in conventional garb, with a slight ironic smile about his lips.

"Do you believe me now?" Vizaphmal queried.

"Yes, I believe you."

"Are you willing to accept my offer?"

"I accept it." A thousand questions were forming in Alvor's mind, but he dared not ask them. Divining these questions, the stranger spoke as follows:

"You wonder how it is possible for me to assume a human

shape. I assure you, it is merely a matter of taking thought. My mental images are infinitely clearer and stronger than those of any earth-being, and by conceiving myself as a man, I can appear to you and your fellows as such.

"You wonder also as to the modus operandi of my arrival on earth. This I shall now show and explain to you, if you will follow me."

He led the way to an upper story of the old mansion. Here, in a sort of attic, beneath a large skylight in the southward-sloping roof, there stood a curious mechanism, wrought of a dark metal which Alvor could not identify. It was a tall, complicated framework with many transverse bars and two stout upright rods terminating at each end in a single heavy disk. These disks seemed to form the main portions of the top and bottom.

"Put your hand between the bars," commanded Alvor's host.

Alvor tried to obey this command, but his fingers met with an adamantine obstruction, and he realized that the intervals of the bars were filled with an unknown material clearer than glass or crystal.

"You behold here," said Vizaphmal, "an invention which, I flatter myself, is quite unique anywhere this side of the galactic suns. The disks at top and bottom are a vibratory device with a twofold use; and no other material than that of which they are wrought would have the same properties, the same achievable rates of vibration. When you and I have locked ourselves within the framework, as we shall do anon, a few revolutions of the lower disk will have the effect of isolating us from our present environment, and we shall find ourselves in the midst of what is known to you as space, or ether. The vibrations of the upper disk, which we shall then employ, are of such potency as to annihilate space itself in any direction desired. Space, like everything else in the atomic universe, is subject to laws of integration and dissolution. It was merely a matter of finding the vibrational power that would effect this dissolution; and, by untiring research, by ceaseless experimentation, I located and isolated the rare metallic elements which, in a state of union, are capable of this power."

While the poet was pondering all he had seen and heard, Vizaphmal touched a tiny knob, and one side of the framework swung open. He then turned off the electric light in the garret, and simultaneously with its extinction, a ruddy glow filled the interior of the machine, serving to illumine all the parts, but leaving the room around it in darkness. Standing beside his invention, Vizaphmal looked at the skylight, and Alvor followed his gaze. The fog had cleared away and many stars were out, including the red gleam of Antares, now high in the south. The stranger was evidently making certain preliminary calculations, for he moved the machine a little after peering at the star, and adjusted a number of fine wires in the interior, as if he were tuning some stringed instrument.

At last he turned to Alvor.

"Everything is now in readiness," he announced. "If you are still prepared to accompany me, we will take our departure."

Alvor was conscious of an unexpected coolness and fortitude as he answered: "I am at your service." The unparalleled occurrences and disclosures of the evening, the wellnigh undreamable prospect of a plunge across untold immensitude, such as no man had been privileged to dare before, had really benumbed his imagination, and he was unable at the moment to conceive the true awesomeness of what he had undertaken.

Vizaphmal indicated the place where Alvor was to stand in the machine. The poet entered, and assumed a position between one of the upright rods and the side, opposite Vizaphmal. He found that a layer of the transparent material was interposed between his feet and the large disk in which the rods were based. No sooner had he stationed himself, than, with a celerity and an utter silence that were uncanny, the framework closed upon itself with hermetic tightness, till the jointure where it had opened was no longer detectable.

"We are now in a sealed compartment," explained the Antarean, "into which nothing can penetrate. Both the dark metal and the crystalline are substances that refuse the passage of heat and cold, of air and ether, or of any known cosmic ray, with the one exception of light itself, which is admitted by the clear metal."

When he ceased, Alvor realized that they were walled about with an insulating silence utter and absolute as that of some intersidereal void. The traffic in the streets without, the rumbling and roaring and jarring of the great city, so loud a minute before, might have been a million miles away in some other world for all that he could hear or feel of its vibration.

In the red glow that pervaded the machine, emanating from a source he could not discover, the poet gazed at his companion. Vizaphmal had now resumed his Antarean form, as if all necessity for a human disguise were at an end, and he towered above Alvor, glorious with inter-merging zones of fluctuant colors, where hues the poet had not seen in any spectrum were simultaneous or intermittent with flaming blues and coruscating emeralds and amethysts and fulgurant purples and vermilions and saffrons. Lifting one of his five arms, which terminated in two finger-like appendages with many joints all capable of bending in any direction, the Antarean touched a thin wire that was stretched overhead between the two rods. He plucked at this wire like a musician at a lute-string, and from it there emanated a single clear note higher in pitch than anything Alvor had ever heard. Its sheer unearthly acuity caused a shudder of anguish to run through the poet, and he could scarcely have borne a prolongation of the sound, which, however, ceased in a moment and was followed by a much more endurable humming and singing noise which seemed to arise at his feet. Looking down, he saw that the large disk at the bottom of the medial rods had begun to revolve. This revolution was slow at first, but rapidly increased in its rate, till he could no longer see the movement; and the singing sound became agonizingly sweet and high till it pierced his senses like a knife.

Vizaphamal touched a second wire, and the revolution of the disk was brought abruptly to an end. Alvor felt an unspeakable relief at the cessation of the torturing music.

"We are now in etheric space," the Antarean declared. "Look out, if you so desire."

Alvor peered through the interstices of the dark metal, and saw around and above and below them the unlimited blackness of cosmic night and the teeming of uncountable trillions of stars. He had a sensation of frightful and deadly vertigo, and staggered like a drunken man as he tried to keep himself from falling against the side of the machine.

Vizaphmal plucked at a third wire, but this time Alvor was not aware of any sound. Something that was like an electric shock, and also like the crushing impact of a heavy blow, descended upon his head and shook him to the soles of his feet. Then he felt as if his tissues were being stabbed by innumerable needles of fire, and then that he was being torn apart in a thousand fragments, bone by bone, muscle by muscle, vein by vein, and nerve by nerve, on some invisible rack. He swooned and fell huddled in a corner of the machine, but his unconsciousness was not altogether complete. He seemed to be drowning beneath an infinite sea of darkness, beneath the accumulation of shoreless gulfs, and above this sea, so far away that he lost it again and again, there thrilled a supernal melody, sweet as the singing of sirens or the fabled music of the spheres, together with an insupportable dissonance like the shattering of all the battlements of time. He thought that all his nerves had been elongated to an immense distance, where the outlying parts of himself were being tortured in the oubliettes of fantastic inquisitions by the use of instruments of percussion, diabolically vibrant, that were somehow identified with certain of his own body-cells. Once he thought that he saw Vizaphmal standing a million leagues remote on the shore of an alien planet, with a sky of soaring many-colored flame behind him and the night of all the universe rippling gently at his feet like a submissive ocean. Then he lost the vision, and the intervals of the far unearthly music became more prolonged, and at last he could not hear it at all, nor could he feel any longer the torturing of his remote nerve-ends. The gulf deepened above him, and he sank through eons of darkness and emptiness to the very nadir of oblivion.

Alvor's return to consciousness was even more slow and gradual than his descent into Lethe had been. Still lying at the bottom of a shoreless and boundless night, he became aware of an unidentifiable odor with which in some way the sense of ardent warmth was associated. This odor changed incessantly, as if it were composed of many diverse ingredients, each of which predominated in turn. Myrrhlike and mystic in the beginning as the fumes of an antique altar, it assumed the heavy languor of unimaginable flowers, the sharp sting of vaporizing chemicals unknown to science, the smell of exotic water and exotic earth, and then a medley of other elements that conveyed no suggestion of anything whatever, except of evolutionary realms and ranges that were beyond all human experience or calculation. For a while he lived and was awake only in his sensory response to this potpourri of odors; then the awareness of his own corporeal being came back to him through tactual sensations of an unusual order, which he did not at first recognize as being within himself, but which seemed to be those of a foreign entity in some other dimension, with whom he was connected across unbridgeable gulfs by a nexus of gossamer tenuity. This entity, he thought, was reclining on a material of great softness, into which he sank with a supreme and leaden indolence and a feeling of sheer bodily weight that held him utterly motionless. Then, floating along the ebon cycles of the void, this being came with ineffable slowness toward Alvor, and at last, by no perceptible transition, by no breach of physical logic or mental congruity, was incorporate with him. Then a tiny light, like a star burning all alone in the center of infinitude, began to dawn far off; and it drew nearer and nearer and grew larger and larger till it turned the black void to a dazzling luminescence, to a many-tinted glory that smote full upon Alvor.

He found that he was lying with wide-open eyes on a huge couch, in a sort of pavilion consisting of a low and elliptical dome supported on double rows of diagonally fluted pillars. He was quite naked, though a sheet of some thin and pale yellow fabric had been thrown across his lower limbs. He saw at a glance, even though his brain-centers were still half benumbed as by the action of some opiate, that this fabric was not the product of any terrestrial loom. Beneath his body, the couch was covered with gray and purple stuffs, but whether they were made of feathers, fur or cloth he was quite uncertain, for they suggested all three of these materials. They were very thick and resilient, and accounted for the sense of extreme softness underneath him that had marked his return from the swoon. The couch itself stood higher above the floor than an ordinary bed, and was also longer, and in his half-narcotized condition this troubled Alvor even more than other aspects of his situation which were far less normal and explicable.

Amazement grew upon him as he looked about with reviving faculties, for all that he saw and smelt and touched was totally foreign and unaccountable. The floor of the pavilion was wrought in a geometric marquetry of ovals, rhomboids and equilaterals, in white, black and yellow metals that no earthly mine had ever disclosed; and the pillars were of the same three metals, regularly alternating. The dome alone was entirely of yellow. Not far from the couch, there stood on a squat tripod a dark and wide-mouthed vessel from which poured an opalescent vapor. Some one standing behind it, invisible through the cloud of gorgeous fumes, was fanning the vapor toward Alvor. He recognized it as the source of the myrrh-like odor that had first troubled his reanimating senses. It was quite agreeable but was borne away from him again and again by gusts of hot wind which brought into the pavilion a mixture of perfumes that were both sweet and acrid and were altogether novel. Looking between the pillars, he saw the monstrous heads of towering blossoms with pagoda-like tiers of sultry, sullen petals, and beyond them a terraced landscape of low hills of mauve and nacarat soil, extending toward a horizon incredibly remote, till they rose and rose against the heavens. Above all this was a whitish sky, filled with a blinding radiation of intense light from a sun that was now hidden by the dome. Alvor's eyes began to ache, the odors disturbed and oppressed him, and he was possessed by a terrible dubiety and perplexity, amid which he remembered vaguely his meeting with Vizaphmal, and the events preceding his swoon. He was unbearably nervous, and for some time all his ideas and sensations took on the painful disorder and irrational fears of incipient delirium.

A figure stepped from behind the veering vapors and approached the couch. It was Vizaphmal, who bore in one of his five hands the large thin circular fan of bluish metal he had been using. He was holding in another hand a tubular cup, half full of an erubescent liquid.

"Drink this," he ordered, as he put the cup to Alvor's lips. The liquid was so bitter and fiery that Alvor could swallow it only in sips, between periods of gasping and coughing. But once he had gotten it down, his brain cleared with celerity and all his sensations were soon comparatively normal.

"Where am I?" he asked. His voice sounded very strange and unfamiliar to him, and its effect bordered upon ventriloquism—which, as he afterward learned, was due to certain peculiarities of the atmospheric medium.

"You are on my country estate, in Ulphalor, a kingdom which occupies the whole northern hemisphere of Satabbor, the inmost planet of Sanarda, that sun which is called Antares in your world. You have been unconscious for three of our days, a result which I anticipated, knowing the profound shock your nervous system would receive from the experience through which you have passed. However, I do not think you will suffer any permanent illness or inconvenience; and I have just now administered to you a sovereign drug which will aid in the adjustment of your nerves and your corporeal functions to the novel conditions under which you are to live henceforward. I employed the opalescent vapor to arouse you from your swoon, when I deemed that it had become safe and wise to do this. The vapor is produced by the burning of an aromatic seaweed, and is magisterial in its restorative effect."

Alvor tried to grasp the full meaning of this information, but his brain was still unable to receive anything more than a mélange of impressions that were totally new and obscure and outlandish. As he pondered the words of Vizaphmal, he saw that rays of bright light had fallen between the columns and were creeping across the floor. Then the rim of a vast ember-colored sun descended below the rim of the dome and he felt an overwhelming, but somehow not insupportable, warmth. His eyes no longer ached, not even in the direct beams of this luminary; nor did the perfumes irritate him, as they had done for a while.

"I think," said Vizaphmal, "that you may now arise. It is afternoon, and there is much for you to learn, and much to be done."

Alvor threw off the thin covering of yellow cloth, and sat up, with his legs hanging over the edge of the couch.

"But my clothing?" he queried.

"You will need none in our climate. No one has ever worn anything of the sort in Satabbor."

Alvor digested this idea, and though he was slightly disconcerted, he made up his mind that he would accustom himself to whatever should be required of him. Anyway, the lack of his usual habiliments was far from disagreeable in the dry, sultry air of this new world.

He slid from the couch to the floor, which was nearly five feet below him, and took several steps. He was not weak or dizzy, as he had half expected, but all his movements were characterized by the same sense of extreme bodily weight of which he had been dimly aware while still in a semi-conscious condition.

"The world in which you now dwell is somewhat larger than your own," explained Vizaphmal, "and the force of gravity is proportionately greater. Your weight has been increased by no less than a third; but I think you will soon become habituated to this, as well as to the other novelties of your situation."

Motioning the poet to follow him, he led the way through that portion of the pavilion which had been behind Alvor's head as he lay on the couch. A spiral bridge of ascending stairs ran from this pavilion to a much larger pile where numerous wings and annexes of the same aerial architecture of domes and columns flared from a central edifice with a circular wall and many thin spires. Below the bridge, about the pavilion, and around the whole edifice above, were gardens of trees and flowers that caused Alvor to recall the things he had seen during his one experiment with hashish. The foliation of the trees was either very fine and hair-like, or else it consisted of huge, semi-globular and discoid forms depending from horizontal branches and suggesting a novel union of fruit and leaf. Almost all colors, even green, were shown in the bark and foliage of these trees. The flowers were mainly similar to those Alvor had seen from the pavilion, but there were others of a short, puffy-stemmed variety, with no trace of leaves, and with malignant purple-black heads full of crimson mouths, which swayed a little even when there was no wind. There were oval pools and meandering streams of a dark water with irisated glints all through this garden, which, with the columnar edifice, occupied the middle of a small plateau.

As Alvor followed his guide along the bridge, a perspective of hills and plains all marked out in geometric diamonds and squares and triangles, with a large lake or inland sea in their midst, was revealed momently. Far in the distance, more than a hundred leagues away, were the gleaming domes and towers of some baroque city, toward which the enormous orb of the sun was now declining. When he looked at this sun and saw the whole extent of its diameter for the first time, he felt an overpowering thrill of imaginative awe and wonder and exultation at the thought that it was identical with the red star to which he had addressed in another world the half-lyric, half-ironic lines of his ode.

At the end of the spiral bridge, they came to a second and more spacious pavilion, in which stood a high table with many seats attached to it by means of curving rods. Table and chairs were of the same material, a light, grayish metal. As they entered this pavilion, two strange beings appeared and bowed before Vizaphmal. They resembled the scientist in their organic structure, but were not so tall, and their coloring was very drab and dark, with no hint of opalescence. By certain bizarre indications Alvor surmised that the two beings were of different sexes.

"You are right," said Vizaphmal, reading his thoughts. "These persons are a male and female of the two inferior sexes called Abbars, who constitute the workers, as well as the breeders, of our world. There are two superior sexes, who are sterile, and who form the intellectual, esthetic and ruling classes, to whom I belong. We call ourselves the Alphads. The Abbars are more numerous, but we hold them in close subjection; and even though they are our parents as well as our slaves, the ideas of filial piety which prevail in your world would be regarded as truly singular by us. We supervise their breeding, so that the due proportion of Abbars and Alphads may be maintained, and the character of the progeny is determined by the injection of certain serums at the time of conceiving. We ourselves, though sterile, are capable of what you call love, and our amorous delights are more complex than yours in their nature."

He now turned and addressed the two Abbars. The phonetic forms and combinations that issued from his lips were unbelievably different from those of the scholarly English in which he had spoken to Alvor. There were strange gutturals and linguals and oddly prolonged vowels which Alvor, for all his subsequent attempts to learn the language, could never quite approximate and which argued a basic divergence in the structure of the vocal organs of Vizaphmal from that of his own.

Bowing till their heads almost touched the floor, the two Abbars disappeared among the columns in a wing of the building and soon returned, carrying long trays on which were unknown foods and beverages in utensils of unearthly forms.

"Be seated," said Vizaphmal. The meal that followed was far from unpleasant, and the foodstuffs were quite palatable, though Alvor was not sure whether they were meats or vegetables. He learned that they were really both, for his host explained that they were the prepared fruits of plants which were half animal in their cellular composition and characteristics. These plants grew wild, and were hunted with the same care that would be required in hunting dangerous beasts, on account of their mobile branches and the poisonous darts with which they were armed. The two beverages were a pale, colorless wine with an acrid flavor, made from a root, and a dusky, sweetish liquid, the natural water of this world. Alvor noticed that the water had a saline after-taste.

"The time has now come," announced Vizaphmal at the end of the meal, "to explain frankly the reason why I have brought you here. We will now adjourn to that portion of my home which you would term a laboratory, or workshop, and which also includes my library."

They passed through several pavilions and winding colonnades, and reached the circular wall at the core of the edifice. Here a high narrow door, engraved with heteroclitic ciphers, gave admission to a huge room without windows, lit by a yellow glow whose cause was not ascertainable.

"The walls and ceiling are lined with a radio-active substance," said Vizaphmal, "which affords this illumination. The vibrations of this substance are also highly stimulating to the processes of thought."

Alvor looked about him at the room, which was filled with alembics and cupels and retorts and sundry other scientific mechanisms, all of unfamiliar types and materials. He could not even surmise their use. Beyond them, in a corner, he saw the apparatus of intersecting bars, with the two heavy disks, in which he and Vizaphmal had made their passage through etheric space. Around the walls there were a number of deep shelves, laden with great rolls like the volumes of the ancients.

Vizaphmal selected one of these rolls, and started to unfurl it. It was four feet wide, was gray in color, and was closely written with many columns of dark violet and maroon characters that ran horizontally instead of up and down.

"It will be necessary," said Vizaphmal, "to tell you a few facts regarding the history, religion and intellectual temper of our world, before I read to you the singular prophecy contained in one of the columns of this ancient chronicle.

"We are a very old people, and the beginnings, or even the first maturity of our civilization, antedate the appearance of the lowliest forms of life on your earth. Religious sentiment and the veneration of the past have always been dominant factors among us, and have shaped our history to an amazing extent. Even today, the whole mass of the Abbars and the majority of the Alphads are immersed in superstition, and the veriest details of quotidian life are regulated by sacerdotal law. A few scientists and thinkers, like myself, are above all such puerilities; but, strictly between you and me, the Alphads, for all their superior and highly aristocratic traits, are mainly the victims of arrested development in this regard. They have cultivated the epicurean and esthetic side of life to a high degree, they are accomplished artists, sybarites and able administrators or politicians; but, intellectually, they have not freed themselves from the chains of a sterile pantheism and an all too prolific priesthood.

"Several cycles ago, in what might be called an early period of our history, the worship of all our sundry deities was at its height. There was at this time a veritable eruption, a universal plague of prophets, who termed themselves the voices of the gods, even as similarly-minded persons have done in your world. Each of these prophets made his own especial job-lot of predictions, often quite minutely worked out and elaborate, and sometimes far from lacking in imaginative quality. A number of these prophecies have since been fulfilled to the letter, which, as you may well surmise, has helped enormously in confirming the hold of religion. However, between ourselves, I suspect that their fulfilment has had behind it more or less of a shrewd instrumentality, supplied by those who could profit therefrom in one way or another.

"There was one vates, Abbolechiolor by name, who was even more fertile-minded and long-winded than his fellows. I shall now translate to you, from the volumen I have just unrolled, a prediction that he made in the year 299 of the cycle of Sargholoth, the third of the seven epochs into which our known history has been subdivided. It runs thus:

"When, for the second time following this prediction, the two outmost moons of Satabbor shall be simultaneously darkened in a total eclipse by the third and innermost moon, and when the dim night of this occultation shall have worn away in the dawn, a mighty wizard shall appear in the city of Sarpoulom, before the palace of the kings of

Ulphalor, accompanied by a most unique and unheard-of monster with two arms, two legs, two eyes and a white skin. And he that then rules in Ulphalor shall be deposed ere noon of this day, and the wizard shall be enthroned in his place, to reign as long as the white monster shall abide with him."

Vizaphmal paused, as if to give Alvor a chance to cogitate the matters that had been presented to him. Then, while his three eyes assumed a look of quizzical sharpness and shrewdness, he continued:

"Since the promulgation of this prophecy, there has already been one total eclipse of our two outer moons by the inner one. And, according to all the calculations of our astronomers, in which I can find no possible flaw, a second similar eclipse is now about to take place—in fact, it is due this very night. If Abbolechiolor was truly inspired, tomorrow morn is the time when the prophecy will be fulfilled. However, I decided some while ago that its fulfilment should not be left to chance; and one of my purposes in designing the mechanism with which I visited your world, was to find a monster would would meet the specifications of Abbolechiolor. No creature of this anomalous kind has ever been known, or even fabled, to exist in Satabbor; and I made a thorough search of many remote and outlying planets without being able to obtain what I required. In some of these worlds there were monsters of very uncommon types, with an almost unlimited number of visual organs and limbs; but the variety to which you belong, with only two eyes, two arms and two legs, must indeed be rare throughout the infra-galactic universe, since I have not discovered it in any other planet than your own.

"I am sure that you now conceive the project I have long nurtured. You and I will appear at dawn in Sarpoulom, the capital of Ulphalor, whose domes and towers you saw this afternoon far off on the plain. Because of the celebrated prophecy, and the publicly known calculations regarding the imminence of a second two-fold eclipse, a great crowd will doubtless be gathered before the palace of the kings to await whatever shall occur. Akkiel, the present king, is by no means popular, and your advent in company with me, who am widely famed as a wizard, will be the signal for his dethronement. I shall then be ruler in his place, even as Abbolechiolor has so thoughtfully predicted. The holding of supreme temporal power in Ulphalor is not undesirable, even for one who is wise and learned and above most of the vanities of life, as I am. When this honor has devolved upon my unworthy shoulders, I shall be able to offer you, as a reward for your miraculous aid, an existence of rare and sybaritic luxury, of rich and varied sensation, such as you can hardly have imagined. It is true, no doubt, that you will be doomed to a certain loneliness among us: you will always be looked upon as a monster, a portentous anomaly; but such, I believe was your lot in the world where I found you and where you were about to cast yourself into a most unpleasant river. There, as you have learned, all poets are regarded as no less anomalous than double-headed snakes or five-legged calves."

Alvor had listened to this speech in manifold and ever-increasing amazement. Toward the end, when there was no longer any doubt concerning Vizaphmal's intention, he felt the sting of a bitter and curious irony at the thought of the role he was destined to play. However, he could do no less than admit the cogency of Vizaphmal's final argument.

"I trust," said Vizaphmal, "that I have not injured your feelings by my frankness, or by the position in which I am about to place you."

"Oh, no, not at all," Alvor hastened to assure him.

"In that case, we shall soon begin our journey to Sarpoulom, which will take all night. Of course, we could make the trip in the flash of an instant with my space-annihilator, or in a few minutes with one of the air-machines that have long been employed among us. But I intend to use a very old-fashioned mode of conveyance for the occasion, so that we will arrive in the proper style, at the proper time, and also that you may enjoy our scenery and view the double eclipse at leisure."

When they emerged from the windowless room, the colonnades and pavilions without were full of a rosy light, though the sun was still an hour above the horizon. This, Alvor learned, was the usual prelude of a Satabborian sunset. He and Vizaphmal watched while the whole landscape before them became steeped in the ruddy glow, which deepened through shades of cinnabar and ruby to a rich garnet by the time Antares had begun to sink from sight. When the huge orb had disappeared, the intervening lands took on a fiery amethyst, and tall auroral flames of a hundred hues shot upward to the zenith from the sunken sun. Alvor was spellbound by the glory of the spectacle.

Turning from this magnificent display at an unfamiliar sound, he saw that a singular vehicle had been brought by the Abbars to the steps of the pavilion in which they stood. It was more like a chariot than anything else, and was drawn by three animals undreamt of in human fable or heraldry. These animals were black and hairless, their bodies were exteremely long, each of them had eight legs and a forked tail, and their whole aspect, including their flat, venomous, triangular heads, was uncomfortably serpentine. A series of green and scarlet wattles hung from their throats and bellies, and semi-translucent membranes, erigible at will, were attached to their sides.

"You behold," Vizaphmal informed Alvor, "the traditional conveyance that has been used since time immemorial by all orthodox wizards in Ulphalor. These creatures are called *orpods,* and they are among the swiftest of our mammalian serpents."

He and Alvor seated themselves in the vehicle. Then the three *orpods,* who had no reins in their complicated harness, started off at a word of command on a spiral road that ran from Vizaphmal's home to the plain beneath. As they went, they erected the membranes at their sides and soon attained an amazing speed.

Now, for the first time, Alvor saw the three moons of Satabbor, which had risen opposite the afterglow. They were all large, especially the innermost one, a perceptible warmth was shed by their pink rays, and their combined illumination was nearly as clear and bright as that of a terrestrial day.

The land through which Vizaphmal and the poet now passed was uninhabited, in spite of its nearness to Sarpoulom, and they met no one. Alvor learned that the terraces he had seen upon awaking were not the work of intelligent beings, as he had thought, but were a natural formation of the hills. Vizaphmal had chosen this location for his home because of the solitude and privacy, so desirable for the scientific experiments to which he had devoted himself.

After they had traversed many leagues, they began to pass occasional houses, of a like structure to that of Vizaphmal's. Then the road meandered along the rim of cultivated fields, which Alvor recognized as the source of the geometric divisions he had seen from afar during the day. He was told that these fields were given mainly to the growing of root-vegetables, of a gigantic truffle, and a kind of succulent cactus, which formed the chief foods of the Abbars. The Alphads ate by choice only the meat of animals and the fruits of wild, half-animal plants, such as those with which Alvor had been served.

By midnight the three moons had drawn very close together and the second moon had begun to occlude the outermost. Then the inner moon came slowly across the others, till in an hour's time the eclipse was complete. The diminution of light was very marked, and the whole effect was now similar to that of a moonlit night on earth.

"It will be morning in a little more than two hours." said Vizaphmal, "since our nights are extremely short at this time of year. The eclipse will be over before then. But there is no need for us to hurry."

He spoke to the *orpods*, who folded their membranes and settled to a sort of trot.

Sarpoulom was now visible in the heart of the plain, and its outlines were rendered more distinct as the two hidden moons began to draw forth from the adumbration of the other. When to this triple light the ruby rays of earliest morn were added, the city loomed upon the travelers with fantastic many-storied piles of that same open type of metal architecture which the home of Vizaphmal had displayed. This architecture, Alvor found, was general throughout the land, though an older type with closed walls was occasionally to be met with, and was used altogether in the building of prisons and the inquisitions maintained by the priesthoods of the various deities.

It was an incredible vision that Alvor saw—a vision of high domes upborne on slender elongated columns, tier above tier, of airy colonnades and bridges and hanging gardens loftier than Babylon or than Babel, all tinged by the ever-changing red that accompanied and followed the Satabborian dawn, even as it had preceded the sunset.

Into this vision, along streets that were paven with the same metal as that of the buildings, Alvor and Vizaphmal were drawn by the three *orpods*.

The poet was overcome by the sense of an unimaginably old and alien and diverse life which descended upon him from these buildings. He was surprized to find that the streets were nearly deserted and that little sign of activity was manifest anywhere. A few Abbars, now and then, scuttled away in alleys or entrances at the approach of the *orpods*, and two beings of a coloration similar to that of Vizaphmal, one of whom Alvor took to be a female, issued from a colonnade and stood staring at the travelers in evident stupefaction.

When they had followed a sort of winding avenue for more than a mile, Alvor saw between and above the edifices in front of them the domes and upper tiers of a building that surpassed all the others in its extent.

"You now behold the palace of the kings of Ulphalor," his companion told him.

In a little while they emerged upon a great square that surrounded the palace. This square was crowded with the people of the city, who, as Vizaphmal had surmised, were all gathered to await the fulfilment or non-fulfilment of the prophecy of Abbolechiolor. The open galleries and arcades of the huge edifice, which rose to a height of ten stories, were also laden with watching figures. Abbars were the most plentiful element in this throng, but there were also multitudes of the gayly colored Alphads among them.

At sight of Alvor and his companion, a perceptible movement, a sort of communal shuddering which soon grew convulsive, ran through the whole assemblage in the square and along the galleries of the edifice above. Loud cries of a peculiar shrillness and harshness arose, there was a strident sound of beaten metal in the heart of the palace, like the gongs of an alarm, and mysterious lights glowed out and were extinguished in the higher stories. Clangors of unknown machines, the moan and roar and shriek of strange instruments, were audible above the clamor of the crowd, which grew more tumultuous and agitated in its motion. A way was opened for the car drawn by the three *orpods,* and Vizaphmal and Alvor soon reached the entrance of the palace.

There was an unreality about it all to Alvor, and the discomfiture he had felt in drawing upon himself the weird phosphoric gaze of ten thousand eyes, all of whom were now intent with a fearsome uncanny curiosity on every detail of his physique, was like the discomfiture of some absurd and terrible dream. The movement of the crowd had ceased, while the car was passing along the unhuman lane that had been made for it, and there was an interval of silence. Then, once more, there were babble and debate, and cries that had the accent of martial orders or summonses were caught up and repeated. The throng began to move, with a new and more concentric swirling, and the foremost ranks of Abbars and Alphads swelled like a dark and tinted wave into the colonnades of the palace. They climbed the pillars with a dreadful swift agility to the stories above, they thronged the courts and pavilions and arcades, and though a weak resistance was apparently put up by those within, there was nothing that could stem them.

Through all this clangor and clamor and tumult, Vizaphmal stood in the car with an imperturbable mien beside the poet. Soon a number of Alphads, evidently a delegation, issued from the palace and made obeisance to the wizard, whom they addressed in humble and supplicative tones.

"A revolution has been precipitated by our advent," explained Vizaphmal, "and Akkiel the king has fled. The chamberlains of the court and the high priests of all our local deities are now offering me the throne of Ulphalor. Thus the prophecy is being fulfilled to the letter. You must agree with me that the great Abbolechiolor was happily inspired."

The ceremony of Vizaphmal's enthronement was held almost immediately, in a huge hall at the core of the palace, open like all the rest of the structure, and with columns of colossal size. The throne was a great globe of azure metal, with a seat hollowed out near the top, accessible by means of a serpentine flight of stairs. Alvor, at an order issued by the wizard, was allowed to stand at the base of this globe with some of the Alphads.

The enthronement itself was quite simple. The wizard mounted the stairs, amid the silence of a multitude that had thronged the hall, and seated himself in the hollow of the great globe. Then a very tall and distinguished-looking Alphad also climbed the steps, carrying a heavy rod, one half of which was green, and the other a swart, sullen crimson, and placed this rod in the hands of Vizaphmal. Later, Alvor learned that the crimson end of this rod could emit a death-dealing ray, and the green a vibration that cured almost all the kinds of illness to which the Satabborians were subject. Thus it was more than symbolical of the twofold power of life and death with which the king had been invested.

The ceremony was now at an end, and the gathering quickly dispersed. Alvor, at the command of Vizaphmal, was installed in a suite of open apartments on the third story of the palace, at the end of many labyrinthine stairs. A dozen Abbars, who were made his personal retainers, soon came in, each carrying a different food or drink. The foods were beyond belief in their strangeness, for they included the eggs of a moth-like insect large as a plover, and the apples of a fungoid tree that grew in the craters of dead volcanoes. They were served in ewers of a white and shining mineral, upborne on legs of fantastic length, and wrought with a cunning artistry. Likewise he was given, in shallow bowls, a liquor made from the blood-like juice of living plants, and a wine in which the narcotic pollen of some night-blooming flower had been dissolved.

The days and weeks that now followed were, for the poet, an experience beyond the visionary resources of any terrestrial drug. Step by step, he was initiated, as much as possible for one so radically alien, into the complexities and singularities of life in a new world. Gradually his nerves and his mind, by the aid of the erubescent liquid which Vizaphmal continued to administer to him at intervals, became habituated to the strong light and heat, the intense radiative properties of a soil and atmosphere with unearthly chemical constituents, the strange foods and beverages, and the people themselves with their queer anatomy and queerer customs. Tutors were engaged to teach him the language, and, in spite of the difficulties presented by certain unmanageable consonants, certain weird ululative vowels, he learned enough of it to make his simpler ideas and wants understood.

He saw Vizaphmal every day, and the new king seemed to cherish a real gratitude toward him for his indispensable aid in the fulfilment of the prophecy. Vizaphmal took pains to instruct him in regard to all that it was necessary to know, and kept him well-informed as to the progress of public events in Ulphalor. He was told, among other things, that no news had been heard concerning the whereabouts of Akkiel, the late ruler. Also, Vizaphmal had reason to be aware of more or less opposition toward himself on the part of the various priesthoods, who, in spite of his life-long discretion, had somehow learned of his free-thinking propensities.

For all the attention, kindness and service that he received, and the unique luxury with which he was surrounded, Alvor felt that these people, even as the wizard had forewarned him, looked upon him merely as a kind of unnatural curiosity or anomaly. He was no less monstrous to them than they were to him, and the gulf created by the laws of a diverse biology, by an alien trend of evolution, seemed impossible to bridge in any manner. He was questioned by many of them, and, in especial, by more than one delegation of noted scientists, who desired to know as much as he could tell them about himself. But the queries were so patronizing, so rude and narrow-minded and scornful and smug, that he was soon wont to feign a total ignorance of the language on such occasions. Indeed, there was a gulf; and he was rendered even more acutely conscious of it whenever he met any of the female Abbars or Alphads of the court, who eyed him with disdainful inquisitiveness, and among whom a sort of tittering usually arose when he passed. His naked members, so limited in number, were obviously as great a source of astonishment to them as their own somewhat intricate and puzzling charms were to him. All of them were quite nude; indeed, nothing, not even a string of jewels or a single gem, was ever worn by any of the Satabborians. The female Alphads, like the males, were extremely tall and were gorgeous with epidermic hues that would have outdone the plumage of any peacock; and their anatomical structure was most peculiar. ... Alvor began to feel the loneliness of which Vizaphmal had spoken, and he was overcome at times by a great nostalgia for his own world, by a planetary homesickness. He became atrociously nervous, even if not actually ill.

While he was still in this condition, Vizaphmal took him on a tour of Ulphalor that had become necessary for political reasons. More or less incredulity concerning the real existence of such a monstrosity as Alvor had been expressed by the folk of outlying provinces, of the polar realms and the antipodes, and the new ruler felt that a visual demonstration of the two-armed, two-legged and two-eyed phenomenon would be far from inadvisable, to establish beyond dispute the legitimacy of his own claim to the throne. In the course of this tour, they visited many unique cities, and the rural and urban centers of industries peculiar to Satabbor; and Alvor saw the mines from which the countless minerals and metals used in Ulphalor were extracted by the toil of millions of Abbars. These metals were found in a pure state, and were of inexhaustible extent. Also he saw the huge oceans, which, with certain inland seas and lakes that were fed from underground sources, formed the sole water-supply of the aging planet, where no rain had even been rumored to fall for centuries. The sea-water, after undergoing a treatment that purged it of a number of undesirable elements, was carried all through the land by a system of conduits. Moreover, he saw the marshlands at the north pole, with their vicious tangle of animate vegetation, into which one one had ever tried to penetrate.

They met many outland peoples in the course of this tour; but the general characteristics were the same throughout Ulphalor, except in one or two races of the lowest aborigines, among whom there were no Alphads. Everywhere the poet was eyed with the same cruel and ignorant curiosity that had been shown in Sarpoulom. However, he became gradually inured to this, and the varying spectacles of bizarre interest and the unheard-of scenes that he saw daily, helped to divert him a little from his nostalgia for the lost earth.

When he and Vizaphmal returned to Sarpoulom, after an absence of many weeks, they found that much discontent and revolutionary sentiment had been sown among the multitude by the hierarchies of the Satabborian gods and goddesses, particularly by the priesthood of Cunthamosi, the Cosmic Mother, a female deity in high favor among the two reproductive sexes, from whom the lower ranks of her hierophants were recruited. Cunthamosi was worshipped as the source of all things: her maternal organs were believed to have given birth to the sun, the moon, the world, the stars, the planets, and even the meteors which often fell in Satabbor. But it was argued by her priests that such a monstrosity as Alvor could not possibly have issued from her womb, and that therefore his very existence was a kind of blasphemy, and that the rule of the heretic wizard, Vizaphmal, based on the advent of this abnormality, was likewise a flagrant insult to the Cosmic Mother. They did not deny the apparently miraculous fulfilment of the prophecy of Abbolechiolor, but it was maintained that this fulfilment was no assurance of the perpetuity of Vizaphmal's reign, and no proof that his reign was countenanced by any of the gods.

"I can not conceal from you," said Vizaphmal to Alvor, "that the position in which we both stand is now slightly parlous. I intend to bring the space-annihilator from my country home to the court, since it is not impossible that I may have need for it, and that some foreign sphere will soon become more salubrious for me than my native one."

However, it would seem that this able scientist, alert wizard and competent king had not grasped the full imminence of the danger that threatened his reign; or else he spoke, as was sometimes his wont, with sardonic moderation. He showed no further concern, beyond setting a strong guard about Alvor to attend him at all times, lest an attempt should be made to kidnap the poet in consideration of the last clause of the prophecy.

Three days after the return to Sarpoulom, while Alvor

was standing in one of his private balconies looking out over the roofs of the town, with his guards chattering idly in the rooms behind, he saw that the streets were dark with a horde of people, mainly Abbars, who were streaming silently toward the palace. A few Alphads, distinguishable even at a distance by their gaudy hues, were at the head of this throng. Alarmed at the spectacle, and remembering what the king had told him, he went to find Vizaphmal and climbed the eternal tortuous series of complicated stairs that led to the king's personal suite. Others among the inmates of the court had seen the advancing crowd, and there were agitation, terror and frantic hurry everywhere. Mounting the last flight of steps to the king's threshold, Alvor was astounded to find that many of the Abbars, who had gained ingress from the other side of the palace and had scaled the successive rows of columns and stairs with ape-like celerity, were already pouring into the room. Vizaphmal himself was standing before the open framework of the space-annihilator, which had now been installed beside his couch. The rod of royal investiture was in his hand, and he was levelling the crimson end at the foremost of the invading Abbars. As this creature leapt toward him, waving an atrocious weapon lined by a score of hooked blades, Vizaphmal tightened his hold on the rod, thus pressing a secret spring, and a thin rose-colored ray of light was emitted from the end, causing the Abbar to crumple and fall. Others, in nowise deterred, ran forward to succeed him, and the king turned his lethal beam upon them with the calm air of one who is conducting a scientific experiment, till the floor was piled with dead Abbars. Still others took their place, and some began to cast their hooked weapons at the king. None of these touched him, but he seemed to weary of the sport, and stepping within the framework, he closed it upon himself. A moment more, and then there was a roar as of a thousand thunders, and the mechanism and Visaphmal were no longer to be seen. Never, at any future time, was the poet to learn what had become of him, nor in what stranger world than Satabbor he was now indulging his scientific fancies and curiosities.

Alvor had no time to feel, as he might conceivably have done, that he had been basely deserted by the king. All the nether and upper stories of the great edifice were now a-swarm with the invading crowd, who were no longer silent, but were uttering shrill, ferocious cries as they bore down the opposition of the courtiers and slaves. The whole place was inundated by an ever-mounting sea, in which there were now myriads of Alphads as well as of Abbars; and no escape was possible. In a few instants, Alvor himself was seized by a group of the Abbars, who seemed to have been enraged rather than terrified or discomforted by the vanishing of Vizaphmal. He recognized them as priests of Cunthamosi by an odd oval and vertical marking of red pigments on their swart bodies. They bound him viciously with cords made from the intestines of a dragon-like animal, and carried him away from the palace, along streets that were lined by a staring and glibbering mob, to a building on the southern outskirts of Sarpoulom, which Vizaphmal had once pointed out to him as the Inquisition of the Cosmic Mother.

This edifice, unlike most of the buildings in Sarpoulom, was walled on all sides and was constructed entirely of enormous gray bricks, made from the local soil, and bigger and harder than blocks of granite. In a long five-sided chamber illumined only by narrow slits in the roof, Alvor found himself arraigned before a jury of the priests, presided over by a swollen and pontifical-looking Alphad, the Grand Inquisitor.

The place was filled with ingenious and grotesque implements of torture, and the very walls were hung to the ceiling with contrivances that would have put Torquemada to shame. Some of them were very small, and were designed for the treatment of special and separate nerves; and others were intended to harrow the entire epidermic area of the body at a single twist of their screw-like mechanism.

Alvor could understand little of the charges being preferred against him, but gathered that they were the same, or included the same, of which Vizaphmal had spoken— to wit, that he, Alvor, was a monstrosity that could never have been conceived or brought forth by Cunthamosi, and whose very existence, past, present and future, was a dire affront to this divinity. The entire scene—the dark and lurid room with its array of hellish instruments, the diabolic faces of the inquisitors, and the high unhuman drone of their voices as they intoned the charges and brought judgment against Alvor—was laden with a horror beyond the horror of dreams.

Presently the Grand Inquisitor focussed the malign gleam of his three unblinking orbs upon the poet, and began to pronounce an interminable sentence, pausing a little at quite regular intervals which seemed to mark the clauses of the punishment that was to be inflicted. These clauses were well-nigh innumerable, but Alvor could comprehend almost nothing of what was said; and doubtless it was as well that he did not comprehend.

When the voice of the swollen Alphad had ceased, the poet was led away through endless corridors and down a stairway that seemed to descend into the bowels of Satabbor. These corridors, and also the stairway, were luminous with self-emitted light that resembled the phosphorescence of decaying matter in tombs and catacombs. As Alvor went downward with his guards, who were all Abbars of the lowest type, he could hear somewhere in sealed unknowable vaults the moan and shriek of beings who endured the ordeals imposed by the inquisitors of Cunthamosi.

They came to the final step of the stairway, where, in a vast vault, an abyss whose bottom was not discernible yawned in the center of the floor. On its edge there stood a fantastic sort of windlass on which was wound an immense coil of blackish rope.

The end of this rope was now tied about Alvor's ankles, and he was lowered head downward into the gulf by the inquisitors. The sides were not luminous like those of the stairway, and he could see nothing. But, as he descended into the gulf, the terrible discomfort of his position was increased by sensations of an ulterior origin. He felt that he was passing through a kind of hairy material with numberless filaments that clung to his head and body and limbs like minute tentacles, and whose contact gave rise to an immediate itching. The substance impeded him more and more, till at last he was held immovably suspended as in a net, and all the while the separate hairs seemed to be biting into his flesh with a million microscopic teeth, till the initial itching was followed by a burning and a deep convulsive throbbing more exquisitely painful than the flames of an *auto da fe*. The poet learned long afterward that the material into which he had been lowered was a subterranean organism, half vegetable, half animal, which grew from the side of the gulf, with long mobile feelers that were extremely poisonous to the touch. But at the time, not the least of the horrors he underwent was the uncertainty as to its precise nature.

After he had hung for quite a while in this agonizing web, and had become almost unconscious from the pain and the unnatural position, Alvor felt that he was being drawn upward. A thousand of the fine thread-like tentacles clung to him and his whole body was encircled with a mesh of insufferable pangs as he broke loose from them. He swooned with the intensity of this pain, and when he recovered, he was lying on the floor at the edge of the gulf, and one of the priests was prodding him with a many-pointed weapon.

Alvor gazed for a moment at the cruel visages of his tormenters, in the luminous glow from the sides of the vault, and wondered dimly what infernal torture was next to follow, in the carrying-out of the interminable sentence that had been pronounced. He surmised, of course, that the one he had just undergone was mild in comparison to the many that would succeed it. But he never knew, for at that instant there came a crashing sound like the fall and shattering of the universe; the walls, the floor and the stairway rocked to and fro in a veritable convulsion, and the vault above was riven in sunder, letting through a rain of fragments of all sizes, some of which struck several of the inquisitors and swept them into the gulf. Others of the priests leapt over the edge in their terror, and the two who remained were in no condition to continue their official duties. Both of them were lying beside Alvor with broken heads from which, in lieu of blood, there issued a glutinous light-green liquid.

Alvor could not imagine what had happened, but knew only that he himself was unhurt, as far as the results of the cataclysm were concerned. His mental state was not one to admit of scientific surmise: he was sick and dizzy from the ordeal he had suffered, and his whole body was swollen, was blood-red and violently burning from the touch of the organisms in the gulf. He had, however, enough strength and presence of mind to grope with his bound hands for the weapon that had been dropped by one of the inquisitors. By much patience, by untiring ingenuity, he was able to cut the thongs about his wrists and ankles on the sharp blade of one of the five points.

Carrying this weapon, which he knew that he might need, he began the ascent of the subterranean stairway. The steps were half blocked by fallen masses of stone, and some of the landings and stairs, as well as the sides of the wall, were cloven with enormous rents; and his egress was by no means an easy matter. When he reached the top, he found that the whole edifice was a pile of shattered walls, with a great pit in its center from which a cloud of vapors issued. An immense meteor had fallen, and had struck the Inquisition of the Cosmic Mother.

Alvor was in no condition to appreciate the irony of this event, but at least he was able to comprehend his chance of freedom. The only inquisitors now visible were lying with squashed bodies whose heads or feet protruded from beneath the large squares of overthrown brick, and Alvor lost no time in quitting the vicinity.

It was now night, and only one of the three moons had arisen. Alvor struck off through the level arid country to the south of Sarpoulom, where no one dwelt, with the idea of crossing the boundaries of Ulphalor into one of the independent kingdoms that lay below the equator. He remembered Vizaphmal telling him once that the people of these kingdoms were more enlightened and less priest-ridden than those of Ulphalor.

All night he wandered, in a sort of daze that was at times delirium. The pain of his swollen limbs increased, and he grew feverish. The moonlit plain seemed to shift and waver before him, but was interminable as the landscape of a hashish-dream. Presently the other two moons arose, and in the overtaxed condition of his mind and nerves, he was never quite sure as to their actual number. Usually, there appeared to be more than three, and this troubled him prodigiously. He tried to resolve the problem for hours, as he staggered on, and at last, a little before dawn, he became altogether delirious.

He was unable afterward to recall anything about his subsequent journey. Something impelled him to go on even when his thews were dead and his brain an utter blank: he knew nothing of the waste and terrible lands through which he roamed in the hour-long ruby-red of morn and beneath a furnace-like sun; nor did he knew when he crossed the equator at sunset and entered Omanorion, the realm of the empress Ambiala, still carrying in his hand the five-pointed weapon of one of the dead inquisitors.

It was night when Alvor awoke, but he had no means of surmising that it was not the same night in which he had fled from the Inquisition of the Cosmic Mother; and that many Satabborian days had gone by since he had fallen totally exhausted and unconscious within the boundary-line of Omanorion. The warm, rosy beams of the three moons were full in his face, but he could not know whether they were ascending or declining. Anyhow, he was lying on a very comfortable couch that was not quite so disconcertingly long and high as the one upon which he had first awakened in Ulphalor. He was in an open pavilion, and this pavilion was also a bower of multitudinous blossoms which leaned toward him with faces that were both grotesque and weirdly beautiful, from vines that had scaled the columns, or from the many curious metal pots that stood upon the floor. The air that he breathed was a medley of perfumes more exotic than frangipani; they were extravagantly sweet and spicy, but somehow he did not find them oppressive. Rather, they served to augment the deep, delightful languor of all his sensations.

As he opened his eyes and turned a little on the couch, a female Alphad, not so tall as those of Ulphalor and really quite of his own stature, came out from behind the flower-pots and addressed him. Her language was not that of the Ulphalorians, it was softer and less utterly unhuman, and though he could not understand a word, he was immediately aware of a sympathetic note or undertone which, so far, he had never heard on the lips of any one in this world, not even Vizaphmal.

He replied in the language of Ulphalor, and found that he was understood. He and the female Alphad now carried on as much of a conversation as Alvor's linguistic abilities would permit. He learned that he was talking to the empress Ambiala, the sole and supreme ruler of Omanorion, a quite extensive realm contiguous to Ulphalor. She told him that some of her servitors, while out hunting the wild, ferocious, half-animal fruits of the region, had found him lying unconscious near a thicket of the deadly plants that bore these fruits, and had brought him to her palace in Lompior, the chief city of Omanorion. There, while he still lay in a week-long stupor, he had been treated with medicaments that had now almost cured the painful swellings resultant from his plunge among the hair-like organisms in the Inquisition.

With genuine courtesy, the empress forbore to question the poet regarding himself, nor did she express any surprize at his anatomical peculiarities. However, her whole manner gave evidence of an eager and even fascinated interest, for she did not take her eyes away from him at any time. He was a little embarrassed by her intent scrutiny, and to cover this embarrassment, as well as to afford her the explanations due to so kind a hostess, he tried to tell her as much as he could of his own history and adventures. It was doubtful if she understood more than half of what he said, but even this half obviously lent him an increasingly portentous attraction in her eyes. All of her three orbs grew round with wonder at the tale related by this fantastic Ulysses, and whenever he stopped she would beg him to go on. The garnet and ruby and cinnabar gradations of the dawn found Alvor still talking and the empress Ambiala still listening.

In the full light of Antares, Alvor saw that his hostess was, from a Satabborian viewpoint, a really beautiful and exquisite creature. The iridescence of her coloring was very soft and subtle, her arms and legs, though of the usual number, were all voluptuously rounded, and the features of her face were capable of a wide range of expression. Her usual look, however, was one of a sad and wistful yearning. This look Alvor came to understand, when, with a growing knowledge of her language, he learned that she too was a poet, that she had always been troubled by vague desires for the exotic and the far-off, and that she was thoroughly bored with everything in Omanorion, and especially with the male Alphads of that region, none of whom could rightfully boast of having been her lover even for a day. Alvor's biological difference from these males was evidently the secret of his initial fascination for her.

The poet's life in the palace of Ambiala, where he found that he was looked upon as a permanent guest, was from the beginning much more agreeable than his existence in Ulphalor had been. For one thing, there was Ambiala herself, who impressed him as being infinitely more intelligent than the females of Sarpoulom, and whose attitude was so thoughtful and sympathetic and admiring, in contra-distinction to the attitude of those aforesaid females. Also, the servitors of the palace and the people of Lompior, though they doubtless regarded Alvor as a quite singular sort of being, were at least more tolerant than the Ulphalorians; and he met with no manner of rudeness among them at any time. Moreover, if there were any priesthoods in Omanorion, they were not of the uncompromising type he had met north of the equator, and it would seem that nothing was to be feared from them. No one ever spoke of religion to Alvor in this ideal realm, and somehow he never actually learned whether or not Omanorion possessed any gods or goddesses. Remembering his ordeal in the Inquisition of the Cosmic Mother, he was quite willing not to broach the subject, anyway.

Alvor made rapid progress in the language of Omanorion, since the empress herself was his teacher. He soon learned more and more about her ideas and tastes, about her romantic love for the triple moonlight, and the odd flowers that she cultivated with so much care and so much delectation. These blossoms were rare anywhere in Satabbor: some of them were anemones that came from the tops of almost inaccessible mountains many leagues in height, and others were forms inconceivably more bizarre than orchids, mainly from terrific jungles near the southern pole. He was soon privileged to hear her play on a certain musical instrument of the country, in which were combined the characters of the flute and the lute. And at last, one day, when he knew enough of the tongue to appreciate a few of its subtleties, she read to him from a scroll of vegetable vellum one of her poems, an ode to a star known as Atana by the people of Omanorion. This ode was truly exquisite, was replete with poetic fancies of a high order, and expressed a half-ironic yearning, sadly conscious of its own impossibility, for the ultra-sidereal realms of Atana. Ending, she added:

"I have always loved Atana, because it is so little and so far away."

On questioning her, Alvor learned to his overwhelming amazement, that Atana was identical with a minute star called Arot in Ulphalor, which Vizaphmal had once pointed out to him as the sun of his own earth. This star was visible only in the rare interlunar dark, and it was considered a test of good eyesight to see it even then.

When the poet had communicated this bit of astronomical information to Ambiala, that the star Atana was his own native sun, and had also told her of his *Ode to Antares*, a most affecting scene occurred, for the empress encircled him with her five arms and cried out:

"Do you not feel, as I do, that we were destined for each other?"

Though he was a little discomposed by Ambiala's display of affection, Alvor could do no less than assent. The two beings, so dissimilar in external ways, were absolutely overcome by the rapport revealed in this comparing of poetic notes; and a real understanding, rare even with persons of the same evolutionary type, was established between them henceforward. Also, Alvor soon developed a new appreciation of the outward charms of Ambiala, which, to tell the truth, had not altogether inveigled him heretofore. He reflected that after all her five arms and three legs and three eyes were merely a superabundance of anatomical features upon which human love was wont to set a by no means lowly value. As for her opalescent coloring, it was, he thought, much more lovely than the agglomeration of outlandish hues with which the human female figure had been adorned in many modernistic paintings.

When it became known in Lompior that Alvor was the lover of Ambiala, no surprize or censure was expressed by any one. Doubtless the people, especially the male Alphads who had vainly wooed the empress, thought that her tastes were queer, not to say eccentric. But anyway, no comment was made: it was her own amour after all, and no one else could carry it on for her. It would seem, from this, that the people of Omanorion had mastered the ultra-civilized art of minding their own business.

THE VAULTS OF YOH-VOMBIS

IF the doctors are correct in their prognostication, I have only a few Martian hours of life remaining to me. In those hours I shall endeavor to relate, as a warning to others who might follow in our footsteps, the singular and frightful happenings that terminated our researches among the ruins of Yoh-Vombis. If my story will only serve to prevent future explorations, the telling will not have been in vain.

There were eight of us, professional archeologists with more or less terrene and interplanetary experience, who set forth with native guides from Ignarh, the commercial metropolis of Mars, to inspect that ancient, eon-deserted city. Allan Octave, our official leader, held his primacy by knowing more about Martian archeology than any other Terrestrial on the planet; and others of the party, such as William Harper and Jonas Halgren, had been associated with him in many of his previous researches. I, Rodney Severn, was more of a newcomer, having spent but a few months on Mars; and the greater part of my own ultraterrene delvings had been confined to Venus.

The nude, spongy-chested Aihais had spoken deterringly of vast deserts filled with ever-swirling sandstorms, through which we must pass to reach Yoh-Vombis; and in spite of our munificent offers of payment, it had been difficult to secure guides for the journey. Therefore we were surprised as well as pleased when we came to the ruins after seven hours of plodding across the flat, treeless, orange-yellow desolation to the southwest of Ignarh.

We beheld our destination, for the first time, in the setting of the small, remote sun. For a little, we thought that the domeless, three-angled towers and broken-down monoliths were those of some unlegended city, other than the one we sought. But the disposition of the ruins, which lay in a sort of arc for almost the entire extent of a low, gneissic, league-long elevation of bare, eroded stone, together with the type of architecture, soon convinced us that we had found our goal. No other ancient city on Mars had been laid out in that manner; and the strange, many-terraced buttresses, like the stairways of forgotten Anakim, were peculiar to the prehistoric race that had built Yoh-Vombis.

I have seen the hoary, sky-confronting walls of Machu Pichu amid the desolate Andes; and the frozen, giant-builded battlements of Uogam on the glacial tundras of the nightward hemisphere of Venus. But these were as things of yesteryear compared to the walls upon which we gazed. The whole region was far from the life-giving canals beyond whose environs even the more noxious flora and fauna are seldom found; and we had seen no living thing since our departure from Ignarh. But here, in this place of petrified sterility, of eternal bareness and solitude, it seemed that life could never have been.

I think we all received the same impression as we stood staring in silence while the pale, sanies-like sunset fell on the dark and megalithic ruins. I remember gasping a little, in an air that seemed to have been touched by the irrespirable chill of death; and I heard the same sharp, laborious intake of breath from others of our party.

"That place is deader than an Egyptian morgue," observed Harper.

"Certainly it is far more ancient," Octave assented. "According to the most reliable legends, the Yorhis, who built Yoh-Vombis, were wiped out by the present ruling race at least forty thousand years ago."

"There's a story, isn't there," said Harper, "that the last remnant of the Yorhis was destroyed by some unknown agency—something too horrible and outré to be mentioned even in a myth?"

"Of course, I've heard that legend," agreed Octave. "Maybe we'll find evidence among the ruins to prove or disprove it. The Yorhis may have been cleaned out by some terrible epidemic, such as the Yashta pestilence, which was a kind of green mold that ate all the bones of the body, together with the teeth and nails. But we needn't be afraid of getting it, if there are any mummies in Yoh-Vombis—the bacteria will all be dead as their victims, after so many cycles of planetary dessication."

The sun had gone down with uncanny swiftness, as if it had disappeared through some sort of prestidigitation rather than the normal process of setting. We felt the instant chill of the blue-green twilight; and the ether above us was like a huge, transparent dome of sunless ice, shot with a million bleak sparklings that were the stars. We donned the coats and helmets of Martian fur, which must always be worn at night; and going on to westward of the walls, we established our camp in their lee, so that we might be sheltered a little from the *jaar*, that cruel desert wind that always blows from the east before dawn. Then, lighting the alcohol lamps that had been brought along for cooking purposes, we huddled around them while the evening meal was prepared and eaten.

Afterward, for comfort rather than because of weariness, we retired early to our sleeping-bags; and the two Aihais, our guides, wrapped themselves in the cerement-like folds of *bassa*-cloth which are all the protection their leathery skins appear to require even in sub-zero temperatures.

Even in my thick, double-lined bag, I still felt the rigor of the night air; and I am sure it was this, rather than anything else, which kept me awake for a long while and rendered my eventual slumber somewhat restless and broken. At any rate, I was not troubled by even the least presentiment of alarm or danger; and I should have laughed at the idea that anything of peril could lurk in Yoh-Vombis, amid whose undreamable and stupefying antiquities the very phantoms of its dead must long since have faded into nothingness.

I must have drowsed again and again, with starts of semi-wakefulness. At last, in one of these, I knew vaguely that the small twin moons, Phobos and Deimos, had risen and were making huge and far-flung shadows with the domeless towers; shadows that almost touched the glimmering, shrouded forms of my companions.

The whole scene was locked in a petrific stillness; and none of the sleepers stirred. Then, as my lids were about to close, I received an impression of movement in the frozen gloom; and it seemed to me that a portion of the foremost shadow had detached itself and was crawling toward Octave, who lay nearer to the ruins than we others.

Even through my heavy lethargy, I was disturbed by a warning of something unnatural and perhaps ominous. I started to sit up; and even as I moved, the shadowy object, whatever it was, drew back and became merged once more in the greater shadow. Its vanishment startled me into full wakefulness; and yet I could not be sure that I had actually seen the thing. In that brief, final glimpse, it had seemed like a roughly circular piece of cloth or leather, dark and crumpled, and twelve or fourteen inches in diameter, that ran along the ground with the doubling movement of an inch-worm, causing it to fold and unfold in a startling manner as it went.

I did not go to sleep again for nearly an hour; and if it had not been for the extreme cold, I should doubtless have gotten up to investigate and make sure whether I had really beheld an object of such bizarre nature or had merely dreamt it. But more and more I began to convince myself that the thing was too unlikely and fantastical to have been anything but the figment of a dream. And at last I nodded off into light slumber.

The chill, demoniac sighing of the *jaar* across the jagged walls awoke me, and I saw that the faint moonlight had received the hueless accession of early dawn. We all arose, and prepared our breakfast with fingers that grew numb in spite of the spirit-lamps.

My queer visual experience during the night had taken on more than ever a fantasmagoric unreality; and I gave it no more than a passing thought and did not speak of it to the others. We were all eager to begin our explorations; and shortly after sunrise we started on a preliminary tour of examination.

Strangely, as it seemed, the two Martians refused to accompany us. Stolid and taciturn, they gave no explicit reason; but evidently nothing would induce them to enter Yoh-Vombis. Whether or not they were afraid of the ruins, we were unable to determine: their enigmatic faces, with the small oblique eyes and huge, flaring nostrils, betrayed neither fear nor any other emotion intelligible to man. In reply to our questions, they merely said that no Aihai had set foot among the ruins for ages. Apparently there was some mysterious taboo in connection with the place.

For equipment in that preliminary tour we took along only our electric torches and a crowbar. Our other tools, and some cartridges of high explosives, we left at our camp, to be used later if necessary, after we had surveyed the ground. One or two of us owned automatics; but these also were left behind; for it seemed absurd to imagine that any form of life would be encountered among the ruins.

Octave was visibly excited as we began our inspection, and maintained a running fire of exclamatory comment. The rest of us were subdued and silent: it was impossible to shake off the somber awe and wonder that fell upon us from those megalithic stones.

We went on for some distance among the triangular, terraced buildings, following the zigzag streets that conformed to this peculiar architecture. Most of the towers were more or less dilapidated; and everywhere we saw the deep erosion wrought by cycles of blowing wind and sand, which, in many cases, had worn into roundness the sharp angles of the mighty walls. We entered some of the towers, but found utter emptiness within. Whatever they had contained in the way of furnishings must long ago have crumbled into dust; and the dust had been blown away by the searching desert gales.

At length we came to the wall of a vast terrace, hewn from the plateau itself. On this terrace, the central buildings were grouped like a sort of acropolis. A flight of time-eaten steps, designed for longer limbs than those of men or even the gangling modern Martians, afforded access to the hewn summit.

Pausing, we decided to defer our investigation of the higher buildings, which, being more exposed than the others, were doubly ruinous and dilapidated, and in all likelihood would offer little for our trouble. Octave had begun to voice his disappointment over our failure to find anything in the nature of artifacts that would throw light on the history of Yoh-Vombis.

Then, a little to the right of the stairway, we perceived an entrance in the main wall, half choked with ancient debris. Behind the heap of detritus, we found the beginning of a downward flight of steps. Darkness poured from the opening, musty with primordial stagnancies of decay; and we could see nothing below the first steps, which gave the appearance of being suspended over a black gulf.

Throwing his torch-beam into the abyss, Octave began to descend the stairs. His eager voice called us to follow.

At the bottom of the high, awkward steps, we found ourselves in a long and roomy vault, like a subterranean hallway. Its floor was deep with siftings of immemorial dust. The air was singularly heavy, as if the lees of an ancient atmosphere, less tenuous than that of Mars today, had settled down and remained in that stagnant darkness. It was harder to breathe than the outer air: it was filled with unknown effluvia; and the light dust arose before us at every step, diffusing a faintness of bygone corruption, like the dust of powdered mummies.

At the end of the vault, before a strait and lofty doorway, our torches revealed an immense shallow urn or pan, supported on short cube-shaped legs, and wrought from a dull, blackish-green material. In its bottom, we perceived a deposit of dark and cinder-like fragments, which gave off a slight but disagreeable pungence, like the phantom of some more powerful odor. Octave, bending over the rim, began to cough and sneeze as he inhaled it.

"That stuff, whatever it was, must have been a pretty strong fumigant," he observed. "The people of Yoh-Vombis may have used it to disinfect the vaults."

The doorway beyond the shallow urn admitted us to a larger chamber, whose floor was comparatively free of dust. We found that the dark stone beneath our feet was marked off in multiform geometric patterns, traced with ochreous ore, amid which, as in Egyptian cartouches, hieroglyphics and highly formalized drawings were enclosed. We could make little from most of them; but the figures in many were doubtless designed to represent the Yorhis themselves. Like the Aihais, they were tall and angular, with great, bellows-like chests. The ears and nostrils, as far as we could judge, were not so huge and flaring as those of the modern Martians. All of these Yorhis were depicted as being nude; but in one of the cartouches, done in a far hastier style than the others, we perceived two figures whose high, conical craniums were wrapped in what seemed to be a sort of turban, which they were about to remove or adjust. The artist seemed to have laid a peculiar emphasis on the odd gesture with which the sinuous, four-joined fingers were plucking at these head-dresses; and the whole posture was unexplainably contorted.

From the second vault, passages ramified in all directions, leading to a veritable warren of catacombs. Here, enormous pot-bellied urns of the same material as the fumigating-pan, but taller than a man's head and fitted with angular-handled stoppers, were ranged in solemn rows along the walls, leaving scant room for two of us to walk abreast. When we succeeded in removing one of the huge stoppers, we saw that the jar was filled to the rim with ashes and charred fragments of bone. Doubtless (as is still the Martian custom) the Yorhis had stored the cremated remains of whole families in single urns.

Even Octave became silent as we went on; and a sort of meditative awe seemed to replace his former excitement. We others, I think, were utterly weighed down to a man by the solid gloom of a concept-defying antiquity, into which it seemed that we were going farther and farther at every step.

The shadows fluttered before us like the monstrous and misshapen wings of phantom bats. There was nothing anywhere but the atom-like dust of ages, and the jars that held the ashes of a long-extinct people. But, clinging to the high roof in one of the farther vaults, I saw a dark and corrugated patch of circular form, like a withered fungus. It was impossible to reach the thing; and we went on after peering at it with many futile conjectures. Oddly enough, I failed to remember at that moment the crumpled, shadowy object I had seen or dreamt of the night before.

I have no idea how far we had gone, when we came to the last vault; but it seemed that we had been wandering for ages in that forgotten underworld. The air was growing fouler and more irrespirable, with a thick, sodden quality, as if from a sediment of material rottenness; and we had about decided to turn back. Then, without warning, at the end of a long, urn-lined catacomb, we found ourselves confronted by a blank wall.

Here we came upon one of the strangest and most mystifying of our discoveries—a mummified and incredibly dessicated figure, standing erect against the wall. It was more than seven feet in height, of a brown bituminous color, and was wholly nude except for a sort of black cowl that covered the upper head and drooped down at the sides in wrinkled folds. From the size and general contour, it was plainly one of the ancient Yorhis—perhaps the sole member of this race whose body had remained intact.

We all felt an inexpressible thrill at the sheer age of this shrivelled thing, which, in the dry air of the vault, had endured through all the historic and geologic vicissitudes of the planet, to provide a visible link with lost cycles.

Then, as we peered closer with our torches, we saw *why* the mummy had maintained an upright position. At ankles, knees, waist, shoulders and neck it was shackled to the wall by heavy metal bands, so deeply eaten and embrowned with a sort of rust that we had failed to distinguish them at first sight in the shadow. The strange cowl on the head, when closelier studied, continued to baffle us. It was covered with a fine, mold-like pile, unclean and dusty as ancient cobwebs. Something about it, I know not what, was abhorrent and revolting.

"By Jove! this is a real find!" ejaculated Octave, as he thrust his torch into the mummified face, where shadows moved like living things in the pit-deep hollows of the eyes and the huge triple nostrils and wide ears that flared upward beneath the cowl.

Still lifting the torch, he put out his free hand and touched the body very lightly. Tentative as the touch had been, the lower part of the barrel-like torso, the legs, the hands and forearms all seemed to dissolve into powder, leaving the head and upper body and arms still hanging in their metal fetters. The progress of decay had been queerly unequal, for the remnant portions gave no sign of disintegration.

Octave cried out in dismay, and then began to cough and sneeze, as the cloud of brown powder, floating with airy lightness, enveloped him. We others all stepped back to avoid the powder. Then, above the spreading cloud, I saw an unbelievable thing. The black cowl on the mummy's head began to curl and twitch upward at the corners, it writhed with a verminous motion, it fell from the withered cranium, seeming to fold and unfold convulsively in midair as it fell. Then it dropped on the bare head of Octave who, in his disconcertment at the crumbling of the mummy, had remained standing close to the wall. At that instant, in a start of profound terror, I remembered the thing that had inched itself from the shadows of Yoh-Vombis in the light of the twin moons, and had drawn back like a figment of slumber at my first waking movement.

Cleaving closely as a tightened cloth, the thing enfolded Octave's hair and brow and eyes, and he shrieked wildly, with incoherent pleas for help, and tore with frantic fingers at the cowl, but failed to loosen it. Then his cries began to mount in a mad crescendo of agony, as if beneath some instrument of infernal torture; and he danced and capered blindly about the vault, eluding us with strange celerity as we all sprang forward in an effort to reach him and release him from his weird incumberance. The whole happening was mysterious as a nightmare; but the thing that had fallen on his head was plainly some unclassified form of Martian life, which, contrary to all the known laws of science, had survived in those primordial catacombs. We must rescue him from its clutches if we could.

We tried to close in on the frenzied figure of our chief—which, in the far from roomy space between the last urns and the wall, should have been an easy matter. But, darting away, in a manner doubly incomprehensible because of his blindfolded condition, he circled about us and ran past, to disappear among the urns toward the outer labyrinth of intersecting catacombs.

"My God! What has happened to him?" cried Harper. "The man acts as if he were possessed."

There was obviously no time for a discussion of the enigma, and we all followed Octave as speedily as our astonishment would permit. We had lost sight of him in the darkness; and when we came to the first division of the vaults, we were doubtful as to which passage he had taken, till we heard a shrill scream, several times repeated, in a catacomb on the extreme left. There was a weird, unearthly quality in those screams, which may have been due to the long-stagnant air or the peculiar acoustics of the ramifying caverns. But somehow I could not imagine them as issuing from human lips—at least not from those of a living man. They seemed to contain a soulless, mechanical agony, as if they had been wrung from a devil-driven corpse.

Thrusting our torches before us into the lurching, fleeing shadows, we raced along between rows of mighty urns. The screaming had died away in sepulchral silence; but far off we heard the light and muffled thud of running feet. We followed in headlong pursuit; but, gasping painfully in the vitiated, miasmal air, we were soon compelled to slacken our pace without coming in sight of Octave. Very faintly, and farther away than ever, like the tomb-swallowed steps of a phantom, we heard his vanishing footfalls. Then they ceased; and we heard nothing, except our own convulsive breathing, and the blood that throbbed in our temple-veins like steadily beaten drums of alarm.

We went on, dividing our party into three contingents when we came to a triple branching of the caverns. Harper and Halgren and I took the middle passage, and after we had gone on for an endless interval without finding any trace of Octave, and had threaded our way through recesses piled to the roof with colossal urns that must have held the ashes of a hundred generations, we came out in the huge chamber with the geometric floor-designs. Here, very shortly, we were joined by the others, who had likewise failed to locate our missing leader.

It would be useless to detail our renewed and hour-long search of the myriad vaults, many of which we had not hitherto explored. All were empty, as far as any sign of life was concerned. I remember passing once more through the vault in which I had seen the dark, rounded patch on the ceiling, and noting with a shudder that the patch was gone. It was a miracle that we did not lose ourselves in that underworld maze; but at last we came back again to the final catacomb, in which we had found the shackled mummy.

We heard a measured and recurrent clangor as we neared the place—a most alarming and mystifying sound under the circumstances. It was like the hammering of ghouls on some forgotten mausoleum. When we drew nearer, the beams of our torches revealed a sight that was no less unexplainable than unexpected. A human figure, with its back toward us and the head concealed by a swollen black object that had the size and form of a sofa cushion, was standing near the remains of the mummy and was striking at the wall with a pointed metal bar. How long Octave had been there, and where he had found the bar, we could not know. But the blank wall had crumbled away beneath his furious blows, leaving on the floor a pile of cement-like fragments; and a small, narrow door, of the same ambiguous material as the cinerary urns and the fumigating-pan, had been laid bare.

Amazed, uncertain, inexpressibly bewildered, we were all incapable of action or volition at that moment. The whole business was too fantastic and too horrifying, and it was plain that Octave had been overcome by some sort of madness. I, for one, felt the violent upsurge of sudden nausea when I had identified the loathsomely bloated thing that clung to Octave's head and drooped in obscene tumescence on his neck. I did not dare to surmise the causation of its bloating.

Before any of us could recover our faculties, Octave flung aside the metal bar and began to fumble for something in the wall. It must have been a hidden spring; though how he could have known its location or existence is beyond all legitimate conjecture. With a dull, hideous grating, the uncovered door swung inward, thick and ponderous as a mausolean slab, leaving an aperture from which the nether midnight seemed to well like a flood of eon-buried foulness. Somehow, at that instant, our electric torches flickered and grew dim; and we all breathed a suffocating fetor, like a draft from inner worlds of immemorial putrescence.

Octave had turned toward us now, and he stood in an idle posture before the open door, like one who has finished some ordained task. I was the first of our party to throw off the paralyzing spell; and pulling out a clasp-knife—the only semblance of a weapon which I carried—I ran over to him. He moved back, but not quickly enough to evade me, when I stabbed with the four-inch blade at the black, turgescent mass that enveloped his whole upper head and hung down upon his eyes.

What the thing was, I should prefer not to imagine—if it were possible to imagine. It was formless as a great slug, with neither head nor tail nor apparent organs—an unclean, puffy, leathery thing, covered with that fine, mold-like fur of which I have spoken. The knife tore into it as if through rotten parchment, making a long gash, and the horror appeared to collapse like a broken bladder. Out of it there gushed a sickening torrent of human blood, mingled with dark, filiated masses that may have been half-dissolved hair, and floating gelatinous lumps like molten bone, and shreds of a curdy white substance. At the same time, Octave began to stagger, and went down at full length on the floor. Disturbed by his fall, the mummy-dust arose about him in a curling cloud, beneath which he lay mortally still.

Conquering my revulsion, and choking with the dust, I bent over him and tore the flaccid, oozing horror from his head. It came with unexpected ease, as if I had removed a limp rag: but I wish to God that I had let it remain. Beneath, there was no longer a human cranium, for all had been eaten away, even to the eyebrows, and the half-devoured brain was laid bare as I lifted the cowl-like object. I dropped the unnamable thing from fingers that had grown suddenly nerveless, and it turned over as it fell, revealing on the nether side many rows of pinkish suckers, arranged in circles about a pallid disk that was covered with nerve-like filaments, suggesting a sort of plexus.

My companions had pressed forward behind me; but, for an appreciable interval, no one spoke.

"How long do you suppose he has been dead?" It was Halgren who whispered the awful question, which we had all been asking ourselves. Apparently no one felt able or willing to answer it; and we could only stare in horrible, timeless fascination at Octave.

At length I made an effort to avert my gaze; and turning at random, I saw the remnants of the shackled mummy, and noted for the first time, with mechanical, unreal horror, the half-eaten condition of the withered head. From this, my gaze was diverted to the newly opened door at one side, without perceiving for a moment what had drawn my attention. Then, startled, I beheld beneath my torch, far down beyond the door, as if in some nether pit, a seething, multitudinous, worm-like movement of crawling shadows. They seemed to boil up in the darkness; and then, over the broad threshold of the vault, there poured the verminous vanguard of a countless army: things that were kindred to the monstrous, diabolic leech I had torn from Octave's eaten head. Some were thin and flat, like writhing, doubling disks of cloth or leather, and others were more or less poddy, and crawled with glutted slowness. What they had found to feed on in the sealed, eternal midnight I do not know; and I pray that I never shall know.

I sprang back and away from them, electrified with terror, sick with loathing, and the black army inched itself unendingly with nightmare swiftness from the unsealed abyss, like the nauseous vomit of horror-sated hells. As it poured toward us, burying Octave's body from sight in a writhing wave, I saw a stir of life from the seemingly dead thing I had cast aside, and saw the loathly struggle which it made to right itself and join the others.

But neither I nor my companions could endure to look longer. We turned and ran between the mighty rows of urns, with the slithering mass of demon leeches close upon us, and scattered in blind panic when we came to the first division of the vaults. Heedless of each other or of anything but the urgency of flight, we plunged into the ramifying passages at random. Behind me, I heard some one stumble and go down, with a curse that mounted to an insane shrieking; but I knew that if I halted and went back, it would be only to invite the same baleful doom that had overtaken the hindmost of our party.

Still clutching the electric torch and my open clasp-knife, I ran along a minor passage which, I seemed to remember, would conduct with more or less directness upon the large outer vault with the painted floor. Here I found myself alone. The others had kept to the main catacombs; and I heard far off a muffled babel of mad cries, as if several of them had been seized by their pursuers.

It seemed that I must have been mistaken about the direction of the passage; for it turned and twisted in an unfamiliar manner, with many intersections, and I soon found that I was lost in the black labyrinth, where the dust had lain unstirred by living feet for inestimable generations. The cinerary warren had grown still once more; and I heard my own frenzied panting, loud and stertorous as that of a Titan in the dead silence.

Suddenly, as I went on, my torch disclosed a human figure coming toward me in the gloom. Before I could master my startlement, the figure had passed me with long, machine-like strides, as if returning to the inner vaults. I think it was Harper, since the height and build were about right for him; but I am not altogether sure, for the eyes and upper head were muffled by a dark, inflated cowl, and the pale lips were locked as if in a silence of tetanic torture—or death. Whoever he was, he had dropped his torch; and he was running blindfolded, in utter darkness, beneath the impulsion of that unearthly vampirism, to seek the very fountain-head of the unloosed horror. I knew that he was beyond human help; and I did not even dream of trying to stop him.

Trembling violently, I resumed my flight, and was passed by two more of our party, stalking by with mechanical swiftness and sureness, and cowled with those Satanic leeches. The others must have returned by way of the main passages; for I did not meet them; and I was never to see them again.

The remainder of my flight is a blur of pandemonian terror. Once more, after thinking that I was near the outer cavern, I found myself astray, and fled through a ranged eternity of monstrous urns, in vaults that must have extended for an unknown distance beyond our explorations. It seemed that I had gone on for years; and my lungs were choking with the eon-dead air, and my legs were ready to crumble beneath me, when I saw far off a tiny point of blessed daylight. I ran toward it, with all the terrors of the alien darkness crowding behind me, and accursed shadows flittering before, and saw that the vault ended in a low, ruinous entrance, littered by rubble on which there fell an arc of thin sunshine.

It was another entrance than the one by which we had penetrated this lethal underworld. I was within a dozen feet of the opening when, without sound or other intimation, something dropped upon my head from the roof above, blinding me instantly and closing upon me like a tautened net. My brow and scalp, at the same time, were shot through with a million needle-like pangs—a manifold, ever-growing agony that seemed to pierce the very bone and converge from all sides upon my inmost brain.

The terror and suffering of that moment were worse than aught which the hells of earthly madness or delirium could ever contain. I felt the foul, vampiric clutch of an atrocious death—and of more than death.

I believe that I dropped the torch; but the fingers of my right hand had still retained the open knife. Instinctively—

since I was hardly capable of conscious volition—I raised the knife and slashed blindly, again and again, many times, at the thing that had fastened its deadly folds upon me. The blade must have gone through and through the clinging monstrosity, to gash my own flesh in a score of places; but I did not feel the pain of those wounds in the million-throbbing torment that possessed me.

At last I saw light, and saw that a black strip, loosened from above my eyes and dripping with my own blood, was hanging down my cheek. It writhed a little, even as it hung, and I ripped it away, and ripped the other remnants of the thing, tatter by oozing, bloody tatter, from off my brow and head. Then I staggered toward the entrance; and the wan light turned to a far, receding, dancing flame before me as I lurched and fell outside the cavern—a flame that fled like the last star of creation above the yawning, sliding chaos and oblivion into which I descended. . . .

I am told that my unconsciousness was of brief duration. I came to myself, with the cryptic faces of the two Martian guides bending over me. My head was full of lancinating pains, and half-remembered terrors closed upon my mind like the shadows of mustering harpies. I rolled over, and looked back toward the cavern-mouth, from which the Martians, after finding me, had seemingly dragged me for some little distance. The mouth was under the terraced angle of an outer building, and within sight of our camp.

I stared at the black opening with hideous fascination, and descried a shadowy stirring in the gloom—the writhing, verminous movement of things that pressed forward from the darkness but did not emerge into the light. Doubtless they could not endure the sun, those creatures of ultramundane night and cycle-sealed corruption.

It was then that the ultimate horror, the beginning madness, came upon me. Amid my crawling revulsion, my nausea-prompted desire to flee from that seething cavern-mouth, there rose an abhorrently conflicting impulse to return; to thread my backward way through all the catacombs, as the others had done; to go down where never men save they, the inconceivably doomed and accursed, had ever gone; to seek beneath that damnable·compulsion a nether world that human thought can never picture. There was a black light, a soundless calling, in the vaults of my brain: the implanted summons of the Thing, like a permeating and sorcerous poison. It lured me to the subterranean door that was walled up by the dying people of Yoh-Vombis, to immure those hellish and immortal leeches, those dark parasites that engraft their own abominable life on the half-eaten brains of the dead. It called me to the depths beyond, where dwell the noisome, necromantic Ones, of whom the leeches, with all their powers of vampirism and diabolism, are but the merest minions. . . .

It was only the two Aihais who prevented me from going back. I struggled, I fought them insanely as they strove to retard me with their spongy arms; but I must have been pretty thoroughly exhausted from all the superhuman adventures of the day; and I went down once more, after a little, into fathomless nothingness, from which I floated out at long intervals, to realize that I was being carried across the desert toward Ignarh.

Well, that is all my story. I have tried to tell it fully and coherently, at a cost that would be unimaginable to the sane . . . to tell it before the madness falls upon me again, as it will very soon—as it is doing now. . . . Yes, I have told my story . . . and you have written it all out, haven't you? Now I must go back to Yoh-Vombis—back across the desert and down through all the catacombs to the vaster vaults beneath. Something is in my brain, that commands me and will direct me. . . . I tell you, I must go. . . .

POSTSCRIPT

As an intern in the territorial hospital at Ignarh, I had charge of the singular case of Rodney Severn, the one surviving member of the Octave Expedition to Yoh-Vombis, and took down the above story from his dictation. Severn had been brought to the hospital by the Martian guides of the Expedition. He was suffering from a horribly lacerated and inflamed condition of the scalp and brow, and was wildly delirious part of the time and had to be held down in his bed during recurrent seizures of a mania whose violence was doubly inexplicable in view of his extreme debility.

The lacerations, as will have been learned from the story, were mainly self-inflicted. They were mingled with numerous small round wounds, easily distinguished from the knife-slashes, and arranged in regular circles, through which an unknown poison had been injected into Severn's scalp. The causation of these wounds was difficult to explain; unless one were to believe that Severn's story was true, and was no mere figment of his illness. Speaking for myself, in the light of what afterward occurred, I feel that I have no other recourse than to believe it. There are strange things on the red planet; and I can only second the wish that was expressed by the doomed archeologist in regard to future explorations.

The night after he had finished telling me his story, while another doctor than myself was supposedly on duty, Severn managed to escape from the hospital, doubtless in one of the strange seizures at which I have hinted: a most astonishing thing, for he had seemed weaker than ever after the long strain of his terrible narrative, and his demise had been hourly expected. More astonishing still, his bare footsteps were found in the desert, going toward Yoh-Vombis, till they vanished in the path of a light sandstorm; but no trace of Severn himself has yet been discovered.

FROM THE CRYPTS OF MEMORY

AEONS OF aeons ago, in an epoch whose marvelous worlds have crumbled, and whose mighty suns are less than shadow, I dwelt in a star whose course, decadent from the high, irremeable heavens of the past, was even then verging upon the abyss in which, said astronomers, its immemorial cycle should find a dark and disastrous close.

Ah, strange was that gulf-forgotten star—how stranger than any dream of dreamers in the spheres of today, or than any vision that hath soared upon visionaries, in their retrospection of the sidereal past! There, through cycles of a history whose piled and bronze-writ records were hopeless of tabulation, the dead had come to outnumber infinitely the living. And built of a stone that was indestructible save in the furnace of suns, their cities rose beside those of the living like the prodigious metropli of Titans, with walls that overgloom the vicinal villages. And over all was the black funereal vault of the cryptic heavens—a dome of infinite shadows, where the dismal sun, suspended like a sole, enormous lamp, failed to illumine, and drawing back its fires from the face of the irresolvable ether, threw a baffled and despairing beam on the vague remote horizons, and shrouded vistas illimitable of the visionary land.

We were a sombre, secret, many-sorrowed people—we who dwelt beneath that sky of eternal twilight, pierced by the towering tombs and obelisks of the past. In our blood was the chill of the ancient night of time; and our pulses flagged with a creeping prescience of the lentor of Lethe. Over our courts and fields, like invisible sluggish vampires born of mausoleums, rose and hovered the black hours, with wings that distilled a malefic languor made from the shadowy woe and despair of perished cycles. The very skies were fraught with oppression, and we breathed beneath them as in a sepulcher, forever sealed with all its stagnancies of corruption and slow decay, and darkness impenetrable save to the fretting worm.

Vaguely we lived, and loved as in dreams—the dim and mystic dreams that hover upon the verge of fathomless sleep. We felt for our women, with their pale and spectral beauty, the same desire that the dead may feel for the phantom lilies of Hadean meads. Our days were spent in roaming through the ruins of lone and immemorial cities, whose palaces of fretted copper, and streets that ran between lines of carven golden obelisks, lay dim and ghastly with the dead light, or were drowned forever in seas of stagnant shadow; cities whose vast and iron-builded fanes preserved their gloom of primordial mystery and awe, from which the simulacra of century-forgotten gods looked forth with unalterable eyes to the hopeless heavens, and saw the ulterior night, the ultimate oblivion. Languidly we kept our gardens, whose grey lilies concealed a necromantic perfume, that had power to evoke for us the dead and spectral dreams of the past. Or, wandering through ashen fields of perennial autumn, we sought the rare and mystic immortelles, with sombre leaves and pallid petals, that bloomed beneath willows of wan and veil-like foliage: or wept with a sweet and nepenthe-laden dew by the flowing silence of Acherontic waters.

And one by one we died and were lost in the dust of accumulated time. We knew the years as a passing of shadows, and death itself as the yielding of twilight unto night.

THE SHADOWS

THERE were many shadows in the palace of Augusthes. About the silver throne that had blackened beneath the invisible passing of ages, they fell from pillar and broken roof and fretted window in ever-shifting multiformity. Seeming the black, fantastic spectres of doom and desolation, they moved through the palace in a gradual, grave, and imperceptible dance, whose music was the change and motion of suns and moons. They were long and slender, like all other shadows, before the early light, and behind the declining sun; squat and intense beneath the desert noontide, and faint with the withered moon; and in the interlunar darkness, they were as myriad tongues hidden behind the shut and silent lips of night.

One came daily to that place of shadows and desolation, and sate upon the silver throne, watching the shadows that were of desolation. King nor slave disputed him there, in the palace whose kings and whose slaves were powerless alike in the intangible dungeon of centuries. The tombs of unnumbered and forgotten monarchs were white upon the yellow desert roundabout. Some had partly rotted away, and showed like the sunken eye-sockets of a skull—blank and lidless beneath the staring heavens; others still retained the undesecrated seal of death, and were as the closed eyes of one lately dead. But he who watched the shadows from the silver throne, heeded not these, nor the fleet wind that dipt to the broken tombs, and emerged shrilly, its unseen hands dark with the dust of kings.

He was a philosopher, from what land there was none to know or ask. Nor was there any to ask what knowledge or delight he sought in the ruined palace, with eyes alway upon the moving shadows; nor what were the thoughts that moved through his mind in ghostly unison with them. His eyes were old and sad with meditation and wisdom; and his beard was long and white upon his long white robe.

For many days he came with the dawn and departed with sunset; and his shadow leaned from the shadow of the throne and moved with the others. But one eve he departed not; and thereafter his shadow was one with the shadow of the silver throne. Death found and left him there, where he dwindled into dust that was as the dust of slaves or kings.

But the ebb and refluence of shadows went on, in the days that were before the end; ere the aged world, astray with the sun in strange heavens, should be lost in the cosmic darkness, or, under the influence of other and conflicting gravitations, should crumble apart and bare its granite bones to the light of strange suns, and the granite, too, should dissolve, and be as of the dust of slaves and kings. Noon was encircled with darkness, and the depths of palace-dusk were chasmed with sunlight. Change there was none, other than this, for the earth was dead, and stirred not to the tottering feet of time. And in the expectant silence before the twilight of the sun, the moving shadows seemed but a mockery of change; a meaningless antic phantasmagoria of things that were; an afterfiguring of forgotten time.

And now the sun was darkened slowly in mid-heaven, as by some vast and invisible bulk. And twilight hushed the shadows in the palace of Augusthes, as the world itself swung down toward the long and single shadow of irretrievable oblivion.

In the Bison Frontiers of Imagination series

Gullivar of Mars
By Edwin L. Arnold
Introduced by Richard A. Lupoff
Afterword by Gary Hoppenstand

A Journey in Other Worlds: A Romance of the Future
By John Jacob Astor
Introduced by S. M. Stirling

Queen of Atlantis
By Pierre Benoit
Afterword by Hugo Frey

The Wonder
By J. D. Beresford
Introduced by Jack L. Chalker

Voices of Vision: Creators of Science Fiction and Fantasy Speak
By Jayme Lynn Blaschke

At the Earth's Core
By Edgar Rice Burroughs
Introduced by Gregory A. Benford
Afterword by Phillip R. Burger

Beyond Thirty
By Edgar Rice Burroughs
Introduced by David Brin
Essays by Phillip R. Burger and Richard A. Lupoff

The Eternal Savage: Nu of the Niocene
By Edgar Rice Burroughs
Introduced by Tom Deitz

The Land That Time Forgot
By Edgar Rice Burroughs
Introduced by Mike Resnick

Lost on Venus
By Edgar Rice Burroughs
Introduced by Kevin J. Anderson

The Moon Maid: Complete and Restored
By Edgar Rice Burroughs
Introduced by Terry Bisson

Pellucidar
By Edgar Rice Burroughs
Introduced by Jack McDevitt
Afterword by Phillip R. Burger

Pirates of Venus
By Edgar Rice Burroughs
Introduced by F. Paul Wilson
Afterword by Phillip R. Burger

Tanar of Pellucidar
By Edgar Rice Burroughs
Introduced by Paul Cook

Tarzan at the Earth's Core
By Edgar Rice Burroughs
Introduced by Sean McMullen

Under the Moons of Mars
By Edgar Rice Burroughs
Introduced by James P. Hogan

The Absolute at Large
By Karel Čapek
Introduced by Stephen Baxter

The Girl in the Golden Atom
By Ray Cummings
Introduced by Jack Williamson

The Poison Belt: Being an Account of Another Amazing Adventure of Professor Challenger
By Sir Arthur Conan Doyle
Introduced by Katya Reimann

Tarzan Alive
By Philip José Farmer
New Foreword by Win Scott Eckert
Introduced by Mike Resnick

The Circus of Dr. Lao
By Charles G. Finney
Introduced by John Marco

Omega: The Last Days of the World
By Camille Flammarion
Introduced by Robert Silverberg

Ralph 124C 41+
By Hugo Gernsback
Introduced by Jack Williamson

The Journey of Niels Klim to the World Underground
By Ludvig Holberg
Introduced and edited by James I. McNelis Jr.
Preface by Peter Fitting

The Lost Continent: The Story of Atlantis
By C. J. Cutcliffe Hyne
Introduced by Harry Turtledove
Afterword by Gary Hoppenstand

Mizora: A World of Women
By Mary E. Bradley Lane
Introduced by Joan Saberhagen

A Voyage to Arcturus
By David Lindsay
Introduced by John Clute

Before Adam
By Jack London
Introduced by Dennis L. McKiernan

Fantastic Tales
By Jack London
Edited by Dale L. Walker

Master of Adventure: The Worlds of Edgar Rice Burroughs
By Richard A. Lupoff
With an introduction to the Bison Books Edition by the author
Foreword by Michael Moorcock

Preface by Henry Hardy Heins
With an essay by Phillip R. Burger

The Moon Pool
By A. Merritt
Introduced by Robert Silverberg

The Purple Cloud
By M. P. Shiel
Introduced by John Clute

Lost Worlds
By Clark Ashton Smith
Introduced by Jeff VanderMeer

Out of Space and Time
By Clark Ashton Smith
Introduced by Jeff VanderMeer

The Skylark of Space
By E. E. "Doc" Smith
Introduced by Vernor Vinge

Skylark Three
By E. E. "Doc" Smith
Introduced by Jack Williamson

The Nightmare and Other Tales of Dark Fantasy
By Francis Stevens
Edited and introduced by Gary Hoppenstand

Tales of Wonder
By Mark Twain
Edited, introduced, and with notes by David Ketterer

The Chase of the Golden Meteor
By Jules Verne
Introduced by Gregory A. Benford

The Meteor Hunt: The First English Translation of Verne's Original Manuscript
By Jules Verne
Translated and edited by Frederick Paul Walter and Walter James Miller

The Croquet Player
By H. G. Wells
Afterword by John Huntington

In the Days of the Comet
By H. G. Wells
Introduced by Ben Bova

The Last War: A World Set Free
By H. G. Wells
Introduced by Greg Bear

The Sleeper Awakes
By H. G. Wells
Introduced by J. Gregory Keyes
Afterword by Gareth Davies-Morris

The War in the Air
By H. G. Wells
Introduced by Dave Duncan

The Disappearance
By Philip Wylie
Introduced by Robert Silverberg

Gladiator
By Philip Wylie
Introduced by Janny Wurts

When Worlds Collide
By Philip Wylie and Edwin Balmer
Introduced by John Varley

University of Nebraska Press

Also of Interest by E.E. "Doc" Smith:

THE SKYLARK OF SPACE
Illustrated by O. G. Estes Jr.
Introduction by Vernor Vinge

The *Amazing Stories* publication of *The Skylark of Space* in 1928 heralded the debut of a major new voice in American pulp science fiction and ushered in its golden age. This commemorative edition features the author's preferred version of the story, the original illustrations by O. G. Estes Jr., and a new introduction by acclaimed science fiction writer Vernor Vinge.

ISBN: 0-8032-9286-4; 978-0-8032-9286-4 (paper)

SKYLARK THREE
Illustrated by A. J. Donnell
Introduction by Jack Williamson

In this exhilarating sequel to *The Skylark of Space*, momentous danger again stalks genius inventor and interplanetary adventurer Dr. Richard Seaton. Featuring even more technological wizardry, alien worlds, and all-out action than its predecessor, *Skylark Three* is hailed by many as the imaginative high point of the Skylark series.

ISBN: 0-8032-9303-8; 978-0-8032-9303-8 (paper)

Order online at www.nebraskapress.unl.edu or call 1-800-755-1105.
Mention the code "BOFOX" to receive a 20% discount.